P9-DCY-140

# STORM OF LOCUSTS

Also by Rebecca Roanhorse

The Sixth World
*Trail of Lightning*

The Sixth World : Book Two

# STORM OF LOCUSTS

Rebecca Roanhorse

LONDON SYDNEY NEW YORK TORONTO NEW DELHI

1230 AVENUE OF THE AMERICAS, NEW YORK, NEW YORK 10020

 · For information about special discounts for bulk purchases, please contact Simon & Schuster Special Sales at 1-866-506-1949 or business@simonandschuster.com. · The Simon & Schuster Speakers Bureau can bring authors to your live event. For more information or to book an event, contact the Simon & Schuster Speakers Bureau at 1-866-248-3049 or visit our website at www.simonspeakers.com. · Also available in a Saga Press paperback edition · Design by Nick Sciacca · The text for this book was set in Times New Roman. · Manufactured in the United States of America · First Saga Press hardcover edition April 2019 · 10 9 8 7 6 5 4 3 2 1 · Library of Congress Cataloging-in-Publication Data · Names: Roanhorse, Rebecca, author. · Title: Storm of locusts / Rebecca Roanhorse. · Description: First Edition. | London ; Toronto ; New York : Saga Press, [2019] | Series: The Sixth World ; book 2 | Includes bibliographical references and index. · Identifiers: LCCN 2018017646 (print) | ISBN 9781534413528 (hardcover : alk. paper) | ISBN 9781534413535 (pbk) | ISBN 9781534413542 (eBook) · Subjects: | GSAFD: Fantasy fiction. · Classification: LCC PS3618.O283 S76 2019 (print) | DDC 813/.6—dc23 · LC record available at https://lccn.loc.gov/2018017646

To all the women who are hard to love, and to the people who love them anyway

# Chapter 1

Four men with guns stand in my yard.

It's just past seven in the morning, and in other places in Dinétah, in other people's yards, men and women are breaking their fast with their families. Husbands grumble half-heartedly about the heat already starting to drag down the December morning. Mothers remind children of the newest Tribal Council winter water rations before sending them out to feed the sheep. Relatives make plans to get together over the coming Keshmish holiday.

But these four men aren't here to complain about the weather or to make holiday plans. They certainly aren't here for the pleasure of my company. They've come because they want me to kill something.

Only it's my day off, so this better be good.

"Hastiin," I greet the man on my front steps. He's all weathered skin and hard, lean muscle in blue fatigues, skull bandanna hanging loose around his corded neck, black hair shorn skull short. He's also wearing a small arsenal. An M16 over one shoulder, a monster of a Desert Eagle at his hip, another pistol in a clip holster in his waistband. And I know he's got a knife tucked in his heavy-soled boot, the left one, and another strapped to his thigh. He didn't used to do that, dress for a worst-case scenario. But things have changed. For both of us.

"Hoskie." Hastiin drawls my last name out. Never my first name—Maggie—always just the last, like we're army buddies or something. Likely his way of trying to forget he's talking to a woman, but that's his problem, not mine. He shifts in his big black boots, his gear jingling like tiny war bells. His fingers flex into fists.

I lean against my front door and cross my arms, patient as the desert. Stare at him until he stops fidgeting like a goddamn prom date. I've learned a lot about Hastiin in the last few weeks, and I know the man shakes like an aspen in the wind when he's got something on his mind. Some remnant of breathing in too much nerve gas on the front lines of the Energy Wars way back when. Which doesn't bode well for me. I can see my day off slipping away with the edges of the dawn. But I won't let him have my time that easy. He's going to have to work for it.

"You lost?" I ask him.

He chuckles low. Not like I'm funny. More like I'm irritating. "You know I'm not lost."

"Then I'm not sure why you're here. Thought we'd agreed this was going to be my day off. I promised Tah that I'd . . ." I frown, scanning my yard. "Where're my dogs?"

Hastiin's mouth cracks slightly in what passes as a grin, and he jerks his chin toward one of his men farther back near the gate. Young guy in fatigues, a fresh-scrubbed face that I don't recognize, hair tied back in a tsiiyéél. He's kneeling down, rubbing the belly of a very content mutt.

"Traitor," I mutter, but my dog doesn't hear. Or doesn't care. All three of my mutts don't seem to register Hastiin and his Thirsty Boys as a threat anymore. If we keep this business arrangement going, I'm going to have to work on that. I turn back to Hastiin. "So, what's this all about?"

He squints dark eyes. "Got a bounty come in. Something big and bad over near Lake Asááyi."

Most of the lakes around here have dried up. Red Lake, Wheatfields. But Asááyi has stuck around, fed by an underground aquifer that even this record drought couldn't kill. It seems doubtful that whoever or whatever Hastiin was hunting over by the lake couldn't be done without me. Which means—

"If this is you trying to apologize again for not having my back at Black Mesa . . ."

"Shit." He drawls that out too. Spits to the side like it tastes bad in his mouth.

"I've already said you don't owe me anything. You can stop offering me gigs to try to make it up to me."

"That's not it."

"Then what?"

He shrugs, a spare lift of a knobby shoulder. "It's worth big trade," he offers. Unconvincingly.

"I don't need the money."

"Thought you might. What with Grandpa staying with you."

"No, you didn't."

He scratches a knuckle across his scruff. Sounds somewhere between resigned and hopeful when he says, "Could be something big and bad. Maybe fun."

"And your Thirsty Boys can't handle it?"

"You're the Monsterslayer." He gives me another squinty stare. "Me and the Boys are just a bunch of assholes with guns."

He's throwing my words back at me, but he says it with a small smile, and I know he doesn't really mean it. And it occurs to me that maybe, just maybe, this is his idea of friendly. He's inviting me because he does, in fact, want the pleasure of my company. Something inside me shifts. Unfamiliar, but not entirely unappealing.

"All right," I say with an exaggerated sigh. No need to let him know I'm pleased at the gesture. "I'll go. But at least tell me what the job is."

"Tell you on the way. Clock's ticking and all."

I look over my shoulder back into the house. "One problem. I promised Tah I'd take him up the mountain to cut some good logs. He wants to build a new hogan."

Hastiin blinks a few times. "In Tse Bonito?"

"Here. On my land. He's staying."

He nods approvingly. "Tell you what," he says. "You help me with this bounty today, me and the Boys'll help Grandpa build his hogan tomorrow."

It's a good trade, and better than me hauling the logs down the mountain by myself. In fact, I'd call it a win, and it's been a while since I had one of those.

"Let me get my shotgun."

It doesn't take me long to get ready. I'm already wearing what Hastiin calls my uniform, which is fairly rich considering he and his Thirsty Boys actually wear a freaking uniform. He tried to get me into a set of those blue fatigues when I first joined up with the Thirsty Boys right after Black Mesa, but I told him that it felt like I was playing soldier, and if there was one thing I'm not, it's a soldier. I'm surprised I've made it this long working with the Boys, but I guess I didn't feel much like being alone after everything that went down. I hate to admit it, and I intend to deny it if he asks, but I like Hastiin. Well, maybe "like" is a bit strong. But I could get to like.

I do change my T-shirt. Same black, but it smells markedly better than the one I slept in. I tighten my moccasin wraps. Tuck my throwing knives into the edges just below the knee. One obsidian blade, one silver. Both made to kill creatures that might not be hurt by steel. My new Böker knife is all steel, and it goes in the sheath at my waist. It's a recent replacement for the one I lost in the fighting arena at the Shalimar and the first thing I bought with the trade I earned hunting with the Thirsty Boys. I thumb the hilt of the big knife, memories of the Shalimar wanting to surface, but there's nothing good there and I've spent enough time replaying that night in my head. What I need more than anything is a fresh start. I'm tired of carrying around old ghosts.

As if the threat of memories alone is enough to compel me, I find myself on my knees, reaching behind the narrow space between the head of my mattress and the wall. My hand hits cloth, and beneath it I feel the pommel of a sword. I know the rest of the sword is four feet long, its blade forged from the raw lightning that the sun gifted to his son as a weapon. His son who was once my mentor, once the only man I ever thought I'd love. But I tricked that man, trapped him and imprisoned him in the earth. I know I didn't have a choice, that it was either him or me. And as much as I loved him, I loved myself just a little bit more.

So now the sword is mine.

I leave the sword where it is. It's not meant for a simple bounty hunt. It's too sacred, too bound in power and memories for me to take hunting with Hastiin. But one day maybe. Until then it stays put.

My shotgun rests on the gun rack next to my bed. It's a beauty. Double-barrel-pump action with a custom grip. I take it from the rack and slide it into my shoulder holster. Adjust it so it sits just right, an easy draw from the left. Glock comes too. It rides on the hip opposite from my Böker. I pat it all down, reciting my list of weapons softly to myself, just to make sure everything's where it's supposed to be.

Tah catches me as I come out of my bedroom, a mug of Navajo tea in his wrinkled hands. "I thought I heard you in there," he says cheerfully. "I'm ready to go. Just need to find my hat . . ." He trails off as he sees my weapons.

"Hastiin's here," I explain. "Some kind of emergency at Lake Asááyi and he needs backup. But he said he and the Boys'll help us build your hogan tomorrow. They'll even do all the heavy lifting."

Tah's thin shoulders fall forward in disappointment. For a moment he looks all of his seventy-odd years.

And I know that's my fault, even before today's small disappointment.

But Tah straightens, smiles. "Well, tomorrow's just as good

as today. I made some tea. Want to at least take a cup? It's not coffee. . . ." He shakes his head, chuckles a happy laugh. "Remember when my grandson brought me all that coffee?"

"And the sugar, too," I say. "I remember."

I smile back, but it's not much of a smile. In fact, it feels like I'm trying to smile past the broken place in my heart. We haven't much talked about Black Mesa and what happened with Kai. And he hasn't asked. But I saw him once, head together with Hastiin's, when he thought I wasn't listening, and I'm sure the mercenary told him what I did. Well, at least his side of the story, anyway. But Tah's never asked me. Maybe he doesn't want to know the truth.

"Just you wait, Maggie. He'll come. Kai will come. And then maybe you'll quit your moping."

I look up, surprised. "I thought I was doing okay."

He shakes his head. "Maybe we'll both quit our moping." He folds his hands tight around his mug of tea. Stares out the window at nothing. Or maybe he's staring all the way across Dinétah to the All-American, where his grandson is alive and well.

Alive and well for more than a month and he hasn't come to us. To me. When I asked Hastiin if he knew why Kai hadn't come, he said, "Ask him yourself." But I can't. I'm too proud, or too scared to push it. If Kai doesn't want to see me, I have to respect that. Even if I crawl into bed every night to stare at the ceiling and think about him. Even if I stumble out of bed bleary-eyed and restless a handful of hours later, still thinking about him. Even if every day starts and ends with the image of him lying dead at my feet. My last and most terrible deed, even worse than betraying my mentor. All of it eating me alive.

"When he's ready," Tah says quietly, more to himself than to me. "When Kai is ready he'll come to us."

I want to ask Tah when he thinks that will be, but he doesn't know any more than I do. So I check my weapons again, my fingers lingering on the comfort of cold metal, and leave.

# Chapter 2

Hastiin and the Thirsty Boys are gathered by their vehicles. Three of us pile into an armor-fitted jeep, Hastiin in the driver's seat, me at shotgun with my shotgun literally across my lap, and another Thirsty Boy, the young one who was petting my traitorous pup, in the back. Two other Boys climb onto terrain-friendly motorbikes and lead us out. My dogs escort us, tails wagging, as far as the cattle guard that marks the edge of my property.

"Take care of the old man," I tell my dogs, as the jeep rattles its way over the metal grating. They bark a happy farewell before turning back toward the trailer. Hastiin pulls out onto the road and turns us west.

"So how far to Asááyi these days?" I ask. "I hear that road's shot to shit."

"Half an hour."

"Half an hour?" I ask, incredulous. "It's eight, ten miles tops. Your jeep can't go any faster than that?" Granted the road isn't much more than a winding suggestion up the side of a mountain and down into the canyon and drought has pockmarked the red earth with massive potholes, but there's no reason we shouldn't get there in half the time Hastiin suggests.

"He drives like an old man," the Thirsty Boy in the back remarks cheerfully. I glance back. He's young, fifteen. Sixteen, maybe. Hair in a traditional bun, nice brown eyes. Somebody's kid brother. No, check that. Now that I'm closer, I can see. Somebody's kid sister.

"A girl?" I ask Hastiin. "I didn't think you had it in you."

Hastiin frowns. "Just 'cause I don't like you much, Hoskie, doesn't mean I don't like women."

I snort. "Yeah, right."

"I'm the best tracker in Dinétah," the new girl says. "He had to bring me if he wants to catch the White Locust. He didn't have a choice."

"I thought I was the best tracker in Dinétah," I say.

The new girl's eyes get big, and I give her a smile to let her know I'm not serious. Turn in my seat to get a good look at her. That almost bony frame, the crooked nose, the dimple I can see clear enough on her cheek, but that Hastiin hides behind his scruff of a beard. I turn back to Hastiin. "You're related, aren't you?"

He grumbles something.

"Speak up, Hastiin."

"He and my mom are cousins!" the girl says. "Brother-sister, Navajo way."

I used to think Hastiin was a hard-ass, one of the grizzled mercenary types that had seen it all and learned not to give a shit. Granted, he was always a dick to me before Black Mesa, so I might have been biased. But these past few weeks I've spent a lot of time with the man, and I've learned that underneath that rough exterior is a bit of a softie. I'm starting to appreciate him, and I think he feels the same way. I won't ask him though. He'll just deny it and demand that I crawl through a field of prickly goat's head to prove how much he doesn't care. But it doesn't mean I can't tease him.

"Our tracker's got a point about your driving, Hastiin. Why don't you let me drive?"

"Why don't you sit there and look pretty, Hoskie?"

"Why don't you retire while you still can, old man?"

Hastiin's niece makes a choking sound. He looks back in alarm. "You okay?"

"No," I say, "she's not okay. She's dying, very slowly, because it's taking too long to drive to Lake Asááyi."

Hastiin snorts, amused at my dumb joke. The jeep jerks forward as he presses the accelerator. I don't even crack a smile. Like I said. Softie.

We make it to Asááyi in under twenty minutes.

# Chapter 3

"What are we up against?" I ask, sliding out of the jeep parked at the edge of the lake. My moccasins kick up swirls of red dust. Around us stretch the red and white striated cliffs of Bowl Canyon. Pine trees dot the sides of the rock face, incongruous spikes of determined survival in a world made of hard surfaces and callous time. Long before the Big Water, before even the Diné became the Earth-Surface People that we are today, this part of the world used to be the floor of a great sea. The bilagáana scientists call that continental shift geology. We Diné don't disagree exactly. We find the same strange ocean-born fossils in our rocks, the same signs of a world before ours, foreign and unfamiliar. We just attribute the current face of our homeland to different sources.

"Have you heard of the White Locust?" Hastiin asks me as he comes around the back of the jeep.

"Not until your niece mentioned her. Him. They?"

"He's the leader of a group that call themselves the Swarm. You can blame your boy for that," he says, digging around in the back of the jeep. My boy. He means Kai. He pulls out a bullet-resistant vest and throws it at me.

I catch it. "I need body armor?"

"Ever since his storm cloud's been hanging over Canyon de Chelly"—he points with his lips in the direction of the sacred canyon even though we can't see it from here—"people have been getting crazy ideas. End of the world. Beginning of the new world."

"Isn't the apocalypse a little 'been there, done that'? I mean, didn't we just have a massive world-destroying flood? Earthquakes? Wars? What, did they miss the memo?"

The new girl laughs, and I give her a grin. Either I'm getting funnier or apocalypse jokes are low-hanging fruit.

"Put the damn thing on," he says when he sees I'm not strapping on the vest. "I fully expect these people are armed to the teeth."

"You do remember I'm fast, don't you?"

He frowns. Hastiin hates when I bring up my clan powers. Most of the time he pretends I don't have them. The rest of the time he's relying on me to use them to get us out of a jam. What he doesn't seem to understand is that I can't turn them on and off when I want to. They come on their own schedule, usually when I'm personally in danger, and leave just as abruptly when the adrenaline spike that drive them fades.

"You're not faster than a bullet," he says, but there's no conviction in his voice.

I grin at even getting that small admission out of him. I actually don't know if I'm faster than a bullet. But I do know that I'm faster than the human that is holding the gun that is shooting the bullet. And my clan power, Honágháahnii, will show me where that bullet is heading in plenty of time for me to get out of the way. And that usually means I'm a pretty good bullet dodger. I must have a smart-ass look on my face because Hastiin grumbles, "Humor me."

I stare at him. He stares back. I consider whether this is really the hill I want to die on and decide it's not. "Fine." I lay my shotgun across the seat of the jeep. Shrug out of my back holster. Place it and my leather jacket in the vehicle. "So these people think Kai's storm cloud is a sign of another Big Water?"

"You know the story of the Emergence?" Hastiin asks.

"Some," I acknowledge, remembering the stories Coyote liked to tell me about the creation of the world. "I know that the First World was a red world, inhabited by insect people. Beetle, dragonfly—"

"Locusts."

"—locusts. But they screwed up their world and were forced to flee to the Second World, the Blue World."

"And what made them flee?"

"Uh . . ."

"Floods. A storm."

"So this White Locust guy fits in how?"

"When the Air-Surface People escaped the First World and traveled to the Second World, they sent out scouts to try to find a place to live. One of those scouts was White Locust."

"So this White Locust guy thinks he's . . . what? Scouting for a new world?"

"Something like that," he admits. "Says the Big Water was some kind of moral punishment and it's his job to lead us to a new land."

"I like the land we're on just fine. Besides, the Big Water didn't flood Dinétah." That was a sobering thought. The Big Water drowned most of the continent, hell most of the world. The coastline these days starts somewhere in West Texas, the island chain of the Appalachians being the only land until somewhere near the Alps. The western half of the continent fared a little better. California was below twenty feet of sea water, but places like New Denver had risen, a chaotic but prosperous place, from what I'd heard. Salt Lake City had extended its influence over most of Utah, Nevada, and what was left of northern Arizona to become the Exalted Mormon Kingdom. Albuquerque was the Burque, a volatile city-state run by Hispanic land-grant families and water barons.

“The White Locust is just another New Ager turned doomsday prophet,” Hastiin says. “Men like him can’t be happy with living. They got to be praying for the end of the world. They thrive on death. Convince weaker men that only they can save them, but it’s all bullshit. Don’t trust those death-dealers, no matter how sweet their words. They only want to die and take you down with them.”

I stare until, under the weight of my gaze, Hastiin looks up. “What?”

“That’s the longest speech I’ve ever heard you make.”

He narrows his eyes, annoyed. “Check her straps,” he says to his niece. She follows orders, although she looks a little reluctant. No, a little scared. Like I might bite if she gets too close. I lift my arms, an invitation, and she approaches me with a small smile. I wince as she tightens my vest.

“Sorry,” she mutters.

“It’s okay. What’s your name?”

“Ben.”

“Ben what?”

“Just Ben.”

“Well, thanks, just Ben.”

She finishes up. Gives me a shy nod and steps back to the jeep and tries to look busy moving equipment around.

“So how’d you get involved with this White Locust?” I ask Hastiin.

“Tribal Council’s put a bounty out on him. Seems the White Locust has been buying up every piece of dynamite in Dinétah. Trading posts. Black markets, too. Not just TNT, but anything that will make things go ‘boom.’ Camped up here at the lake with all his bombs in some hidey-hole. Got the Tribal Council worried. They decide they should have a sit-down, just to talk. So they send a representative out to do just that. Only the rep doesn’t come back. Nobody’s heard from him since.”

"You think he's dead?"

"That's what they're paying us to find out."

"So, what's the plan?"

Hastiin looks at Ben. "Go on. You can tell her."

Ben straightens, tries to look authoritative. "We believe that he and a handful of followers are camping in the caves along the top ridge of the mesa. I tracked one of them back up there when she came down for a first aid kit last week at the medical depot. Her knuckle was all busted and she threw away a bloody bandage, right there in the common trash. She thought nobody saw her. She was real careful, running the switchback, but I'm good on the mountain trails. The best, actually." She barely blushes at the brag.

I press my lips together. Consider young Ben. "Good on the mountain trails?"

Hastiin exhales loudly and pointedly, and Ben reddens for real this time. "Keha'atiinii," she admits, "born for Bįįh Dine'é." Her chin comes up, proud.

Foot-trails People, born for Deer People. A potent combination for a tracker.

"Good for you," I say. I don't ask her what life-threatening trauma brought on her clan powers. Us trauma survivors try to respect each other's boundaries. And I'm fairly impressed that she's not hiding her powers. I did when I was her age. Actually, I just lived with a supernatural warrior and avoided human contact. We all deal in different ways.

"I'm sending Ben up first because of her . . . talents. She's only going to scout it out and report back. Not engage." He glares at his niece, who looks sufficiently cowed. "Then you and I will follow, Hoskie. Atcitty and Curley are circling around the other side of the canyon as we speak. They'll come down from the east." Atcitty and Curley must be the other Thirsty Boys, the ones on the bikes.

“Check her straps,” Hastiin says to Ben. Ben’s eyes crinkle, and I hold up a hand to stop her.

“Seems straightforward enough, Hastiin. Go up, find the guy, maybe find the Tribal Council rep, dead or alive. Nothing we haven’t done a dozen times in the past month. What’s making you so nervous?”

“What are you talking about?” he says, voice thick with irritation.

“You’re fidgeting like I asked you to tell me how you feel about your mother loving her other sons the best, and you told Ben to check my straps twice.”

Hastiin looks taken aback. He stills for a moment, something I rarely see him do, before he grunts and hawks another mouthful of tobacco on the ground. “It’s nothing.”

“Say it.”

His shoulders tense. “I said it’s nothing. Just some dreams I’ve been having.”

A shiver of alarm dances down my spine, my monster instincts flaring. “What kind of dreams?”

“Did Ben tell you there’s rumors that the White Locust can fly?” he says, a clear attempt to change the subject.

“Okay,” I say carefully. I’m not quite ready to let the subject of his dreams go, but I also want to know more about our bounty. I decide I’m not going to get much more out of him about his nightmares, or whatever he’s been having, so I let it go for now. Decide to concentrate on the issue at hand. “There’s a lot of strange things in Dinétah after the Big Water. It’s weird, but it’s not out of the realm of possibility. Clan powers? Or something else?”

“Nobody’s sure. But they say he’s got other powers too. Dark medicine maybe.”

“Like witchcraft?” I shudder. If that’s it, Hastiin’s right to be nervous.

“Nobody said that. But there’s something not right with him and his people.”

“Who exactly are his people?”

Hastiin squints up at the mesa ridge. “Rumor is there’s a whole mess of them. Converts, I guess.” He reaches into a back pocket and pulls out a folded piece of paper. Hands it over. I open it and read the big block lettering.

ARE YOU READY FOR THE NEXT WORLD?
WILL YOU HEED THE SIGNS?

Below the words is a picture of the four sacred mountains being overcome by a cresting wave. People flee in terror. And hovering above it all, like some sort of dark angel, is a man with locust wings. He points a finger at the drowning people in judgment.

“He seems nice,” I remark.

“Tribal Council would probably let it go if they weren’t stockpiling explosives. Nobody wants a bunch of doomsdayers with the means to enact their madness.”

“Well, let’s go relieve them of their means, then,” I say. “Maybe knock a few heads together. Return the Tribal Council representative to the Tribal Council.”

“They are so screwed!” Ben chirps enthusiastically.

Hastiin looks at me and then Ben, lines creasing his face.

“Well, don’t look so damn happy about it, you two,” he mutters before he slings his pack over his shoulders and motions for Ben to lead the way.

# Chapter 4

The path we follow is steep and narrow, an animal trail that wanders up the side of the mountain from the lake. It's peaceful here before the heat of the day's settled in, the glint of the water visible through the trees every time we hit a curve in the trail. But it's steep, steeper than it looked from down where we parked the jeep, and twenty minutes in Hastiin and I are huffing under the weight of our body armor and packs. Ben seems none the worse for wear, despite wearing the same heavy flak jacket we are, as she flits up the trail ahead of us and then circles back every few minutes to let us know we're still on the right track.

"What do you think of her?" Hastiin asks me, lips thrust forward, pointing toward the place Ben disappeared down the trail in front of us.

I turn sharply. Hastiin has never asked me what I thought about anything expect the caliber of ammo he needs to take down a runner from fifty yards away.

"I mean, she's good, right?" He nods like a proud uncle, which I guess he is. "Yeah, she's good."

"Jesus, Mary, and Joseph," I say, borrowing a curse from Grace Goodacre.

The old mercenary growls at me. “Forget I asked, Hoskie.”

“I will.”

He stiffens, then hurries his gait, moving away from me at apace.

I roll my eyes, but he can’t see it. “Okay, okay,” I say, jogging to catch him. “She seems good. I mean, she found the trail, right?”

He slows a little, allows me to match his stride. “She did. She’s a natural.”

I open my mouth to remind him of her clan powers, but I shut it when I see the look on his face. Why ruin his familial pride with a few pesky supernatural facts?

He coughs. “Promise me something, Hoskie,” he growls. “No. Don’t give me that look. Just promise.”

“I’m listening,”

Something flashes silver on the path ahead, Ben headed back to us. Hastiin sees her too, and his words come out in a fast tumble. “If anything happens to me, you take care of her. She wants to be a Thirsty Boy, but the Boys won’t know what to do with her. She needs another . . . female. You’re a female.”

“Nice of you to notice.”

“I’m not asking you to take her in, but just look out for her. Be a role model.”

“Now I know you’re delusional.”

“C’mon, Hoskie. You’re not that bad. I mean, you did pay me back that money you owed me, and Grandpa Tah thinks you’re okay.”

“I’m not so sure about that.”

“He understands more than you give him credit for.”

“Whatever. Wait. Is that why you invited me along today? You wanted me to meet Ben?”

He nods.

“Sonofabitch.” So much for some budding friendship. He wants something like everyone else does. I shouldn’t feel that prick of disappointment in my chest, but I do.

"Don't look so sour," he says. "I wouldn't ask you if I did think you were worth—" He cuts off as Ben bounds down the hill to join us.

"Their hideout is just around the next turn," she announces. "You'll be able to see the mouth of the cave from there. And there's someone up there for sure. I saw movement."

Before either of us can say anything, she pivots on her toes and bounces back the way she came, the white yarn of her tsiiyéél bright in the sun, a glint of silver from her hair clip catching the light.

I blink. How had I not noticed before? How had Hastiin not noticed?

"Ben," I warn, the dread hitting me fast and hard. I push up the hill behind her, legs turning. But she's supernaturally light, like the deer clan she draws her power from. She hits the clearing first before I can reach her.

"Your hair clip!" I shout.

"Ben!" Hastiin growls behind me. He must have noticed the silver clip, the same thought hitting him like it did me. "Get down!" he shouts to her. "If you can see them, they can see you!"

Ben skids to a stop. Loose pebbles shake free under her feet. I expect her to backtrack toward us, or at least get down behind the grove of creosote bushes that line the path. But she turns to us, eyes wide with wonder.

"What are you doing?" Hastiin shouts to her in a low whisper. He's still a good ten feet behind me, his gear rattling as he presses up the mountain.

"Do you hear that?" Ben asks. She turns to us, a beatific look on her face.

Hastiin lets out a string of curses and hustles past me toward his niece. For a moment the only sound is the noise of his shoulder holster, the slap of the knife belt as he passes me.

But I'm stopped dead in my tracks. Because I hear it too.

"It's music," Ben says, her voice suffused with awe. "Someone's singing."

A sweet chorus, like the best summer day you ever had. Sticky with grape snow cones and staying out too late at the creek with your cousins as the locusts sing their mating songs.

Locusts. My monster instincts scream a warning that shakes through my bones.

"It's a trap!" I yell. But I'm too late.

I watch helpless as Hastiin reaches for his niece, pulling her to the ground. Just as the arrow that was meant for Ben strikes him. Dead center through his throat.

His eyes bulge in surprise. His mouth opens to speak. But no words come out.

Another arrow. Ripping through his eye.

And Hastiin falls down dead at my feet.

# Chapter 5

Ben screams.

I hit the ground, rolling for cover. Whoever killed Hastiin is shooting from somewhere above us, an insurmountable vantage point.

Another arrow flies and strikes Hastiin in the meat of his thigh. It makes an ugly thudding sound. He doesn't flinch. He's dead.

Ben stands there, staring at her uncle's body. She makes a keening sound, something low and broken.

"Get to cover!" I hiss at her. "He's gone. You can't help him!"

But Ben isn't listening. She drops to her knees. Falls against Hastiin's chest, wraps arms around his still frame.

"Move, Ben! You're a targ—" An arrow flies past my cheek, close enough that I feel a kiss of air as it passes. It's only a matter of time before an arrow finds one of us. Cursing, I glance around, looking for the other two Thirsty Boys, who took the alternate path up the mountain, but they're nowhere in sight. I'm on my own.

I focus on the ridge, scanning the switchback for movement. I can feel my clan powers awakening, kindled to life by the danger. My vision sharpens, and my mind shows me the fastest way up the mountain. A thrill of blood lust rises, hot and urgent.

I roll to my feet and run, Honágháahnii fast. Not up the curving path where I'm a nice fat target, but straight up the side of the hill, hands grappling for holds. Branches yank at the sleeves of my shirt. Something sharp rips across my forehead. I ignore it all. Keep moving, tacking slightly north from where the archer should be.

Thirty feet up and I see an echo of something bright on the cliff side to my left. Something pearlescent, diaphanous, and delicate like a dew-soaked spiderweb caught in the sunlight. My mind can't quite figure out what I'm seeing. Is it fabric? Metal? But it doesn't matter as a human face rises from behind an oversize boulder. Then shoulders. Chest. The dull black of a compound bow rises above the edge of the rock as the archer raises it to aim down the mountain.

The archer is a Navajo woman dressed in loose white cotton pants and wearing an open-backed shirt. She has a sighting device over one eye, and fingerless gloves grip her bow. She looks formidable. But what has me slowing in my tracks isn't so much her deadly technology, but the thin membranous insect wings that sprout from just below her shoulder to drape down the length of her back.

She's focused down mountain, oblivious. She doesn't even look my way.

She opens her mouth, and a high humming song flows from her lips. It surrounds me, and for a moment I feel that sun-soaked warmth of late summer again, something fragile and beautiful from an idyllic childhood. But it's a childhood that was never mine. It's fake, something pretty that has nothing to do with me. An approximation of a perfect childhood too foreign a seduction to lure me in.

She's still singing when I launch myself onto the path. She startles to silence. Her eyes bulge in shock. She seems to forget that she's holding a weapon, and by the time she remembers, it's too late.

I grip the bow, twisting as I rip it from her hands. She cries out as I hurl the weapon over the ledge. I spin back to face her, but she's no longer standing on the trail. Instead, she's hovering five feet off the ground, wings buzzing. She's holding a flimsy-looking knife in her hand.

Her eyes dart toward where the bow went over the ledge. Her fingers work nervously on the hilt of her knife. I have a feeling she's never used that knife for more than eating dinner. I almost feel bad for her. But then I remember Hastiin and the sound Ben made over his body, and any sympathy in me goes dead.

She dives for the bow, headfirst. I run toward the boulder, leap. Plant my foot on the rock and launch myself into the sky. Grab her ankle. Drag her down. She screams as we both crash to the ground.

We grapple, but I'm bigger and stronger and she's not a fighter. I've got her pinned, my weight planted on her chest, in seconds.

She glares at me, brown eyes shining with hate I haven't earned. Opens her mouth wide, and that strange locust song pours forth. I think I'm immune to it, but it's obviously some kind of weapon, so I'm not taking any chances.

I hit her in the face, hard. Her jawbone connects with my knuckles. Her song cuts off abruptly as her cheek slams into the dirt.

"Quit that shit," I warn her. "Or I'll tape your mouth shut." I don't have any tape, but that's a small detail.

Besides, I've got my own kind of song to contend with. Even now K'aahanáanii is crooning in my ear, urging me to spill her blood. And it would be justified for what she did to Hastiin. But this is a bounty hunt. We're supposed to bring the White Locust and his followers in to face murder charges, not be murderers ourselves.

And I promised Kai I was going to try something else besides being a killer.

I draw my Böker and her eyes go from hate to fear. I've decided to let her live, but she doesn't know that. For a moment I savor the terror I elicit, the control I have over her. It's a dark emotion, something I'm not proud of, but it's there nonetheless.

I flip my Böker around. Bring the hilt down full force against her temple. Her eyes roll back, and her face goes slack. I press my fingers under her nose and feel air. She'll live, but she'll wake up with a hell of a headache.

Instinct more than sound tickles something in my awareness. I twist as I draw my throwing knife. Release it before I can think twice.

It flies true, striking my target in the chest, right over his heart.

The Thirsty Boy stares at the knife protruding from his protective jacket. Swallows loudly enough for me to hear.

I grimace, irritated that he almost made me break my new vow not to kill people. If he thinks I'm going to apologize, he's got the wrong girl. "Don't sneak up on me," I snap. "That'll get you killed."

He nods, his face bloodless.

I sigh, brace my hands on my thighs and push myself up off the unconscious archer. "You're lucky I didn't aim for your eye."

He says nothing. Smarter than he looks. "You are . . . ?"

"Atcitty," he says. "Marvin Atcitty."

I nod an acknowledgment. Walk over. Brace a hand against his chest and pull my knife from his flak jacket. He lets me do it all without comment. "You see anyone else up here, Marvin? Any more like this one, or maybe the White Locust himself?"

He shakes his head. "Curley went down to help Hastiin. I've cleared the perimeter. There's a cave up the trail"—he gestures higher up the path—"but it looks abandoned. I—I haven't checked. I heard the commotion"—he means Ben—"so I came as fast as I could to help Hastiin."

"Hastiin's dead."

Marvin bristles. "Curley went down to help him."

I get it. He won't believe until he sees it for himself. I run a hand over my face, feeling exhausted. My clan powers are draining, and the reality of Hastiin's death is starting to sink in. And that broken sound Ben made. I never want to hear that again.

"I'm going to take a look at the cave. Restrain this one." I kick at the archer. "And make sure you cover her mouth. She's got some sort of weaponized singing thing."

He slides his pack of supplies off his shoulder in reply.

I press past him, up the trail toward where he said he found the cave. I guess I need to see for myself too. See if there's any sign of the White Locust. Get a feel for what kind of monster he is.

Plus, if I'm honest, I can't deal with Ben right now. Because if I do, I'll have to explain her uncle's dying wish.

# Chapter 6

The cave is empty, or, more correctly, abandoned. It's clear someone's been living here, and more than one someone. There are shallow shelves carved in the walls that still hold a stash of canned goods. A spatula and a wooden spoon hang next to each other from hooks forced into the cracks in the rock, and a tub of soapy water sits next to a Coleman camp stove, both on an old Walmart folding table. A metal chair is pushed back from the table in front of the remains of someone's breakfast, hastily left unfinished. The archer was definitely living here. But it looks like she was living alone, at least for now. But if they'd all fled, why leave one woman behind alone? To protect something? To punish her?

There are papers on the table next to the Coleman. I dig through them, looking for some sign of where the White Locust and his people might have gone. I find a guard schedule, penciled in neat, precise handwriting. A list of traveling supplies. An inventory of weapons.

The weapons list gives me pause. Hastiin was right. The White Locust has a shitload of explosives. And not just explosives. Compound bows, likely similar to the one the archer was using. Small firearms. Long guns. Grenades. I'm starting to think we were lucky we missed visiting with the White Locust. Guns are one thing, but a grenade?

A map catches my eye. Lake Asááyi is clearly marked with a "RV." No idea what that means. Black pencil limns the road back to the main highway and then down through Tse Bonito, all the way to the southern Wall. The markings end abruptly at Lupton, a small border town on the edge of the Wall. Beyond Lupton, on the other side of the Wall, is the old highway. Route 66, they used to call it, and then Interstate 40.

I pocket the map in case the Thirsty Boys want to take a look, but I can guarantee that the Thirsty Boys won't cross the Wall for any amount of trade, or revenge. The truth is that Dinétah got off easy when the rest of the world went to shit. Outside that wall is the horror of what happened to everyone else. And it may sound truly selfish, but I've had enough horror in my life. I don't want to know about other people's horrors too.

I walk past the makeshift kitchen to find at least a dozen crudely dug holes, wide enough to accommodate a human and about ten to fifteen feet deep. I bend to look down into one and see blankets piled at the bottom. Sleeping holes? Prisons? Whatever they are, people were living in them. In the last hole I find him. The Tribal Council representative. Dead. But there's no smell, so he can't have been dead long. A day, two days max.

A sound comes from outside the cave. A high-pitched keening, the sound of a girl in mourning, that instinctively makes me want to cover my ears and run away.

But as much as I'm tempted to run, I don't have the option. I owe Hastiin for the month he took me in, gave me a purpose with the Thirsty Boys so that I wouldn't dwell on what happened at Black Mesa, what I'd done there. The blood staining my hands. I owe him for his friendship, prickly as it was. For his forgiveness of my social transgressions. For being there, in his own way, when everyone else was ready to give up on me.

And so, mouth set in a grim line and soul aching, I leave the cave to face Hastiin's niece.

# Chapter 7

Marvin Atcitty's splayed the archer out on her back, tied and staked spread-eagle. She's got a skull bandanna stuffed in her mouth, and her eyes roll wildly between Atcitty, the other Thirsty Boy, and now me.

"What's going on?" I ask. I expected them to have the prisoner tied up and ready to take back to Tse Bonito to be turned over to the police or the Law Dogs or whoever's in charge of paying out the bounty. "Why is she staked to the ground?"

Ben rises to her feet. The front of her shirt is covered in blood I know isn't hers.

"Maggie," she says. Her voice is a teary whisper. Her eyes are red-rimmed and so hard to look at that I have to stop myself from turning away.

"Maggie?" she says again, but this time her voice is heavy with a question. More than a question. A demand.

She wants something from me. Something terrible that I recognize. Hastiin must have told her stories about me. About the bloodthirsty monsterslayer. About the indiscriminate killer.

And now she's asking me to be that person for her. To kill the archer.

I know it.

But it's a request that I have no interest in fulfilling. My stomach hardens like a rock. My jaw clenches, the frustration so acute that I dig my fingernails into my palm for relief. I relax my hand, but the tiny moons shallow with blood stay carved in my flesh.

"No, Ben," I say, my voice firm. It's not her fault that Hastiin misled her, but I won't be that monster for her. I can't.

She whimpers. Looks to my hip where my Böker is sheathed.

"Ask Atcitty," I tell her, somewhere between weary and angry. "Or that other guy. I don't owe you this."

"My uncle said it would be you. If I got in trouble, I should ask you. That the Boys weren't . . ."

"Weren't what?"

"Killers." She looks right at me as she says it. Hard, uncompromising. Older than sixteen.

I must have looked the same way when I was her age and faced down the men who killed my nalí. It's not a good thing.

I curse. Something crude enough to make Atcitty shuffle his feet uncomfortably. The archer between us writhes in her bonds, looks at me with big brown eyes, pleading for her life. A cut mars her cheek, blood smeared across her face from where I punched her.

"Don't ask me this, Ben."

"I have to."

"You don't."

"I—please."

I flinch back like she hit me. So dumb. Such a small word, trite even. But I can't ignore it. My surrender must show in the set of my shoulders, the way I shift on my feet, because Atcitty comes forward to unstake the archer's hands and legs and pull her up on her knees. He stretches her arms up high behind her, pulls her head back, exposing her throat.

So easy.

I glance at the other Thirsty Boy, but he's looking down into the valley where somewhere below us Lake Asááyi glitters in the late-morning sun. "Coward," I mutter, and watch him recoil.

As I come to her, the archer's strange wings flare momentarily. They look like spun lace in the sunlight, fine and delicate. Atcitty struggles to hold her. I lay the tip of the Böker against the delicate skin in the hollow of her throat. She stills, wings drooping to her sides.

One cut, one small thrust of my hand, and the blade is in her brain. But I wait, pull the bandanna from her mouth, and ask instead, "Who are you?"

She opens her mouth, and I tap her chin with the tip of my knife. "Words," I warn her. "I hear singing and it's the last noise you'll make."

"What are you doing?" Ben shouts, confused. "I don't care who she is. I want her dead."

"We need information," I say. Not a lie, but I'm definitely stalling. "You want to know about the White Locust, don't you? We won't know anything if she's dead."

"I don't care about—"

"Ben," Atcitty says gently. "We should find out."

Ben stares at him as if he's betrayed her, but she quiets anyway.

"You seek the White Locust," the archer says, her voice ringing, "but he is gone. You will get nothing from me."

"Break her wing," I instruct Atcitty.

The archer makes a strangled cry and Atcitty glares at me. I shrug, unimpressed with his disapproval. "It's either that or I just kill her outright," I tell him, "but if you want her to talk . . ."

Atcitty twists the thin wire at the top of the membrane, and the archer's wing crumbles. She screams and buckles, folding her body over her right shoulder as if she could protect it. We wait until she calms, her breath coming in slow, painful pants.

The other Thirsty Boy, Curley, curses darkly and walks away. Fucking cowards, all of them.

"You won't find him!" the archer says, barely above a whisper. Her face is slick and fevered with sweat. "You're too late. You can torture me, but it won't matter. He's gone!"

"Gone where?" I ask.

"To call for a reckoning. To cleanse the unworthy from this world."

"Original," I say.

"She's not going to—" Atcitty begins, and then cuts off abruptly as Ben rushes forward.

"Do you know who this is?" Ben screams in the archer's face, spittle flying. She thrusts a finger in my direction. "She's the Monsterslayer," Ben hisses. "Have you heard of her? If you've heard of her, then you should be afraid."

I stare at Ben. What exactly did Hastiin tell her? Do I even want to know? I want to tell her I'm not some sort of boogeyman, no matter what her uncle said.

But Hastiin's niece won't look at me. Her eyes bore into the woman kneeling in front of her. "She slit the throat of Coyote because he double-crossed her, and she buried alive Naayéé' Neizghání, the hero of Dinétah, even though she really loved him. She shot a powerful medicine man through the heart. So, who are you? Who are you that she won't slit your throat? That she won't bury you alive? Or slice off your wings inch by inch? Or cut out your tongue out to make sure you never sing again!"

Holy fucking hell.

The woman looks at me, eyes huge. She mouths something I can't quite follow. Again, less than a whisper. Again, growing louder until I can make out what she is saying.

"Godslayer."

"Godslayer," she says again, louder, as she starts to tremble.

"Godslayer!" she screams. She shakes, spasms of fear juddering through her body. She shrieks the word again, bending in half and convulsing painfully. Her good wing flares, and she jerks forward. Ben stumbles back, thrown off-balance.

The archer wrenches away from Atcitty. And for a moment she's free.

Ben surges forward to meet her, something in her hand. She thrusts her arm forward. Blood sprays, hitting me in the face. The archer falls.

The knife, the flimsy little knife the archer had before, is planted in her lower torso. The woman gasps, hands grasping for the hilt. But Ben falls on her, grabbing the knife and stabbing her again. Twice more until the knife breaks off at the handle. And then Ben starts beating her with her bare hands.

"That's enough!" I yell, dragging her off. "Stop it, Ben! Enough!"

I shake her until she stops struggling. Her hands tremble, palms coated in blood. Her face is drained of color, and she looks at me with huge lost eyes.

Dammit.

Atcitty's eyes meet mine, and he glances down at the archer. Shrugs. Not dead, despite Ben's best efforts. A belly wound with a knife like that may cause a lot of blood, but it will take more than that to kill.

"I never killed anyone before," Ben whispers, head against my chest.

"Of course you haven't killed anyone," I tell Ben, trying to sound soothing. I don't have the heart to tell Ben that the archer will probably live if the Boys can get her medical care in time. I nod to Atcitty, who nods back in understanding.

I wrap an arm around her shoulders and lead Ben away, down the mountain, careful to keep her turned until we're far enough away that she can't look back.

"I—I was just so angry," she sobs. "And she was going to get away. I—I had to kill her, didn't I? I had to."

Probably not, to both of those, but no need to tell Ben that now.

"My uncle's going to be so mad."

I close my eyes. "Ben . . ."

"Oh." She nods. "Right. He's dead."

Her knees give. I catch her just before she hits the ground.

# Chapter 8

We don't speak on the drive home. Ben curls up in the passenger's seat of the jeep, a small ball of grief. I keep my eyes on the road, try to avoid the worst of the potholes and keep the jostling to a minimum. We get back to my trailer with the setting sun, the vehicle rattling over the cattle grate. The noise wakes Ben from her stupor. She looks around, confused.

"We're at your place?" she asks, as I guide the vehicle up the sloping hill to my house. The lights are on above the porch, and in the front window, a warm glow that tells me Tah is in there making an early dinner or afternoon tea. At the thought, my muscles slide loose and some of the horror of the afternoon fades. I decide right then and there to clear the air with Tah and fix the rift I've let fester. If that means talking about Kai, so be it. It's time I made things right between us.

But that vow holds only until Tah opens the door, a cup of broth in his hands. He doesn't say anything, just takes one look at Ben, wrung-out and blood-spattered, and hustles her into the house. I can hear him fussing, probably getting her out of those bloody clothes and making her wash up before he puts her to bed.

I collapse on the couch, mindful of my own bloody face and

clothes, but too tired to do much about it. Dealing with a shell-shocked teenager seems to have compounded my fatigue.

Confident Tah's got Ben in hand, I close my eyes. Just a moment of rest before I figure out what comes next.

I wake up to Tah standing over me, holding out a cup of broth. I take it, grateful and silent, and we sit together, stealing a moment of peace. He waits until I've finished my broth to ask what happened.

"Hastiin's dead." I don't equivocate. "Arrow through the throat. The brain. She saw it all."

Tah sighs, long and heavy. "He was a good man."

"No, he was a complete ass," I say, tired, "but he was my friend in the end. And I don't have many of those."

Tah nods. "And who is the girl?"

"His niece. A tracker with clan powers."

Tah's eyes are tired. "So she's a bit like you, then, Maggie."

"I hope not." He looks surprised at my vehemence. "I don't want anyone to go through what I went through, Tah. It would be better to be dead. I mean it."

"But she's already come into her clan powers. So she's already suffered. And her clans aren't . . . She's not . . ."

He's trying to say she's not K'aahanáanii, so she won't suffer the same blood lust as me. She won't become a killer.

"She's Foot Path, born for Deer People, or something like that," I acknowledge. "But she did try to kill that woman today, up on the ridge. The one who killed Hastiin." And she said some awful things about me, but I don't tell Tah that.

"Ah . . . ," Tah says, sounding disappointed. Weary. "Ah."

"There's something else. Before Hastiin died, he asked me to watch after her."

Tah fiddles with a silver ring, a habit Kai had too. It makes me smile. And then it makes me unconscionably sad.

"And what did you say, Maggie?"

“To Hastiin? Nothing. He died before I could answer him.”

“What will you do?”

I rub a hand across my face, belatedly realize that I’m raining flakes of dried blood onto my shirt. “Honestly, Tah? I haven’t got a clue.”

He pats my knee. He takes the empty cup from my hand and stands. “Tomorrow, then,” he says.

I nod, close my eyes, and fall asleep sitting up on the couch.

# Chapter 9

I wake to barking dogs. Watery dawn filters in through the curtains of the living room, and at first I think my pups must be doing their morning all-clear. But then I hear voices, definitely human and definitely outside my window.

"Maybe she's not here." A male voice.

"Her truck is here," says a female voice.

"But—"

"Just knock before I shoot one of these fucking dogs."

I know those voices. And the shock of hearing them after all these weeks makes me momentarily forget the horrors of the day before. My pulse ticks up, and a fluttery feeling tickles my stomach. If Rissa and Clive Goodacre are here, then maybe he is too. Maybe Kai's finally come.

I realize I'm still in my blood-crusted hunting clothes, so I hurry to the bathroom and scrub my face clean. No time to change, so I'm stuck in the same shirt, but I wear black for a reason—it hides bloodstains. I think about brushing my hair or doing something—I'm not sure exactly what—to make myself look more presentable. My hands are suddenly clumsy, and I wipe them on my pants, telling myself to calm down. That if he's waited this long, maybe it's not what I think it is. Maybe this isn't some happy reunion. Maybe he's not here at all.

My heart slows back to normal with that sobering thought, just as a thick hand hammers on my front door. I retrieve the Glock from where I left it last night. I raise the gun to eye level, shift my angle up slightly to adjust for the twins' height, and pull the door open.

Despite having a gun in his face, the man on my doorstep breaks into a grin. His brown face brightens under the relative dimness of my porch light, the freckles on his cheeks glowing like tiny brown stars. I can't see his kinky red hair under the black beanie he's wearing, but I know it's there. He's wearing a dark green bomber jacket over a tan T-shirt only a shade lighter than his skin. The T-shirt stretches taut over athlete-size shoulders, showing off impressively massive muscles. But Clive's muscles are the last thing on my mind.

"Is he here?" I ask, my breath hitching on the last word.

He doesn't need to ask who. The man shakes his head, his smile dimming.

I press my lips together, hold back something that feels like a wail. Swallow that down and blink my eyes to clear the unfamiliar tears. It's a moment of weakness I resent, and more than anything, I hate that someone saw it. But I'm still holding a gun, so that helps a little.

"I don't mean to be rude," I say, my voice sounding falsely nonchalant, "but what do you want, Clive?"

Footsteps and Clive's twin comes forward out of the night. She's wearing the same jacket, tan shirt, and dark green pants tucked into combat boots, the same assault rifle slung over her shoulder. But no hat and her thick red curls are braided in two long plaits down her back. Something about Rissa seem to repel the light, coiling in shadows around her head. I know they're twins, but there's something hard about Rissa that her brother doesn't possess. Something more dangerous. Something that pricks my senses and tells me to "Beware."

"We come in peace," she says.

I shift the gun to point at her. "I heard you threaten my dogs. You touch my dogs?"

"No." She sounds irritated, but I heard what she said, and I take Rissa's threats seriously, whether they're against my dogs. Or against me.

I scan the yard for my pups. They've gone back to their patrolling now that I'm at the door and taking care of things. Satisfied Rissa was only being an ass, but still wary of the twins' intentions, I say, "Speaking of threats, you know what my next question is going to be, Rissa."

She nods. Holds up her hands in innocence. "I said we come in peace."

"Because last time we saw each other you said you'd try to kill me if you ever saw me again."

Clive makes a surprised face and looks back at his sister. Interesting. Did Clive not know?

"Things have changed," Rissa says.

"And?"

"And what?"

"And I think you owe me an apology," I say.

She sighs audibly, and her brother frowns. I can tell Rissa would rather eat nails than apologize. Too bad. I'm not going to forget the way she ran me out of Black Mesa at gunpoint, threats of murder over my head. Even if was a misunderstanding. Hastiin came and apologized, so Rissa can too.

Oh, Hastiin. The twins don't know.

"It's not my fault that you and that medicine man were keeping secrets," Rissa says. "How was I supposed to know he could come back from the dead? And you still put Neizghání in that trap. He's the hero of Dinétah. It's still wrong what you did. And I don't owe you shit."

*That medicine man?* Is that how she sees Kai now? A knot of uneasiness twists in my belly. Something's wrong. Something's wrong with Kai. There's a reason he's not here. Relief, quickly followed by worry. But I'll be damned if I let Rissa see that.

"Then we're done here," I tell her. "See yourselves out of my yard."

"I knew she wouldn't help us," she says, throwing up a hand in irritation.

"Maggie, wait," Clive says, reaching out as if to touch my arm. I arch an eyebrow at his outstretched hand. He freezes, maybe remembering what happened the last time he tried to touch me without permission. Not that I'd draw a knife on him now, but you never know. I'm jittery like that.

"Rissa's just upset. She doesn't mean it."

"Sounds like she means it."

Clive looks meaningfully at his sister. "She doesn't. We need to talk to you. Can we come in?"

"What do you want, Clive? Why are you here?"

"That's why we've come," he says. "Kai's in trouble."

Reluctantly, and against my better judgment, I let the Goodacre twins in. They squeeze into my living room, broad shoulders taking up all the space, Rissa's attitude sucking the air out of the room. Whatever it is, my demand that she apologize or something else that's bothering her, hangs like a foul cloud around us.

I gesture with the Glock for them to move past me so I can stay close to the door. They do as they're told.

"Can we put our hands down now?" Rissa asks.

"No."

She stops in the act of lowering her hands and raises them back up. Gives me a look of disgust. But it's fine. I'm getting used to her disapproval. Clive waits, his face patient.

"Lower your hands," I say. "But keep them where I can see them. You carrying anything besides those rifles?" It's sort of a rhetorical question. I remember well enough both the Goodacres' love of a firearm.

Rissa hesitates.

"A .44," Clive says. "Rissa's got a .44 Magnum in a shoulder holster under her jacket."

"Jesus, asshole," she mutters.

"Hey, be grateful," I say. "Clive is the only thing keeping you inside my door right now, so I suggest you thank your brother for his honesty."

"This is so unnecessary. I already said that I come in pea—"

I cut her off with a look.

"Fine." She tears open her jacket and reaches for the sidearm.

"Slow."

She grimaces, but moves nice and slow, holding the gun away from her body. Lays it on the floor. They both do the same with the ARs.

Clive takes a few steps back until his big body is framed by the kitchen door. Rissa flops onto the chair next to him. It's my second favorite chair, and I only have two. Confident they are far enough away from their guns that they can't surprise me, I lower my Glock.

"So, tell me what's wrong."

Rissa gestures to her brother like she's finished talking to me and it's Clive's turn. Clive shifts on his feet. "Well, it's not that we think he did it. At least I don't. Rissa doesn't agree, but she doesn't know Kai like I do. Like you do too, I mean. I just don't see him doing something like that, do you?"

I'm trying to follow what Clive is saying, but he's not making a lot of sense. "From the beginning."

He flushes, showing red at the neck. "Well, I don't remember much of Black Mesa. Rissa can tell you what happened after you left."

"No," I say, exasperated. "Not that beginning. Why are you here?" The one thing I really want to know sits on the tip of my tongue, demanding I ask. But what if they say he's left Dinétah? Gone back to the Burque or somewhere else I can't follow. What if they say he doesn't want to see me?

"He's missing," Rissa says, an answer to my questions, asked and unasked.

"Kai?"

"Not just him. Caleb, too."

"Who's Caleb?"

"Our little brother."

I remember. The teenager at the gatehouse when I brought Kai to the All-American for the first time. We had been running from the Law Dogs, and Kai had been bloody from the beating he'd taken from Longarm. That was before I knew he had healing powers. But I'd never learned the youngest Goodacre's name. Just called him Freckles.

"What do you mean they're 'missing'?"

The siblings exchange a look.

"Maybe you want to sit down," Clive says, his voice gentle enough to make me nervous.

Rissa's face darkens, angry. "Clive, I said no."

"She deserves to know."

"And we'll tell her. But not here. Mom said to bring her back. That the only way she would understand is if she saw."

Clive sighs and pushes himself up. "She's right, Maggie. It'd be better if we just showed you. Every minute we waste here is a minute they both get farther away. Plus, I think it'd be better to explain it there, with Mom"—he shoots his sister a look—"and stuff."

"But Kai's not dead," I say, keeping the tremble out of my voice this time.

Rissa snorts, irritated. "If you recall, you put a bullet through his heart. If that didn't kill him, then I'm pretty sure he's not dying anytime soon."

"Maggie?" a voice calls from my bedroom doorway.

The twins both reach for their knives. Clive's on his lower back, Rissa her ankle. I mark the locations before greeting Tah.

"Are these my grandson's friends?" he asks.

Clive understands first and reaches forward to shake Tah's hand. "Sir," he says, suddenly formal. Rissa stands and offers her hand too. Even if she's pissed at Kai for some reason, she hasn't lost all her manners. Point for Grace's home training.

"The Goodacre twins," I explain to Tah. "Clive and Rissa."

"Ah," Tah says, smiling. "I know you mother, Grace. How is she?"

"She's been better," Clive admits. "That's why we're here."

Tah's brow furrows. "And did I hear you say that my grandson is missing?"

"We've come to ask Maggie's help in finding him. We think he and my brother might have been taken against their will."

"Kidnapped?"

"We're not sure."

Tah looks at me. "Maggie will help you."

And just like that Tah calls my bluff. Because the truth is that nothing in the world could keep me from going to the All-American to find Kai.

I run a hand through my hair, thinking. "I'll need some things," I tell the twins as I turn toward the bedroom.

Tah, behind me, says, "Can I make you both some tea?"

# Chapter 10

"Who's out there?" Ben asks, a small dark lump in the middle of my bed. I'd forgotten she was here.

"Some people I know," I say, stepping over Tah's makeshift pallet on the floor.

"Friends?"

"Not exactly." Ben watches me as I pull the sword scabbard from the closet. Run my hands along the black leather. The baldric is elaborately hand-tooled with Western swirls and filigrees. It's beautiful and something I would have never considered myself, but Tah said it was important to have the proper house for such a sacred weapon when he gifted it to me. Where it came from and how he could afford such a thing is beyond me. But I'm grateful. It's a work of art created by a master leatherworker. I lay the scabbard across the foot of my bed. Ben sits up to get a better look.

"Move," I tell her.

"What?"

I gesture for her to get up, and she slides off mattress. I drop to my knees and reach into the space between the mattress and the wall and pull out Neizghání's sword. Reverent and fully aware that I'm holding a supernatural weapon, I unwrap the sword from the soft cloth. It's close to four feet long, with a one-handed grip. Its core is a black wood I'm not familiar with, the edges a series of sharpened obsidian laid together so closely that they almost appear as a single edge, the slight differentiation resembling forked lightning. Legend says that the Jo'hanaa'ei, the sun, gifted Neizghání and his brother with four weapons. From these weapons Neizghání made two of his own: the lightning dagger that pierced my side in the arena at the Shalimar and this sword. The dagger is with him underneath the earth of Black Mesa.

And the sword is mine.

I've never used it, but I've seen what it can do. In Neizghání's hands, it became a living thing, a weapon of white fire. With it, he could call lightning from the sky. Take the head of a man in a single sweep. Rouse sheet lightning to wipe out armies in a single blinding blow. It's the weapon of a hero, but I'm going to have to do for now.

Ben's standing next to me, eyes glued to the sword. I give her a tight smile as I slide it into the scabbard, keeping the hilt wrapped in black cloth, secured with a length of suede tie. Wordless, she helps me lift the scabbard over my shoulder and secure the baldric across my chest.

"Are you leaving?" Ben asks, her voice small.

I nod.

"Can I come?"

"I don't think that's a good idea."

"Why not?" she asks. "Because I killed that lady?"

I pause, close my eyes. I still can't decide if it would hurt her more to know she killed the archer or that she didn't. If it were me, it would be the latter, so I go with that, at least for now.

I take a deep breath to release the tightness in my chest and turn to her. "No, Ben. It's because we don't really know each other, do we? And the Thirsty Boys will be back for you later today, and they're your family, not me. So why would I want to take you with me?"

My words are harsh, and I expect her to cringe, maybe even cry, but instead she raises her chin, her eyes blazing. "Because my uncle asked you to."

So she knows about Hastiin's request. That's unexpected.

"I know he asked you to watch after me," she continues. She steps toward me, hands on her hips. "He said that if anything happened to him . . . if he . . ." She takes a deep breath and practically shouts, "You owe him!"

"I owe him nothing," I growl through a clenched jaw.

"Then you owe me!" she says, just as defiant. We stare at each other, and even though I've faced down gods and monsters, I've got nothing on a stubborn, grieving, and annoyingly righteous teenager.

"Tell me about your clan powers."

She blinks at my quick change of subject. "What?"

"Tell me about your tracking power, and I'll let you come." Because it hasn't escaped my notice that Ben might not be a burden when I'm looking for Kai, but an asset.

She flushes. Works her jaw.

"Your choice," I say. "Tell me how they work, or you can stay with—"

"Blood," she blurts. "It's blood."

"Explain."

"I—I can find someone by the taste of their blood."

Well, that's different. "You used them up on the mountain today, but you weren't in immediate danger. I've never heard of that. How did you do it?" Something I'd noticed but hadn't had the opportunity to ask her about, all things considered.

She flushes, smooths her hair unconsciously. "Something to do with the blood part, I think. I . . . I don't really know. And I've never had anyone to ask about it before. None of the Thirsty Boys have clan powers, and my uncle doesn't . . . didn't . . . approve."

"You should ask Tah." Or Kai. Kai would know. Or at least he could figure it out. "It's a powerful thing, using your clan powers at will. It could change things." For better or worse.

"So, can I go with you or not?" she asks.

I consider. I want to know more about how her powers work, but that can wait until we have Kai back. I utter the three words I know I'll come to rue.

"You can come." I sling my bag over my shoulder. "But there are conditions."

She bounces lightly on her feet before settling down, face serious. "Like what?"

"First, you follow my rules. Second, no killing people without permission, and third, no . . . annoying me."

She grins. Actually grins.

"Get dressed and get your stuff. You've got five minutes, and then I'm leaving, with or without you."

"Yes, sir! Ma'am!" she corrects herself hastily.

"This is not the Thirsty Boys," I say. "We are not playing soldier. I am not your commanding officer. Just call me Maggie."

"Yes, Maggie," she says, giving me a sharp salute, hand to forehead.

It's not too late to change my mind. It's not. But I don't.

"One more thing, Maggie," she says, making me pause in the doorway.

She hesitates.

"What is it?"

"Can I borrow a gun?"

# Chapter 11

Back in the living room, Tah and the Goodacres are settled around my makeshift coffee table, steaming mugs of tea in hands. Tah is gesturing broadly with one hand, and Clive and Rissa are laughing. Laughing.

Then Rissa sees me and the lightness in the room cuts off like it never was. Clive sobers too. I realize they're both looking at the pommel protruding over my shoulder. Oh well. It wasn't like it was a secret.

Tah turns in his chair and sees me. He grins like he's proud of me, and I'm stupidly grateful.

"I'm ready to go!" Ben says brightly as she rushes into the room behind me. Both the Goodacres' eyebrows shoot up.

"This is Ben," I say. "She's coming with us."

"What? Why?" Rissa protests.

Clive grins. "Since when did you get a mini-me?"

I glance at Ben. Oh God, Clive's right. Ben's dressed in the same leggings and T-shirt I always wear. The only difference is she's got her big lace-up combat boots on instead of moccasins and her long hair is pulled pack in a tsiiyéél, where mine is not long enough to reach my shoulders.

“What happened to your clothes?” I ask her. “The blue fatigues?”

“Still drying,” Tah says. “They had to be washed.”

“Well, go get them. You can change when we get to the All-American.”

“I think she looks great!” Clive says, and Ben grins. “And we can always use another shooter.”

“She’s a tracker,” I explain.

“Born for Keha’atiinii,” Ben says brightly. “Foot-trails People.”

“And how exactly did she end up with you?” Rissa asks, still doubtful.

I have to tell them sooner or later. “Hastiin was her uncle.”

Clive catches the past tense, looks up. “*Was?*”

“Ben, go wait outside,” I tell the girl.

“I don’t need to—”

“Come on,” Tah says gently, coming forward to take her by the arm. “You can help me feed the dogs. They like you. Especially the little one, Ladygirl.”

Ben looks like she wants to stay, but after a forlorn glance over her shoulder, she lets Tah lead her out the door. Once it’s closed firmly, I tell the twins what happened at Lake Asááyi, what happened to Hastiin. And the final favor he asked me.

Rissa’s the first to speak. “And you’re going to do it?”

“I don’t see that I have a choice.”

“You have a choice,” she says. “You always have a choice.”

“What kind of friend would I be if I didn’t?”

“I wasn’t aware that the two of you were friends,” Rissa says dryly.

“She wants to come.”

“Of course she wants to come,” she says. “She thinks this is an adventure.”

“She’ll be with the three of us,” Clive says. “That’s actually pretty safe. Maybe safer than being with the Thirsty Boys, especially if they decide to go after that White Locust. Explosives, huh?"

"A lot. A whole arsenal. Enough to take out a town."

"Wonder what he wanted them for . . ."

"Can you both focus?" Rissa says. "We're talking about a child."

"A child I watched attempt to stab a woman to death yesterday."

Rissa waves my words away. "She was emotionally distraught. In the heat of the moment."

"That was a hell of a temper tantrum."

"Clan powers," Clive muses thoughtfully. "She could be dangerous." His eyes cut to me. "No offense."

"None taken, because you're right. She could be. Which, as you pointed out, would mean she's in good company. So we're bringing her along."

Rissa frowns.

"Bring her along, then," she says finally. "She gets killed, that's on your head." Rissa stands and, without another word, heads for the door, pausing long enough only to retrieve her guns. She passes Tah and Ben coming back in, not bothering to acknowledge them. Ben watches the Goodacre twin go, chewing worriedly on her lip, no doubt afraid that Rissa somehow vetoed her ride along.

"Don't worry. You're still in," I reassure her.

Ben grins and rushes out the door like she's afraid I'll change my mind. Clive whispers a thanks to Tah for the hospitality, grips his hand briefly, and is gone.

It's just me and Tah now. I go to shake his hand, and he gives me a hug. I'm aware of the myriad weapons strapped to my body, making me hard to get close to, but Tah hugs me anyway. His bones feel bird-thin under his shirt, and I'm reminded how fragile he is, how old.

Doubt hits me like a hammer. How did I end up here? Ben to watch over, Rissa hating me, Clive indifferent, and Kai missing. And Hastiin dead. I consider going back to my room and crawling into bed, forgetting about all these people who want something from me, expect me to be someone that I'm not.

"Don't worry about the Goodacres," Tah says, like he's reading my mind. "They'll come around. You just make sure that you take care of Ben. She's yours now."

"I know."

"And bring Kai home, Maggie. He's yours too."

# Chapter 12

Since I'm not sure how long we'll be gone, I leave my truck behind for Tah. I don't want him stuck without a vehicle. The twins came on their motorbikes, big monsters with knobby oversize tires and serious off-road suspensions, black on black so that they can't be seen at night when the Goodacres are up to more nefarious things than running a honky-tonk.

Ben's already climbing on behind Rissa. Rissa hands her a pair of goggles, which she puts on dutifully.

"You got something warm for your head?" she asks the younger girl, all her concerns about Ben tagging along seemingly gone.

"No," Ben says. "Do I need something?"

Rissa digs around in her pocket and produces a black beanie, twin to the one Clive's wearing. "Wind was rough coming up," she explains. "Cold, too. You're going to want this."

Ben pulls the beanie on, tucking her bun underneath. It's so big that Rissa reaches back to roll up the edge so the smaller girl's eyes aren't covered. Ben grins in her beanie and goggles, looking like a slightly dangerous but very nearsighted prairie dog. Rissa laughs. Turns the key in the ignition and revs the engine.

Shaking my head at the two of them and their sudden sisterhood, I head over to Clive.

"Rissa warmed up to Ben quickly," I observe.

He's been watching their exchange too. "I don't think she meant anything bad before. She's just . . . protective."

"I meant what I said earlier—that she's only coming to help us track."

He gives me a skeptical look. "Did I not see her with a gun?"

"It's mine. I'll take it away if I need to."

"Good luck with that."

"I mean it, Clive. I'll make sure she gets back to the Thirsty Boys in one piece. I didn't actually promise Hastiin I'd take care of his niece, but I plan to do it anyway."

He nods, thoughtful, before he leans back to say, "Glad you decided to come. Kai's my friend too. I want him back just as much as you do."

Our eyes meet. "Not just as much."

He holds my gaze for a moment before he says, "No. Maybe not."

Rissa pulls forward first, Clive and I follow, and my dogs escort us out.

Grace's All-American looks the same as the last time I saw it. Long strips of gray paneling line the rectangular box of a building, trying their best to look like wood but mostly looking like the cheap aluminum siding that it is. An old Budweiser banner hangs limply from the twenty-foot-high metal fence, the edge caught in a curling spool of razor wire. The All-American is usually a welcome sight, a kind refuge beyond the jurisdictional reach of the Law Dogs or just a place to have a drink and not be alone. But in the harsh light of the early-December morning, the place looks defeated. It's unsettling. Wrong.

The yard is silent, dry gravel and gray dirt. The line of garages that usually house a variety of illegal or otherwise suspect vehicles is shuttered. But it's the guardhouse that drives it home. Last time I was here Freckles stopped me there, his hands like oversize puppy paws around his assault rifle. Fierce kid, bright-eyed, innocent in a lot of ways I liked, despite having a mouth like an old rodeo hand. And me and Kai here because we were running and needed Grace's help. I'd owe Grace this, even if Kai weren't missing.

We stop at the entrance, and Rissa gets off her bike to key the heavy bolt locks and pull the gate open. Clive drives through, and I catch a glimpse of the inside of the gatehouse through the open door. The floor is stained an unmistakable brownish red. The door itself has an amoeba-like splash the same ugly color right above center. I know what it is.

Blood.

Unease flickers in my stomach, making my throat dry. The twins didn't say anything about violence.

I tap Clive on the shoulder and motion for him to cut the engine. He obliges, bringing the bike to a halt a few feet inside the gate.

"I want to look around," I say, sliding off the back. "Then I'll come meet you at the house."

"What about Mom?"

I pull my goggles off, hand them to Clive. "Tell Grace what I'm doing. She'll understand."

He doesn't argue. Just starts the bike up and winds down the driveway to disappear behind the bar.

I step into the gatehouse first. It's a modified shed, the kind people used to buy at hardware depots to store their yard tools, but this one's been decked out with an extra layer of thick concrete bricks along the interior wall that faces the road and around the entrance surrounding the metal door. No windows. There's a small table and two chairs, a dartboard with a handful of darts all stuck in the bull's-eye, and a stack of old paperback books, mostly with spaceships on the covers. All of it looks fairly undisturbed, as if whoever works here stepped out and expects to come back the next day. Certainly no signs of struggle or forced entry. Just the blood.

The blood looks like an impact stain of some kind. Something or someone was hit hard enough to spatter. Gunshot is my first thought even though the concrete bricks are intact. I examine the walls opposite me, but they're clean too. Which means that if the blood was back spatter from a gunshot, there'd be front spatter too. And there's nothing. It's possible that whoever shot the gun got hit with most of the front spatter, but surely some would have reached the walls. Plus, the twins said nothing about hearing a gunshot. But then they didn't say anything about bloodstains either. I'm not going to rule it out, but my gut says no guns.

My next thought is some kind of knife wound, and at this height, maybe to the throat. But there's no arcing patterns to suggest spray. In fact, the pattern is more like clumps of mist, almost like wisps of clouds against the walls. Kind of pretty, if it weren't, well, blood. I'm not sure what to make of it.

I pull the blue bandanna from around my neck and shake it out. Hold it flat in my palm and use my Böker to dig a few flakes of the dried blood into it. Sheathe the knife and carefully fold the bandanna closed. Tuck it in my pocket and step outside into the sun.

I walk a wide circle around the gatehouse, eyes on the ground. Slow, careful where I step, searching for prints. As much as Dinétah needs rain, for once I'm glad for the drought. No rain means footprints stick around forever, and the clay-colored dust here in Grace's yard holds prints exceedingly well. I see at least three distinct ones. A heavy boot, a moccasin, and what looks like a partial print of a bare foot.

I can eliminate the first two sets as Caleb's boot and Kai's moccasin respectively. I bend to get a closer look at the last one. Too many nasty things out here in the desert to go barefoot anywhere. Besides, the ground itself is too hot to walk on for any distance without a good pair of shoes. Wouldn't make sense for anyone to be barefoot.

I trace my finger along the outline of the print. A partial print. A graceful foot, with a high arch. As if a dancer rested only briefly here, touching on the ball of their foot. Light, too, shown by the shallow imprint.

A shadow moves between me and the sun. I look up to find Rissa coming my way, fine white gravel breaking under her feet.

"Did you see this?" I say as she joins me.

She glances down at the partial print. "Yeah. Mom's waiting for you back at the house."

"What did you make of it?" I ask, ignoring her implied command.

"I didn't. It's a footprint."

"A bare foot. That doesn't seem strange?"

She shrugs. Looks away into the sun.

I sigh. "Work with me here. We're on the same side, right?"

She exhales, annoyed. But bends to run a finger around the edge of the print, careful not to disturb it. "I guess I didn't think much about it. We get a lot of customers through here. Most of them not at their best by the end of a night bellied up to the bar, if you know what I mean. Unusual, but not impossible, for someone to lose a shoe on the way out."

"Well, whoever it was seems light on their feet."

She snorts. "Most people aren't light on their feet after a night at the All-American."

"That's my point."

She stands and brushes the dust from her hands. "You done? Mom wants to see you. It's rude to keep her waiting."

I rise too. "Don't you have cameras out here?"

"Closed circuit, feeds to an old DVR back behind the bar."

"Did it record?"

A shadow crosses her face, dragging the edges of her mouth down in disapproval. "It recorded."

"But something's wrong?"

"It recorded Kai shutting off the camera."

"I don't understand."

"There's some audio. You can hear him talking, but it's mostly incomprehensible. Then he comes into the frame, looks right at the camera." She rubs her hands up and down her arms. "I hear Caleb scream, and then . . ." She exhales and fixes me with a stare. "And then Kai come back on, clear as fucking day. Reaches up and shuts off the feed."

There's a beat of silence between us when I have no idea what to say. "Are you sure?" I finally manage.

She shakes her head. "You can see for yourself. I kept the tape."

No wonder Rissa's so angry, and no wonder she thinks looking at footprints is a waste of time. She's already convinced Kai is responsible for hurting Caleb.

"Anything else?" she asks.

"I just want to . . . If you give me a minute . . ." I walk away from Rissa's accusing glare. Head outside the gate, where there are more prints. There is a series of crisscrossing tire tracks here, but with all the traffic that comes and goes from Grace's All-American, that doesn't mean much.

Rissa joins me. "We've been closed since it happened. Those are the last prints anyone made." They're tire tracks, wide tread and off-road, which isn't unusual for Dinétah.

"So, this is the vehicle that took them. You're sure."

"I'm not one hundred percent sure, but I'm pretty sure."

"When did it happen?"

"Day before yesterday."

Almost seventy-two hours. So why wait to come to me? One look at Rissa's stormy face and I don't have to ask. I was a last resort. If she'd had any other options, I would never have found out that Kai was even missing.

"Those two would come out here together for morning duty," she continues. "I mean, usually there's nothing to worry about. We're a bar, mostly. There's deliveries sometimes, but otherwise not a lot of traffic during daylight hours. But they liked to sit together and have coffee. Caleb really liked Kai." She smiles a little. "Like a puppy the way he took to him."

"A lot of people do that. Kai's charming."

He faces darkens with suspicion. "Doesn't he have some clan power that makes him like that?"

"He does," I say carefully. Rissa's made it clear she's not a fan of clan powers. "But a lot of his charm is just the way he is. Clan powers don't work like that. They only come when you're in some sort of life-threatening situation, and they're exhausting. It's not like you go around using them all the time, and he wouldn't use them on Caleb unless he felt threatened." I don't mention Kai's superhealing, which allows him to use his clan powers more often than other people might. And I definitely don't mention Ben's seeming ability to use hers at will. I'm sure Caleb and Kai's friendship had nothing to do with Bit'ąą'nii.

She shrugs. "Well, whatever. They were friends."

Which makes this even worse in her mind. I get it.

"Nothing different about that morning?"

"If there was, I don't remember it now."

"When did you notice they were gone?"

"Clive noticed. Maybe around dusk. He usually goes out for guard duty around then. Me or him, and it was his turn. I was working the door at the bar. Anyway, Caleb's usually inside, complaining that he's starving or whatever, but he didn't come back. So, finally,

Clive went to look, and . . ." She trails off. Glances back at the gatehouse with the bloodstain.

"Did you go after them?"

She glares at me. "Of course we went after them. But the trail faded out in Tse Bonito and no one in town had seen a thing, and by that time it was dark anyway. There was nothing we could do."

"And day two?"

"We went back. Asked more questions. Got shit-all. And that's when Mom said we should . . ." Her whole face seems to bunch up in distaste.

"Grace said to come find me." I know I'm going to have to deal with this enmity between Rissa and me. I know it's left over from Black Mesa, and Caleb's disappearance has just compounded it. Maybe we can hash it out over a bottle of whiskey, or maybe we'll end up meeting at dawn and drawing down OK Corral style. Whatever it takes. But it's going to have to wait. "I'd like to get a look at that closed-circuit recording."

She slaps a hand against her leather pants. "Suit yourself. You're not going to see anything."

"Humor me. That's why I'm here, isn't it? Another set of eyes? Someone who might see something you missed."

She starts to answer me but cuts herself off. Turns on a heel and heads back to the bar, leaving me to follow. Or not. Because I have to fight the urge to curse her name and go the opposite direction, head out the fence and leave Rissa and her hostility behind. I don't need the Goodacres. I'm perfectly capable of finding Kai on my own.

But I don't leave. Too many people are involved now. Clive and Grace. Tah. Even Ben, in a way. So I swallow my choice words and jog a little to catch up.

"There was one weird thing about that tape," Rissa admits reluctantly, once we're walking side by side again.

"What's that?"

"It doesn't make a lot of sense. At first I thought it was just Caleb, but we listened to it half a dozen times. It's definitely not my brother."

"What is it?"

"Right before Kai shuts off the tape."

"Yeah?"

"I swear you can hear someone singing."

# Chapter 13

I sit at the bar while Rissa queues up the video recording. The All-American looks much the same as last time I was here. One big room, cloaked in perpetual dive-bar twilight. A wooden dance floor bordered by a smattering of low round wagon-wheel tables and squat matching chairs. Walls a dull gray-washed wood paneling that match the dull gray-washed wood-paneled exterior, decorated with a half dozen now-dark neon signs of beer makers long dead in the Big Water. Advertisements for St. Louis and Lynchburg and Milwaukee and a handful of other places that no longer exist. A long wooden bar stretches the length of the front wall, and above the bar, attached to the wall and leaning slightly toward the line of barstools, are three wide flat-paneled televisions.

Back before the Big Water, the TVs piped in the weekend football games, local teams from Dallas and Phoenix the big draws. But now there's no satellite, no networks either. The TVs are hooked to a closed-circuit feed that can show old DVD movies or pick up the feed from the security cameras Grace has around the place.

Rissa clicks a button and the whole wall of TVs comes alive at once, a grainy rain of static. She sets the remote control on the bar in front of where I've taken a seat. She turns to leave. Hesitates. "You want a drink or something?"

"Hmm?" I say, surprised she's offering.

"From the bar." Her gesture encompasses the smoky glass bottles of hooch, the double tap for Grace's homebrewed beer.

"I'm good."

She grunts, sounding dubious. "Well, if you change your mind, you know . . . after you watch it. The good whiskey is under the bar, glasses on the shelf."

"Is it that bad?"

She doesn't say anything. Just gives me a long look that could pretty much mean anything, but I think may be actual sympathy. It really is that bad.

"Thanks." I don't know what else to say.

She nods. "You know how to work the remote?"

"It's been a while, but I remember the basics. Arrow means go. Square means stop."

"And that one's rewind. And this is pause."

"Got it."

"Yeah." She stands there, arms hanging at her sides. Her mouth is twisted up like she wants to add something else, and there's a heavy double line across her forehead. I'm pretty keyed up myself. Anxious to see what's on the tape and not interested in bickering with her again.

"Got it," I repeat, my voice heavy with "go away."

She looks down at the bar, jangles the keys she has in her hands. "Mom's not well. She . . ." She clears her throat. "She thinks Caleb's dead."

It's hard to imagine Grace as anything less than the formidable woman who rules her criminal kingdom with an iron fist. But I remember how small she looked when we came back from Rock Springs, Rissa bleeding out. How vulnerable. Even then I wondered if losing another child would be the grief that would finally break her.

"I don't think he's dead," I offer.

She looks up sharply. "How would you know? You saw the blood."

"Because he's with Kai. And you of all people should know that Kai wouldn't let him die."

She pulls back a little, blinking. Her hand unconsciously moves to her stomach. Her fingers flex over the spot where the monsters ripped her belly open. Hopefully she's remembering that Kai saved her life, and that should mean something, should matter when she's ready to throw him over as some sort of traitor.

She stares at me, her hazel eyes weary. Scared. "I hope you're right. I really do."

Once Rissa's gone, I turn back to the bank of TVs. Take a deep breath. And pick up the remote. I press play. Hold it for a second, afraid to let go. The feeling of the button is a dull rubbery firmness that belies the anxiety of the moment.

"Better to know," I tell myself. And let go of the button.

The picture comes up in triplicate. At first there's nothing, just empty space and a camera trained at the door of the gatehouse, a good view of any vehicle trying to enter Grace's compound. And then someone steps into frame. The back of Caleb's head. There's the sound of an engine, but the vehicle doesn't pull in, staying out of the entryway and out of view. Caleb says something, and someone outside the frame answers. A female voice.

And then there's another voice.

A voice I know all too well. It is the one I feared I might never hear again.

Kai's voice is a soothing tenor. He's the child of college professors, and it showed in the way he talked. Never nonplussed, an observational quality in the lilt of his words. It always seemed like nothing much bothered him. When we first met, I thought that was just Kai. Calm, cool, and collected. I wonder now how much of that easygoing facade was real, how much of that was a cover to hide some of the darkness that was haunting him. Even so, hearing his voice now, that same voice that pulled me back from getting lost in my own misery, rips my heart open.

I pause the recording to gather myself, and when the cool dark quiet of the bar has got me settled again, I press play.

A woman's voice answers Kai. And then a murmured question from a new voice, not Kai or Caleb but masculine. So that means that there's at least four of them, a man and a woman in the vehicle and then Kai and Caleb.

Caleb answers, sounding angry, and I catch a " . . . fucking kidding me . . ." I can't hold back the smile. That sounds just like what I remember of Freckles.

Kai again, soothing intervention. But this time his voice sends a chill dancing down my spine. It's neither quite that easygoing tenor nor the crisp professor, but something else.

Something a shade deeper, a touch sharper. I know what it is. Bit'ą́ą́'nii. He's using his clan power. Kai once referred to his clan power as "a way with words," but it's more than that. Kai possesses the power of persuasion, making him as deadly as anyone with a firearm, maybe more. Because why shoot someone when you can talk them into shooting themselves?

Not that he would. Kai was unwilling to even hold a gun, much less kill someone. Maybe this time he should have.

I sit forward, punching the little button to raise volume. Hit it again and again until it's as high as it will go. But without the visual cues, the audio feels distant, too garbled for me to follow.

Then the woman's voice, and this time she's arguing with Kai.

Impossible.

Kai's power persuaded gods.

And then singing. Beautiful, soft and rhythmic, a lilting melody I recognize immediately.

Uneasiness churns in my gut. I'm pretty sure I'm immune to that singing, but I rapidly tap the button to bring the volume down to zero. No need to take a chance.

I know who's got Kai. Caleb, too. Someone with powers of persuasion all their own.

I reach out to tap the pause button, ready to go share my discovery with the Goodacres, when Kai's face fills the screen. My finger freezes, hovering.

Just like the first time I saw him, I let out a little gasp.

His face is still perfect, an impossibly unfair combination of flawless warm-brown skin, blue-black hair, graceful features. When he looks into the camera, I swallow hard. Last time I saw him, his eyes had bled out a liquid silver, something to do with his clan powers. A mystery that neither he nor Tah understood. Part of me expected to see those eyes, the eyes of a man so strange and powerful that he could come back from the dead. But instead his eyes are normal. No, not normal. Never just normal. Beautiful. A rich reddish brown that seem to even now reflect the warmth and kindness of the man they belong to.

He looks directly into the camera. Directly at me. Mouths a sentence I can't quite follow.

And the feed shuts off.

Nothing but blank screens that, after a moment, bleed to gray rain.

I scramble to replay the video, watching it again. Not so much looking for clues as just waiting to see his face.

A second time, he looks into the camera, lips moving silently on a final phrase, ending in a blank screen.

I watch it again.

By the fourth time, when I pause the feed on Kai's face, my

hands are shaking and I'm holding back some emotion that if I let it out might shatter me whole. A joy that he's alive. A fear that I've lost him all over again. Because I've figured out what he says in that final frame, and I know his words are meant for me.

*I love you. Don't follow me.*

Six words. Simple words. Words that leave my heart stuttering in my chest, my breath coming short, but my feelings conflicted. Because the words don't make sense. If he loves me, why would he tell me not to follow him? If he was going to leave, why bother to say he loved me? Kai is smart. He would know what those six words would do to me, how they would make me want to destroy worlds to reach him, how they would send me reeling toward something as terrible as hope.

Why would he say that? Why? Unless he really thought he was saying good-bye. A thought that sends me spiraling into a future I have no interest in living.

And there it is. Clear as a desert morning. I am not willing to give Kai up. No matter my posturing about letting him come to me, no matter my fears and insecurities. No matter what he'd done in the past. Tah said that Kai was mine now, and it's true. But what he didn't say was the other half of that. I am Kai's.

And there's no way in hell I'm losing him again.

I don't even hear Ben come up behind me until she says, "Mama mercy, who is that?"

I shove my feelings down somewhere deep. Look over my shoulder at my new ward. Ben is staring at the screens, eyes wide and mouth gaping like someone just knocked her on the head with a hot-boy stick. I know the feeling.

"Don't sneak up on me," I mutter.

"Footpath People clan," she says absently. "Makes me sneaky. I can't really help it."

"Yeah, well, Footpath clan or not, I'll put a knife in your gut if you sneak up on me again."

Her eyes flicker my way, like she can't believe I just threatened her and she's not sure how to take it.

I sigh. "Just don't push your luck. My reaction time can be . . . fast."

"Wow," she says, and then, "Sorry." Not sounding all that sorry. Sounding more like a teenager who just decided I was dramatic instead of dangerous. She slides onto the barstool next to me. "That guy on the screen had me distracted. I'm bi, but I usually don't go for boys. Too much ego, if you know what I mean, but I can appreciate the lovely wherever I see it."

"So, is that the guy we're trying to find? I mean, the other one. Your Kai. He's clearly not a red."

By "red" she must mean a Goodacre. Not sure if the twins would find that insulting, but I'll leave it for her to find out on her own.

"That's Kai," I acknowledge as I hit the button and turn off the screen.

She sighs and drops her chin onto her hand, elbow propped up on the bar. "You didn't tell me he looked like that. No wonder you agreed to this gig."

I give her a tight smile but don't answer her. I can tell she wants to hear more, maybe a story about Kai. How we met. What we mean to each other. Why I shot him. But I'm not offering.

*I love you. Don't follow me.*

Ben's watching me. But she doesn't ask me what's wrong, or why I turned the video off. Instead she spins the barstool around, surveying the All-American. "This is a cool place. Very cowboy." She hops down and walks behind the bar.

"What are you doing?" I ask, suspicious.

"Having a drink," she says, eyes roaming over Grace's limited inventory. Even though the All-American is one of the more prosperous establishments of its kind, there's really only a few options for the drinker in a post–Big Water world. Grace's specialty is beer, something her and her kids brew themselves in vats out back in one of the garage bays. But on occasion she has other stuff. It's really the luck of the draw, what's coming across the Wall from New Denver or the Burque.

"You want a drink?" Ben asks me.

"Aren't you a little young to be drinking?"

Ben rolls her eyes. "Pretty sure there's no drinking age in the apocalypse." She tilts her head to give me a look. "You're not going to start mothering me, are you?"

I stare, horrified. Is that what I was doing? "Good whiskey's down there, second shelf. Glasses behind you."

She grins. Bends down to find the bottle of whiskey. She puts it on the bar triumphantly and reaches back to retrieve two glasses from the shelf. She's careful to measure us each out a shot, not too generous, but not stingy either. "Where'd you learn to pour?" I ask her.

"Thirsty Boys are my uncles," she says by way of explanation. Which I guess is pretty much all the explanation needed.

She pushes my glass over to me. I pick it up, and we briefly clink the cheap imitation crystal together in a toast. I sip mine. Watch as Ben takes a drink and immediately breaks out into a gagging cough. I raise an eyebrow and wait for her to catch her breath.

"Confession," she chokes out hoarsely, swallowing hard to clear her throat. Her face looks pained. I don't even crack a smile. "I've never drank alcohol before. My uncle would never let me. I poured for the Boys"—she waves her hand in a vague gesture—"but I never drank it. I just wanted to try it."

I don't say a word.

She coughs some more. Finds Grace's jug of drinking water and fills a clean glass. Chugs it down and, with a disgusted look on her face, tips her whiskey glass and pours the rest of her shot into mine. "Take it," she says.

Now I laugh. I figure I've let her keep her dignity long enough.

"Jesus," she mutters, wiping at her mouth. "Why on earth would people choose to drink that stuff?" She disappears behind the bar again. "Especially when . . . I thought I saw . . ." Her voice drifts off as she rummages around. I sip my whiskey, waiting. Happy for the distraction Ben provides. Trying not the see Kai's face every time I close my eyes. Hear his words. *I love you. Don't follow me.*

"Found it!" she declares, holding up a brown-and-white aluminum can.

I come back from my reverie. Notice what she's holding. "Is that . . . ?" I gasp.

"Shasta! Yes. I heard Clive mention something about soda pop to his mom, so I figured where else would you keep your rare sugary carbonated beverages but behind the bar?"

I narrow my eyes. "So you didn't come looking for me. You came to pilfer soda."

"Don't take it personally," she says. "I came to check on you too. Looks like some huge dust storm's rolling in from the west, and Clive said we should all get together in one place to wait it out. But this." She frames the soda can with her hands like a game show hostess. Something she's too young to have ever seen in person, but maybe the gesture's universal.

"You know that's probably Grace's secret stash."

"I know."

"So maybe you shouldn't drink it."

"Do you think she'll care?" She looks crestfallen.

"No," I lie, amused. Thinking of the lecture Grace would lay on Ben if she were her normal feisty self instead of what Rissa feared her mother had become. A mother heavy with the belief that she's lost her youngest child.

Ben pops the can open with a soft hissing sound. The distinctive smell of cola, a smell I would have sworn I forgot but remember as clearly as my own name, fizzes in my nose. She pours half the soda into her glass and the rest into my recently emptied whiskey glass, then comes around and sits next to me. We toast and drink. The bubbles dance against my lips, and I can't help but smile.

"So what's the plan? I figure you got a plan. If that were my boyfriend, I'd have a plan." She holds the glass to her mouth. "Even if you did shoot him."

I ignore that. Jabs from Rissa cut deeper than I'd like to admit, but Ben's feel more like teasing. Meant to make me laugh more than bleed.

I sigh. Back to business, and Ben needs to know anyway.

"Listen to this." I touch the screen, bring the video back to life. Rewind to where I want it. Bring the volume back up. "Hear that singing? Isn't that just like what we heard on the mountain?"

Her face is an open book. Horror and fascination and grief. She rolls the glass in her hands, looks up at me with big eyes. "That's the same ones who killed my uncle?"

"I think so."

"And that woman. That's the same one, isn't it? The one I killed."

"Could be," I say. "Maybe. Probably. Which means they came here first."

"And then, what? Back to Lake Asááyi?"

"Or they split up. Who knows? But the timing is right." I down the rest of my Shasta, the aftertaste of whiskey dulled by the sugary drink. "Let's go, before the dust storm hits."

I turn off the video feed. Slide off the bench. Take a few steps before I realize Ben isn't following me.

"What is it?"

She's rocking back and forth on the barstool, eyes down and hands tucked in the sleeves of her shirt. She looks young. Alone. All that teenager sass from earlier vanished like it never was.

"We're going to kill him, aren't we?" she says, her voice hard. "The White Locust?"

I think about what Kai said on that tape. He didn't know, couldn't know that Caleb's disappearance would threaten to destroy Grace, that the White Locust's follower would kill Hastiin, that his cheii would be desperately waiting for him. And I think about my vow to myself, that I'm not the indiscriminate killer I was before, definitely not the boogeyman Ben described me as up on the mountain. But before I can answer her, the walls of the All-American give a little shake. We stop still, listening, as the roar of a dust storm rolls over us.

"Damn," I mutter. "You didn't say it was coming in that fast."

We can hear the *thunk* of something hitting the roof loud enough to make me flinch. It sounds like a hail storm, but there's no way it's hailing. The weather in Dinétah doesn't vary much from dry and sunny.

The sound of objects hitting the roof gets louder, more steady.

Ben hops down off the barstool and walks toward the back door, the one facing the trailer. There're no windows in the All-American, so if we want to see what's going on, we're going to have to open a door.

"Wait," I tell her. I reach around the bar to find a couple of Grace's ubiquitous bar rags. Hand Ben one, and we tie them around our faces, covering noses and mouths. By now the sounds of the storm have become so loud I have to raise my voice to be heard.

"What's going on?" Ben asks, her voice scared. We both flinch again as something heavy lands on the roof.

"I don't know, but that doesn't sound like a normal windstorm unless it's tossing around boulders. You better let me do it." I step in front of Ben, moving her protectively behind me. She grasps the back of my shirt in her fist, holding on. "I'm going to open the door," I tell her, trying to keep my voice reassuring, "and we're going to make a run for it. On the count of three. Okay?"

She pulls a little harder at my shirt, so I take that for a yes. It's less than fifty feet to Grace's porch. Whatever is raining down on us, we can make it.

I grip the door handle. "One . . . two . . ."

But I don't get to three before the door comes crashing inward, forcing me to step back and almost knocking Ben, who's too close to me, over. I reach back to steady her as a hulking figure fills the empty space. I catch a glimpse of the storm before Clive slams the door shut.

"What in the . . . ?" I whisper, awe in my voice, my eyes still staring beyond that flimsy door.

"Locusts," Clive says grimly. He shakes his shirt out. Shudders as three insects fall to the floor. They are about an inch to an inch and a half long, a dull dusty-brown color, with the shimmering wings of a dragonfly and the long back legs I associate with a grasshopper. Clive immediately stomps on the bugs, crushing them under a heavy boot. The crunch of their carapaces is drowned out by the roar of the swarm outside.

Ben makes a choking sound as they splatter against the hardwood floor, and I'm not far behind.

"What in the hell is going on?" I ask.

Clive shudders as something huge thumps against the closed door. "That's not a windstorm out there," he says grimly. "It's a locust swarm."

"What are they?" Ben asks, her voice shaking. "Why are they here? Why are there so many of them?"

"All good questions," Clive assures her. "But right now we've got to get back to the house with Rissa and Mom. The bar's not going to hold up to this."

As if to prove Clive's point, something strikes the roof hard enough to shake a piece of the ceiling free. Plaster and Sheetrock rain down a dozen feet from us, and through the hole they leave,

I can see daylight. Or at least the place I expect daylight to be. Because all I see out there is a dark cloud of living shadow.

"Not good," I murmur.

We all watch as a single locust squeezes through the hole. And then another.

"Gotta go," Clive repeats. He hands us each a pair of goggles, which we gratefully put on. "Tuck your shirts in too. Tighten your sleeves, if you can. And make sure those towels don't leave any holes for them to get into. They stick to you"—the big man shudders again—"so move fast. They get in your hair, but there's no way to avoid it. If one gets in your clothes, don't stop. Get in the house and we'll deal with it then."

"Look!" Ben says. Crawling through the growing hole in the ceiling is what can only be called a giant. More than twice the size of the other locusts, it is at least four inches long, with iridescent wings and long spiked back legs. It swivels its huge head back and forth, mandibles snapping.

"Tell me that thing can't actually see us," I say, my voice high with a primal fear of crawling six-legged things.

"There's no way . . . ," Clive starts, but he drifts off as the giant locust settles its huge eyes on us. I swear it looks right at me.

"Run!" I shout, pushing Ben to the door. Just as the swarm breaks through the ceiling and the giant locust launches free.

# Chapter 14

There are many times I've faced down monsters in my life. Frightening creatures that made my blood run cold. But there is something about insects, the mindlessness of the horde, that is particularly terrifying.

Ben screams, Clive curses, and I move.

Honághàahnii wakes. Time slows to the pulse of an insect's wings, the sustained scream of a young girl, and between one beat and the next, my hand finds the throwing knife tucked in my moccasin. I release the blade, an impossible throw, that splits the giant locust in half. It breaks. Falls.

And then Clive's wrenching the door open, and the roof is collapsing under the weight of the insects, and we're running. Stumbling into hell.

The darkness is alive, clutching at our clothes, our hair, our skin. A million tiny claws, grasping, hungry. Honághàahnii shows me each creature clearly, a tiny individual nightmare, There's so many that there's nothing I can do but hold back the fear, keep moving, and try to shield Ben.

Ben stumbles. Trips on the stairs of the porch and goes down. I grab for her, yank her up by her shirt, but she slips from my grasp.

The swarm seems to solidify around her, a blanket of unnatural blackness. I do the only thing I can think to do.

I draw Neizghání's sword.

I lift it high, like I've seen him do a hundred times. And . . . nothing. The sword stays as it is, black obsidian on black wood, no fire. No lightning.

Shit.

But even without the lightning, it's a powerful weapon, like a sharp-edged club.

I swing it. Cleave through the swarm. Again and again, until I can get to Ben. She's struggling on hands and knees to crawl up the stairs. I reach down with my free arm and grasp Ben around the waist. Heave her up and throw her forward up the stairs. She stumbles to her feet, and then Clive is there, pulling her through the open door.

I jump the remaining stairs in a single leap, swing the sword one last time to clear my path, and tumble backward through the door. Clive slams it shut, and I hear the heavy smack of bugs against the wood.

Hands are on me, Rissa and Grace, knocking locusts from my clothes and hair. I hold my arms out, careful with the sword, as Grace whacks me with a long-handled broom.

"You're clear," Rissa says. I nod thankfully and hobble to the familiar chair by the sofa.

Ben's sitting on the floor, sniffling quietly but generally holding it together. Maybe not holding it together well, but I can't blame her. I'm not sure how well I'm holding it together and I'm used to the monsters.

Rissa and Clive are pushing furniture against the door to help it hold. And Grace . . . Oh, Grace. Rissa was right. Her mom looks frail, a bad tiding away from broken. But she's got a pair of heavy black combat boots on, and she's sweeping the bugs into piles and stomping them like she's crushing grapes for harvest.

"It won't hold," I tell the twins, breathless. "The door. There's too many, and they're not natural."

Rissa looks up. "What do you mean?"

"I mean this swarm is not natural." I catch my breath a little before I continue. "I don't believe it."

"There's been locust swarms in the past. Famous ones, that last days and cover a hundred miles. There's no reason to think this isn't one of those. I mean, they're destructive, but they'll pass. We just have to wait—"

"It looked right at us."

Grace stops her stomping to stare at me. "What?"

"The giant locust inside the bar," I say, sheathing the sword. A little tricky the first time, but I manage. "Before I killed it. It looked right at me."

"It's a bug. Be serious."

"It—it did." Ben sniffles, her arms wrapped tightly around her knees. She rocks slightly to comfort herself. "I felt it too. Like a presence. It was. . . . smart. It knew we were there."

Rissa looks grim. "What are you saying?"

"That this door isn't going to hold. That they know we're here and it's only a matter of time. They'll find another way in. There's no waiting them out because they're not going away."

"So we fight our way out," Rissa says.

"To where?" I ask. "You said it yourself. This swarm could be a hundred miles wide."

"The tunnels," Grace says.

We all turn to Grace. She may look feeble, but her eyes are sharp and her mouth is set in a determined line.

"Mom?" Clive asks.

Grace drops her broom and heads for the back bedrooms. Clive helps Ben to her feet, and we all hustle after her, the steady beat of insects striking the side of the trailer all around us.

"Help me move the bed, son," Grace says once we're in her bedroom. Dutifully, Clive pushes the mattress to the side. Rissa and I move to the other side to pull, and soon the floorboards are exposed. Sure enough, there's a trapdoor there, square and big enough to fit a person through. The lock is rusted shut, like it hasn't been used in years.

Grace goes to the dresser next to the bed and opens the top drawer. Pulls out a small key, the kind that would fit into a padlock like the one on the trapdoor. "Open it," Grace says, handing the key to Clive. He bends to fit the key in the lock. It takes a little muscle, but he gets the lock to turn. He slips the bolt off, and the door swings inward. Stale air wafts out, rich with the smell of dirt and age.

"Where does this go?" I ask.

"It's an old smuggling tunnel," Grace explains. "Used to use it to move bootleg booze and the occasional human when the Wall first went up. This is checkerboard land—Navajo police got no jurisdiction at the All-American—but there's plenty of jurisdiction between here and the Wall. So we needed a better way."

"Are you saying this tunnel goes all the way to the Wall?"

The older woman lifts a shoulder. "Used to. Now, maybe. Maybe not. Maybe it's caved in."

Rissa says, "The Wall's twenty miles east of here. We're not crawling underground in the dark for twenty miles."

"And it's the wrong direction," I say. "Caleb and Kai's trail goes west toward Tse Bonito."

"We're not crawling," Grace says. "The tunnel also goes right out to the garage, where there's some perfectly fine motorbikes that can certainly outrun a bunch of damn bugs."

Clive grins. He picks his mom up and twirls her around, planting a kiss on her cheek.

"Put me down," she complains, slapping his hands away. "Good Lord. You're going to break something."

Rissa laughs. “You’re full of secrets, Mom.”

She sighs as her son sets her gently on her feet. “A woman’s got to keep secrets. Else who is she?”

“You can’t come back here, you know,” I say. “At least for a while.”

The Goodacres look at me like I spoiled the party. I look pointedly at the walls, the ceiling, where we can still hear the constant noise of locusts.

“Grace, you can go to my house in Crystal. Tah’s there, and it’s safe enough. Thirsty Boys can help you out if there’s trouble. And the rest of us will stick to the plan. We go after Kai. And Caleb. The locusts will follow us.”

No one says anything. Rissa still looks dubious, like maybe I’m a little crazy. Like I haven’t been fighting supernatural creatures since I was fifteen.

“You think this is a coincidence?” I hiss, my voice angry. “You think some guy calling himself the White Locust just shows up, steals your son away, and then coincidently, a monster swarm of killer locusts shows up and tries to break your door down?”

“What?” Rissa and Clive say at once.

“How the hell do you know that?” Rissa asks.

“Who is the White Locust?” her brother asks at the same time.

Grace is staring at me hard, part like it’s the first sign of hope she’s had in days and part like I was keeping secrets and she’s pissed. “You better explain, Maggie.”

“There’s not really time,” I say.

“We’ll make time,” Rissa says through gritted teeth.

Grace motions her daughter to silence. “Just tell us the basics, Maggie. We have time.”

I want to argue. The locust swarm has become a black mass pressing against the windows, and that tells me different. But Grace asked, and she deserves an answer. “Hastiin and the Boys were hired to find this guy, the White Locust. It was one of his followers who killed Hastiin."

"Hastiin's dead?" Grace asks, surprised.

Ben whimpers somewhere behind me.

I nod, grim.

Grace makes a little motion, touching her head and her chest. "Then what, Maggie?" she says, voice subdued.

"Then I saw the videotape, the one from the guardhouse, and I think I recognized the woman on the tape. I think she's the same woman who killed Hastiin. She has a clan power or something similar that gives her the ability to sing this song. . . ."

I can tell Grace isn't following.

"Anyway, I'm sure it's the same people. The ones who killed Hastiin and the ones who took Kai and Caleb. And they all tie back to the White Locust."

"You still haven't told us who he is," Clive says.

"He's a cult leader," Ben volunteers. "Believes in the end of the world, cleansing Dinétah of its sins or something like that."

"What does he want with Caleb, then?" Clive asks.

"Maybe nothing," I admit. "Maybe he was just in the wrong place at the wrong time."

"You mean he came for Kai and Caleb was in the way."

"So it *is* Kai's fault," Rissa says, jaw clenched.

"You don't think Caleb's dead, do you, Maggie?" Grace asks.

"I don't. You know Kai, Grace. He wouldn't let Caleb die. He's a healer. He . . . wouldn't."

"Unless he's the one who hurt Caleb to begin with," Rissa says, "because your theory about a cult leader is great, but there's only your word for it. And it doesn't explain the bloodstains. Or what he said on that tape."

Rissa knows. She knows what Kai said to me. And in her mind, he left because he did something terrible, something unforgiveable, like kill Caleb. She believes it was his good-bye, and while I don't believe he would hurt Caleb, it's hard to argue with the rest.

"No," Grace says, voice firm. "Maggie's right. I know Kai. He's a good young man. He wouldn't hurt Caleb, and if Caleb was hurt by this White Locust man, Kai would heal him. I know that."

"How can you know that, Mom?" Rissa asks.

"Because he did the same for you."

Mother and daughter lock eyes for a moment. The room is quiet except for the growing song of the locusts outside. We all hold our breath.

And then the sound of shattering glass fills the room as the bedroom window breaks.

Chaos, as we scramble for the trapdoor and the tunnel to safety.

Rissa drops first, gun drawn, no hesitation. Clive helps his mom follow, and then Ben.

Clive shouts, "Maggie, you go fi . . ." His voice dies as he looks back at me over his shoulder. His face pales, the expression draining away in fear. Whatever he sees behind me is not good. "Maggie . . . ?" he whispers, his voice soft with terror.

I draw Neizghání's sword.

"Go!" I shout.

Without a word, Clive drops through the trapdoor.

I can feel it now, whatever horror Clive saw. It's behind me, reaching for me.

I turn and swing.

And strike a man.

I almost pull up short, I'm so shocked. But I'm moving too fast and he's too close, so I cleave him in half. Locusts splatter and break, the rotten-pork smell of their guts filling the bedroom.

And the man re-forms, his body a mass of locusts. Crawling over one another, singing their strange shrill song. He smiles, dripping locusts from his mouth, a black carapace for a tongue.

I strike again. He re-forms.

I take his head off, but it doesn't matter. As soon as the blade is clear, he re-forms.

This time, when his head re-forms, his mouth opens. His voice is the buzz of a thousand winged creatures, the song of nightmares long buried underground, the cry of a million hungry mouths. And he says one word:

"Godslayer."

Horror shudders through my body. The same word the archer called me after Ben's wild accusation.

I run.

Honágháahnii has me diving for the tunnel entrance headfirst. I hit something fleshy that grunts. Clive. He puts me on my feet and slams the trapdoor closed. Slides the bolt closed. But it won't hold long. Already locusts are trying to get in around the thin edges at the seams. Once enough are through to make a man again, I have no doubt they will.

I get to my feet, and we both sprint, sightless, through the earth. Cobwebs cling to my face, something skitters down my cheek. I slap at it, too terrified to scream. The tunnel seems to go on for miles, hours, even though logic tells me that the garage is only a few dozen yards away. But logic has no claim here, and when Clive and I finally spot hazy daylight, we stagger toward it like it's our last hope in the world.

There's a rope ladder, and I drag myself up it. Ben sticks a hand out and helps me up the last rungs. Clive is next. And we slam that door shut too.

"Where's Rissa?" I pant, my heart still hammering in my chest. "And Grace?"

"Already gone," Ben says. "They went out the back way, headed for Crystal, like you said."

"Already?" Clive asks, incredulous.

"I thought that was your plan," Ben says, looking back and forth between us, worried.

"It was," Clive says. "Until we saw that . . . thing."

"What thing?" Ben didn't see the locust man.

"No time," I say, moving toward the closest bike. "We go. We'll worry about meeting up with Rissa later."

Clive doesn't argue. Just gets on the bike. Ben slides on behind him. I climb onto the other bike, where my pack and shotgun are still tied to the rack, secure my goggles, and adjust the cloth over my nose and mouth.

"Here," Clive says, handing me a small metal device, curved to fit the shape of my ear.

"What is this?"

"Sort of like a walkie-talkie. A short-range communication link. I call it a commlink. Not the most original name, but as long as it works, right? This way we can talk to each other on the bikes."

I tuck it over my ear, the round center clicking into place. A thin wire hangs loose against my neck.

"Tap it to turn it on. Tap it again to turn it off."

"Did you build this?"

"Try it," he says.

I tap the commlink. "Can you hear me?" he asks, clear as if he were standing next to me.

I nod, then remember to talk. "I can hear you."

He gives one to Ben, who slips hers on and taps the device. "Hello!" she shouts.

I wince. "Okay, so we know they work. Let's go, and remember: Whatever you see—and I mean whatever—do not stop. Understood?"

"I know." Clive kicks the bike alive. "Where are we going?"

"Tse Bonito for now. And then"—I look over at Ben and pat the bloody bandanna in my pocket—"we'll find a way."

We skip opening the garage bay, opting to sneak out the back door single file. The swarm is still hovering around the trailer and the bar, which look as though a black blanket has been thrown over the structures themselves. I know it won't be long before the swarm figures out where we went and follows. We're buying hours, not days.

"Fire," Clive mutters over the communication link.

"What?" I speed up as we come off the dirt path and hit the paved freeway. He accelerates to stay close, Ben huddled low against his back.

"Just like the tsé nayéé', we can burn those locusts with fire."

"I don't think so. There's thousands, maybe millions, and they're smart enough to avoid it. Plus, your mom won't appreciate it if we burn her house down. We'll think of a better way."

"What if we don't?"

I have no idea what to say to that, so I don't say anything at all.

# Chapter 15

Nothing after that. Just a breakneck push to Tse Bonito, and soon the town comes into view. Tse Bonito is the main hub of activity for southeastern Dinétah, located at a T-shaped stretch of asphalt where the two main highways meet. Its busy roads are filled with shops and stew stands, interrupted by the occasional hogan or trailer, all tucked within the embrace of tall white cliffs. I hate it. Always have. And I hate it even more since everything with Longarm went down. But I can't avoid it today.

We move through town, weaving through afternoon traffic. I'm pretty covered up—goggles, rag over half my face—and I have no reason to think the Law Dogs might be looking for me, but I keep my eyes peeled, wary of every glimpse of khaki I catch out of the corner of my eye. Mostly it's Diné people, going about their business. Oblivious to the swarm of locusts thirty miles behind us.

Clive leads us to the dusty parking lot of a pawn shop just off the main drag. The lot is crisscrossed with a hundred different tire tracks. He kills the engine and gets off. The pawn shop looks like pretty much every pawn shop I've ever seen. A long rectangular building with a white concrete exterior, one of those cheap buildings they built when the economy was booming and people were more worried about speed and practicality than beauty. The long flat front has no windows, just two glass doors huddled at the west end of the building. Above the doors is a sign that says CAFÉ & PAWN.

"This where we're stopping?" I ask.

"We'll wait here for Rissa."

"Isn't this a little public?"

"This is where their trail ended." He kicks at the dusty parking lot, sending up swirls of dirt, disturbing the patterns of a hundred vehicles and footprints. "She'll know to come here."

No wonder they lost the trail here. If Kai came through this parking lot, there's no way we'd be able to distinguish which tracks were his just by looking with our eyes. But we aren't just looking with our eyes, or even just our noses. We have a secret weapon.

Who right now is checking her profile in the glass doors, striking various cool poses on the back of Clive's bike.

"Go on," I tell Clive. "I want to talk to Ben for a minute."

She stops the modeling and turns to me.

"About what?"

"Girl stuff." I smile flatly.

Clive frowns, no doubt remembering just how hard he had to work to get me into a full face of makeup before. But he doesn't ask questions. Just shakes his head and goes inside, boots making a heavy clatter on the concrete step.

I lean back on my bike and strip off my leather gloves. Reach into my pocket and gingerly pull out my blue bandanna. Unfold it.

Ben slides off the bike to come over and look. "What is that?"

"Come see."

"Does it have to do with girl talk?" she asks suspiciously.

"No," I admit. I hold the bandanna out to her. "I want you to do your thing."

She blanches, looks up at me. "Do what thing?"

"Born for Keha'atiinii, right?"

She nods, wary.

"I took this blood from the guardhouse. It's either Kai's or Caleb's. And you said your power works with blood. I assume that means you track people by their blood."

Her eyes are as big as fry breads.

I say, "Stop me if I'm wrong here."

"Not wrong," she whispers.

"Good. So here's your blood sample. We're in the last place we know Kai and Caleb were. So"—I wave a hand—"do your thing."

She takes a step back from me, and another, her eyes fixed on the flakes of blood in the cloth.

I sigh. She seemed so proud of her clan power. I didn't expect her to get stage fright. "Is there a problem?"

"No," she says quickly. "It's just . . ." Brown eyes look up at me. And I think I get it. I fold up the bandanna carefully. Hold it in my hand, which I fold in my lap.

"You want to know how I got my clan powers? My nalí and I were attacked by monsters. Monsters who murdered her in front of me. They were going to murder me, too. But something happened, and they didn't. Because I murdered them all first." I shift in my seat. "I killed them all, Ben. Violently. Brutally. And I loved it."

"You did?" A whisper.

"Never felt better in my life."

"How old were you?" she asks, her voice so soft it's almost lost to the wind.

"Fifteen."

She looks up, a little less scared.

"So, if there's something not so pretty about your clan power . . ." I shrug. "It's not going to faze me."

She swallows. "Okay, but not here. It's too public." She walks away, disappearing around the corner of the building, where a narrow alley separates it from some sort of fueling station. I follow her. She's waiting for me in the shadows.

"You sure I don't need to threaten you or something?" I ask, feeling a little awkward. "Put you in danger?"

"No. Besides, I would have to believe it, Maggie. Even if you threatened me, I would know you didn't mean it."

"Oh, I can make you believe I mean it."

She bites the edge of her lower lip, considering. "I can never tell if you're serious," she finally admits.

"I'm always serious."

She stares at me a little longer before she sighs. "Well, it doesn't matter. I don't need it. So . . ." She holds out a hand, gesturing for the bandanna. Her face is eager now, almost hungry. I hand her the cloth, and she holds it up to her face. I expect her to sniff it, but she doesn't. She licks it. Licks it again until she's licked off all the blood. Smiles like it was sugar candy.

Unexpected, but I promised not to freak, so I press my lips together and keep my word.

Her slender form shudders, and something supernatural rolls across her like a wave of heat I can almost feel. Instinctively, I take a step back. Her eyes close, and she lets out a moan of what in other circumstances I might mistake for pleasure. She rolls her head ear to shoulder. Left and then right and then left again before she straightens. And inhales like she could suck down the whole world.

She opens eyes narrowed to pinpricks of dark ink in a sea of white.

Okay.

She spins slowly, like she's looking for something. Something in the crowded streets that only she can see. She stops, points a steady hand. And exhales a pale red mist. It hangs in the air for a moment before it rolls thinly southwest.

"Damn," I whisper, at a loss for anything more eloquent.

She shudders and blinks, and her irises expand back to normal, brown islands growing large. She looks a little unsteady, so I lead her over to a metal guardrail that doubles as a bench. She leans forward, arms braced against her knees and head down, looking tired. Clan powers exhaust.

"Now what?" I ask her after she's had a few moments to recover.

"Now we follow the blood mist."

"It's gone."

She shakes her head. "Not to me. That person, I know them now. Could find them anywhere. I don't actually need to follow the mist. I can . . . feel them inside me."

I sit next to her, thinking. "Do you want to tell me how you got your clan powers?"

She looks up. "Please don't make me."

"Never," I reassure her, part of me already regretting prying and part of me relieved she doesn't want to share. "But if you want to talk . . ." *Please don't want to talk.*

She gives me a small smile. She reaches over and squeezes my hand. "My uncle was right, Maggie. You make a great auntie."

We find Clive inside at the small café. The café is not much, just a collection of half a dozen square tables and mismatched chairs where a woman named Cat, if her name tag is anything to go by, has informed us of the day's menu and brought Clive a plate of grease-soaked yeast bread. He's happily stuffing the thick bread in his mouth like he hasn't eaten for days. Around bites he says, "So how'd the girl talk go?"

"Great!" Ben chirps, and I think she means it.

I look up briefly as Cat brings another plate of bread, dripping with mutton grease. She also sets down a bowl of corn stew. All in front of Ben. There isn't much meat in the stew, but the kernels of steamed corn are plentiful, and the broth looks rich. My stomach grumbles as I realize that I haven't eaten today and didn't eat anything but Tah's broth yesterday. I wait for Cat to come back with more bread and another bowl.

"I'm not saying you're wrong, Ben," Clive is saying. "But shouldn't we get some kind of outside confirmation? The only thing south of here is the Wall."

I must have missed some part of the conversation. Ben must have told him what she'd done. Probably not the details, but enough.

"They were kidnapped, remember?" I say, my mind still on my potential meal. The woman, Cat, is back over behind the counter, not looking like she's planning to bring me anything, and my hunger is quickly turning to irritation.

"Yes, but even if . . ." Clive continues, but I'm not really listening. I'm staring a hole in Cat's head, willing her to look my way. She finally does, and I point to Ben's food suggestively.

"I'm all out," she says impassively before turning back to whatever it is she's doing besides feeding me.

I lean back, tipping the front of my chair off the tile floor, and gaze back behind the counter to the two-burner she's running. A hug metal pot bubbles gently under a low fire, smelling like steamed corn and fresh chilé. Clearly there's more stew.

Clive finally notices I'm not listening and stops talking. His eyes flicker between Cat and me, picking up on the strange tension. Ben, however, keeps eating, making happy noises as she shovels another spoonful of corn stew into her mouth. I try not to take Ben's teenage metabolism personally.

"Seems there's more stew," I say evenly, eyes on Cat.

She sniffs and folds her arms below her breasts. Gives me a look usually reserved for naughty children. "For them. For you? I'm all out."

I can hear Clive sigh heavily. Ben finally looks up from her bowl. "What's going on?" she asks, her mouth full.

"What *is* going on?" I ask Cat.

She narrows her eyes. "You don't recognize me, do you, child? Do your eyes not see? Can your nose not scent?"

She stares at me, a challenge.

I stare back. "I don't give a—"

"Maggie," Clive warns. "Drop it."

"But—"

He shakes he head. "Don't go borrowing trouble from strangers. We've got bigger problems right now."

"Then you can share," I say, reaching over and pulling his half-full bowl to me.

He doesn't argue. In fact, he rips his bread in half and hands me some. I eat. A few more bites stop my stomach from complaining, but it's not enough to fill me, to replenish what I spent fighting the locusts earlier, what I spent on the mountain the day before. But it will have to do.

I pass the bowl back to Clive. Shoot a glance toward the counter where Cat was, but she's turned away from us, busy in her tiny kitchen.

"What were you saying about the Wall?" I ask Clive, ready to listen.

"Just that the direction Ben's suggesting, there's nothing there. Only empty desert until you hit the town of Lupton, and from there, the Wall."

"The map!" I exclaim, remembering. In the chaos of the afternoon, I'd forgotten all about the map. "There was a map, back at the camp at Lake Asááyi. There was a route marked that led to Lupton. I'd forgotten about it until now."

"What's at Lupton?" Ben asks.

"It's the southern entrance into Dinétah. There's a refugee post, like Rock Springs. Remember Rock Springs, Maggie?" He turns back to Ben. "They process people wanting to enter, check your CIB, find a relative who will vouch for you. Immigration stuff."

I scratch absently at my neck, thinking. The southern entrance. That means it's also the southern exit. But surely not . . .

"Do you think they left Dinétah?" Ben asks, the very thing I was thinking.

"No." Clive's voice is definite. Final. "Nobody *wants* to go to the Malpais."

"The Malpais?" Ben asks. A tiny piece of corn flies out of her mouth and lands on the table. I give her a look. She wipes it away, sheepish.

"It's everything south of the Wall, along the old highway," I explain. "What was it called?"

"Interstate 40," Clive says. "And it's a wasteland."

"It was Route 66," a voice behind me interrupts. I look over my shoulder as Cat sets a fresh bowl of stew in front of me. Bread, too, the grease shining under the artificial light. I look at Clive. He shrugs. Ben shakes her head and mouths, *Poisoned?*

To my shock, Cat pulls out the empty chair to my left and sits. Tears off a piece of my bread, runs it through the grease, and starts eating. "It was always Route 66. Some terrible men called it I-40 for a while, but that didn't make it so. It didn't change its soul. It will always be Route 66."

She smiles when she says it, like the name means something. And maybe it does. Maybe giving a road a name is not so different from giving a person a name. Outside of the main highways, most roads on the rez don't even have names. They're simply "the road right after the big red rock" or "the road near that abandoned school bus." Easy enough. But maybe when you give a road a name, it changes it.

"Sometimes they called her the Mother Road," Cat says, eyes still dreamy. "She ran from Chicago all the way to the ocean in Santa Monica."

"What's a Chicago?" Ben asks, sounding confused. "Or for that matter, a Santa Monica?"

"They were major cities before the Big Water," Clive says. "We learned about them in school and on TV shows. They're long gone now. But part of the road is still there. She's right about that. I think it's a refugee road now. It starts somewhere around the Burque and ends at Flagstaff, or wherever the ocean starts these days."

"What do you know about the road?" I ask our new suddenly friendly tablemate.

"They wrote songs in her honor," she says, chin in hands. "Built museums so generations would know her greatness."

"We're still talking about a road, right?" I ask.

"Yes. A place a cat—" She clears her throat almost delicately. "A place that I have dreamed of seeing."

"It's probably not much to look at now," Clive says.

The woman doesn't seem to hear him. She starts softly humming a tune I've never heard before, maybe one of her road songs.

I have a thought. "So, you know this road, then?"

She rubs her cheek against the back of her hand and smiles. "I have a treasure collection here at the pawn shop devoted to her."

"And in this collection, do you have a map?"

"Of course. Several."

"And pictures, maybe? Landmarks? Postcards? Things like that?"

She runs the back of her hand across her forehead. "Certainly."

"Can we see them?"

She pauses her grooming. Looks questioningly at me.

"Because it looks like that's where we're headed," I explain.

She shifts her eyes to me, focusing. Nods a slow, deliberate yes. "You may see it all, everything I have. The maps, the cards, the tiny cars replicas. For a price." Her eyes blink slowly, shifting from brown to yellow, her pupils becoming vertical slits. "Battle Child."

Ben gasps. Clive chokes on his food.

I turn to our waitress. And I greet the shape-shifting cat, former bookie at the Shalimar, purveyor of all things macabre, and the only person who has ever called me "Battle Child."

"Hello, Mósí."

# Chapter 16

Mósí the human grooms herself in a decidedly feline way as we all finish our meal, and then with a swish of her long skirt, she leads us to a corner of the trading post. Sure enough, there's a treasure trove of toys, trinkets, key chains, coffee mugs, aprons, candies, postcards, and yes, tiny replica cars, devoted to Route 66. Or at least the Americana that was America's Freeway.

"Come, child," Mósí commands, waving a thick rectangular paper in my direction. "Let me show you the Mother Road."

She's holding a map, folded over six ways, with a picture of the Window Rock on the front. Across the top it reads ROAD MAP OF THE NAVAJO NATION in a font that's vaguely Indian feeling, a sort of generic Southwest print pattern filling in the blue letters. Mósí unfolds the map and lays it out in a space she clears on a table. Motions us closer.

The map itself is a couple of feet across, wider than it is long. Hundreds of town names cover the face, the boundaries of Dinétah clearly marked by a solid black border. I immediately look for Crystal, my home, mentally tracing the road that runs between it and Tse Bonito. I wonder if Rissa and Grace made it to Tah's okay.

My eyes cut across, almost unwillingly, to Black Mesa. The

exact place where I trapped Neizghání won't be marked on any map, but I search for it anyway.

"This is where we are," Mósí says, pointing with her thumb to Tse Bonito and pulling my attention back to the present. "And this is where the Mother Road runs, just below Dinétah." Sure enough, there's a long red line there, following almost parallel with the southern border. "The only way out of Dinétah on the southern side is here." She points to a place about fifty miles southwest of Tse Bonito, a town called Lupton. "You cross here to enter the Malpais."

"But do we head east or west?" Clive asks.

"If Kai were going east, he would have left through the eastern wall at Rock Springs. Why go this far west just to backtrack?"

"The silver-eyed boy?" Mósí purrs. "Is that who you hunt?"

Clive starts to answer her, and I raise my hand to stop him. I remember what Neizghání said at Black Mesa, that Mósí was the one who told him of Kai's clan power. If she hadn't spoken, who know what would have happened? Maybe Neizghání wouldn't have felt compelled to make sure Kai was dead before he left. Maybe my heart wouldn't have been shattered into a million pieces by Kai's deceitfulness. Maybe I wouldn't have had to shoot him. I don't blame the Cat for what happened, but I don't trust her either.

"And what if it is?" I ask carefully. "Why do you care?"

"He would make a fine mate, now that you want nothing more from Neizghání."

"And that doesn't bother you? I know you are close to Neizghání's mother."

She lifts a shoulder, coyly touching it to her cheek. "Time will tell all, Battle Child. For you and the silver-eyed boy and the Monsterslayer himself. Your paths are far from decided. There are still many trials. Most you will fail because failure is your nature. But others . . ." She shrugs.

And just like that I'm reminded how much I dislike Mósí.

"What do you want for the map?" I say, already tired of talking to her.

She smiles, showing dainty fangs. And I know it's going to be something I have absolutely no desire to give.

"I want to come with you, of course."

"To the Malpais? Can your kind even leave Dinétah?"

She raises an eyebrow. "My 'kind'?"

"You know. The Bik'e'áyéeii."

"Do you think we don't exist outside the borders of Dinétah? That we aren't real in our own right? That we endure only at the whim of the five-fingereds, and if you do not believe, then nothing?"

"I honestly have no idea."

"I will go to the Malpais with you." Her tone is decisive, expecting to be obeyed.

"We're not exactly going on a pleasure cruise," I say. "They call it the Malpais for a reason. And we're not giving you any special treatment. You're going to have to pull your weight just like everyone else. And I expect you to be part of the team."

I say that all with a serious face, and I'm pretty sure part of me means it. But the rest of me knows I'm full of shit. When did I become part of a team? Hell, when did I become its leader?

Clive's looking at me like he can't believe those words came out of my mouth either. I give him a face that means keep it to yourself. Whatever it takes to keep the Cat in line, right?

Mósí leans back against the display case, bracing herself with her hands and crossing her ankles prettily. Her black bob falls forward to brush her shoulder as she tilts her head. Her pose is somehow both demure and alluring, a challenge and an invitation. "Do you know what happened to my establishment after your visit?" she asks softly.

I glance at Clive. He's the one who told me.

"It was struck by lightning," he says.

"Struck by lightning," she agrees. "And destroyed. Everything that was mine. Gone. And did anyone worry about what would happen to me? How I, a poor cat, could ever repair the damage that the fire has done to my home, my business? Did you, Battle Child, ever even spare a thought for me?"

"No," I answer her honestly.

"No," she repeats, her voice vibrating with emotion. "Of course you did not. And that is why I am here, at this terrible place. Forced to collect the treasures of others, live in the daylight when one such as I prefers the night. Cook food for five-fingereds! It is a travesty. And it is your fault." She looks directly at me.

She has got to be kidding me. "How it is my fault? You set up the fight. You got in bed with Ma'ii—" Her eyes widen theatrically, obviously offended at my word choice, but I'm pissed now, her pity-party routine grating across my already worn nerves. "You made that damn deal with Ma'ii. If anything, you owe me."

Her eyes narrow to tiny yellow slits. "And what would I owe you, exactly?"

"You can start with an apology."

I hear Clive sigh.

"Am I wrong?" I ask him, voice raised. "I'm not wrong."

"Maybe we can call it even," he says diplomatically. "I mean, we did destroy the Shalimar."

"'We'? That was Ma'ii. Or Neizghání. One of them. I didn't destroy anything."

"Just hear her out, Maggie."

"Why should I?"

"Just . . ." He shakes his head, like I'm the unreasonable one. "What is it you want, Mósí? To go to the Malpais with us? What else?"

"Not because I owe you," I say hotly. "But as trade. For your map, for your help, which you *will* give us. For supplies." I wave my hand to encompass the shelves of goods in the store.

Her eyes narrow. "Very well," she says. "I will give you this map, my aid, and any knowledge I may have of the Malpais in exchange for your protection on the Mother Road to a destination of my choosing."

"No. We're on a timeline here. The longer it takes to find Kai and Caleb, the more likely . . ." Well, the more likely Caleb will be dead, at least. But I don't say that. No need to remind Clive of the facts.

"It's a fair deal, Maggie," Clive says. "This map is old. Before the Big Water. Who knows what it's like out there now? It might be good to have someone like her with us."

"She's probably more trouble than she's worth."

"Only one way to find out."

"Fine." I motion toward the Cat. "Name it. Where do you want to go?"

"I will let you know my final destination once we arrive," Mósí says primly. "Until then, it is my secret to keep. Now, are we ready? I thought time was of the essence to . . . your kind. And yet here we are, dillydallying."

"This is not going to end well," I mutter to Clive as we bring the last of our new supplies out to the bikes.

"She is kind of right that we owe her," he says. "I mean, we did destroy her home."

I stop, balancing a six-pack of Spam against my hip so I can wipe the sweat from my face. "I don't know who this 'we' that you keep referring to is. As I recall, I was tricked into a fight to the death and at that moment was probably bleeding out on the floor. I don't owe that cat anything."

"I still think it's a good omen that she wants to come," Clive says, glancing over his shoulder. It turns out Mósí has a sidecar that attaches to Clive's bike, and she's settled herself in the small seat, donned a pair of black sunglasses, and tied a flower-patterned scarf over her hair. She's waiting demurely while we do the work. "She probably has powers that we don't even know about."

"Her only power is self-preservation. I don't trust her as far as I can throw her."

"We don't have to trust her. It's a mutually beneficial relationship as long as we're going in the same direction. If self-preservation is her power, then maybe that will work in our favor."

"And maybe it will get us killed."

He snorts, sounding dubious.

"You don't know them like I do, Clive. They're all tricksters, ready to stab you in the back as soon as it's convenient."

"And maybe you can't see this clearly, Maggie."

"What does that mean?"

"Not everyone is a Coyote or Neizghání," he says. "Or even a Kai."

"Fuck you, Clive." I pick my crate of Spam up and stomp over to the bikes.

"Maggie—" Clive starts behind me, but I wave him away. I don't want to hear it. Mósí sits silently, facing forward, humming her road song. I don't even bother to look in her direction.

Clive joins me. He looks up at the setting sun. "Rissa should be here soon. Wonder what's taking her so long?"

"Hey, you guys?" Ben says from the back of my bike, where she's patiently waiting. Her voice is high and scared.

"What is it?" I ask, instantly alert.

"Do you hear that?" she asks.

I listen. And sure enough, there it is, a low rumbling buzz, like a freight train far away but inexorably heading your direction. Mósí stops humming, shifts to look over her shoulder, and raises her designer sunglasses to look east. "Well, child, it looks like you have a very angry swarm of locusts headed in your direction. I supposed that's not your fault either. Even so, I'd suggest we make haste out of town before there is no more town."

Without another word, Clive and I shift our packing to high gear. We're done and ready in a matter of seconds. I slide onto my bike, Ben huddles in behind me. She wraps her arms around me, and I can feel her shaking. I try to think of something reassuring to say, but I've got nothing. I put my commlink on and motion for her to do the same. Strap on my goggles and pull the rag up over my nose.

"Which way?' Clive asks, his voice a lie of calm.

"What about Rissa?" Ben asks.

"We can't wait for her," I say. And with the swarm on our tail, I wonder if Rissa is even coming. Maybe we overestimated the safety of sending her and Grace to Crystal. Clive must be thinking it, too, but if he is, he's keeping it to himself. Doesn't argue with me. Which tells me he's scared too.

"Lead them out of town," Mósí says. She's not wearing a commlink, but I can hear her clearly.

"What?"

"The locusts will destroy any and everything they touch. They are devourers by nature. If they come through Tse Bonito, there will be no more Tse Bonito. Lead them out of town, Battle Child. And quickly!"

I realize even the Cat is scared.

Well, that makes all four of us.

I hit the gas and tear out of the parking lot, shouting for Ben to hang on. She clutches me tightly. We ride due south across open desert, hoping to turn the swarm. No roads here, but no town, either. The shops and trailers that mark the edges of Tse Bonito quickly disappear, and all that's left is the wind whipping around us as we race for the Lupton. Driven by the surety that somewhere behind us there's a monster following.

# Chapter 17

We ride at full speed south across the open desert.

After half an hour, we hit a paved road and a sign pointing us to Lupton. The road is pockmarked by time and weather, but it's better than the bare suggestion of a trail we've been on. Finally, the Wall comes into view.

The Tribal Council built the Wall. Protection from not just the natural disasters of the Big Water that rained down on the earth—the storms and earthquakes—but for all the man-made horrors too. The Energy Wars that gutted the Midwest, the fracking engines shaking the earth until she broke, the oil pumps bleeding her dry. But Dinétah was spared, safe behind the Wall.

And here I was about to leave willingly.

Clive's voice comes through the speaker in my head. "Guardhouse on the left, coming up fast."

"I see it," I say, throttling down. I glance around the camp itself. "That's strange."

"What's strange?" Ben says, her voice anxious in my ear. She hadn't said anything the whole ride from Tse Bonito, but she stayed tight up against my back, her arms holding on to me like I was the last life preserver on a sinking ship.

Clive answers first. "There's no one here."

There's a refugee camp here in Lupton, much like the one I remember from Rock Springs. Probably four dozen tents of various shapes and sizes, some nylon camping tents and some canvas, some just makeshift lean-tos held up by wooden poles. The tents spread out between the sparse piñon trees and brush along an open field in the shadow of the Wall. There's a few more solid-looking buildings here and there. Something that looks like a meeting hall. Another building with a big red cross on the roof that marks it as a medical facility. A hogan for ceremony.

But just like Rock Springs, Lupton is empty. Back in Rock Springs it was because the people had fled the flesh-eating monsters and hid in smuggling tunnels. We never found them, but news came back that that's where they'd been. The people had clearly left Lupton, too. But to where? Through the Wall into the Malpais? Somewhere else in Dinétah? And more important, why? What could have made them all abandon the hope of a new home?

A shiver runs down my back as I realize the most obvious answer. They followed the White Locust to whatever new home he promised them, swelling the numbers of the faithful, building his Swarm.

"Hand me my shotgun," I mutter to Ben through the comm. Ben keeps one hand around my waist and pulls my shotgun free from the side rack with the other. We drive slowly through the ghost town, our engines the only noise. I maneuver around a metal tent pole that's left abandoned in the road, like a windstorm had come through. Windstorms make me think of Kai. He could have done this, but why? He was so careful with his power, worried about hurting people. I can't see him destroying a whole town even if it was within his ability. But if the White Locust made him? If somehow he has control of Kai and his powers?

"Gates are open," Clive says. There, fifty feet in front of us, the road leads us to a gatehouse and, just past it, a massive gate. The gate is a heavy steel door set on a huge pulley system that would take at least three men to operate. I imagine it would close with crushing force if recklessly released. To get that door open and closed is no small task. But now the door is wide-open, listing dangerously off the single metal chain that it's still attached to. Something, or someone powerful, ripped that door free from its hinges. Something with supernatural force. Someone with clan powers.

I swallow, uneasy. And then something above the gate catches my eye, and my unease turns to horror. Because high above the top of the gate, hammered into the turquoise rock itself, is a body.

"Up there," I whisper. "Above the door."

The body is slight, young. Too hard to tell the person's gender so high up and half-hidden in the shadows of the Wall. They are nailed to the rock, their arms spread Christ-like, held by some sort of stakes through their shoulders that look like railroad spikes. The spikes hold all their weight, which isn't much. But it's enough to leave the legs hanging uselessly and their head lolling senselessly on a bent neck. It's a terrible thing that's been done, and my stomach threatens to bring back my hard-won lunch at the sight.

Then I realize who it is staked into the Wall, and my whole being shudders in revulsion.

"Oh God," Clive moans, a strangled cry as he sees the same shock of red hair I do. Comes to the same inevitable conclusion.

"Caleb."

# Chapter 18

Clive is off his bike in seconds. He rushes forward, eyes riven to the scene above him. His hands clutch ineffectually at the Wall, searching for holds.

I turn off the engine and wait. Take a deep breath and try to ease the tightness in my chest. I've killed more people than I care to count, no doubt inadvertently caused pain to their friends and family. But whoever did this wanted to be deliberately cruel. Caleb was tortured, meant as a message for whoever found him. For us, most likely. I have no doubt that whoever did this is a monster.

Clive's efforts to scale the Wall are getting more frantic, his hands turning bloody as his fingernails scratch uselessly at the hard turquoise. A fine sheen of blue dust rains to the earth around his feet, but he's not making any progress unless he intends to tear down the Wall molecule by molecule with his bare hands. Which no doubt he would attempt if he thought it would help his little brother.

"Stay put," I murmur to Ben. "Keep your eyes open for trouble."

She swallows, her face scared, her back rigid.

My steps are steady and hushed as I approach Clive. He's finally found a small shallow foothold in the Wall, and he's trying to dig his toe in and push himself up through will alone. But the man is built like a wall himself. Six four and two hundred and twenty pounds on a bad day. He's just not going to get up. His foot slips, and he crashes to his knees, his palms scraping raw against the uneven rock. He doesn't cry out, doesn't make a noise, but his whole body is trembling.

I reach out and touch the Wall. The turquoise is cold and rough, jagged stone under my palm. I don't know how the White Locust got Caleb up there, but we're not climbing this without a ladder or a rope or something. At least Clive and I aren't.

"Ben," I call calmly over my shoulder. "Come here."

I hear her approach, her footsteps dragging uncertainly.

"Can you climb this?" I ask, my eyes still studying the Wall, looking for some kind of weakness, something that will help us.

She comes up beside me and presses her own small hand to the Wall. She gulps nervously, blinks too quickly. "Maybe?"

"I saw how you handled the trails as Lake Asááyi," I say, willing her confidence.

But she shakes her head, looking overcome and out of her league. Something falls from above us, blood like a raindrop. It strikes Ben on the cheek. Her hand flies to her face in horror. "It's him!" she whispers before she turns, stumbling back to the bikes. I hear her gagging and then the sound of vomit striking the ground.

"I can climb it," comes another voice from behind me. Mósí.

"Will you?" I ask, not hiding my surprise that she's offering. "I didn't think you were the helping kind."

"After your convincing lecture at the pawn shop? How could I not be? Who is this unfortunate soul?" she asks, her voice soft with wonder.

Clive's voice cracks as he says, "It's Caleb, my brother." His shoulders heave, and for the first time since we got here, he lets out a sob. Struggles to hold in more, but they escape in strangled cries.

Mósí tilts her head, yellow eyes studying Clive, feline inscrutable.

I think of Clive as the guy who clapped Kai on the back, laughing after we killed the monsters in Rock Springs. Teasing me about Kai dancing with him instead of me. Tormenting me with a tube of mascara. But now he is in pain, and I know I should help him. But the only way I know to help him is to hurt whoever did this to his brother. And since he's not here, I'm useless.

"Why did they kill him?" Ben asks quietly, coming up beside me. Tears run freely down her cheeks.

I start to answer that I don't know why, when Mósí says, "But he's not dead."

I jerk my head around. "What did you say?"

Clive looks up, the hope in his face frightening.

Mósí blinks rapidly, her vertical pupils dilating, clearly startled at our response. She takes a moment to straighten her scarf and smooth her hands over her clothes before she says, "Can you not smell the blood moving through his veins? His heartbeat is sluggish, but it is there."

"Get him down," Clive says, pleading. "Please. Can you get him down?"

The Cat looks at him a long moment and nods once. We all move back a few feet to give her space. She removes her flowered scarf from her head and hands it to me absently. For once I don't mind the implicit order. She slips her flat shoes off her feet and stretches her back, arching, and then her hands, fingers interlaced. Finally, she approaches the Wall. Bows her head, and when she raises it again, I can see the feline in her, almost like it's interposed across her human features. Vibrissae, a button nose, and almost soft fur-like texture to her skin. And her fingers have sprouted curved claws. I expect her to scale the Wall like I've seen cats do to trees, but instead she crouches low, coiling like a spring, and launches herself skyward thirty feet. She lands just parallel to Caleb's head, scrambling to some ledge we can't see. Balancing on clawed toes, she leans in over his face. She opens her mouth and lowers her chin, panting. Like she's breathing him in.

"What is she doing?" Ben asks.

"I have no idea," I murmur.

"Please," Clive begs urgently. "Can you hurry?"

Mósí looks down at him, unbothered by his pleas. "He smells . . . sweet," she murmurs. With her small pink tongue, she leans in to lick his cheek.

"Mósí!" I shout, worried that the Cat is losing focus. "Get the boy down."

Her shoulders stiffen. If she had a tail, it would be twitching. "I am only assessing his health. Your ignorance is irritating, to say the least." But she does reach over and, with supernatural strength, rip the first stake from Caleb's shoulder. She lets it drop, clattering to the ground, catching his body against her own and cradling him with one arm while the other holds the Wall. Caleb moans and shudders, his weight sagging.

"Caleb!" Clive screams, relieved. "We're here, brother. I'm here. We're getting you down. Just hold on!"

Shifting his weight so her hand is free, Mósí stretches across his body and grips the remaining stake. "I suspect he'll fall when I release him, despite the lovely wings. Do be ready to catch him."

"Wings?" I look closer, and she is right. Just like the archer at Lake Asááyi, Caleb has delicately veined wings—two sprouting from the joints of his shoulders like shortened angel wings and two shorter ones at the top of his rib cage. Both made of some kind of shimmering gossamer.

Mósí wrenches the other spike free, and Caleb unceremoniously drops. Clive catches his brother in his arms, taking his weight with a small grunt. He lowers him gently to the ground, murmuring insensible words of comfort.

Mósí turns, ready to jump down. And freezes, eyes sharpening on something in the distance. My adrenaline spikes. I turn toward the road, shotgun raised.

"Someone's coming," the Cat says as she drops soundlessly on bare feet. She slips on her flats and comes forward. "I can hear a motorbike."

"How many?"

I assess our situation. Clive is no good right now, lost in grief and trying to care for his brother. Ben's brought him her canteen, and he's washing Caleb's face and chest reverently. A quick glance reveals Caleb's bleeding only from the places the spikes pierced his skin, and the blood loss has trickled to almost nothing now. I don't see any other obvious wounds, if you don't count the wings grafted to his back. I remember the archer at Lake Asááyi had them too, and they were functional. Which suggests to me that, as wild as it sounds, the wings weren't meant to kill Caleb, but to make him fly. No severe bleeding, no wounds, so he's most likely in shock. Dehydrated. Starved. I wonder how long he's been up there.

Ben's hands are shaking slightly, and she still looks unwell. She might be in shock too. I thought maybe she'd seen this kind of bad before, but it's starting to seem like maybe Hastiin kept her from the ugly stuff. Which might have seemed kind back then but won't be of service to her now.

So, it's me and the Cat, and I'm not sure Mósí's willing to fight. But maybe she doesn't have to be.

"Only one," she says, straightening, and I relax as well. One I can take no problem.

We wait as the bike comes over the hill and pulls into camp. Winds its way slowly through the tattered tents and past the guard station. Pulls up short not twenty feet away. The rider rolls gracefully off the bike and pulls off a black mirrored helmet, shaking out two long red braids.

"Caleb?" Rissa's voice is shaky with disbelief. "Caleb!"

Caleb opens his eyes just in time to greet his sister. And screams.

# Chapter 19

"Is Caleb going to be okay?" Ben asks. She and I are sitting across from each other at a long table in the building that was once Lupton's refugee mess hall. Enough room for fifty people to sit and eat at once, but it's only me and Ben now, and her voice echoes around the place like a bat in a cave.

"I think he'll be okay," I tell her, rubbing my eyes, and I'm pretty sure that's not a lie. My nerves are so frayed it's hard to tell. Once Rissa arrived, Caleb started screaming, and he didn't stop for the better part of an hour. Nothing the twins did could calm their brother. Finally, Rissa found a flask of some kind of booze in the guard barracks and forced some down his throat. He seemed to calm after that, rolling in and out of consciousness, which was better than the alternative, I guess. The three Goodacres were still holed up in the infirmary, but I'd begged off, saying I needed some air and should check on Ben. Mósí had wandered off somewhere, as cats do, and I found Ben in here, listlessly picking at a can of Spam with a fork.

I say, "Clive's got him stabilized and he's resting. It's a good thing there's a medical facility here. If we'd been out on the road, things might be a little bleaker."

"Is Clive a doctor? Or, I mean, was he a doctor before the Big Water?"

"No, but I think he did some EMT training or something. He knows what he's doing. And he's got plenty of hands-on experience from dealing with the lot who end up staying at Grace's. Most of us roll in with some kind of damage."

"He patch you up before?"

"Not me, but Kai. Before we knew about his Medicine People clan power."

Ben gives me a beleaguered smile. "Why do you think they did it? To Caleb?"

"I don't know. As a warning? Once Caleb's able to talk, we'll know more. Until then . . ."

"The White Locust is a monster," she says, voice hard as the Wall outside. "Just like his followers. They all deserve to die." She stabs the potted meat with her fork.

"Ben," I start. I consider telling her she didn't kill the archer, but once again I decide the timing is shit. Besides, there's nothing she can change about it now, and I'm not sure whether the truth would help her or hurt her more. "Don't think like that. It's not good."

"It's funny," she says. "I've never felt like I had a purpose. Like, I used to wonder why I survived the Little Keystone Massacre when my parents and everyone I knew at the camp died. It never felt right."

The Little Keystone was one of the last battles of the Energy Wars, and calling it a battle would be overly generous. The Protectors' camp housed whole families, sitting in protest at the site of a proposed pipeline through Osage territory. The Osage and the oil companies were tied up in court, since many of the battles were fought with lawyers and legal briefs as much as they were with guns. But there was a posse of violent men who worked to support the corporations. Those men's souls were as dark and as slick as the crude itself, so most folks just called them "Oilers." The Oilers decided the courts weren't moving fast enough. They took it upon themselves to clear Protector camps by any means necessary. Little Keystone had been one of those.

"I didn't know there were any survivors at Little Keystone," I say.

"I hid." Simple words, but her voice is anguished.

I know that shame. It's all too familiar. And even though I don't believe it about myself and my nalí's death, I try to offer her something. "You were a child." She's still a child, but I don't tell her that. She's lived through the kind of thing that strips one's childhood away.

"Doesn't matter," she says, voice flat. "Other kids didn't hide."

"If you hadn't hidden, you would have died."

She looks up at me. "If I had died, my uncle would still be alive."

I could try to tell her she doesn't know that for a fact, that a lot happens between one person's life and another's death to make things fall out a certain way. But what do I know about why things happen the way they do? Maybe she's right.

"I'm too soft," she says, like an admission. "I thought I was tough, because of . . . stuff. But I couldn't take seeing Caleb like that." She pushes the fork into the flesh of her hand, the tines making little indents.

"Ben."

"Don't make excuses for me, Maggie," she says, her voice low with anger.

"I wasn't going to."

She gives me a half smile, like she's relived. "It's okay. I get it now. I know what I'm supposed to do."

I lean forward, arms folded on the table, not sure I like the sound of that. "What exactly do you think you are supposed to do?"

"Kill the White Locust." Her eyes meet mine, hard and uncompromising. "I'm supposed to avenge my uncle. Caleb, too."

"It's not your job to avenge anyone."

Her jaw tightens, fingers flexing around the fork she's still holding. "If not me, then who? Who fights the evil in this world?"

"I kind of thought that's what I was doing."

Her mouth twists, cynical. "Did you really?"

I blink, caught off guard. But I can't lie. "No. Maybe. Sometimes."

She nods, confirmed. "My uncle told me about you."

"I gathered that from what you said back at Lake Asááyi."

"Don't be mad at him. He only told me the truth. You can't help what you are. None of us can. And you do have some good qualities." She rolls the fork back and forth across the table. "You have a gift for violence. I—I don't have that naturally, but I can find that in myself. I know I can."

"You don't want that," I say gently.

"I do if I'm going to kill the White Locust. And I am going to kill him. I need you to understand that."

"I do, but—"

"It's my new purpose. You get that, don't you? Having a purpose?"

"Yes, but—"

"I just can't do it alone. I need your help. And Clive and Rissa, probably, too." Her face falls, like she just remembered something. "What do you think they'll do now that they've got Caleb back? Do you think they'll go home? Forget about us?"

"I don't know what they'll do," I admit.

She straightens. "They won't leave," she says, sounding confident. "They know the right thing to do. They're going to want revenge too."

"You know this is a rescue mission, right?"

"Do you think Caleb can travel?" she asks like she didn't hear me. "He'll have to. Maybe Mósí will let him sit in her sidecar. Do you think she'll share?"

"Speaking of Mósí," I say, grateful for the chance to change the topic, "do you know where she went?"

"She said something about going back over by the gate where we found Caleb."

I stand up, eager to end the conversation. "Did she say why?"

Ben looks at me a long minute, and I feel like I should say something, but I got nothing. I don't really do platitudes, and she asked me not to lie. Finally, she nods. "It's okay, Maggie. I appreciate you trying." She puts a forkful of Spam in her mouth and chews. "And no. I don't know why Mósí went back to the gate. I mean, I didn't ask her why. I just assumed it was a cat thing."

Sure enough, I find Mósí standing in front of the open gate. She's sitting primly, legs tucked under, back straight, and hands folded in her lap. And she's staring through the open gate into the space beyond. Into the Malpais. In the chaos of finding Caleb, I hadn't even thought to get a look through the gate at the lands beyond Dinétah. If I'm honest, the idea of leaving still makes me queasy.

I approach, my moccasins silent on the paved road. She turns slightly to acknowledge that she knows I'm here, and no doubt to remind me that I can't sneak up on a cat.

"What do you see?" I ask, curious. I know her eyesight is better than mine. Her hearing, too. I've reconsidered my initial reluctance to have her along, admitting—to myself at least—my prejudice. I know full well that Caleb might still be hanging from that wall if it weren't for her.

"What do I see, child?" she says, her voice soft with wonder. "I see darkness. And monsters moving in the darkness." She twists her body to face me. "A great force came through here to remove these people. When you come face-to-face with it—and you will—do not underestimate it."

"Was it Kai?" I ask, remembering the metal pole littering the road.

"No," she says, "but don't underestimate him, either. Chaos

trails him like death trails you. But no, what happened here was not his doing. The people of Lupton left here willingly."

"Kai could convince them."

"With Bit'ąą'nii? No. They would be no threat to him, and the effects of Bit'ąą'nii . . . It cannot make you a slave. It cannot convince you to do something you don't already want to do."

"I don't know much about it," I admit, interested. "He never explained."

"You mean before you killed him?"

Damn cat. "Yes."

She smiles in a way that makes me decidedly uncomfortable. "Bit'ąą'nii is like a lover's whisper. It persuades, but it does not destroy the will. It is a subtle power. This"—she looks around the empty town—"was not subtle. They abandoned their home for something they wanted more than a home."

"I don't understand that. A home is all I've ever wanted."

She tilts her head. "You know much of want, Battle Child. Careful it is not your undoing."

I step forward to stare into what feels like a solid wall of black beyond the Dinétah border. "Why is it so dark out there? The sun is still up for a few more hours. Is there no daylight on the other side of the Wall?"

"There are many places the sun does not reach, and darkness can be a balm to those who belong to the night."

"But there is daylight out there?"

"What is illuminated does not always—"

"Just answer the question. No riddles."

Her whole body flickers with annoyance. "There is daylight."

"Good." I shake off a shiver and rub my arms to try to get warm. The afternoon sunlight on this side of the Wall suddenly doesn't feel like enough. "So, you're still coming with us, right? You haven't changed your mind?"

She blinks, surprised. "Oh, no. Not at all. Why would I when I have a monsterslayer as my bodyguard who wields the sword of a great warrior?" She glances back at Neizghání's sword still strapped to my back.

"About that." I take a steadying breath, ready to admit the truth. "I'm more of a sword escort."

Her small face wrinkles in concern. "Can you not wield the sword? Did he never teach you how?"

"I was more the guns and knives side of the duo."

"You cannot wield the lightning sword," she says flatly. Her face falls in disappointment.

"I just need some time to practice," I protest. "Figure out a few things." Like how the hell it works.

"You promised to keep me safe."

"And I will. Just not with the sword. I still have all my guns."

She smooths her hands across her lap. "I suppose I do not care how you do it, as long as we are agreed. To break a promise of safe passage is an offense to the Diyin Dine'é. Plus, it is very rude." She looks over her shoulder. "Someone is coming. One of the red ones."

I hear it too. Heavy footsteps and the quiet slap of an automatic rifle against padding. I turn to see Clive, a lone figure coming toward us up the road.

"How is he?" I ask as he gets into earshot.

His face is set in a grim mask, lips thinned to nothing, hazel eyes dark and haunted. "He's awake. And talking. And he's asking for you."

# Chapter 20

Clive, Mósí, and I walk back to the infirmary in silence. Whatever Caleb says is going to decide what the Goodacres do next, and from Clive's grim face, it seems like it might not be anything I want to hear.

Clive opens the door and I walk through first. Caleb is propped up on a cot, white sheets and a rough wool blanket tucked around his thin frame. His freckles are stark against his light brown skin, and his deep auburn curls are slicked back from a gaunt face. He looks up at me, smiles. I smile back. And then his eyes widen in warning just as I see movement to my right. Disbelief slows my response time, and I forget to move as Rissa's fist comes flying toward my face.

I take the hit directly on the cheek. Stumble back a few steps, shocked. But then my clan powers flare, and I've got a knife in my hand faster than I can think. I lunge forward, instinct driving me. I have a blade at her neck in seconds.

My hands are trembling. K'aahanáanii is singing so loudly in my head to do it, to kill her, to spill her blood for her transgression, that I can't even hear my own stuttered breath. The only thing keeping her alive right now is that her hands are empty. Her chin is raised in stubborn defiance, head thrown back like a dare. But she's not trying to fight me, and even I know, through the haze of clan power blood lust, that killing her for punching me in the face is excessive. But I'm still raging.

"What the fuck?!" I scream at her from inches away, my knife still raised between us. "I could have killed you!"

Clive hustles in behind me, shouting at his sister. He pushes her away from me with a rough shove. "What are you doing, Clarissa?"

"She deserved it!" Rissa screams. "She brought him to us. If Kai hadn't come, none of this would have happened! Caleb wouldn't have gotten hurt."

I'm still panting, fighting to get my clan powers under control. K'aahanáanii is still demanding that I kill Rissa, that she's a threat, but I take a few deep breaths to tamp down the adrenaline. Remind myself that I'm trying not to kill people these days.

I run my tongue around my mouth, feeling for a loose tooth. I bit the shit out of my cheek, but no teeth feel out of place. I turn my head and spit a mouthful of blood on the dirt floor, making a note that Rissa packs a hell of a right hook.

"Are you okay?" Clive asks me, hand still braced against his sister's shoulder. Although I don't think he's holding her back as much as he's keeping her away from me. Like he's more worried about what I might do to her than what she could do to me.

"Do you really want to do this right now, Rissa?" My Böker is still bare in my hand, my voice tinged with some kind of awful anticipation. "You've been promising to kill me since Black Mesa. Maybe it's time we step out and settle this."

Her eyes narrow to slits of green and her fists clench. I grin, show teeth still stained red. And let K'aahanáanii croon a little song, something written in Rissa's blood. It flows from my lips as a tuneless melody, a promise of violence. And, God, it feels good.

"Stop it!" It's Caleb, his voice a hoarse shout that slices through the tension like a cleaver. "Just stop it!"

Rissa blanches, turns worried eyes to her brother in bed. "I'm sorry, Caleb," she says, sounding abashed. "I didn't mean to upset you." She throws Clive's hands off and rushes over to sit next to her little brother. She takes his hand in hers, squeezing his fingers in reassurance.

"Don't apologize to me. Apologize to Maggie."

She shoots me a glance that says, *Not in a million years*, before turning back to her brother. Whatever. I'm fully aware that even if Rissa managed to mouth an apology my way, she wouldn't mean it.

"Are you okay?" she asks him, running a hand over his forehead. "Do you need more water? Another blanket? Clive, bring Caleb a blanket."

"I'm fine," her little brother says, heat in his voice. "Stop fussing over me."

I come up on the other side of Caleb's bed. "You're alive," I greet him. Maybe not the most diplomatic thing I could say, but I believe in cutting to the chase.

"Yeah," he says.

"You wanted to tell me something?"

He hesitates. "It's why Rissa's mad, but she doesn't understand."

"Ca—" she starts, but he silences his older sister with a look.

"It's about my wings. How it happened."

I shift a little closer. "How did it happen?"

"Kai did it."

I stare stupidly. It takes me a moment to register what he said. Mósí giggles somewhere behind me. "I'm sorry. I don't understand."

"Not the wings themselves. Gideon made them. Well, grew them, maybe? I'm not sure. But he's amazing. He can make anything out of metal. They're metal, but you can't tell. They look real, don't they?"

I'm tempted to reach out and touch the wings, but I stay my hand.

“Gideon did the surgery,” Caleb’s rushes on, “but Kai helped with the healing time. It used to take weeks, and some people rejected the implants. But Kai helped me so there weren’t any problems.” His eyes are bright with wonder, not the horror I expected, and his breath is short with excitement.

I’m afraid to ask, but I want to know. “Does Kai have wings too?”

He shakes his head. “He told Gideon it would be better if he didn’t, and Gideon agreed. He said Kai was special and he had another purpose.”

“Another purpose? What kind of purpose?”

“You hear that, Monsterslayer?” Rissa says, cutting in, her voice sharp with accusation. “Without your boy helping, Caleb wouldn’t even be like this.”

“No. He said without Kai, it might have been worse.” I turn back to Caleb, picking my words carefully. “You make it sound like he was helping this . . . Gideon? But we saw the tape, Caleb. You were kidnapped. That was your blood on the wall, wasn’t it?”

Caleb flushes. “I was being stupid, you know? I didn’t understand what Gideon wanted. So I fought him. Ziona hit me. That’s what that blood was in the guardhouse. He yelled at her for it. Made her stay behind at their old camp as punishment. It was my fault.”

“So Gideon is the one who took you? He’s the White Locust?”

And that explains who our archer was and why she was left behind. If I had to guess, I’d bet that Gideon knew exactly what would happen to anyone he left behind. He wanted her dead for some reason, and he came damn close to getting exactly what he wanted.

“Sounds like Kai isn’t the Boy Scout you keep trying to convince yourself he is,” Rissa says, picking up where she left off.

“Why would he hurt Caleb?” I ask. “He went out of his way to never hurt anyone.” *Except you, Maggie*, a voice inside me whispers. *He hurt you.*

"Hurt me?" Caleb says. "He didn't hurt me."

"Then how did you end up with wings, child?" Mósí says somewhere behind me.

Caleb's eyes search her out, and his smile is beatific. "I volunteered. Just like I volunteered to stay behind. To be the messenger."

"The messenger for what?" I ask sharply, a chill rolling down my spine.

His head turns to me. His eyes are too big, the whites too white. He looks crazed, and I fight an urge to get away from him. My monster instincts are dinging. Hard. I remind myself that this is just Freckles. Not a monster, even with those wings and that terrible look on his face.

"The message is for you."

The place on my cheek where Rissa hit me throbs.

"What is the message?" I ask.

"Tell the Godslayer to come to Amangiri."

The four of us leave Caleb to sleep. Step outside into the cooling evening, the empty town.

"What do you think?" I ask no one in particular.

Clive sighs, rubs a hand over his face and through his hair. "I think Caleb's only fifteen and he's been through some traumatic stuff and maybe he's not thinking straight."

"He said he volunteered."

"I don't know what that means," he admits. "In his mind, I mean. You said this White Locust is a cult leader of some kind. Maybe he talked him into it and Caleb doesn't even realize it."

"Maybe he has a clan power like Kai's," Rissa says. "What is his called? Talks-in-Blanket? Maybe he can talk people into doing stupid shit. Hell, maybe Kai talked him into it himself."

"Kai didn't make Caleb volunteer for some kind of wing-implant surgery. He definitely can't make him climb up there to be nailed to a wall. His powers don't work that way."

"Why not? You frame it the right way—"

"Perhaps," Mósí interrupts. "Perhaps the why of the thing doesn't matter."

"Easy for you to say," Rissa fires back. "That wasn't your brother pinned to a fucking wall like an insect." She gasps. "Oh my God. With wings even. Jesus . . ." She lets loose a string of curses under her breath.

I rub my forehead. I'm getting a headache.

"Who do you think is the 'Godslayer'?" Clive asks.

I realize he didn't hear what the locust man back at Grace's trailer said to me, and Ben isn't here to tell him what the archer on the mountain said either. But it doesn't matter. Rissa gets it.

"Oh, seriously, Clive? You don't know?" She looks at me pointedly.

"I did not kill a god," I protest.

"Whatever you call him," she says, exasperated. "Hero. God. It's semantics."

"It's definitely not semantics, whatever that means."

"Well, he's dead, isn't he? Who else could it be?"

I stare, dumbstruck. "He's not dead," I finally manage, but it even sounds weak to my ears.

Rissa just snorts and folds her hands across her chest, unimpressed.

"So, what now?" I ask, changing the conversation to a subject that doesn't send me to the dark, unforgiving places in my head. "You've got your brother back. You clearly hate Kai—and me, for that matter. Does that mean you and Clive are bailing?"

"Why shouldn't we?" she says before Clive can answer.

I have a million reasons why they shouldn't. Because I don't understand the White Locust's power. Because Caleb being nailed to the Wall and then *praising* the man who did it to him scares the shit out of me. Because I don't want to do this alone.

"You don't want our help finding Kai, Maggie?" Clive asks, sounding hurt.

The words feel awkward as they leave my mouth, but I say, "Yes, I want your help!"

I turn to Rissa. She's cradling her hand slightly, the one she hit me with. It must hurt. That cheers me up a little, but I still can't believe I'm really going to say what I'm about to say. But . . . I am. Because I told Kai that I wanted to try something different, and maybe that something different also means admitting shit like this.

"You're a pain in the ass," I tell Rissa, "and I think you might have a worse attitude than me, which is saying a lot of nothing nice about you. But you're good with a gun, and a fist"—I touch my cheek pointedly, and she has the grace to blush—"and I'm going to need help. Mósí thinks the people left Lupton under the influence of a powerful force, something that makes Kai's Bit'ąą'nii clan power look like a polite suggestion. And we know Caleb volunteered for"—I point back toward the infirmary—"that. We're up against something—someone—I'm not sure how to fight. I don't know what to expect, but I know I don't want to face him alone if I don't have to. Because I will bring Kai back home or I will die trying. I promised Tah. And I promised myself." *And Kai said he loved me.* I take a deep breath, and the words tumble out before I can second-guess myself. "I haven't seen Kai since he came back. You both have. And it"—I exhale, not sure I want to admit this but knowing that they need to hear it—"and it's killing me. I need to see him. Alive. I need to know I didn't . . . I just need to find him, okay?"

Rissa gapes at me for a moment, but her surprise quickly turns to wariness. She presses her lips together, clearly considering my words, before she finally says, "One of us has to stay with Caleb."

"I'll stay," Clive says. "I'm the one with the medical knowledge. I can take care of him until I can get him to Tah."

Rissa starts to protest, but Clive stops her. "I'm the better choice and you know it. If the two of you can just rein in your bullshit for a few days and work together."

She looks at her brother, and something passes between them, whole conversations in the raising of eyebrows and the tilt of a chin.

"Fine," Rissa says. "I'm going back to check on Caleb, and then we'll get the hell out of here. The sooner we finish this, the better." And she's gone, I assume to Caleb for her good-byes.

Clive sighs, eyes on his sister's back.

"I can handle Rissa," I reassure him.

"I know you can, Maggie. But I wish you wouldn't. She didn't mean anything. She was just worried about Caleb and needed a target to take it out on, that's all."

"I'm not volunteering. She sucker punched me, and you and I both know she's lucky I didn't kill her for it."

He shakes his head. "Putting you two together is like sticking two cats in a bag." He glances at Mósí, looking sheepish. "Sorry. I just hope you don't tear each other apart before you get to Kai. She's angry, but she knows it's not Kai's fault, not really."

"Are you sure?"

He studies me for a moment. "You two are a lot alike," he says.

I make a noise.

"No, seriously. Rissa's fierce because she loves her family. She would do anything for us. I'm the same. I get that."

"If you recall, I don't have a family."

"I remember," he says. "And I think maybe you like it that way."

"What?"

"Don't take it the wrong way. I just mean that when something is part of your identity for so long, even if it's not a good thing, it's hard to let it go. Even if maybe you should."

"I let Tah move in, didn't I? And before this, I was working with the Thirsty Boys. Hell, I'm watching over Ben, wherever she is. I'm practically a goddamn auntie!"

"Maybe not quite, but it's a start," he admits, his mouth leaning into a smile. "I mean, for someone with your rep. Look, just remember, Rissa's my sister, Grace's daughter. We love her."

"That's your problem."

His smile becomes a full-on grin. "I suppose it is. Just try not to stab her, okay?"

"I won't unless she hits me again."

He raises his hands in surrender. "That's all I can ask. I'll go fetch Ben. She in the mess hall?"

Once Clive is gone, Mósí and I head back to the bikes. But something's not right. Mósí keeps making little noises, blowing her breath out in short exasperated puffs. Clearly agitated.

"What's wrong?" I ask her, worried that there's something bad that I'm missing.

She blinks big eyes at me, hands on her hips. "Cats in a bag!" she exclaims. "Who is putting cats in a bag?! Is this a common five-fingered activity?"

"It's a figure of speech."

She glares at me, trying to decide if I'm lying. Finally, she huffs out a breath and says indignantly, "I never!"

# Chapter 21

We head through the gate in the Wall about an hour before nightfall. Ben rides with me, and Rissa on the bike with Mósí's sidecar. The darkness Mósí and I saw through the gate turns out to be more of an accident of the Wall's height throwing shadows into the canyon beyond and not something ominously supernatural. A hundred yards out, we leave the deep shade of the Wall behind, and a gray winter sky reveals itself—blotchy clouds scuttling high and thin across a fading evening sky. Sunlight, or at least a weak semblance of it.

The path we are on curves through high sandstone walls, striped white and orange and brown by the shifting desert. Sand eddies in pools under a seemingly constant wind that howls low and mournful through the rocky canyons. No signs of life here, not even the dull hum of insects. Which, after our encounters with the locust, I don't mind as much as I probably should.

A deep uneasiness settles over me as we enter the Malpais. Leaving Dinétah feels like ripping something vital from my body, something I need to keep breathing, keep my heart beating in my chest. Maybe it's sentiment, but all my life I've believed that the Diyin Dine'é put us between the four sacred mountains for a reason.

That we Diné are part of this land as much as any mountain or valley or stream. We are it, and it is in us, and out here, in this wasteland, none of that feels true. Mósí said being Diné is a constant, something that cannot change. That one cannot stop being Diné, even in a place where Dinétah cannot be reached. So maybe if the Bik'e'áyéeii can do it, a simple five-fingered girl like me can too.

I shiver, cold. Huddle down on the bike and try to ignore the uneasy feeling, the sense of being forsaken. But it's not easy.

We follow the dirt path for half an hour as it wends its way out of the cliffs until it dead-ends into a four-lane highway. The blacktop on the highway is still smooth in some places. Worn but whole. In others it's gutted, broken up to rubble like some massive hand came down and smashed the earth. The god-size potholes make for slow going. Better on our nimble bikes that can thread through breaks in the road than in wider, four-wheeled vehicles that will have to find more difficult ways to get around. We know from the surveillance tape that Gideon is in a car or truck of some kind, so maybe that works to our advantage. A thin hope, but that's all I've got.

There are signs other travelers have passed this way. That smell of oil, for one, thick in the air. And the graveyard of abandoned vehicles around us, some left in the middle of the highway, most pulled to the side before they gave out in the heat of the day or ran out of fuel. But no people.

"Where is everyone?" Ben asks through her commlink, clearly thinking the same thing.

"Most travelers settle in somewhere safe once the sun starts to set," Mósí says. "Probably in the cliffs around us, out of sight. The Mother Road is not safe in the dark."

"Now you tell us," Rissa quips, but she's not serious. We already know. Danger flavors the air out here. We know something will come for us. We just don't know what. Or when.

"If Mósí's map is right," I say, "we've got a couple of hours until we hit Joseph City. We should be able to rest there. Refuel. Maybe someone there's heard of Amangiri." Amangiri, the place where Caleb said we should bring the Godslayer, which, for now, I admit must mean me. We looked over the map but couldn't find anywhere called Amangiri along Route 66, so for now we head west and hope the place reveals itself to us somewhere along the way.

"What's in Joseph City, again?" Ben asks.

"It's a Mormon settlement. There's a handful of independent wards scattered through the Malpais, separate from the Kingdom. Joseph City is one of them. My brother used to go there sometimes to trade."

"Clive?" Ben asks, sounding curious.

"My older brother," Rissa says. "Cletus."

"Oh, I didn't meet him. Was he at the All-American?"

"He's dead," Rissa says, voice sounding normal enough, but over the static of the wind in the earpiece, it's hard to tell.

"Oh . . . sorry, Rissa," Ben says.

"It was a while ago."

Silence falls around us, just the sound of engines and wheels over gravel. It lasts a full two minutes before Ben says, "So, are we there yet?"

"Stay off the commlink, Ben," I tell her, tired of her nervous chatter. "And keep your eyes open. When it comes for us, we won't have much warning."

"It?" she squeaks, shifting on the seat behind me. She moves closer to me, wrapping her arms tighter around my waist and leaning against my back.

The sun inches steadily downward, the darkness growing. There's no moon, and what stars there should be are lost to thickening cover. The only light for miles is a narrowing band on the far horizon and that's fading quickly. Rissa flips on her headlight, and

I follow her lead. I lean into the headlight almost instinctively. But I can tell immediately that the bright light compromises my night vision, and if I want to see more than fifteen feet in front of me, I'm going to have to lose the headlight. So I flip the switch to kill it. And in that split second between light and dark, I see it.

A flash of movement high and to my right.

I whip my head around, but my sight hasn't recovered. A strong breeze passes close to my face, a feeling of a presence. The wind screams in my ear. I instinctively swerve.

Ben shouts behind me, her grip tightening.

"Maggie?" Rissa's voice is high and worried.

"Did you see that?" I shout.

"See what?"

I strain through the darkness, searching for whatever came close to my face. Nothing. "I felt . . ." But what did I feel? The wind? A bird? No. It's dead out here. No birds in this wasteland.

"What was it?" Rissa demands.

"I don't know, but—"

Rissa shouts, and I hear her tires slide on the asphalt. She recovers and accelerates back up to come parallel to me.

"Something's out there, flying around," she says, voice grim. "I can't see it, but it's out there."

Of all the things we considered, an assault from the air was not one of them. I search the tops of cliffs, looking for motion, a shine, anything that may give away the location of whoever's got eyes on us. But it's just black, as the last of our sunlight dies.

"Should we stop?" Ben asks anxiously.

"And make it easy for them?" Rissa says "Hell no."

"You see anything, Mósí?" I ask the Cat, the one with supernatural senses. But the Cat is asleep, curled up in an uncomfortable-looking ball in her sidecar. Impossible. "Will somebody wake that damn cat—"

"What is that?" Ben shouts. She's behind me, so I can't see where she's looking. But I don't have to. I can feel it. A thrust of air so strong that it catches my bike and sends it sideways. I wrench the bike upright against the sudden gale. Ben clutches my waist and presses her head into my back.

Sweat breaks out on my forehead, sudden and cold, and I tighten my grip. I'm well aware that if I lose control out here, going this fast, we're both roadkill.

Ben hammers on my shoulder, frantic. She points up.

"Is that a . . . ?" Rissa's voice trails off.

The airplane buzzes low, feet from our heads, a dense winged shape in the dark. We can sense more than see it arc wide, turning to make another pass. The roar of a propeller's steady *tap, tap, tap* fills the air. And behind the plane, small dark shapes trail like ducklings. Battery-powered drones, the eyes on the Malpais, waiting for travelers like us.

"They're going to try to run us off the road," I yell, searching for somewhere to take cover. I spot a narrow entry, a path snaking between a break in the canyons. It looks wide enough for the bikes but impossible for the plane's wingspan. The drones will follow, but the twisting canyon will make us harder to target. "There!"

"Do we take it?" Rissa shouts. "It could be a trap." The plane has completed its turn and is coming in fast, the trajectory of its dive putting us directly in its path.

"It's going to try to bring us down. We either run for the canyon or we're road splatter."

The rumble of the engine permeates the sky, the turn of the propeller filling my vision.

"Maggie?!"

"Wait for it. . . . Wait . . ." And when the plane is so close that I can see the pilot briefly illuminated in Rissa's headlight—a hunched figure in a leather aviator cap and googles—I yell, "Now!"

I wrench the bike right, barreling off the road and onto the rocky terrain. Bounce hard and come down, teeth rattling. Ben's arms crush my ribs so hard I can't breathe. I hear Rissa's wheels hit dirt behind me and we haul ass for the crevice. The plane buzzes past, the wind from its passing pushing against my back.

We hit the canyon at full speed, walls closing around us immediately. Rissa kills her headlight too, and we fly blind, inches from the rocks on either side. Honágháahnii flares, and my vision improves, but the night is dense, almost a physical thing, and we're moving fast. I squint into the darkness, clocking cliffsides and looming boulders as we speed past. My arm catches a jutting rock. Pain rips across my biceps, bright and hot. I bite my lip to keep from crying out, let off the throttle instinctively.

A wall comes up fast. I slam the brakes, dirt flying. Make the turn and keep going.

"You okay, Ben?" I ask, panting through the stinging pain on my arm. I reach back to feel the spot, and there's a rip in the leather, and under that, wetness.

"You're bleeding!" Ben says.

"I'm fine. It just hurts like a sonofabitch. Are you okay?"

"I'm okay. But I can't see Rissa."

I brake, the back wheel spinning. Brace my feet on the ground. Turn the bike until we're facing back the way we came. She's right. No Rissa. I wait a few minutes to see if she'll appear, but nothing. Maybe she couldn't make that tight turn with the sidecar.

"Hold on. We're going back."

I accelerate slowly, moving back toward the mouth of the canyon. "We're headed back to you, Rissa," I say through the commlink. "Eyes open." There's no answer. And that worries me more than the possibilities of a sudden collision.

"They couldn't have just disappeared," I mutter to myself. "Unless—"

Light bursts bright and blinding in front of me. I skid to a halt. Raise my hand to my eyes, trying to block the sudden flood of light and preserve my night vision.

"Turn off your engine," comes a voice from somewhere in the brightness. Male, commanding. The kind of voice that expects to be obeyed. No way I trust that voice. I rev the motor, ready to make a run for it.

"I know you are considering disobeying. I would advise against that. Any lack of cooperation on your part won't go well for your friend."

He has to mean Rissa. Damn. I let the engine idle and think about making a run for it. Because it's better if Ben and I make it out of here than if no one makes it out of here. I have no idea what to expect from this man hiding behind the spotlight. But this is the Malpais, and I've never heard anything good about the people who survive out here. Bandits, thieves, and worse. For all I know, Rissa and Mósí could already be dead. Surrender could do us no good, and there's still a chance we could make it out, hide somewhere deep in the canyons where they can't find us. And I could still make it to Kai. Or at least one of us could make it to Kai.

"Off the motorcycle, if you please," says the voice again, the irritation ratcheted up a notch. "I must insist."

"I can't see!" I shout, stalling. And hoping to get a better look at our odds. "Turn off the light and I'll turn off the engine."

"If you run, I will have Aaron put a bullet through your friend's head. Is that understood?"

Not dead, then. "Understood."

The lights dim, enough for me to see the outlines of half a dozen vehicles, lights mounted on the roofs. Human figures, too, carrying weapons. I squint, looking for a rifle or other kind of long gun, but they appear to be armed only with blades—a man on the left holding a spear, the one next to him cradling a crossbow. All homemade, by the looks of it. No match for my guns at this distance and with Honágháahnii speed.

K'aahanáanii sighs, happy. A smile bleeds across my face.

"Maggie?" Ben's voice, small and scared.

Ben. I'd forgotten about Ben, so caught up in K'aahanáanii. I refocus on getting us out of here in one piece instead of turning these men in bloody pieces. Remind myself that I vowed I wouldn't kill anyone. And I won't, at least not on purpose. But "kill" and "grievously wound" are different things.

"Remember how you promised not to argue with me?" I ask Ben, my voice a low whisper.

A soft exhale of acknowledgment in my ears.

"I want you to run. Use your clan powers and get the hell out of here. Find out where Amangiri is, what Caleb meant. Can you do that? And I want you to get Kai out, away from this Gideon person. Whatever it takes. Go back for Clive, bring the whole of fucking Dinétah if you have to, but you find him. You promise?" It's a ridiculous thing to ask. But I have to give her a reason to run and keep running.

"And kill the White Locust. I promise," she whispers. Touches her hand briefly to the wound on my arm, smearing my blood across her fingers and then sticking them in her mouth.

I kill the engine. Silence, sudden and stark, fills the canyon. I hold my hands high in surrender.

"Very good," says the voice again, sounding relieved. "Now, if you'll just step forward please."

I swing my leg over the bike. Honágháahnii waits, alert and ready. And I move.

Pull my shotgun free in one smooth motion. Fire at the row of people, light flaring from my gun. And scream at Ben. "Run!"

She takes off.

I pump and fire. Wish for a moment for Rissa's automatic rifle, but the scattershot of the shotgun is doing its job, spreading pain and chaos over the enemy. Shouting and panic. The lights pop on again, blinding. I shoot them out, bulbs breaking and glass showering down. Someone screams in the darkness. I take the opportunity to drop more shells into the double barrel. Shake it closed. Keep firing.

Someone rushes me, just a bulky mass of human flesh in the corner of my eye. I flip my shotgun, catch the barrel in my gloved hand, and swing at his head. Impact, and a grunt of pain as the enemy goes down. Another one comes in fast, swinging a baseball bat wrapped in barbed wire. I duck, drop the shotgun, and draw my Böker. Slide under his guard and come up. Rip my knife across his stomach. Another figure, this one wearing some kind of animal mask. She swings a six-foot pike at my chest. I rear back, safe by inches. Spin and kick. Knock the weapon from her hands. Twist and land another kick to the back of her knee. And another to her head. And keep moving.

Two more attack, and I take them out too. But Honágháahnii will start to wane soon. I can feel the adrenaline dropping, the disastrous fatigue not far behind. I've got to stop fighting and get out of here. I scan the cliffs, looking for escape.

"Maggie! Help me!"

I freeze. Ben? Did she not get away?

I hear sounds of struggle, then a cry, abruptly cut off, and I know they have Ben.

With Honágháahnii still hot, I could run. Make it to the cliffs. Scramble up and maybe disappear. But I can't leave Ben. I promised, didn't I? Assured Rissa I was responsible for Ben's life. And Tah said she was mine, my life to keep safe.

"Weapons! On the ground!"

A single light flickers on. A flashlight, bright and directly in my eyes. Only a dozen feet away. Too close to be the man with the voice.

I drop my Böker.

"Everything!"

I drop my throwing knives too.

A low murmur of voices in the distance and then. "Aaron, if you would."

A man with the flashlight comes forward. He's wearing a leather aviator's cap like the pilot in the plane, goggles pushed up high on his forehead. A bilagáana face, long and gaunt, dominated by a large nose and startlingly white eyebrows. Tufts of bleached white hair escape his cap to fall down over pale eyes. He glances up at me. His brows and eyelashes are white too, and there's a thick mess of scar tissue near his left eye, the result of a burn. Those eyes meet mine for a brief second before he quickly looks away.

He tucks the flashlight under an arm and bends to gather my weapons. Dumps the knives into a rucksack, retrieves my shotgun and tucks it under his arm before scurrying away. One of the bigger lights pops on, revealing another figure. A large man who swaggers forward, a clever grin splitting his face wide. Bilagáana too. Skin pale as milk and hair the yellow of chamisa blossoms. He wears a button-up white shirt closed tight all the way up to his chin, long sleeves and black suspenders over a wide chest.

"Good girl," he says with an ugly smile that sends my stomach plummeting.

"Where's Ben?" I ask.

"Ben?" He frowns like the name is distasteful, thin lips turning down. "What is a Ben?"

"Do you have her or not?"

"Ah," he says. "The girl is Ben. We'll have to change that name. What kind of name is that for a pretty little laurel? Well, thanks to you, the girl Ben is safe." He grins, showing a mouthful of silver-capped teeth. "Unlike you."

He gestures around us, taking in the injured warriors that

surround us. People that I made that way. He looks pointedly at the fresh blood spattering my clothes.

"They're not dead," I say, a small protest, considering the situation. And maybe not entirely true, but I did try. That should count for something.

"So much violence," he chides me. "I had hoped to spare you, maybe take you to auction, but you're much too dangerous. Imagine the scandal if I sold you to a client only to have you . . ." His face falls, as if he's truly disappointed. Shakes his head like I've let him down. "No, I'm afraid not. I hate to waste a breedable woman, but it's the Harvest for you."

He takes a step back, raises his hand and snaps his fingers. Rough hands grab me, force me down to my knees. A heavy strike between my shoulders forces me flat on the ground. I bite my tongue. Dirt and blood fill my mouth. Someone knees me hard in the back and grabs my arms, twisting. I feel the cold metal of handcuffs against my wrists before I'm dragged back up to my feet.

The man in the white shirt studies me for a minute. The hairs on the back of my neck rise under that blue gaze. His eyes linger for a moment on my face before traveling over my body. Evaluating. Like I'm something he's considering buying. Or something he thinks he already owns.

On impulse, I spit my mouthful of blood on his shirt. His freezes, before his face purples in rage. He takes a cloth from his pocket and carefully wipes the mess away.

"Bag her," he says tersely, already walking away. "And take her to the Reaping Room. And in the name of the prophets, fetch me a clean shirt!"

Someone pulls rough black fabric over my head, I feel a sharp sting at the back of my neck like a bug bite, and everything goes black.

# Chapter 22

I wake up, lying on a cold concrete floor. My head's pounding like a sledgehammer against my temples, and my mouth is as dry as the desert. I blink through blinding light blasting down on me and try to get my bearings. "What is the deal with these people and light?" I mutter, squinting to try to see around me.

"She lives," comes a familiar surly voice.

"Rissa?" The Goodacre twin is here, flashing me a relieved smile that belies the annoyed tone of her voice. She offers me a hand, pulling me into a sitting position. Gives me a canteen, which I take gratefully. Her usually neat braids are wild and loose around her head, and a huge bruise covers the side of her face. "What happened?"

"I fought back. Until . . ." She holds her hand to the wound on her face. "I suppose it's a bit of justice."

"I wasn't going to say that."

"You didn't have to."

I run fingers gingerly across my neck. Feel the spot where they injected me with whatever they used to knock me out.

"Still better than whatever they pumped into you to put you to sleep. You've been out for hours." She grins. "You must have scared the shit out of them."

"Maybe they're not used to clan powers."

"Poor five-fingereds," she says in a very good imitation of Mósí. "Didn't know what hit them."

"Speaking of, any sign of Mósí? Or Ben?"

"No. The Cat disappeared before they caught us. She's out there. Somewhere."

Well, at least that's one bit of good news. If Mósí's free, our chances of getting out of this place go up. Assuming she decides she wants to help us.

"And no Ben?"

She shakes her head.

I sit up straighter, shade my eyes, and take a good look around, wondering where exactly "here" is. Rissa and I are alone, and in a cage of some kind, thick iron bars on four sides of us, a concrete floor sloping toward the middle of the room. There's a drain in the center. I can see other cages like ours along the wall. They're all empty, but there are fresh stains on the cement. I can smell the lingering odors of piss and worse things. Empty meat hooks hang from the ceiling at various intervals, swinging idly. Massive steel tables take up most of the space. A room straight out of a fucking horror movie.

I look at Rissa, who gives me a tight terrified smile. I hadn't noticed before, but her hands are shaking.

"He called this the Reaping Room," I say, feeling some of that same dawning revulsion. "Is this a . . . ?"

"Body shop. That's what this is. I've heard people talk about them, but I didn't think they existed. But this sure looks like the real deal."

"Cannibals?" I ask, the word thick on my tongue.

"No. A body shop harvests your organs, sells them to the highest bidder."

"Harvest," I repeat. I remember what the bilagáana man with

the blue eyes said about sending me to the Harvest. This must be what he meant.

"I've heard they take everything," Rissa says. "Skin, hair, organs. There's a booming market for body parts. A man came to the All-American once. Approached Mom about getting into the business. But she turned him down flat. Reported him as a Harvester, and they ran him out of Dinétah."

"Grace was going to get into the Harvesting business?"

"Never." Rissa shudders. "Mom would never. But I learned a bit about it after that. Morbid curiosity, I guess."

"So, what happens after you get Harvested?"

"Does it matter? We'll be dead."

She's got a point.

I push myself to my feet. Pace around the cage, rattling the bars, testing their strength. "Any idea where we are? I mean, besides hell, generally?"

"Pretty sure this is Knifetown. It used to be one of those places Mósí was talking about along Route 66. 'Come see the largest collection of knives in North America.' That kind of thing. Now . . ." Her eyes travel over the cages, the surgical tables. "And Knifetown came up more than once when I was doing my research. I got the feeling it was infamous."

"Great. So we're prisoners of the most infamous body shop in the Malpais. Is that what you're telling me?" I run my hands over my face, trying to think. "How far is that from where we were headed? That Mormon settlement?"

"Joseph City? Not far. Less than twenty miles. We were almost there."

"Figures."

"They wouldn't help you in Joseph City," comes a voice from behind us. We whirl to find the pilot from before, the one in the aviator's cap with the bleached eyebrows and lashes, walking through a door marked EXIT in red glowing letters. "They're scared of Bishop out in J City, just like the rest of them. If you'd stopped there, they would have just brought you here, only made a little trade in the in-between."

"Who are you?" Rissa asks.

"Aaron," I say, remembering what the man in the white shirt called him. "He took my weapons."

"Nothing personal," he says, his lips quirking in a sideways grin. He pulls a wallet-size pack from his pocket. Lays it flat in his palm and unzips it along the side. Inside gleam four sharp-looking needles. He pulls a long vial of liquid from the other side of his kit.

"I'm guessing he's also the one who drugged me," I say to Rissa.

"Again," Aaron says, "not personal."

"I took it pretty personally, Aaron."

"Then you're really not going to like this." He holds up the vial to the light. "My sincere apologies for what comes next, but Bishop's got guests tonight and he needs you both asleep until he's done entertaining."

"Asleep?" I ask, eyeing that needle warily. "Or dead?"

"What makes one ride the Malpais at night?" he asks conversationally as he sticks a needle into the top of the vial. He pulls the plunger, and we all watch it fill. "Everybody knows this is Bishop's territory, and what comes through here belongs to Bishop. Too easy to catch something like you. You ladies don't look that brainless. Are you that brainless?" He looks up at us, like he's waiting for us to answer.

"Technically it was dusk," I mutter.

His shoulders shake in what might be laughter. "Well, technically, you're screwed."

"Was that you flying that airplane?" Rissa asks.

Now he really does smile, showing a mouthful of silver teeth. "What gave it away? Was it the cap?" He touches a hand to his head.

"So, you're a pilot?" I ask, trying to keep him talking instead of shooting us up with whatever is in that vial.

"I *was* a pilot," he corrects me. "Before the Big Water. Shuttling tourists around the South Rim of the grandest canyon of all in one of those high-winged little Caravans. Nice little craft. I miss flying her."

"We're a long way from the Grand Canyon. How'd you end up here?"

He lifts a shoulder, noncommittal. "Lucky, I guess. Same as you." He grins. "Now, where were we?"

"What would it cost us to get you to fly us out of here?" Rissa asks in a rush.

Aaron stills. Just a moment's hesitation, but it's there. "Neither of you ladies have that kind of trade," he scoffs, his tone dismissive.

"I do," Rissa says, her voice sweet as honey and just as seductive. "My family is Dinétah wealthy, not this Malpais gangland ghoul shit like your boss. You get us out of here, we'll bring you across the border. Get you papers, make sure you're set up real nice. Whatever you want."

He licks his lips, eyes narrowed on Rissa. "Across the Wall? You're not Diné," he says suspiciously. "You got no sway over there on the other side."

"Have you heard of the Goodacres?"

His eyes light up. He leans back against one of the big stainless-steel tables, crossing his arms. Rolls the needle between his fingers like another man might a coin. "Everyone knows the Goodacres. Cletus Goodacre was famous in the Harvesting business. A goddamn legend!"

I shoot a startled glance at Rissa. *Didn't know if they were real, eh? Never in the business. Mom would never*, she said. But her older brother's a goddamn legend?

She shifts uncomfortably, caught out in a lie. Embarrassing, but we both know our priority is getting out of here. My moral outrage can come later.

"You're talking to Clarissa Goodacre," she says, stepping forward, hands on her hips.

He looks doubtful at first, but slowly the knowledge seems to dawn. "The red hair. Should have known. Can't be too many reds like you left in the world. But I always thought Cletus was part-Navajo," he says. "Used to joke about being the same clan."

"You're Navajo?" I ask, surprised.

"You actually knew him?" Rissa asks.

"'Course. We all knew him. Until . . ." He makes a gesture, something to ward off evil. Curious. I've never asked Grace what happened to Cletus. How he died. I just assumed it was in the Energy Wars or in some horrible accident like her husband.

"So, are you going to get us out of here?" I ask.

He looks back to me. Hesitates, glances down at the needle still in his hand. "You'll get me into Dinétah. Set me up, a wealthy man."

Rissa nods.

"Exactly how much wealth are we talking?"

"Enough to make it worth your while. You knew Cletus, so you know that I'm good to my word."

He taps the needle against his cheek. "Tempting. But if I get caught, I'll be the next one in that cage."

"You won't get caught because you'll come with us," Rissa practically croons. "We make it to that airplane, no one's catching us."

I can see the greed practically shining from his eyes, in the way he twirls the needle between his fingers, contemplating. He swallows hard as Rissa swaggers forward, hips swinging in her fitted brown leathers. She leans folded arms against the bars. She's close enough to reach out and touch him if she wants.

"So, what do you say, Aaron?" she drawls. "Want to be rich?"

# Chapter 23

Aaron decides he does indeed want to be rich. He pockets the needle and pulls a ring of keys from his belt, deftly finding the one that opens our cage. Turns the lock and I'm swinging the door open before he's even finished. I'd never been in a cage before and I can't say I cared for the experience. Don't think I'll do it again.

Aaron lets me pass and then turns back to Rissa. Gives her a little bow as he holds the door open for her. She returns the gesture with a predator's grin. He reaches out and takes her hand. Kisses her knuckles. "An honor, Ms. Goodacre," he murmurs.

I have to stop myself from gagging. "Really? Ms. Goodacre?"

"No reason we can't be civil," she says, giving me a fuck-off kind of smile.

I want to point out that ten minutes ago Aaron was willing to cut her into pieces and sell her liver to the highest bidder. But I don't. Instead I say, "Be civil all you want. Let's just get out of here."

And that's when we hear it. Voices coming from the stairwell. Two men at least, maybe more.

"Were you expecting backup?" I ask, tense.

Aaron goes rigid. "No. Everyone's supposed to be at the auction. No one's allowed in the Reaping Room when there's prisoners."

I scan the room, looking for weapons. Four metal tables, way too heavy to lift. Bare bulbs hanging in intervals from the ceiling. Meat hooks. And along the wall, medicine cabinets. I hadn't really noticed them before, but now that I have, I'm guessing they are full of surgical equipment. The kind one might use to remove organs.

"Fuck!" Aaron hisses, striding for the door. There's a small window at eye level. He hunches down to peek through, looking up the stairs. "You've got to be shitting me." He runs a shaky hand across his head. "What are they doing here?" He claps his hands together sharply. "Think, Aaron, think." He looks up, eyes bright. "Quick, back in the cage."

"Like hell," Rissa says for both of us.

"If you're out, the jig is up."

"There is no jig." I walk to the closest cabinet. Slam my elbow against the flimsy lock and it comes open. Sure enough, sharp metal gleams back at me in deadly little rows. I grab what looks like a scalpel, careful not to cut myself. Slip two razors on long handles into the places where my throwing knives usually go.

"What are you doing?" Aaron whisper-shouts at me. "These are my buddies. You're not going to chop them up."

"Watch me," I say, tucking a particularly ugly blade into my sleeve.

"No!" he says, grabbing at my arm. I shake him off, give him a look that's frightened braver men than him, and he backs down.

"Okay, all right, all right." He paces the floor. "Rissa!" He hurries to Rissa, who's resting her butt against one of the steel tables, eyeing the meat hooks above her thoughtfully. "You're the sane one in the girl group, am I right?"

"I heard that," I say.

"Can you talk your friend there into getting in the cage? I won't lock it, and we already have a deal, right? You know I wouldn't go back on a deal. Not with Cletus's sister. But let me see what my buddies want. Maybe it's a mistake. Maybe they can walk away, eh? Before it gets violent."

Rissa crosses her arms. The voices are getting louder, laughing and joking as heavy footsteps come down the stairs.

"What do you say, Maggie?" she asks me, leaning forward a bit. "Should we give them a chance?"

"Or," I say, shutting the cabinet. "We could just kill them."

Aaron groans.

"I thought you were turning over a new leaf," Rissa says to me. "Trying not to kill people."

"I was, but that was yesterday. Today, with the whole captured and drugged thing? I'm feeling pretty aggro."

Rissa gestures to Aaron like there's nothing she can do.

"Unless," I say, cutting off whatever he was going to say next. "Unless you help us find Ben."

"Sure, sure, whatever you want. Let me—let me open that door and I will help you with your Ben, no problem."

"Okay." I look to Rissa. "Okay?"

"You armed?" she asks.

I nod, a feral smile leaking from my lips. "I've even picked out a few for you. I know you prefer a gun, but it's good for a woman to learn to use a blade."

"That's nice, Maggie. I appreciate you thinking of me."

"No reason I can't be civil, Ms. Goodacre."

Aaron's dancing from foot to foot, sweating. If I weren't convinced we were going to have to fight our way out of this place in the next sixty seconds, I'd laugh. But instead I saunter over to the cage, and Rissa follows. Aaron starts to close the door, but I stop it with my foot. Hold out my hand. He slaps the key ring down in my palm, so I move my foot and let him close the door.

"Now lie down," he says, eyes darting between us and the door. "So it looks like I drugged you."

We can hear that Aaron's friends have arrived, so we don't argue. Rissa and I hit the concrete. I fling an arm out to cover my face, but I make sure I can see the door. Aaron practically sprints for the stairwell, slapping the bright lights off as he hits the wall. He catches the knob and pulls it open just as two men barrel through.

"My brothers!" he shouts, overly friendly. "What are you doing here?"

Aaron's friends freeze. The one in front, a big guy with an unkempt beard and a broad sloping belly, stutters out, "A-Aaron. We thought you'd be up at the auction with everyone else." His eyes dart around the room, clearly looking for something, someone. Us. But the dark has rendered Rissa and I into indistinct lumps. "Bishop sent me down to check on the prisoners."

The other one laughs nervously. "Oh yeah, same. We were just checking."

"Funny," Aaron says in a voice as empty as the Malpais. "He didn't mention he was sending you two down. In fact, I was supposed to dose them and lock them up for the night. You know the rules."

His friends exchange a look. The bearded one shrugs, shoulders slumping in defeat. But the other one, fair-haired and lean, isn't willing to give up so quickly. "So, listen, Aaron," he says, leaning in conspiratorially. "We heard they were women. Young ones. Pretty ones. And you know how it is. We don't get to see a lot of those. We just wanted to take a look."

"While they're knocked out cold?" Aaron asks, finger against his chin like he's confused.

His friend stares a hard moment and then lifts his hands. "You got us!" he says, exasperated. "We're men, aren't we?"

"Virile men," Beard agrees.

The blond shoots his friend an annoyed look before turning back to Aaron. "So maybe we want to do more than look. But what's the harm? They're scheduled for Harvesting tomorrow. They won't care because they'll be dead."

Something changes in Aaron's posture. A subtle thing. I recognize it only because I know a fighting stance when I see it. A relaxing of the shoulders, a shift of his weight as he bends his knees. "Pete," he says, his voice a degree colder than it was before, "please tell me you're not saying what I think you're saying."

Pete takes a step back, clearly not expecting his friend's reaction. "We know the rules, Aaron, but what's a little rule bending between friends?"

"They're just women," his bearded friend says. "And strangers at that. Who cares what we do to them?"

"It's a sin. Especially because they are strangers. Especially because they are women."

Pete exhales, loud and exasperated. "Get over yourself, Aaron. If you think about it, we're doing this trash a favor—"

It happens so fast I almost miss it. One minute Pete's standing in the threshold of the door, hands braced on the doorjamb. The next he's got a needle protruding from his eye.

Pete screams, clawing for his eye.

Aaron grabs Pete's head, drives it down into his knee, forcing the needle farther into the socket. He twists Pete's neck and the scream cuts off abruptly. He throws Pete into the room, and his body slides awkwardly across the tile, clearly dead.

Aaron's other friend stares in shock. But not for long.

He swings, a blade hidden in his hand, slicing open Aaron's face right above his eye. Aaron staggers back, cursing. And his friend takes off running. Not back up the stairs, a death trap, but across the room to the exit door on the far end.

Aaron looks up. He's bleeding, blood dripping into his eye, blinding him. He wipes at it ineffectively, trying to stanch the flow. He's not going to catch him.

I move.

His friend doesn't make it ten feet before I'm tackling him from behind. He hits the tile, face-first, me on his back. I grind my knees into his shoulder to hold him still. Grab his hair and have a surgically sharp blade at his throat, all Honágháahnii fast.

"Shhhhh!" I whisper in his ear. "Or I cut your throat."

"Cut his throat," Aaron says, coming up behind me with Rissa. Blood streams down his cheek in rivulets, following the lines of his scar, spattering onto his white double-breasted.

I say, "I thought they were your friends and we weren't supposed to hurt your friends."

Aaron presses at the wound on his forehead. "I thought so, too, but they're not friends of mine. Did you hear what Pete said? What he and Wyatt had planned?"

Wyatt whines under my hand, and I pull his hair a little tighter to shut him up. "I heard. Not very original. I'd be more impressed if they were sneaking down here to steal our kidneys or something."

"Teeth," Rissa adds. "You all could use some better teeth than this silver crap you got filling your mouths."

"I don't abide rapists," he says with such vehemence that I turn all the way around, shifting to drive my knee into Wyatt's neck just because I can.

"I can't say I care for them myself, but that sounds personal," I observe carefully.

Aaron stares at me. He lost his aviator's cap somewhere along the way, and his hair trails down his back in a long line, the sides of his head completely shaved but for the strip of hair down the middle. He looks wild, fierce in a way he didn't before. But his eyes are bright and wet. Hurt. He blinks white lashes at me, the look on his face answer enough.

I sigh, conflicted. "I'm trying not to kill people," I explain. "It's a new thing I'm trying. I mean, I know I said all that stuff before . . ."

He takes a moment before he nods. "Then I'll do it."

I look over at Rissa. She's watching Aaron, head tilted, evaluating. I catch her eye and she shrugs. Clearly not our problem.

"And murder's not a sin to you?" I ask. Not that I'm interested in whatever flavor of religion Aaron seems to be so strongly devoted to, but I am curious.

"Those who disobey, even in thought, are deserving of death."

"That seems harsh. We could just lock him in one of these cages."

Aaron seems to think about it. "There is a punishment Bishop decrees that is short of death for those that are tempted by lust."

"Fine. Do that."

Aaron nods once, flicking blood across his white jacket.

I slam Wyatt's head down against the concrete. Hard. He grunts, dazed.

I stand up, hand the blade to Aaron, and step back. "He's all yours."

Aaron stands there, blade in hand. Unmoving. I'm worried he's in shock until he opens his mouth and says, "You know the rules and you chose to break them. You know the punishment."

Wyatt moans, a sound that sends a tremor through the room.

"Just kill me," he wails.

But Aaron is unbending. "Choose, Wyatt."

"I—I can't!"

"I take your tongue or I take your balls. Choose."

Rissa's eyes widen. I grab her arm and pull her toward the stairwell door, Wyatt's pleas for death trail us, growing more hysterical. "We'll wait out here," I call back. We sidestep Pete's body to clear the entrance.

"Don't take too long!" Rissa says as I close the door.

The lights of the stairwell are stark and the air is warm compared to the temperature in the lab, but I still feel cold. "Holy shit! Who are these people?"

Rissa doesn't say anything. Just climbs a few stairs and takes a seat. She's still got the thoughtful look on her face.

I frown. "What is that look? Oh no. Don't tell me you like him."

She glances up, surprised. Blushes under the bright lights. "He's interesting," she admits.

"He's some kind of religious fanatic."

"Believing in sin doesn't make him a fanatic."

"He's in there right now butchering a man he called his friend five minutes ago."

"He doesn't like rapists. That seems like an excellent quality to me."

I exhale some of the adrenaline from Honágháahnii, shake out my arms. "Don't ever say I have bad taste in men again."

She snorts. "That was my mom, not me. Although I still think Kai—"

The door opens, and we both turn. Aaron comes through, gently closing the door behind him. He's cleaned up. Traded his bloodied white jacket for a new spotless one. The cut on his head has a crude bandage on it that the blood has already begun to soak through.

"You're going to need stitches for that," I say, gesturing toward the wound.

"I can do it," Rissa offers. "It will only take a minute. I've got lots of experience sewing people up."

Aaron looks up at us, tears caught in his lashes. "I'm sorry you had to see that, ladies." His whole demeanor has changed. He's a different man than the one that swaggered into the room earlier.

"I've seen worse."

I want to ask her where and when, but I don't think I want to know.

Aaron holds his hand out, offering up a bottle of superglue and a spray bottle of Bactine. "I think glue will do the trick. It's not deep."

Rissa frowns but takes the bottle from him. "I'll try it."

"I just don't like a needle so much," he says, without a hint of irony. "Bad memories, you understand."

I don't, but whatever. Aaron's obviously a man with a collection of nasty stories, none of which I need to hear to believe that this place is a hellhole and the sooner we're all out of here the better.

Aaron lets Rissa clean his wound and apply the superglue. We wait a few seconds for the glue to set, and then Rissa gently wipes Aaron's skin clean. "Good enough," she says, giving her work a critical eye.

"Then let's go," Aaron says, his voice subdued. "I'm done here."

# Chapter 24

"The Tank is on the top floor of the building, at ground level," Aaron explains as we make our way up the stairs. He's somber. The lightness in his personality seems to have leeched out of him along with his friends' blood. We didn't ask what ultimately happened to Wyatt, because we didn't want to know. But Aaron doesn't seem worried about anyone following us, so that's likely explanation enough.

"The Reaping Room was at the bottom level, four floors down. Once we get to the Tank, we grab your weapons, load the plane, and leave. If we're lucky, everyone will be at the auction, where they're supposed to be, and no one will even notice we're missing until we're airborne."

"There's one thing you forgot," I remind him. "Ben."

He looks at me blankly.

"You promised you'd help us find our friend Ben. The girl who was on the bike with me, out in the canyon. We need to rescue her, too."

"Ahhh . . . ," he says, scratching at the scars on his face. "That might be a problem."

"How's that?" I ask, my voice as sharp as a surgical blade.

"I'm afraid it's too late for her."

"Too late?"

"She's not dead," he says quickly. "She's getting married."

I stop, plant my feet on the stairs. "Explain."

He hesitates, mouth twisting up like he's searching for the words. "I'll tell you everything," he says finally, "But keep moving."

The landing in front of us is marked with a big number two. Halfway there. I glare at him but start back up the stairs.

"Every second month, Bishop holds an auction. People come from all over. The Burque, Hopiland, the Kingdom. A delegation even came from New Denver once upon time, looking for a real specialty item. And these are important people. Wealthy." He rubs two fingers together. "People looking for goods they can't get anywhere else, if you catch my drift."

"Body parts," I say flatly. "We've established that. What else?"

"We make knives, of course. It's in the name. Guns, too. Explosives. But we also sell labor and the occasional exotic."

I frown. "Exotics? Labor?"

"Slaves," Rissa says, her voice sounding tired. "He means slaves."

I stare, aghast. "You're selling Ben as a slave?!"

"Not me!" he says quickly, hands raised. "Bishop. I got no part in that side of the business."

"You clearly have a part in it if you're here, serving him, working for him."

His rubs at his scars again. "My choices are obey or end up downstairs on a steel table. What would you have me choose?"

I breathe in, try to steady myself. "What happens to Ben if she goes to auction?"

"A young girl like that? She could go as a house girl, but most likely she'll go as a wife." He narrows his eyes. "She's bled, right? She can have babies?"

"What the fuck, Aaron?"

He shrugs. "It matters."

"And how is that different from rape?" Rissa asks. "How is that different from what your two buddies were thinking they could do to us?"

He looks genuinely taken aback. "It's marriage. She'll have babies, raise a family."

"And what if she doesn't want any of that?!"

"All women want that."

Rissa and I exchange a look over Aaron's shoulder. He shakes his head, clearly confused. We're at the top of the stairs, facing a thick gray metal door. There's a caution sign on our side, warning against cross traffic. Aaron looks up as if he's contemplating the caution sign.

"It's the best life that the Malpais can offer. She'll have a rich husband if he can afford the auction. And a home of her own. Better by yards than what happens to most kids who grow up out here. Better than what we had planned for you both."

"But Ben didn't grow up out here. She's from Dinétah. She's with us."

He shrugs, still not getting it. "Shitty luck. Just didn't go her way, then."

"Hey," Rissa says, grabbing his arm. "She's a sixteen-year-old girl. You're going to help us, right?"

He looks at her like a drowning man looks at the shore—wondering why he ever left and wishing like hell he could get back. He exhales heavily, bending over, his hands on his hips. He shakes his head violently like he's trying to shake off whatever emotion he's feeling. And then he kicks the door in front of us. Once, twice. He's wearing a steel-toed boot, and the door bends where he makes contact. He slams his head against the door with a strangled growl, hard enough to leave a dent.

We watch in silence.

Finally, he stops. Leans forward on the door, arms folded and head resting on his forearms. "Okay," he says, mostly to himself. "Okay." He scrubs a hand across his face before he stands straight and faces us. "I'll help you get your Ben, but then you are taking me to Dinétah."

"That was the deal," Rissa says.

He nods once. "There are some things you should know. This is the Tank, but the auction will be across the road in the big tent. There's only two ways in and out of the tent. One in the front and one straight back. Like a barn. There'll be security. The auction draws a big crowd."

"How big?" I ask.

"Tonight? A hundred? Maybe more. The Familias were already arriving when I came down to the Harvest Room. And I'm sure there'll be some representative from the Kingdom. Even a Swarmer or two from Amangiri."

I look up. "Amangiri?"

He nods.

"You know Amangiri?"

"Yeah."

My heart ticks up a beat. "Can you take us there? In your plane?"

"That wasn't the deal."

"We can talk about that later," Rissa interjects, throwing a pointed look my way. "Right now we need to focus on getting Ben out."

It hurts, but I let Amangiri go for now. Knowing Aaron knows about it, that it's a real place that actually exists at all, is enough for now. Rissa's eyes linger on me until she's sure I'll keep my mouth shut before she turns back to Aaron.

"Is there anything else we need to know?" she asks.

He says, "Bishop's a crazy man. Not reasonable like me. And you can't buy him over, neither. He catches us, we'll be made an example of." His fingers run across his scars again unconsciously. "For stealing his property, he'll cook up something extra nasty, I suppose. A skin flailing. Feedings us to the sporting dogs. Maybe a chase down in the desert." He shudders. "He's a monster."

I want to yell at him that Ben is no one's property, but the adrenaline's kicking in now, and I can feel my clan powers rising again, waiting. Hungry. I still plan to keep my promise not to kill anyone, but I can certainly make these sick bastards suffer.

"I know we haven't officially been introduced, Aaron," I say, "but they call me the Monsterslayer. I think I can handle Bishop."

The Tank is a massive hanger. The center is dominated by the airplane we saw out on the road, and around it are the outfitted battle trucks and metal-plated cars like the ones that chased us down. There's also a dozen motorcycles, and at the end of a line, up on blocks and in parts, our bikes. They've claimed them as their own.

"Well, there's no getting those back," Rissa says, sounding bitter.

"Everything for a price," Aaron says.

"They're my bikes," she says, outraged.

"Not anymore."

"What's in the cage?" I ask, eyeing a fenced metal cage at least the size of my trailer. My question is a little rhetorical because I can clearly see what's in the cage—shelf after shelf, case and case, filled with weapons.

"Holy crap," Rissa whispers as we make our way over. I rattle the door. It's locked.

"You still got those keys?" Aaron asks. I hand him the key ring, and he unlocks the weapons cage.

"If you have all these weapons, why did you come after us with blades and baseball bats?"

"There were guns if we needed them, but Bishop says guns are too easy. He wants to see us get bloody. Says it keeps us sharp."

"Sharp? Or dead."

Aaron shrugs. "Better to know sooner than later if you can't survive in the Malpais."

"These are all for sale?" Rissa asks, eyes on the massive arsenal.

"We hold them here until the auction's finished. No weapons are allowed inside, 'cept each representative gets a personal bodyguard. Personal weapons only. The auction operates under truce."

"Honor among thieves," I say. "Great for us."

Rissa admires what looks to be modified Heckler assault rifles. "It's like early Keshmish," she whispers, running a hand over the gun.

I laugh, and she laughs back. Gives me a genuine smile.

Aaron hauls up a plastic crate in which our stuff has been unceremoniously dumped. "I was going to sort it and categorize it tomorrow, but I guess I don't have to now." He gestures to the crate. "Have at it."

I take my knives out first. Tuck them back in place next to the razors, which I decide to keep because why not. I put my Böker into the sheathe on my hip. Retrieve my shotgun. Attach my ammo belt. And there, still in its scabbard, still wrapped in black cloth, a thin ribbon of suede tying it all closed at the hilt, is Neizghání's sword. I exhale a nervous breath, relieved to see it.

Rissa's rearmed, too, her familiar AR over her shoulder, a Sig on her hip. She runs a hand over one of the Hecklers again, hefts it up, testing the weight. "It wants me to take it home," she murmurs. "Don't you, baby?"

"I helped modify those myself," Aaron says.

"That's nice," I say. "Rissa, bring an extra gun for Ben. I don't want her defenseless."

"Maggie!" Rissa squeals with delight. "Look at this!" She picks up something from a bucket on the floor and holds it up. A hand grenade. She tucks a few in her pocket, looking like a kid who found a candy stash.

"We ready?" I ask.

"I'm ready," Rissa says. "But what's the plan? Do we just go in swinging?"

"If I may," Aaron says, face wrinkling in concern. "It's just, seeing you like this, Rissa, it occurs to me . . ."

Rissa looks suspicious. "Seeing me like what?"

"I was thinking," he says. "If we're going to have a chance of getting to your friend, we might need to be more subtle than"—he swings an arm, taking in the weapons cage—"all this."

"I'm not putting my guns back," I say.

"Not you. No one would believe you as a fine lady. But Ms. Goodacre . . ." He turns and gives Rissa a little bow. I feel like I should be offended, but I'm so far from offended. Being a fine lady sounds like a fucking nightmare.

"What's going on?" Rissa asks, suspicious.

"How would you like to make your auction debut as the heir to the Goodacre empire and a rising player in the Harvesting business?"

Rissa's face darkens. "What do you mean?"

"You won't have to buy anything. Just look the part."

"How?"

"Any and everything for sale, including a closet for a queen." He gestures toward another section of the Tank, where I can see mountains of fabric and discarded clothes. Rissa's eyes follow, too, and I watch as she takes it all in.

"Do I get to wear a fancy suit?" she says finally.

He grins. "You can wear a tiara if you want."

"No," she says, already putting her guns back where they came from. "We'll do this right."

# Chapter 25

The air outside is decidedly cold. I'd forgotten somehow that it was December, just a few days before Keshmish. Since Neizgháni didn't celebrate the holiday and my past years had been spent solely in his company, it had kind of slipped my mind. I remember the Keshmishes of my childhood, but only in the most limited notion. I remember my nalí always got us a tree. Sometimes they were cheap, something secondhand or a freebie from the tribe, but I didn't know the difference at the time. All I knew was that I loved the way it shined. The lights, the ornaments. Gifts weren't much. New socks from the trading post, some hand-me-downs from one of the ladies at the chapter house. Even then I mostly liked the wrapping paper more than the presents themselves. Since most gifts came in old newspaper or paper bags folded and taped closed, the ones with the shine, no matter how gaudy and metallic, were my favorite.

I'm thinking about that now, as we make our way through all the shiny representatives here for the auction, dressed up in color and spectacle as they mill around outside. Rissa, Aaron, and I maneuver through the crowd, trying to blend in. There's a break in the action and people have come outside to socialize, gathering around small bonfires, drinking hot alcoholic drinks of some kind and waiting for things to resume inside. There's a decidedly festive feeling to the night, not what I was expecting from a bunch of criminals and slave traders. It's disconcerting to think that a few levels beneath our feet, Rissa and I were in a cage awaiting vivisection just an hour ago. I shudder involuntarily, remind myself that a pretty veneer does not mean these people aren't monsters.

Aaron sidles up to us, handing Rissa a drink. She takes it with only the slightest acknowledgment, playing her role as representative to the hilt. I don't get a drink. Aaron explained it would be weird for a representative's bodyguard to drink anything at all. So I tuck my hands in my sleeves, duck my head a little deeper into the heavy black cowl I'm wearing to cover my hair and most of my face, and wait.

"They're going to be starting up again soon," Aaron says, leaning in so we can both hear. "We got lucky. Exotics haven't come up yet."

"Do you have to keep calling them that?" Rissa says, her voice low and angry.

Aaron blinks, caught off guard. "I didn't mean to offend."

Rissa huffs, waves his apology away. "Just . . . call them something else."

Aaron looks crestfallen in the wake of Rissa's admonishment.

"What else can you tell me about Amangiri?" I ask.

"Why do you want to know?" he asks, not sounding like he wants to share.

"I've heard of a cult leader from there, the White Locust."

Aaron stills, and his strange eyes meet mine. "Do you know him?" he asks, his voice tight.

"Only by name," I say, working not to give anything away, thrown by his sudden intensity.

"You thinking of joining up?" he asks sharply.

"No."

He studies me for a moment before he decides something. Whatever it is, he relaxes. He throws off one of his careless shrugs, like he's not really invested in my answer. A lie. "The White Locust has been buying up the market in things that go boom. That's about all I know."

"Anyone know why?"

"Who cares why, as long as he's paying?"

"I heard he wants to destroy the world."

Aaron laughs, loud enough for a few curious people around us to turn and look. "This is the apocalypse, lady. Who cares if some nutjob with wings wants to blow some shit up?"

"Your boss, maybe?"

"My ex-boss. And profiteering is Bishop's middle name. We're making the explosives, aren't we? You don't kill the goose laying the golden egg."

If that's true, I wonder why Aaron has such a strong reaction to me asking about him. But I don't feel like arguing about it, so I scan the crowd, looking for Amangiri's representative. How many people with wings can there be?

"You are going to get us up close to the front, right?" Rissa asks, leaning in to talk to Aaron. "Once we are inside the auction tent?"

"I let the guard know that Cletus Goodacre's little sister was here and that his family's looking to get back into the Harvesting business. He promised to find you prime seating."

Rissa pales a little. She pulls the long gold coat Aaron found her closer around her body. Despite being a little shaky around the edges at the prospect of pretending to be in the market for body parts, she looks downright regal. She's unplaited her hair, letting it loose around her head in a halo of burnished copper. Her brown skin glows in the ruddy firelight, her massive hoop earrings flicker brightly, and the gold-flocked three-piece suit she's wearing hugs her body worshipfully. But it's really in the way she carries herself.

The high tilt of her head, the set of her shoulders. She was born to the role, looking every inch the wealthy criminal heir.

And Aaron can't stop staring at her. Or bringing her things. His infatuation might be amusing under other circumstances, but right now I just find it disturbing. I can still hear him asking his friend to choose between losing his tongue or his balls, a very sharp scalpel in his hand.

"Don't I know you?" comes a voice to my left. We all turn, my hand going for my gun.

The woman who spoke shifts her gaze from Rissa to lift an over-arched and heavily drawn-in eyebrow in my direction. Pale skin made paler by a thick application of powder, bloodred lips outlined in black, a long, thin nose made for looking down on her lessers. Her black hair coils in intricate ropes around her head, adorned with a dragon's den of colorful jewels. More jewels drip from her ears and neck, an ostentatious show of wealth.

"I don't think I've had the pleasure," Rissa says, her voice pitched to match the haughtiness of the woman before us.

"Elena Urioste," the older woman introduces herself, her tone clear that we should already know who she is.

And I do know that name. The Uriostes of the Burque, infamous water barons and land-grant heirs, the old-school Hispanic royalty of the newly developed city-states of the Southwest. And the family responsible for beating Kai half to death to prove a point about their daughter's nonexistent virginity.

Elena holds out a hand to Rissa, who introduces herself as Rissa Goodacre. They touch fingers briefly, a Diné handshake. Elena's dark eyes linger after Rissa removes her hand.

"I understand you are in the Harvesting market?"

"Inquiring," Rissa corrects her smoothly. "Not here to buy, simply to observe. We, my family, haven't made a commitment yet."

Elena purses her lips. "If you are looking for potential growth opportunities, perhaps we should speak at length. The Uriostes have had an interest in expanding into Dinétah, and if you decide to move forward, certainly the Burque has a surplus of resources we would be happy to supply." She laughs, high and artificial. "I have to say, I admire what your mother has done in Dinétah. We've been trying for a foothold there for a while, but tribal red tape." She clicks her tongue. "A ruse of delay, I'm afraid. They favor their own. Your family is one of the few exceptions."

"Maybe they just don't want to do business with you," I say.

They all turn to stare.

"Pardon?" Elena Urioste says, her tone suggesting I'm a bug that suddenly learned to speak and she doesn't approve.

"Why don't you go get me another drink," Rissa says coolly, but her message is clear enough. I've overstepped, forgotten my role. I bite my tongue, remind myself why I'm here and that none of this matters. That if I wanted Elena Urioste dead, she would be in seconds, bodyguard or not.

"Now, Maggie," Rissa says, her jaw tight.

I nod curtly and turn toward the place I saw Aaron get the drinks earlier. But I'm saved from servant duty as a dull gong sounds somewhere close to the tent, signaling that the auction is starting up again.

Rissa inclines her head, a small bow in Elena's direction. "Until next time."

Elena smiles, and I've seen more sincere smiles on rattlesnakes. Aaron motions Rissa toward the tent, and I follow, eyes on Elena Urioste and her goon, hand on my gun.

She watches me back, her eyes laughing, brimming with poison.

"Monsters everywhere," I mutter.

She cocks her head like she heard me. I guess she did. I give her a little salute, and once I'm convinced she's not a threat, at least not right now, I walk into the auction tent.

* * *

Aaron's friend was true to his word, finding us a table in the center of the room. The place is filled to capacity, a series of small round tables spaced intermittently throughout the room, surrounded by straight-backed chairs. In the center of the room is a raised circular stage probably twenty feet in diameter. A spotlight shines down on the stage, which at the moment is empty.

"Are you sure we won't be recognized by your people?" I ask Aaron.

"You don't look the same as when you came in, and it's not so unusual for me to be escorting a representative around. Besides, nobody can see good once the house lights are off, and all attention will be on the baby in the middle."

"Baby?" Rissa asks, horrified.

"An expression," he reassures her. "No babies."

"Just teenagers," I murmur.

We take our seats, the conversation around us still lively and loud. I scan for anyone who might be a threat, but all the representatives seem engrossed in whatever socializing or business has brought them here. I see a tall bilagáana woman in a full-length white dress, high-necked and long sleeves, a pattern of flowers around the hem. She's leaning on the arm of a man in a black suit, white shirt, and thin black tie. His brown hair is parted neatly and slicked back close to his head. He reminds me of the Mormon missionaries who used to travel the rez when I was a kid. Which means he and the woman are probably from the Kingdom. The woman catches my eye, and I turn away before I'm forced to interact.

Others roam the room. I haven't see a representative from Dinétah, but there's a young woman in a deep blue one-shouldered dress, her hair split into two symmetrical buns on the side of her head like butterfly wings. Hopi Nation. But no winged people. It seems the White Locust is only interested in purchasing explosives.

The lights blink twice, and conversation falls. A lone man walks purposefully down the aisle through the center of the room, crisp white shirt clean once again. Bishop hops nimbly up on the stage and raises his hands for silence. The crowd's murmur fades obediently.

"Yá'át'ééh, bienvenidos, and welcome, to honored guests and scoundrels alike," he says, spreading his arms wide, his voice pitched theatrically. "Tonight, Knifetown is honored to offer you a very special evening, a revel of commerce just in time for your Keshmish shopping."

At that the crowd laughs, applauding lightly, and Bishop gives them a little bow.

"Perhaps Granddad needs a new liver. Or your new bride a house girl to do the dirty work. Or maybe you're in the market for a bride yourself. Someone young enough to give you a rise when you need it most!" The representatives twitter knowingly, and I struggle to hold back the bile rising in my throat. I glance over at Rissa. Her face is demure, her eyes focused on the show up front. But her hand is clasping the bidding paddle so hard her knuckles are white.

"Look no further! Knifetown has it all. Every need, every want, every pleasure once forbidden in the old world has been reborn in the new! Some say the Big Water ushered in a broken age, but here at Knifetown we say it brought in a golden one! For those with the wealth and the will to seize it!" He mimes gripping something in a fist, pulling it close to his chest. "Because everything in Knifetown is for sale. Just you ask, and Bishop will do his best to make sure you receive!"

At this the crowd claps for real. There's even a few whistles and shouts, which echo around the room in excitement.

"I thought Bishop was all about sin?"

"Commerce is sacred in all its forms," Aaron mutters.

"And now . . . !" Bishop throws his arm out with a flourish. The spotlight splits in two. Once half of the light stays put, but the other rotates over to a corner of the stage that was dark before. It rests on a bald bilagáana man in a bright red jacquard tuxedo jacket. The man looks up into the light, a layer of sweat evident on his pate. He wipes at it with a handkerchief, looking nervous, and motions Bishop over.

Bishop, his salesman smile still firmly in place, bows slightly to the crowd. A few voices call out, wondering what the delay is. He apes an overly dramatic shrug and then puts his hands together as if praying, begging patience from the crowd. But I can see his face as he turns back to the auctioneer, and it's half rage . . . and half fear. He can feel it too. The promise of violence in the air. Despite the veneer of civility, the people in this tent are a wrong word away from tearing one another apart. Aaron may talk big about the auction operating under a truce, but all this friendly mingling is clearly a sham.

The two men put their heads together, whispering furiously. They argue back and forth until the other man throws up his hands in frustration, and with the flair of a performer, stomps off the stage.

Someone *boo*s, the Hopi woman.

"What's going on?" I ask Aaron quietly. I can feel the shift in the crowd. Eager before for flesh to buy, they are now growing eager for something else. Maybe Bishop's head.

"Never seen this before," he admits, rubbing at his burn scars. "But if the auctioneer's done left, something's wrong."

Bishop turns to the crowd, his smile looking a little sickly around the edges. He clears his throat, wringing his hands. "It seems we have a small delay," he says, his voice trying for reassuring but coming across as one step below desperate.

"What's the problem, Bishop?" the black-suited man from the Kingdom yells. "We've come a long way for tonight."

"I want a wife!" another man shouts.

"You promised me a houseboy!" someone else says.

And suddenly everyone is shouting at once, demanding the things—the *people*—Bishop promised them.

Bishop swallows. Under the spotlight, the otherwise invisible outline of the old stains on his white shirt stand out like amoebas. He rubs at his neck with a fleshy hand. “I understand you have wants, and Bishop has made promises, but this is unexpected.”

“Spit it out!” the man in the suit shouts.

Bishop clears his throat. “It appears the exotics we had for you tonight have gone missing.”

A shout of disbelief goes up. Another, angry and demanding an explanation. The Mormon woman stands up to leave, turning her back to Bishop.

And that’s when the bomb goes off.

# Chapter 26

A concussive *boom*. Sounds become a distant echo, the screams around me dampened.

I hit the floor, scrambling for cover under the table. Rissa and Aaron do the same. The back end of the auction tent caves in, the wooden support beams cracking and collapsing the heavy canvas down onto the guests inside. A scream, and I turn in time to see the Kingdom representative, a splinter of wood as thick as my wrist protruding from his neck.

A hand touches my shoulder, and I have my knife out and swinging for the offender's neck faster than the Kingdom representative's last breath. It's Ben. She looks like at me with huge eyes. Eyes that are painted with a thick layer of black liner and green eyeshadow. Heavy blush colors her cheeks, and her lips are an unnatural pink. She looks like someone's sick version of a doll.

"Maggie!" she squeaks, and I pull my swing just in time, the knife edge striking the dirt floor inches from her head.

"What in the actual fuck!"

"Ben!" Rissa shouts, crawling toward us. She leans in and gives the girl a brief hug, which Ben returns. "What are you doing here?"

"What are *you* doing here?" Ben asks, breathless. Her eyes cut to me, to the knife just to the left of her cheek, and then back to Rissa.

"We're rescuing you!" Rissa says.

Another massive *crack* echoes through the tent, and the spotlight that was attached to the roof beam crashes to the ground.

"We've got to go," Aaron says urgently. "The whole thing's coming down."

"Who's he?" Ben asks, wary.

"One of the bad guys," I say.

"Who's helping us get out of here." Rissa shoots me an annoyed look. "We'll explain later. Right now we follow him."

Which we do, scrambling through the chaos and noise. The auction tent has turned into a madhouse, people in their ruined finery stumbling through the semi-darkness, tables overturned, half the tent fallen down in a suffocating layer of heavy white canvas. Aaron clambers through the crowd, sometimes on his feet, and other times we're forced to duck and crawl under tables and through the stampeding crowd. It seems like an eternity before we reach the side of the tent. Aaron grabs the edge, heaves it up over his head and motions us under. Rissa first, ducking, and then Ben. Aaron. Me last. The canvas comes down on my head, and there's a moment of darkness and smothering weight. I push blindly forward, trusting that this is the way out. We clear in a handful of seconds. No time to rest, we sprint for the Tank and our waiting plane.

"Where are we going?" Ben asks, as light on her feet as ever, flushed with excitement.

"Aaron was the pilot, from the canyon," I explain. "He can fly that plane. Was that your bomb?"

Ben beams. "I would have waited if I knew you were coming," she says, sheepish. "Didn't mean to ruin your rescue."

She is completely sincere when she says it, and I don't know whether I want to laugh or cuss her out. I settle on, "It's fine. Next time."

We hit the door of the Tank without pause, pushing through just as I hear someone behind us shout my name. I whip my head around and lock eyes with Elena Urioste. She's across the yard, the collapsed tent behind her. Her dark eyes bore into me, an almost physical thing. I feel a hand around my throat and pull up short. It feels so real I stumble forward, gasping, but there's nothing there. I lunge for my throwing knife, twisting to sight Elena, and the pressure of fingers on my neck disappear. She's gone.

"Maggie!" Ben tugs at my sleeve. "Let's go!" I spare one last glance for the matron of the Urioste Familia before I follow Ben inside.

The Tank is the same as it was before. Mercifully empty. I guess when the punishment for stealing is getting fed to the dogs, people become lax about guarding their stuff.

Aaron and Ben sprint for the plane. I run to open the far doors of the hangar, and Rissa detours to the fenced cage where she left her weapons.

That's when I hear Aaron shout. He's standing at the plane, the door on the pilot's side flung open. His stumbles back, his hands raised.

I draw my shotgun, ready to confront whatever terror is inside that plane.

"Stop!" Ben runs toward me with her hands raised, putting herself between me and the plane, warning me off. "It's not what you think!"

I'm not sure what I think. I just know there's something in that plane that's not supposed to be there.

"Aaron?" I ask. Aaron turns to me, his face pale, his expression thunderstruck.

"What is it?" I ask. "Is everything okay?"

"There's a cat in my airplane!"

All that killing adrenaline firing, K'aahanáanii pooling in my stomach, I shoulder Ben out of the way and step forward to look inside to the open cockpit. Sure enough, there's a black cat sitting in the pilot's seat. Back leg in the air, shamelessly grooming herself.

"Mósí," I say. It's not even a question.

The cat looks up at me and blinks.

"Where have you been?" I demand. Not that I expect her to answer. Not that I'm sure she even can in this animal form. "And get out of the way!"

She lowers her leg, flicks her tail once, and then hops to the back seat, her whole demeanor radiating offense. Aaron slides into the vacated pilot's seat and asks, "So, uh, you know that cat?"

"She's with us," I admit. "Marginally."

He nods. Doesn't ask any more questions as he turns knobs and flips switches and does a handful of other things I don't understand to make the plane come to life. Ben and I pile into the six-seater. Rissa's in last, taking the seat next to Aaron.

"Cover," Aaron says tersely. I nudge Ben down below the window and she doesn't argue. Move into position, shotgun aimed back toward the auction tent, as we clear the Tank. Darkness and chaos still reign, and now it looks like the bonfires outside have set fire to the canvas tent. Shapes run back and forth in the shadows, throwing sand on the fires.

I hear Rissa laugh, and I look up in time to see her fling open her door, lean away from the plane, one hand braced against the overhead wing, and fling something back toward the tents. Five, four, three, two, and the grenade goes off with a massive *boom*. Shrapnel flies, and some of the shadowy forms fall, but it's fairly anticlimactic.

"Is that it?" Rissa demands, looking accusingly at Aaron.

He's focused on getting the plane in the air, steadily increasing our speed. "Hang tight. I'll show you what they can do."

Rissa slides back into her seat, shutting the door, just as our wheels leave the ground. Ben makes a strangled-dog sound, and I have to agree. My stomach does a flip-flop as I realize I've never actually been in a plane and maybe hadn't thought this through. Traveling the lightning with a trickster, sure. Flying, maybe not.

But it's too late to protest now. Aaron lets out a shout as we gain air. But all I can see is the black sky around us, a small scattering of lights below where the fires still burn, and then nothing as we pass through thick cloud cover.

"How do you know which way to go?" Ben says anxiously.

Aaron taps the panel of instruments in front of him. "I don't need to see. These see for me."

He climbs for a while before banking the plane, circling back around high above Knifetown. He digs under the seat and hands Rissa something in a black canister. "Try this one," he tells her. She slides a window open and drops the explosive. Six seconds later, with an air-shaking boom, the Tank goes up in flames.

"Now we're talking!" she says, laughing wildly, the fire below throwing light across her face. Aaron laughs, too, *whoop*ing loudly. Ben joins in, and they're all screaming and joking as we turn west into the night sky.

The only one besides me that's not celebrating is Mósí, who has curled up on the back seat and is asleep. Sleep sounds like I great idea, so I move back to the empty seat next to her, pull the cowl I'm still wearing down over my eyes. Despite the knowledge that I am high in the air with nothing between me and a very long fall to the hard earth except a relatively thin layer of metal, the exhaustion takes me, and I fall asleep too.

# Chapter 27

I wake to the murmur of voices. Crack an eye open and look around. Mósí is still next to me, but she's shifted to her human form, pedal pushers and flowered head scarf back in place. She's curled up in her seat, knees to her chest and cheek resting against the window, sleeping. Ben is splayed out across the two seats in front of me, snoring softly. The conversation is coming from the cockpit, Aaron and Rissa whispering quietly to each other.

"It was just me and him for the first years after the Big Water," Aaron says, voice low and quiet, barely audible over the sound of the engine. "As soon as I understood what it meant, the news reports and the TVs going out, I went straight to him because I knew he'd know what to do. But he didn't. He was just as lost as me. We stayed in Joseph City for a while, but when the plague hit, we ran to Knifetown, to Bishop, same as the rest of them." A mocking laugh. "Gideon had always been my protector, from the time we were kids together in foster care. More of a father figure than a big brother, I guess. I owed him better."

"You did what you had to do to survive," Rissa says.

"Maybe. Maybe not. Maybe I wanted to be top dog, prove

myself. Maybe I could have found a way to challenge Bishop instead of . . ." His voice is briefly lost in the roar of the plane. Rissa asks him something. I don't hear her question, but Aaron says, "No. Gideon was a thinker. He was never going to best me in a fight. He didn't have that instinct, you know? He was always trying to save people."

Gideon? The same name Caleb called the White Locust. Could be a complete coincidence. Gideon isn't a common name in Dinétah, but Aaron said they had come from Joseph City. Maybe it was more common in the Mormon community, which meant that maybe the White Locust had Mormon roots. And then there was Aaron's reaction to me asking about the White Locust. Surely that wasn't a coincidence.

"Is he dead?" Rissa asks. "Your brother?"

"I dumped what was left of him in a grove of juniper just outside of the Wall. It's as close to Dinétah as we could get without papers, without someone to sponsor us. Gideon was a quarter Diné, or at least that's what his foster mom told him. I'm more like one-eighth, so they were never going to let me in. We thought about forging CIBs. People do, you know. But it wasn't that. We wanted to go home as prodigal sons, not as fakes. But how could we if didn't even know who we were, what our clans were? Foster care took all that away."

Their conversation seems to die off in the darkness of the night. I'm about to sit up, feign a yawn, and join them up front to ask about Gideon, when Rissa says, "I miss my brother too."

I can only see the two of them in silhouette from the light of the control panel, but Aaron reaches a hand out and rests it on Rissa's knee. She covers his hand with hers, shifts so she's leaning closer to him.

"I knew what he was doing was dangerous," she says. "I should have told my mom. She would have stopped him. He would have listened to her. But I didn't. I'll always regret that. I'll always wish I had said something. To Mom, to Clive. If I had, maybe Cletus would be alive right now."

"Or maybe it wouldn't have made a difference. Maybe he would have done it anyway."

She blows out a breath, nods without making a sound.

"We all carry sins, Rissa." The tone of his voice is heavy with the surety of his wrongdoing. "Some carry a heavier burden than others, but none of us are clean."

"You know, I grew up in the church, but I'm not sure I believe in all that sin stuff."

"I have to believe," he says, his voice intensifying, "because if I don't, then there's no chance of forgiveness. It's the only hope I have."

"There's something wrong with the plane," Mósí says in my ear, so close that I jump.

"Don't sneak up on people!" I whisper-shout at her, but she just blinks at me, unconcerned. "What do you mean 'wrong'?"

"The mechanism that keeps this vehicle aloft is failing. Imminently."

"What?"

She flicks her head in annoyance. "Can you not hear me? Please go tell that bilagáana man flying the plane that we need to land."

"He's actually—"

She exhales, exasperated. Steps around me, slithering up the middle aisle until she's at Aaron's shoulder. "Your airplane is failing," she says.

Aaron startles, veering the plane in a sharp left. We all scream, Ben tumbling from her seat into a pile on the floor.

"Who the hell are you?!" Aaron shouts. I'd forgotten he hadn't seen Mósí in her human form.

"It's okay," Rissa rushes to reassure him. "She's with us. Remember that cat? It's a long story, but that's her." She looks back over her shoulder at me, as if asking for help. Then at Mósí. "She is a friend to the gods of Dinétah. She can . . . shape-shift."

Aaron's righted the plan, and now he turns to stare at Mósí. "A god?" he asks, voice awed.

"Better than a god. I am a Cat," Mósí says. "But now, human child, you need to listen to me. See those lights below us? We need to land there."

Aaron checks something on his controls, looks at a map I hadn't noticed before. It's our map. The one we traded with Mósí for. "There's nothing there," he says. "No cities or towns."

"There is indeed something there," Mósí counters.

"The old casino," Rissa says, leaning over to look at the map. "Twin Arrows."

I step up through the aisle, pausing to help Ben get back in her seat and then taking the empty one next to her. "What do you know about the casino?" I ask Aaron.

Aaron shrugs. "I've heard stories here and there, mostly about scavengers who tried to raid the place and never made it back. They say it's haunted."

"Haunted?" Ben squeaks.

"A good reason to avoid it," Rissa says.

"And we don't have time," I say. "We're already—"

"We will not have a choice," Mósí says firmly.

"Bishop will come for us," Aaron warns. "He won't forget what we've done. He'll track us down. Make an example. We've got to keep moving."

"This Bishop person doesn't matter. We are landing. I am just informing you of events that shall come to pass." And with that she walks back to her seat, pulls the seat belt across her lap, and fastens herself in.

The engine sputters and, with a short burst of smoke from the propeller, all the electrical goes out.

# Chapter 28

Aaron reassures us he can land the plan without the electrical. But he's equally sure he won't be able to take off again. So whatever made the plane fail—and I have my suspicions—Twin Arrows has our total attention.

The casino stands alone on a wide flat plain, the dark shape of mountains low in the east, and to the north, the looming shadow of the Wall. Twin Arrows is actually three buildings connected. At the center is a cylinder-shaped building, maybe three stories high. Two massive bright blue neon arrows jut skyward from the top of the cylinder, a literal interpretation of the casino's namesake. Below the twin arrows is a breezeway held up by five imposing pillars of stone. The breezeway fans out over a driveway, marking the entrance to the casino. To the left of the entrance is a three-story square building that looks like a conference center, and directly behind that an undulating wall of white and red concrete disguising a parking structure. On the other side of the entrance is a five-story hotel. Stretched out on both sides of the casino are asphalt-paved parking lots. Enough parking for a thousand cars, maybe more. The lots make a perfect landing strip. They're even lit, neon pinks and purples marking the long driveway like a welcoming acid trip.

"Looks fun," Ben says, staring out the window, and I can't tell if she's kidding or not.

"What exactly are you wearing?" I'd been meaning to ask her, but we were all a little busy running for our lives.

She runs a hand over the white ankle-length dress, fluffing the layers of taffeta that billow out at her shoulders and hips like frilly layers on a cake. "Do you like it? I kind of like it." She shrugs. "I never thought of myself as much of a girly-girl, but I think it's pretty."

"It's a wedding dress."

"Not that I ever want to get married," she says hastily. "Dudes? Kind of gross. But dressing up to get married is kind of fun."

"They let you marry women these days too," Rissa quips from up front.

"They were going to sell you off to the highest bidder," I say, frowning.

Ben, who had perked up a bit at Rissa's comment, deflates. Of course she knows that, and now I just reminded her of it. I have no idea what she went through in our few horrible hours at Knifetown, but if it was anything like Rissa's and mine, it couldn't have been good. I feel like an ass. "But it's pretty," I say, trying to make up for it a little. "I mean, if you like that kind of thing."

She grins. "I bet you could hide a lot of knives in this fluffy stuff."

"Or bomb-making material."

She flushes, looking proud. "It wasn't that hard. A bottle, a little sugar, bleach. One of the Thirsty Boys taught me once as a joke, but I remembered. And did you see how much stuff they had back there?"

"Everything for sale," I murmur.

We both jolt forward in our seats as the airplane's wheels hit the ground. The craft bounces a bit and then rolls smoothly toward the breezeway and the looming double arrows above the entrance.

"We're going to have to find another way out of here," I say to no one in particular.

"He will help us," Mósí says behind my shoulder. She's shifted again when I wasn't looking, this time into a young Navajo girl around Ben's age. She has her hair back is a tsiiyéél, same as Ben before her Knifetown transformation into a child bride, and she's wearing a traditional red-and-black rug dress, belted at the waist. Traditional moccasins, an earthy red with white wraps, come to her knees. She's sitting demurely, hands folded in her lap, waiting for the plane to stop.

"Who is 'he'?" I ask, pretty sure that my suspicions about who sabotaged the plane are about to be confirmed. "And what's with the outfit?"

"He is ancient but new. Long ago exiled from Dinétah for his crimes but returned with the beginning of the new age. Why? I do not know. And I am dressed this way so that he will recognize a daughter of the Diyin Dine'é when one appears before him."

"That was just a lot of words. You didn't actually tell me anything."

The plane has come to a stop in front of the casino. Mósí gives me a demure smile that still manages to show her delicate cat fangs.

"Come inside, then, Battle Child, and find out for yourself."

She moves quickly to the front of the plane, opening the door and leaping gracefully to the ground. The others pile out behind her, grateful to be on land again. Aaron stretches, hands over his head and mouth wide in a yawn. Ben and Rissa look around, curious. And the last bit of the night fades into the whiteness of dawn.

So I follow.

Or not. Because the casino literally won't let me in.

"I don't understand," Ben says.

"What did you do, Maggie?" Rissa asks.

We are all standing at the main entrance, only I'm on the outside of the bank of glass doors leading into the Twin Arrows and everyone else is on the inside. Aaron's patiently holding the door open, but I can't seem to cross the threshold.

"Try again," Rissa says.

"I've already tried twice. It's like an invisible wall. I just—" I put my hand up to my face, miming running into a solid surface.

"He doesn't want you here," Mósí says, stating the obvious.

"What? I don't even know who he is." I lean closer to the door. Cup my hands around my mouth and shout into the room. "I don't even know who you are!"

From what I can see, the lobby's more than nice. A round room, two stories high, the walls made of interlocking bricks in varying shades of tan stone. A tile floor inlaid with an elaborate arrow pattern, and above it, a massive chandelier—four hoops in directional colors encased in a cascade of crystals and light.

And all of it as pristine as the day the casino opened. The lights still work, the floor is still swept clean. I can hear the whirls and beeps of the slot machines coming through the doors on the other side of the lobby that lead to the casino.

Whoever Mósí's mysterious friend is, he keeps a clean house. Now if he'd only let me in.

"He," Mósí says, "is Nohoilpi. He is an old god, a god of games and gambling."

"A god?" Aaron says incredulously. For a moment he forgets he's holding the door open and it swings toward me, but he catches it right before it closes in my face. *Sorry*, he mouths.

I wave his apology off. I should have figured that this would be Mósí's chosen destination, and that someone like this Nohoilpi would be waiting for us. Because Mósí isn't just a cat, or even just a Bik'e'áyéeii, but a nightlife-loving former bookie of one of the most notorious dens of iniquity in Dinétah. Of course she's tight with the god of gambling.

"We are acquainted," she admits. "But I do not know if he will remember me. He was banished long ago from Dinétah for angering the Diyin Dine'é."

"What did he do?" I ask.

Mósí shrugs. "Only what was in his nature."

"That could literally mean anything."

"Well, he's back now," Rissa says, "and apparently living in a very fancy abandoned casino."

"Which is his prerogative, I guess," I say. "But why can't I come in?"

"You are known to the gods, Battle Child," she says to me. "I have told you this. And"—she cocks her head, considering—"you are wearing a very large sword that once belonged to Naayéé' Neizghání. Before you buried him alive."

"You did what?" Aaron asks. Rissa lays a hand on his arm, shakes her head. *Not now.*

"And how does he feel about Neizghání?" I ask, suddenly feeling hot. And short of breath. And like I might not need to go in this damn casino after all.

"There is nothing between them. I did not think it would matter. But clearly it does. Perhaps he would let you in if you left the sword outside," Mósí suggests.

"Is that wise?" Rissa asks. "He may be your friend, Mósí, but he's still a god. I kind of think we should bring the sword."

"Bring the sword," Ben agrees.

"Definitely the sword," Aaron echoes.

"I'm keeping the sword," I say loudly. Maybe if he knew I can't call the lightning it would make a difference, but I'm not one for telling strangers my weaknesses, and not knowing how to use the sword is definitely a weakness. But I can make one promise that sounds reasonable. "I'm not giving up the sword, but I will keep it in the scabbard. Would that work?"

“And if it is not enough?” comes a voice from the across the casino lobby.

We turn to find a brown-skinned man walking toward us. He’s dressed in a scarlet red suit. The jacket looks expensive under the light of the casino’s chandelier. Fitted at the shoulders, trailing down past his knees, a row of red buttons adorning the closure. Matching red pants are wide and loose at the hip, cuffed at the ankle so that they balloon out over his black-and-white dress shoes. He’s wearing a black hat with a red band and a large brim that keeps most of his face in shadow. A huge piece of turquoise hangs from a gold chain around his neck to rest dead center over a white tie with small polka dots.

“Wow,” Ben says. “Nice threads.”

He smooths knuckles down the line of his lapel, preening. Lifts his chin to get a better look at her wedding dress. “Quinceañera?”

She shakes her head sadly. “It’s a long story.”

“Nohoilpi,” Mósí murmurs with a small bow of her head. “It has been many years since you were banished to live among the Nakai.”

“But you are ever the same, shí heart.” He rests a palm against Mósí’s cheek. She flushes and leans into his touch. “How could I ever forget you?” And a few things come together in my mind.

“Perhaps you can introduce us to your ex, Mósí,” I say, still standing outside the door.

Nohoilpi’s eyes turn to me. “That won’t be necessary. Your fame, Godslayer, precedes you.”

That name again. “Where did you hear that name?” I ask.

“On the tongue of a dying angel, from the mouth of a storm king. It is known.”

There’s something familiar about Nohoilpi, something in the way he talks. I can’t quite place it, but it’s there. “Then maybe you can let me in.”

“Not without reassurances.”

“What kind of reassurances?”

His eyes flicker to the pommel over my shoulder. “That my head stays on my shoulders this time.”

This time? “Have we met before?”

“Perhaps you are hungry? Tired?” he says, ignoring me and turning to the others. “I can provide you with a feast. The kitchens here are vast and well stocked. My predecessor kept everything as it was before. A remarkable skill, even for a god. There are beds with clean sheets, soft pillows, showers with water that falls from a mechanical rain cloud. It is all here, and it is yours.”

Ben and Rissa make agreeable noises and Aaron brightens noticeably. It’s been at least twenty-four hours since we’ve eaten, more since we’ve bathed. Everyone could use food, some rest. The Twin Arrows glows and beckons, a temptation to partake, an oasis from the darkness of the Malpais.

Nohoilpi gestures toward the bounty farther in. “Mi casa es su casa,” he says, his voice as enticing as warm baths and soft sheets and impossible as lost loves found again. And they follow. Every one of them. Even Ben. This time Aaron lets go of the door without even bothering to look in my direction.

“Wait!” I shout, but they are already disappearing deep into the lobby, out of earshot.

The last thing I hear is Ben happily exclaiming over a gift shop.

“It’s a trap!” I shout. I don’t know how, but I’m sure of it. “Don’t listen to him. This isn’t real. It’s not real.”

Nohoilpi appears in front of me so quickly I stumble back. He grabs the door right before it shuts. His nails are long and curved. He lifts his chin, and I catch the gleam of a golden eye hidden under the brim of his hat. He leans out over the threshold and says, “Once I’ve accommodated my new friends, I’ll be back to discuss the price for their return. It is a small matter for a godslayer like you. So, if you would please wait here . . . Magdalena.”

He shuts the door firmly in my face. I stare for a moment, dumbfounded, until the shock wears off. I beat my fists on the glass and scream helplessly as my companions disappear into the depths of the casino.

"Ma'ii!"

# Chapter 29

I'm sitting on the curb, watching the sun climb higher in the sky, when I hear him approach. I think about shooting him on principle, but I don't understand all the forces at play here. Why the casino won't let me in, why Coyote is pretending to be an exiled god, and how the hell I'm going to break whatever spell is holding my companions prisoner.

Granted, it's a luxury kind of prison, but they're in there and I'm out here, both of us stuck all the same.

So, when Ma'ii holds out a bottle to me, just behind my shoulder, I don't rip his arm off like I want to. Instead I turn slightly to get a better look at what he's offering. Winged demons of some kind cavort across a gold-edged label, arms raised and mouths open.

"I hate tequila," I say, reading the label.

"Unsurprising. Your tastes have always been somewhat dull."

I squint pointedly at the sun, still hours away from its zenith. "Besides, isn't it a little too early for booze?"

"What is time to a coyote?" Ma'ii, still in the guise of the god Nohoilpi, sits down beside me. He stretches his red-clad legs out, crosses his feet at the ankles, and straightens the turquoise on the chain around his neck before taking a swig from the bottle.

"Don't suppose you have coffee?" I ask. "I'd kill for a cup of coffee."

"Then I shall endeavor to procure you one in the near future, because killing is exactly what I need you to do for me."

And there it is. Or at least part of it. But I'm not much in the mood to do Ma'ii any favors. "I'm off the killing these days. Trying a new leaf, or whatever you call it."

"The phrase is 'turning over a new leaf.'"

"Yeah, that one."

"You could not have considered this new leaf before our last encounter?"

The last time I saw Coyote, I shot him dead. Slit his throat, cut off his head and threw it off a rooftop for good measure. Clearly, I should have done more. Because here he is, reminding me that the problem with immortals is that they don't stay dead.

"You deserved it."

"That is your opinion, and clearly debatable."

I open my mouth to protest, but he cuts me off. "But I am not here to debate it," he says hurriedly. "I forgive you."

I shrug. I couldn't care less about Coyote's supposed forgiveness. The only reason I'm not taking his head off again right now is because I've got a feeling that I might need his help. Later, after I've rescued the others? We'll see.

"Since when do you drink tequila anyway?" I ask, curious. "I thought you were more of a whiskey man . . . coyote?"

"Well," he says, coughing slightly. "I ran out of whiskey a few weeks ago. The bourbon soon after that. But if you must know, it all began when I imprisoned the real Nohoilpi in the presidential suite of this fine establishment."

"You did what?!"

He stares into the distance, eyes on the horizon. "It seemed reasonable at the time."

"To you."

"Yes, to me," he says, sounding slightly annoyed. "Who else would it sound reasonable to?"

"No one."

"Well," he says with a huff. He takes another drink from the bottle. "So, there I was, fretting about how I was going to escape this particularly tricky situation, and a godslayer literally flies over my head. What are the chances?"

"I'm not a godslayer."

"More's the pity. Because I'm desperately in need of one."

"I don't know where that name even came from. There was this woman near Lake Asááyi . . . What is it?"

Ma'ii's looking at his toes, face decidedly guilty. And I can guess why. "You started it, didn't you? The whole 'godslayer' name? It's your doing."

"It's a bit aspirational, perhaps, but not wholly untrue."

"Damn it, Ma'ii. You've got people calling me that. And some nutjob cult guy thinking it too."

"Interesting. Which god does *he* wish you to slay?"

My mouth drops open. Of course. "I have no idea."

"You should probably find out."

"Yeah . . . ," I say slowly, mind racing with a million scenarios I hadn't considered. "I'll get on that."

Ma'ii sighs and pushes his hat back.

"Does the Cat know?"

"That I am not her long-lost paramour? That the real love of her life is tucked away with a micro-kitchenette and a wet bar? Not exactly."

"When are you going to tell her?"

"In due time, Magdalena." He twists his body to look at me. "Why *were* you flying over my casino?"

"It's a long story."

"And here we are, with all this time."

What the hell. Coyote seemed to genuinely like Kai, so maybe he'll help. "I'm rescuing Kai. Remember that nutjob who wants me to kill a god? He abducted Kai."

"Ah, Kai Arviso," he says wistfully. "A lovely boy. So, you did take him to your bed as I advised? Did you shake the very heavens with your lovemaking?" His voice is sly, suggestive. Confident.

"No," I say flatly. "I killed him, too."

He chokes. Drops the bottle. The tequila sloshes violently, and I reach out a hand to right it before the bottle spills. I stare at it a moment and decide what the hell. I pick it up and tip it back, letting the alcohol run down my throat. "Don't worry," I say after I swallow. "He obviously didn't die either. Huh . . ." I take another swig as the idea occurs to me. "Maybe I really am losing my touch."

"You truly are a marvel," Ma'ii says once he gets his breath back.

My voice is as dry as the Mother Road. "Thanks."

We sit for a while. Watch the sun make its steady ascent. It's starting to get hot. It's my first morning out here beyond the Wall, and the heat is no joke. In the hour I've been sitting here it must have climbed twenty degrees. I'm still wearing the cowl from my disguise last night, and I pull it off, sweating. My hair sticks to my head, cakes around my neck.

"What are you doing out here, Ma'ii?"

Ma'ii fusses with the crease of his pants, smoothing the line between his thumb and forefinger. "It seems I am persona non grata in Dinétah. The Diyin Dine'é were not happy that I borrowed the naayéé'ats'os. Or raised the monsters. I am barred from crossing the Wall."

"Forever?"

He takes a drink. "What is time to a coyote?"

"So why is everyone trapped in the casino? What did you do to them?"

"I did nothing. It is the magic of the place. It has a mind of its own, and it does enjoy company. It will let them out eventually."

"Why didn't it let me in?"

"It didn't want you."

I pull my knees to my chest, feeling myself irrationally offended at being rejected by a sentient casino.

Ma'ii glances at me. "Oh, Magdalena, be reasonable. Perhaps because you wear that sword? Perhaps because you have always been more than what you seem and the tricks that work on others do not work on you. Perhaps because despite your dislike for the appellation, it is not incorrect to call you a godslayer and there is, in fact, a god in residence."

"Whatever," I growl, realizing I'm a little drunk.

He shakes his head, exasperated. "I suppose Nohoilpi could intercede with the casino on your behalf, should you convince him. It is his casino, after all."

I hold out my hand for the bottle. He gives it to me, and I drink one last long swallow. I draw my arm back and throw the bottle as hard and as far as I can. It smashes against the pavement, shattering into a dozen sharp-edged pieces. I pocket the cap, a round, gold-colored top.

"The bottle wasn't empty," Ma'ii protests. "We weren't done."

"We're done," I say, standing. I'm a little unsteady on my feet, but otherwise fine. I think. I start walking back toward the entrance, swaying only a little.

"Where are you going?" he calls.

"To fight your friend. That god."

"Drunk?"

"I'm sure as hell not doing it sober."

"Fair point." He scrambles to his feet, dusting his backside and hurrying after me. "What is your plan?"

"Can you release him? From the presidential suite."

“Of course. It’s actually quite simple. I just—”

“Do it.” I roll my shoulders, stretching my neck. “Now.”

“And what will you do?”

“Just bring him to the front of the casino. You said he’s a god of gambling, right? Like games?”

“Indeed.”

“Then I guess we’ll play a little game.”

Minutes later, Ma’ii rushes out the door to where I told him to meet me. It’s clearly him because he’s looking over his shoulder, his brows bunched up in worry. “He’s coming,” he warns me, “but he’s not happy. Seems the minibar ran out days ago.”

“I don’t need him happy.” I draw Neizghání’s sword from its scabbard.

Ma’ii gasps excitedly behind me. “A battle for the ages!” he exclaims. “Cleaved by the lightning sword! After you defeated Neizghání, I knew it was only a matter of time before you confronted the gods themse—”

He cuts off abruptly as I lay the sword down on the pavement at my feet.

“Give me your shoes,” I tell him.

“Pardon?”

I motion impatiently toward his feet. “Shoes. I need them. Before he gets here.”

I untie my moccasin wraps, unwinding the length of soft elk skin that stretches from my heels to my knees. Pull off my red suede moccasins.

“Is this some sort of clever battle strategy?” he asks, doubtful.

“Give!”

He sighs and slips off his shiny shoes. Toes them over toward me. I line up his pair next to mine. Tuck the tequila bottle cap into Ma’ii’s shoe on the far end. Scoop up a handful of sandy dirt and pour it into Ma'ii's shoe. He makes some sort of gargling noise in protest. I do the same to the remaining shoes until they are all filled with dirt.

I take a seat behind the line of shoes, face toward the doors. Think back to the songs of my childhood, the ones my nalí taught me. The ones sung only in the winter months. The ones that the animals sang.

"The shoe game," Ma'ii murmurs. "You know I invented this game."

I pause my song. "I know you tried to cheat to win."

"This will never work. Where is the yucca? The blankets?"

"Quiet. It'll work. You said he likes games."

He snorts but doesn't respond past that. Instead he takes a seat, sitting back on his heels and waiting, I assume, to see what happens.

I keep singing, low and steady. The minutes pass, and nothing changes. The sun keeps climbing, and my throat is getting dry. The tequila sloshes around in my otherwise empty stomach, making me queasy. Another five minutes of singing and I'm beginning to think maybe this wasn't such a good idea after all.

The sword lies nearby, my other option. But one I want to avoid except as a last resort. To wield the sword is risky enough. The use it against a god? At the behest of a trickster? If there are worse scenarios, I don't know what they are.

Ma'ii clears his throat to catch my attention. I look over toward the doors and smile. Someone's coming across the lobby. Someone in a red suit and a black hat. Someone that looks exactly like Ma'ii.

Nohoilpi opens the door. His eyes dart to Ma'ii, who could pass for his doppelgänger. Nohoilpi's face clouds, and he takes a step toward the trickster. Thunder booms somewhere in the distance, and the wind that didn't exist moments before picks up. I sing louder, stressing the words to turn his attention. It works, and the god comes to stand in front of me.

I keep my voice steady, strong. Try not to show my fear, although I have no doubt he can sense it. He looks at me, studying my face. I let him. His eyes flicker to the sword lying beside me.

He crouches down in front of the shoes, eyes roaming curiously and then eagerly. And just like that, I have him.

"It is an ancient game," he says, his voice probing, curious. "Is it true that the five-fingereds play it still in Dinétah?"

"We do."

"And you think you can beat me?"

"There's only one way to find out."

He taps the stick he's holding against his opposite palm. I didn't see him pick the stick up, or where it came from. My adrenaline spikes, reminding me I'm not just playing the shoe game with a man, but with a god, and this is not the same as that one time I swept the tournament at my grade school gym over Keshmish break. And that Nohoilpi has likely played this game for eons.

He waves the stick over the shoes, back and forth, scrutinizing. His hand moves toward my left moccasin.

"Wait!" I say. "What do I win if you're wrong?"

"Another chance." He grins, smile spreading. "We play until the day changes."

"I win, you help me get my friends back. You talk to the casino, or whatever you have to do, and you get them free."

"And you promise not to harm Ma'ii," Ma'ii adds hastily.

"I don't care what you do to Ma'ii. That's between you and him. But my friends . . ."

Ma'ii's eyes bulge, but I ignore him, keep my focus on Nohoilpi.

"Let us play," Nohoipli says, "and then we shall see."

"You will help me?"

"I will consider your request. Should you win."

And I know that's as good as I'm going to get. "Deal."

I remember the reason that the shoe game is played. To

commemorate when the day and the night were set in place. I probably should have suggested we play roulette instead. But it's too late now. Once we've begun, I can't quit without forfeiting, and I'm not going to forfeit.

Nohoilpi picks. Incorrectly. Ma'ii marks the score.

I turn my back and Nohoilpi resets the game, moving the bottle cap to a new shoe. "Your turn," he says.

I take up the stick. Weave it through the air above the shoes, looking for the one with the cap in it. They all look the same.

"Why do you do it, monsterslayer?" Nohoilpi asks, his voice a slithering worm in my ear.

My eyes flicker up to his face before turning back to the shoes.

"Why do you chase the silver-eyed boy who told you not to follow?"

Uneasiness rolls down my spine. "How do you know about that?" I ask, trying to sound casual, even though all my alarm bells are going off. I hadn't anticipated he would know about Kai. Or what he said to me on the videotape.

"He's trying to distract you," Coyote warns.

"I know." It's part of the game. I'll do the same to him when it's my turn. But for a moment I could swear the shoes have changed. Something subtle in the placement of my last moccasin, the one I was going to pick.

I move the stick across the shoes, deciding.

Nohoilpi's smile is as sharp as a blade. "What if you are making a mistake? Risking your companions' lives for nothing but a fantasy? Chasing this boy, the same way you chased Naayéé' Neizghání."

I wince as the barb strikes home, right in my heart. I resist the temptation to touch the scar Neizghání's dagger left on my flesh. I lose my concentration, the stick almost falling from my fingers.

"Magdalena," Ma'ii hisses. "Focus!"

I blink. Grip the stick. Touch it to a shoe before I can change my mind. Nohoilpi nods, and I dig my hand into the dirt inside. My fingers brush the cap and I pull it free, triumphant. Ma'ii marks the score in my favor. Nohoilpi turns his back and I reset the game, burying the cap in one of Ma'ii's dress shoes. Nohoilpi picks up the stick. We start again.

"What did you do to get yourself get kicked out of Dinétah forever?" I ask him.

Now it's Nohoilpi's turn to grimace. "They were jealous of me."

"That's not what I heard."

"What have you heard?" he asks, a hitch in his voice. "From Neizghání? From others? The Talking God?"

My eyes cut involuntarily to Ma'ii.

"From the trickster," he says, his voice disdainful. "He is a fool."

"He trapped you in the presidential suite."

"I chose to stay," Nohoilpi says roughly. "I will make it my new home. Take everything from unsuspecting travelers the way I did before the Talking God stopped me, tricked me into losing all I had. My wives, my riches, my home."

He taps a shoe. Digs for the cap. A win.

Ma'ii marks the score.

He resets, I pick up the stick, and we go again.

"Why bother with this silly quest?" the god croons, and his voice seems to echo through my head. "Why not go home? Lick your wounds and start again? What do you owe him, this boy?"

"Kai is my friend."

"A strange friend. Did he not lie to you? Use you? Did he not keep secrets?"

"Who told you that?"

"It is known."

"Is it known that he sacrificed his life for me?" I bite back.

In a rush, I pick a shoe. Drop the stick and dig my hand in. No cap.

Nohoilpi's smile widens. "Once again, you have picked wrong."

We reset.

And so it goes, for hour after hour. Winning and losing, Ma'ii keeping score. We go back and forth. Nohoilpi whispering my darkest doubts, trying to break me. Me working to keep his voice out of my head. Trying to find his weak spot.

The sun rises to directly overhead, unbearably hot even in the shade of the breezeway. The air is oppressive, not even a hint of the gentle wind I felt before at his arrival. At some point Ma'ii disappears briefly and comes back with a pitcher of water and a tall glass. When Nohoilpi picks up the stick for his turn, I take the minute of reprieve it offers to guzzle the water down. The tequila has passed from my system, leaving me dehydrated and needing to pee, but I don't know the rules for taking a break. I'm afraid there aren't any. He said until the changing of the day, which I take for sundown. I glance to the sky. Sundown, even in December, is still hours away.

I shift, miserably uncomfortable, trying my best to ignore my aching bladder, the unrelenting sun, and the sea of doubts Nohoilpi's raised in my head.

And we start another round.

"What if the silver-eyed boy does not want to be saved?" Nohoilpi asks.

"Too bad. He's getting saved anyway."

"Destined to make the same mistakes over and over again," he says, shaking his head in mock disappointment.

"No. This is different. Neizghání was never my friend. Kai is. And that's what friends do. They don't give up on someone just because they've fucked up."

Ma'ii's watching me intently. Nohoilpi notices. "Is there no betrayal too large to be unforgiven?"

"We all do things that need to be forgiven," I say, thinking about Rissa's and Aaron's whispered confessions in the plane.

I pick a shoe. Correctly.

Look up at Nohoilpi. His dark eyes are focused on me.

"Indeed," he murmurs. "But forgiveness is not always offered."

"Do you wish you could be forgiven?" I ask him.

"It is my only wish," he whispers.

The lights of the casino flicker on in neons of pinks and gold. I glance around me, realize the sun is going down. We have played through the entire day.

As the last rays of light fade below the horizon and full dark settles in, I set the stick down.

"What's the score, Ma'ii?"

Ma'ii makes a show of counting off the marks. "It is a tie."

Nohoilpi stands, fluid and supple. I unwind myself from my spot, muscles aching from sitting so long, bladder screaming.

"Despite what you might think, some things cannot be changed," Nohoilpi says. "The order of the day. The rising and setting of the sun. And not all things can be forgiven. You will learn this the difficult way, I think."

"I want my friends back."

"As do I. But they have all forsaken me."

"Let them go."

"They are free to leave as they please. If they want to come outside, they will." He touches the brim of his hat, a parting salute. Pauses and fixes his eyes on Ma'ii. "I do not like you. I suggest, brother Ma'ii, that you find a new skin before I peel that one from your body. I learned many new things in my time among the Nakai. Do not force me to demonstrate."

Ma'ii touches the brim of his own hat, a mirror image of Nohoilpi. The god and the trickster stare each other down. Until finally Nohoilpi turns sharply on his heel and heads back through the glass doors. At the threshold he turns back and says, "A word of advice, in exchange for seeing Mósí safely to me. Go to the old man at Wahweap."

"We're going to a place called Amangiri."

"Wahweap first. If you do not, your mission will fail. Mark me, monsterslayer. Wahweap." And with that he's gone.

I look at Coyote. "What is a Wahweap?"

He yawns.

"Thanks."

"He was not deceiving you," he says, eyes lingering on the doors. "Your friends are free to leave the casino should they choose. I suggest you get comfortable and wait the night. You will know with the rising sun."

"Fine, but first I've got to find a bathroom."

# Chapter 30

I'm back on the curb watching another sunrise when I hear her footsteps. After a moment Rissa drops down to sit beside me. She's back in her brown leather pants, but instead of her jacket, she's sporting a tight baby-blue T-shirt that says "Arizona Angel" in a flowery rhinestone-studded script, a little gold halo hanging from the *l*. The morning light catches in the rhinestones, making them they sparkle like diamonds. She has bags under her eyes from lack of sleep, but she's obviously taken a shower, and her red hair haloes around her head in tight curls. She stretches out her long legs and says nothing. She's holding a cup in each hand, steam rising in the morning air. I can smell the heavenly aroma of coffee.

"You look like an angel," I tell her. "A beautiful coffee-bearing angel."

"Screw you," she says good-naturedly. "It was the only shirt in the gift shop in my size. Besides, you don't look that great yourself. That's why I brought you this."

She sets down a cup, reaches into her back pocket, and pulls out a black T-shirt. Slaps it against my chest. I catch it, unfold it. Emblazoned across the chest is a dream catcher, and in the center of the dream catcher, a wolf's head, fur limned in purples and grays, eyes shining in the morning light.

"What is this shit?" I ask.

Rissa shrugs. "Clean is clean, right?"

"I'm not wearing this."

"Fine. Wear your dirty shirt."

I look down at the shirt I'm wearing. There are no visible bloodstains, no holes left behind from knife wounds or gunshots. No, check that. Part of my sleeve is sliced open from my run-in with the canyon rocks, and, if I'm honest, the problem isn't my shirt, it's my smell. "What I need is a shower," I admit.

Rissa leans in for an exaggerated sniff. "Yeah, you do."

"I wonder if the casino will let me in now," I say, handing the wolf T-shirt back. She trades it for the cup of coffee. I take that, more grateful for anything than I've ever been in my life.

"Coffee is from the Coyote," she says. "A parting gift, he said. He also promised there's nothing weird in it, but . . ." She shrugs.

I take a sip. "I trust him."

"I have no idea why."

"Friends close and enemies closer?"

"Speaking of friends," she says, voice catching a bit, "I owe you an apology." She looks over at me, eyes a little fuzzy with some emotion.

I could not have been more surprised if Kai fell from the sky and landed in my lap.

"For what?"

She looks over the edge of her cup at the fading bruise on my cheek.

"Oh, that. Yeah, you do. And for a couple of other things too."

"Running you out of Black Mesa?"

"That's one."

"Being a solid bitch this whole time?"

"Two."

She sighs. "You're not going to make this easy, are you?"

"Am I supposed to?"

"Jesus," she says. "Clive was right. You really are an emotional cripple."

I laugh. She looks at me, trying to gauge my mood. Whatever she reads on my face makes her laugh too. And all the stress and anger and fear that's been dogging me for weeks comes bubbling up in a mix of hysteria and release. And the more I laugh, the more Rissa laughs too, and soon we're both howling like a couple of loons. And for a few minutes on a crumbling curb over a cup of coffee, I feel almost human.

"At least tell me you took a shower," I say. "Got some sleep."

"Less than you think," she murmurs, sipping from her cup. "But the beds are nice."

I arch an eyebrow in her direction. "Does that mean what I think it means?"

"If you think it means me and Aaron spent the night together, then yes."

"Are you forgetting that guy ran a body shop?"

"He didn't run it. He worked there. And he didn't have a choice."

"Aren't you the one saying we always have a choice?"

She sighs. "Okay, then, Maggie. Let's judge him by his worst deeds, shall we?"

"I didn't mean that. I just mean . . . be careful. You don't really know him. He's a murderer."

"And you're not?"

I flinch. "That's a low blow."

She holds up a hand in apology. "You're right. I didn't . . . I mean, we've all got problems, right? Aaron didn't choose Knifetown. He's out now, and he wants to change. Is changing. I'm not forgetting what he's done, but I'm not holding his past against him."

"It's not the past. It was literally two days ago."

"I'm not saying I'm going to marry him." She exhales, brushes her hair back from her face.

"Sorry. I guess I just don't get what you see in him."

She shrugs. Moves some gravel around with her toe. "Life is short, Maggie. Even shorter since the Big Water. Sometimes you just have to take people as they are, not worry about whether they're good for you in the long run. Because what if there is no long run? What if there's just a night in a haunted casino in the middle of the badlands?"

I take a long sip of my coffee. "Kai told me he loved me."

Rissa's expression a mix of curious and concerned. "Yeah, I saw the tape. Do you believe him?"

"I don't know. No one's ever told me that before."

She nods, surprisingly sympathetic. "If it's true, that's something to hold on to. It's rarer in this world that you think."

"I think it's pretty rare."

"Did you and Kai . . . ?"

I shake my head. "I thought about it. Wanted to. In your mom's library, actually."

She sticks out her tongue. "You did not!"

I look over at her, a wave of sadness rolling through by body. "No, I didn't. I couldn't get out of my head. I've got issues, if you haven't notice."

"Oh, I noticed."

"Thanks."

"Hey," she says, pushing gently on my shoulder. "Don't do that. I was wrong about you, okay? I admit it. I mean, not that you don't have issues, because clearly . . . I thought you didn't care about anyone but yourself. But I can see now that you care about Kai. And you care about Ben." She cocks her head and smiles. "And considering that you stuck around Twin Arrows and played the shoe game with a god to try to free us, I think you care about me, too."

"Yeah, well, don't let it go to your head."

"Sorry." She grins, showing teeth. "I'm afraid you're stuck with me now."

"Is that a threat? Because you make that sound like a threat."

"You bet your ass it is."

I sit there for a while, staring out across the parking lot. Feeling something, even if I'm not exactly sure what. A good something, that much I know. A new something. Besides Kai, I haven't had friends since I met Neizghání. Definitely not family. And I'm not sure what that means, what's expected of me to be Rissa's friend. But I'm willing to try.

Another moment passes before Rissa says, "Mósí's not coming."

I nod, unsurprised. "I expected as much. I think coming here was her plan all along."

Rissa gives me a questioning look.

"To find Nohoilpi," I explain. "Back in Tse Bonito when we picked her up, she made a deal with me and Clive. Safe passage to wherever she wanted to go in the Malpais in exchange for maps and supplies. She was secretive about her destination, but I think this place was it all along."

"And that doesn't bother you?"

I shrug. Blow across my coffee, sending the steam swirling. "Not really. It's about what I expect from a cat. Where did Ma'ii get this, by the way?" I hold up my cup.

"There's a whole kitchen in there. Stocked like the day they left it. Anything you want that doesn't rot." She clears her throat. "There's something else you need to know. I think the White Locust is Aaron's brother."

I hesitate, but then say, "I do too."

"We were talking last night after we . . . What? You do?"

"I heard you in the airplane. Not a lot—I wasn't eavesdropping. But I heard enough."

She cradles her coffee tighter in her hands. "Aaron keeps saying he thinks he's dead, but I don't think he really believes it. I don't think I believe it. Gideon can't be that popular a name."

"Maybe it's not such a good idea to have Aaron come to Amangiri with us," I say.

"I didn't say that."

"But you thought it."

"No. I'm not saying we dump him. I'm saying that's information for us to know. That's it. And if it becomes an issue, we'll deal with it then."

"You mean kill him?"

She looks down, runs a thumb around the edge of her cup. "I . . . hope not."

"So it's not just shagging. You have feelings for Aaron."

"He knew my brother, knows that part of my life. And he gets me, you know?" She lowers her head. "He respects who I am." Her mouth quirks up at the side. "And he's got a really big dick."

I spit my coffee on the pavement. She laughs. Slaps my leg. "Come on. Let's go find the others. Did you know there's a lower-level garage full of vintage automobiles here? Aaron and Ben are picking out a car, but I don't really trust their tastes."

"Jesus, Rissa. Does Grace know you talk like that?"

She waggles her eyebrows at me. "Where do you think I learned it?"

She's probably right. I push myself up off the curb, stretching in the morning light. Happy to get back on the road soon. "By the way," I say, "I meant that angel thing as a compliment."

She laughs, and it turns into a belch. "Sure you did, Maggie. Sure you did."

The casino does, in fact, let me in, and after a quick shower, Rissa and I head down to the garage. The car Aaron has picked out of an impressive garage of vintage cars is a 1950 Mercury Cobra, a two-door coupe with a drop-top, painted turquoise blue with a darker lid. It's outrageous, a classic lead sled, the likes of which I've never seen in person. I fall in love immediately.

"Want to drive?" he asks, holding out the keys.

"I'd like to see you try to stop me."

"What about these other cars?" Ben asks. She points to a late-model German import. It looks fast enough, serviceable.

"No style," I tell her. "Why would you pick that when you can drive this—"

"—hunk of metal that is almost a hundred years old if it's a day," Rissa interrupts. "I mean, I don't know. Reliability? Comfort? Safety?"

Aaron's face falls a little, but I say, "You don't know beauty when you see it." I unbuckle the scabbard holding Neizghání's sword and hand it to Ben. Pause for a moment to take in her new outfit. Same big boots with green camo pants a few sizes too big and a plain black T-shirt.

"What happened to the dress?" I ask.

She shrugs one thin shoulder. "You were right. It wasn't very practical. I need to be focused on the task at hand."

"Which is?"

"Killing the White Locust."

"Right." I open the door to the Mercury and slide into the low boxy interior. Feel the leather seats under my ass. Maybe purr a little.

"It's the real deal, too," Aaron says enthusiastically. "They used to build knockoffs, fiberglass wannabes, but this is all Detroit steel."

"Now you're just trying to sweet-talk me, Aaron."

He grins. "Try the engine."

It turns over without a hitch.

"Well, at least it runs," Rissa mutters. "What about fuel?"

"There's enough. Engine's been modified. Extra tank, too. Made for desert crossings. Look at this."

Aaron draws our attention to a complex HVAC system that includes a series of vents, blowers, and a breathing mask. "It's to filter the air," he explains. "And to try to keep it cool during the day, but I'm afraid it's still going to bake like the proverbial oven. Can't be helped. Oh, I almost forgot. I found this."

Aaron hands me a glossy folded brochure. I take it. Smooth out the trifold. In an understated script, it reads: THE AMANGIRI RESORT & SPA, CANYON POINT, UTAH. The inside describes a five-star experience, including luxury accommodations, an award-winning spa, and fine dining.

"Where did you get this?"

"In the lobby of the casino. One of those kiosks with handouts on all the local attractions."

"This has got to be it," I say, looking through the elegant photos of the wealthy and relaxed enjoying the exclusive amenities of Amangiri. "But a luxury resort?"

"Makes sense," Rissa says, looking over my shoulder. "It's probably long abandoned, but it checks all the boxes. Secluded, exclusive. Big enough to house all his minions."

She's right. "How long does it take to get to"—I turn it over to look at the front again—"Canyon Point, Utah?"

"Depends on the road," Aaron says. "I haven't been north of Flagstaff in more than a year, but last time Bishop had us venture up, the road was in pretty good shape. There's a handful of settlements out that way. You're close enough to the Kingdom that there's not too much to worry about safety-wise. Bishop tried to make some headway out there, for our . . . enterprises"—he glances at Rissa, who's looking pointedly at her own fingernails—"but the Kingdom was reluctant. Slaughtered half the crew in a shootout. Called us godless and said don't come back unless it was with a Book of Mormon in our hands."

"But I saw Kingdom representatives at the Knifetown auction," I say.

He shrugs. "I'm no politician. From here, Canyon Point's likely three, four hours, depending on the condition of the roads. Could be longer if there's trouble or if the highway's shot to shit."

"What about Wahweap?"

"What's a Wahweap?"

"The place Nohoilpi said to go. He said that was our way in to Amangiri. Do you see it on the map?"

Aaron dutifully checks the map. "I see it. Just down the lake from Canyon Point. Right on Lake Powell. Looks like we could take a boat from there to Canyon Point, come in on the lakeside, avoid roads. It's smart."

"You think we can make it to Wahweap by noon?" I ask, the thought that by tonight I could see Kai again, could touch him, is almost too much to think about.

"Why not?"

"Sounds like it's time to start thinking about how we're going to kill the White Locust, then," Ben says.

I glance over at Aaron, who's scratching at his burn scars. He's looking at Ben, an expression on his face that's hard to read.

"Get in the car, Ben," I say quietly. She complies, sliding into the back seat. Aaron climbs in next to her, and Rissa joins me in the front.

I run my hands around the steering wheel. Press gently on the gas pedal, and the Mercury answers me like the lover she is. "Yes, baby," I murmur.

From the back seat, Ben shouts, "Get in, losers! We're going to Amangiri!"

# Chapter 31

The drive is long and hot and entirely uneventful. It seems that beyond the horrors of Knifetown and the uncanniness of Twin Arrows, the Malpais is just an uninhabitable desert wasteland. Mile after mile of flat brown earth, characterized by stretches of land where there's nothing at all, not even an obstinate tree to break the monotony. The Mercury hums along happily, glad to stretch her legs after years in that garage, no doubt. I drive, and everyone else sleeps, except Ben, who seems determined to sing the entire catalog of some pop music group I've never heard of.

"You really don't know who Maroon 5 is?" she asks. "They're, like, classic oldies."

"Never heard of them."

She huffs. "They were very popular right before the Big Water. My mom had their whole discography."

"Sorry."

"It's fine," she reassures me. "You're lucky I know all their songs and can sing them for you."

"Lucky isn't the word I'd choose."

But she doesn't catch my sarcasm, or ignores it, and I speed through the wastelands of the apocalypse with Ben's version of some song about what lovers do ringing in my ears.

We make decent time, the roads not as bad as they were right outside of Lupton, but still almost impassable in places. Once we have to get out and clear what looks like intentional road debris. I stand guard, shotgun drawn while the others remove the rubble blocking our way. No one attacks us, but I can almost feel the eyes out there watching us.

Early afternoon finds us climbing the narrow roads around the North Rim of the Grand Canyon.

"Have you ever seen it?" Rissa asks, sitting up in the passenger's seat.

"The Grand Canyon? No, you?"

She nods. "A trip once with my family, when my dad was still alive." She smiles with some memory. "It was the last trip we took together before California went."

It had been a combination of fire, earth, and ultimately water that had taken the West Coast, the entire coast ravaged by wildfires, blackened and ruined. People had tried to flee but had been caught by a massive earthquake that sheared most of the Pacific Northwest straight off the continental shelf, and then the ocean had rushed in to finish the job. Millions gone in a series of days one hot November. By then the East Coast had been suffering through a record hurricane season and there was no help to be had. The federal government had long given up on helping anyone, the message clear that we were all on our own. And on our own, we would die.

I was fifteen then, living with my nalí. California might as well have been Saturn. But we did miss the television stations when they all went. The Internet. Later, we would miss more than that. Much more. But for a long time Dinétah was its own bubble. Only recently had we started to see some of the effects of the Big Water in our day-to-day lives. Less choice at the trading posts, but then we'd never had much choice to begin with. Fruit was always canned and in a syrup. Vegetables were limited to what we could grow in the small backyard plot my nalí tended. Strange that our isolation made the transition to a post Big Water world easier when before I'd only ever seen it as a punishment. But now I could see what a blessing it was.

We curve around the edge of a cliff and hit a wide-open mesa. The view is spectacular, and there, in the distance, is a place that can only be Page. It's a city at the top of a hill, almost like some old medieval city from books. But Page is thoroughly modern. Certainly more than anything in Dinétah. Electrical lights recklessly illuminate everything, revealing every road and structure in stark detail. Page benefits from the massive hydroelectric power plants on its borders. Those plants are fueled by the Colorado River that thunders nearby. Most electricity back in Dinétah comes from gas-powered generators, since we don't have a reservation-wide electrical grid anymore, if there had even been one to begin with. But here in Page, electricity flows like air, turning the city into twenty-four hours of continuous daylight. But the most shocking thing about the city is its color.

"It's green!" Rissa says, and after hours surrounded by nothing alive, it's like finding an emerald in a trash bin.

"Ben!" I call to the back seat. "Look at this." Ben rouses herself from where she's been napping against Aaron's shoulder. She wipes drool from her cheek and leans forward over the front seat to look.

"Whoa!" she says sleepily. "Is that grass?"

"Acres of it," Rissa says. "Damn. What do they do with it all?"

"Eat it?"

"I don't think people eat grass," I say. "At least, not when there's other options."

We come to a fork in the road, the one on the right leading up to the city and the one on the left trailing down to . . .

"What is that?" I ask, awed.

"Glen Canyon Dam," Aaron says. "Glen Canyon Dam is the

second-highest concrete-arch dam in the United States." He continues, his voice taking on the cadence of a tour guide. "Second only to Hoover Dam. Glen Canyon is seven hundred and ten feet high, a mere sixteen feet shorter than its more famous cousin. Built in 1956, it is part of one of the most extensive and complex river resource developments in the world. The dam holds more than twenty-six million acre feet of water in Lake Powell, and it has sustained the drought-stricken southwest part of the United States since its inception. It is truly a marvel of human engineering."

"Nice," Ben murmurs.

"I still got it," he says to her with a wink.

"That sign says Wahweap is on the other side of the dam," I say, pointing with my lips to a green-and-white road sign that designates places and miles to those places. "Eleven miles that way. But how do we cross?"

"We cross over the top of the dam," Aaron explains. "There's a road."

"The hell you say?" Rissa says. "Seven hundred feet in the air?"

"Seven hundred and ten," Ben adds unhelpfully.

"It's fine," Aaron assures us. "People do it all the time. There's even a visitors center if you want to stop."

"We're not tourists, Aaron."

"Right. Sorry."

We're approaching a place where the road turns from a dusty asphalt to a dull light gray concrete. The top of the dam. There's a gate that is used to block the entrance to the dam, but it's open right now, a handful of people in uniforms milling about.

We pass the gate. A woman in a brown and green uniform waves to us as we pass. I instinctively check to see if she has any weapons, but she's unarmed. "I don't understand," I say. "Is that a . . . ?"

"National Park Ranger," Aaron offers. "They stayed on after the federal government collapsed. Called themselves the Alt-Rangers.

Said they had a higher duty to the land than to the government. They still wear their uniforms. It's sort of a calling."

"They're not even armed."

"No one would touch them. They're considered sacred."

I keep my eyes forward as we enter the dam proper. Ben *ooh*s and *aah*s, craning her neck to look over the edge. Aaron provides a running commentary of facts. Only Rissa looks as tense as I do. "Hate heights," she says when I look over at her.

It doesn't take long—maybe ten minutes—to cross the dam, and then we're on the other side and winding along another dirt road, following the signs to Wahweap and Amangiri.

As we get closer to our destination, a pall settles heavy around us. Nerves, no doubt. Each of us is wrapped up in our own thoughts about what we expect from Amangiri, none of us actually knowing what will happen once we get there.

I can see Ben in the back seat, eyes out the window, no doubt looking at Lake Powell and thinking of another lake where she lost her uncle just a few days ago. It seems like weeks since we went up that mountainside and Hastiin died and Ben set her heart on revenge.

Aaron's next to her, looking out the other side of the car and absently rubbing the scars on his face, likely thinking of the White Locust too. Only I'm not sure whether he wants Gideon dead, like his seatmate does, or if he has other plans for his long-lost brother.

And then there's Rissa. I know we had a moment and that she says we're friends now. What I don't know is exactly what that means, and if our newfound friendship was weighed against whatever she has with Aaron, would it come out on top or come out wanting? If Aaron flips on us, will Rissa have my back? Ben's back? Or will she feel some kind of loyalty to Aaron? She said she wouldn't, but I don't know her well enough to know if she's lying. Or if she's telling the truth but likely to change her mind when the shit hits the fan.

The molted red and white cliffs of Lake Powell lead us down toward the water. Aaron starts drumming his fingers against the back of the seat. Rissa turns halfway around to lay a hand across his. He looks at her, surprised, and she gives him a smile. Wends her fingers through his. He smiles back. Ben begins singing softly to herself, a song I recognize, which Hastiin used to hum. Some tune he learned on the front lines of the Energy Wars. Something sad, a mourning song for warriors.

And I wonder, not for first time, what the hell I've gotten myself into.

# Chapter 32

It's midday when we reach Wahweap. The shore slopes down to the water, white rocks turning to a sandier mix beneath our feet. A metal dock that's seen better days reaches out past the shallows, branching into bays, offering room to anchor at least two dozen boats. But all the bays are empty, save one. And what's parked there isn't particularly impressive. A flat-bottomed boat about fifty feet long, give or take. White, with some sort of black and maroon patterned design on the sides that is peeling off like old paint in the heat. A dull white railing circles the boat on both the lower and upper deck, the upper deck open to the sky. Up top are a few old folding chairs, and next to one is a bright orange fishing pole, it's red and white floater bobbing in the water below.

"Looks abandoned," Rissa says, joining me. She holds her hand up to shade her eyes, scanning the lakefront as if there must be more to Wahweap than this. But she's seeing the same limited options I am.

"Why would Nohoilpi say to come here?" I wonder, thinking of the bright modern city just a few miles behind us.

Rissa shrugs. "These gods of yours have a strange sense of humor. I wouldn't put it past him to do it just to mess with us." She steps out on the dock tentatively, and the metal structure rocks under her weight.

I follow after her, the dock swaying. It's a little disconcerting, the way the flimsy structure floats on top of the water. If it collapses, the water is shallow enough that we could simply wade back to shore, but it's unsettling anyway. I've never been on a body of water bigger than Lake Asááyi back home, and Lake Powell could swallow a hundred Lake Asááyis. I'm feeling nervous and having second thoughts about Nohoilpi's advice. But we're here, so I'll see it through.

"Let's go introduce ourselves to whoever owns that thing," I say. "If there's anyone home."

Rissa and I move forward, Ben and Aaron trailing. The docks creaks and moans but holds together.

"Are we supposed to knock?" Ben asks as we reach the dilapidated old boat.

"On what? There's no door." Just an opening in the white railing big enough to fit through. It's a small leap across a narrow strip of water to reach the deck, but it seems rude to invite ourselves.

"Hello!?" I call. And for good measure, "Yá'át'ééh?!"

A water bird squawks and flies out from beneath the edge of the dock not ten feet away. I whirl, startled, my hand automatically reaching for my gun. Rissa does the same. We watch as the bird flaps its wings, climbing into the blue sky and across the surface of the lake. I give her a tight smile. Seems I'm not the only one who's jittery.

"Yíi!" shouts a voice from the upper deck of the boat. "Who's down there scaring my birds?"

I step back to get a better view. An old Diné man who wasn't there before is leaning over the white railing above us, giving me the evil eye. He's wearing a blue terry-cloth robe over matching pajama pants and a ratty blue T-shirt. Thin black hair hangs down in a bowl around his grizzled brown face. He looks at me expectantly, clearly waiting for an answer.

"Sorry about your bird, but we're looking for help."

"Help?" he scoffs. He shuffles across the deck, muttering to himself. Climbs down the ladder to the lower deck. His body sways and rolls with the rocking of the boat, but he's sure-footed in his fuzzy house slippers, clearly accustomed to spending time on the water. He comes to the edge of the deck and grasps the rail. He squints, one eye fixed on me as if he's evaluating whether I'm worthy of his help. But he's not much to look at himself.

"We were sent here from Twin Arrows. We were told you would help."

"Who told you that?"

"Nohoilpi."

"Nohoilpi, eh?" The old man scratches at a scruff of silver hair that lines his cheek. "Well, if Nohoilpi sent you from the Arrows, then you must be rich. What are you paying?"

"We're not rich." I hesitate, unsure how much to tell him, but his eyes are sharp and I didn't miss that he appeared out of nowhere. I decide truth is best. "We have a friend who was kidnapped. We think the people who took him are on the other side of the lake at a place called Amangiri. We just need to get there. Nohoilpi said to come here and look for a boat. That crossing here was the fastest way. And if we didn't get there by tonight, it would be too late."

He cocks his head. "That old greedy bastard said all that?"

"Not word for word, but close enough."

"Talkative bugger. Never used to talk that much when I knew him. Unless he was trying to take your money. And these ones?" He takes in Rissa, Ben, and Aaron with a sharp thrust of his lips. "Do they need my help too?"

"They're with me."

"Well," the old man says, "maybe you aren't rich, but you can't just ride for free. What can you do?"

"Work," I say automatically. "We can work, but we need to cross by sunset."

"Work? What kind of work?"

I start to answer, but Ben cuts me off. "I can catch fish!" she says enthusiastically. "I used to fish a lot with my uncle. He said I was a natural. Fish love me."

"They love you, eh?" He snorts but nods his head begrudgingly. Motions Ben forward, and she makes the short hop across the water with ease, landing gracefully on the swaying deck. "And the rest of you? What work can you do?"

We stand there for a minute. The old man waits.

"I'm good with mechanical things," Aaron offers. "If there's something on your boat that needs repairs, I could help."

"Ah!" The old man claps his hands together. "Now you're talking. Come on, then." Aaron does as he's told, grabbing the railing to pull himself across to the boat.

Rissa folds her arms over her chest, evaluating the old man. "I can cook whatever fish Ben catches. I'm good in the kitchen."

The old man holds his hand out, bowing his head. "Invaluable, my dear." Rissa blinks, startled, and then takes his outstretched hand and lets him help her across the water.

"And you?" he asks me. "I ain't got no enemies that needs killing at the moment, so what can you do exactly?"

My mouth drops a little in surprise. "How did you know . . . ?"

"That sword on your back," he says, eyes narrow as he motions to the pommel over my shoulder. "Glowing big as day. That's a killer's sword."

"It's glowing?" I almost reach out and touch Neizghání's sword in the scabbard.

"And all those weapons you're wearing. Who needs so many sharp pointy things?" He sighs and turns away. "Come on, then. I'll figure out something for you to make yourself useful. Shouldn't be too hard. An old man like me needs a lot of help. Out here on the lake by myself." He looks back at me, impatient. "Well? Are you coming? I thought this was important."

I stop myself from responding to his gibe. Barely. Leap lightly across to the boat and do my best to remember my manners. "Ahéheé, Grandpa," I say. "Thank you."

"You can call me Tó."

"Toe?" Ben asks.

Tó pulls a foot out of his slipper and sticks it out, wiggling. Ben giggles and he beams at her, obviously just as tickled.

"How long will it take?" I ask, looking uplake to the Utah side, knowing Kai isn't far away now.

"Ask him," Tó says, looking at Aaron.

"What? Why?"

"He's the one going to fix the engine, enit? How long is it going to take you to fix that engine?"

"Wait, wait, wait." I step forward, hands raised, because surely I didn't hear that right. "The engine doesn't work?"

"Well, not right now, but it's going to work." He winks at Aaron, who's standing there looking bemused. "I got a real good feeling." He claps Aaron on the shoulder.

"You said you could help us." My voice is low, calm, but I can feel my frustration building.

"And I am. You better get to work, then." He grins at Aaron and pokes a thumb in my direction. "This one's in a hurry."

Aaron shakes his head, smiling. "You have tools, Grandpa?"

"All in the back, by that broken engine. Been working on it all week, but she won't sing for me."

Aaron's face lights up. "I'll get her to sing."

Tó chuckles. "I figured." He shuffles back toward the ladder to the upper deck. Pauses to look over his shoulder at Ben. "Well, come on, then. Come show me how them fish love you." Ben hurries over, and the two of them climb the ladder. I can hear Tó's low voice saying something and Ben's laughing replies. Already two peas in a pod.

"What is going on?" I mutter to no one but myself. Everyone seems to be taking it all in stride, but I feel a step behind.

"What do you think?" Rissa asks, coming up beside me. She has a rag in her hand like she's ready to clean up the place. I can hear Aaron back by the engine, the sound of tools on metal.

"I think you all are acting strange," I mutter. "And I'm tired of trying to figure out what's going on."

"We could try another way."

I look pointedly around the empty marina. "There is no other way."

"We could get back on the road. There's got to be a road into Amangiri."

"No doubt heavily guarded by a bunch of fanatics with explosives. Who knows if that road is even passable."

"It might be worth taking the chance."

Rissa's eyes search mine for some kind of answer. And for the first time, I realize she's willing to trust my lead. That something has changed between us, and it's good. "No. We'll let this play out."

"Maggie!" Tó calls down. "Come on up. I figured out what you can do for me."

I don't even bother to ask how he knows my name. I just head for the ladder.

An hour later, we pull out of the dock. Ben cheers, and Aaron holds up a fist in victory. Rissa's inside the boat somewhere, no doubt dutifully cleaning, but she pops out for a minute to give Aaron an encouraging smile. I'm just glad to be moving.

The old man puts me to work, like he said he would. First he has me pull a shade sail out and string it across the upper deck so he and Ben can fish in relative comfort. Even with the sun quickly moving toward evening, he grumbled that it was still too hot, so he has me connect small misting fans to the poles holding up the sunshades. I do it all with no complaints, but when he asks me if I would go downstairs and make him a nice refreshing iced tea, I give him a look that has him muttering about ungrateful "Native youth" and turning back to his fishing pole.

"I'll do it," Ben says, hopping up from her chair. She places her pole into a bucket next to her feet and steadies the reel on the railing to keep it from spinning. Turns and skips over to the ladder, braces her feet along the sides and slides down like an acrobat.

I fold into her abandoned chair, fanning my face. "Do you really have ice?" I ask, dubious. It's got to be over a hundred, even in the shade. It would be a waste of his generator to keep something frozen, if it were even possible.

"You think I got ice?" he asks. "And here I thought you were smart."

"Then why . . . ?" I wave a hand. "You know what? Never mind."

I adjust the sword as it digs into my spine and stretch out my legs.

"You going to take that thing off?" Tó asks, his dark eyes on my sword.

"No."

He grunts. Reels his line up and casts it out again.

"Was it really glowing?" I ask after a minute, my curiosity getting the best of me.

"You used it yet?"

I shake my head. "Not like it's meant to be used."

"Best to do it now, so there's no surprises. Introduce yourself."

I shift in my seat, turning to face him. "What do you know about it?"

"I know what it can do, which is more than you can say."

I drag myself from the chair and walk to the center of the deck. Tó turns to watch, his face unreadable. I reach behind my right shoulder to grab the hilt and pull the sword free.

It's as beautiful as I remember.

And with that memory comes another. Of Black Mesa. Our last battle. My betrayal. My stomach drops, and I can feel tears, heavy and hot, gathering in my eyes. I lower the sword, let the tip rest against the metal deck, as regret rolls through me.

"Ah . . . ," Tó says quietly, his voice serious. "So it's like that."

I look up. I'd forgotten for a moment Tó was even there. I sheath the sword. "No, it's not like that. It's not like anything."

He grunts.

"Take the sword again." He gestures to me. "I don't judge."

I give him a look, but he's serious. I gather myself, take a breath, and draw the sword a second time. Hold it up in front of me. He comes over, wraps his hand around mine. His palms are warm and dry. He jiggles my hands, checking my grip.

"Next time you touch this, you ask the atsiniltł'ish to come. It's there, waiting for you. It just wants an invitation, jíni?" He looks at me, expectant. Making sure I understand. "Once the lightning is there, it's just power. The sword acts like a . . . conduit. Helping you direct that power. You want to try it?"

"On a boat? In the middle of the lake? Is that safe?"

"Probably not. Tell you what. Just say hello. Introduce yourself so it knows you. And then when you're ready, you invite it to stay."

"Introduce myself," I repeat.

"Go on!"

I exhale, feeling foolish. "Hello, sword," I whisper.

"In Diné!" he says. "Sword don't speak English."

"Yá'át'ééh, sword," I say, feeling even more foolish. "*Shí éí* Maggie Hoskie *yinishyé*."

And to my utter shock, the sword grows warm in my hand, the hilt pulsing like a small fire. "Whoa!" I say.

Tó grunts. "Now it knows you. Now when you need it, ask it. Politely."

"Amazing," I whisper, and as if it heard the compliment, a flash of white fire streaks up the blade, changing the obsidian to white lighting. I gape in wonder. Finally!

"Okay, okay, enough!" Tó says. "Now it's just showing off. Put that thing away before you burn down my boat."

Moments later Ben comes back with Tó's tea. "There wasn't any ice," she complains as she hands him the glass. "I looked everywhere."

He takes the tea. Sips. "At least you tried."

I don't even look at him.

"Aaron said he looked at the map and it's going to take a couple of hours to get to the closest stop to Amangiri. Said the water only goes so far and then we'll have to cross on foot. Not too far. A mile, maybe less."

"Okay."

"We're still going to have dinner, right?" she asks, voice sheepish.

Tó laughs. "Your brains are in your stomach, eh? Okay then, Loved-By-Fish, let's catch some dinner."

I get up to give Ben back her seat and pole. She smiles, grateful. Retrieves her pole. Reels and casts. I have no interest in watching the two of them fish, so I decide to make myself scarce.

"I'll go down and help Rissa," I say, heading over to the ladder.

"Not yet, Maggie," Tó says. "I've got something to show you."

He leans over, rifling through the half dozen small buckets he keeps on the deck. Stands when he can't find what he wants and totters over to another set of buckets on the far side of the deck.

"Here it is," he says finally. He shakes an orange bucket, and something metal rattles around inside. I go over to take a look. The bucket is full of tiny metal discs, like the pennies we used to flatten on the train tracks as kids, but unlike copper pennies, these discs are shiny and silver.

"What are they?" I ask, picking one up. It catches the light, bright and pretty in a bauble kind of way. Something that Mósí would like.

"Watch this!"

Tó totters back to the rail, the bucket of silver discs in hand. Ben's recast, but her line is still, nothing biting yet. Tó reaches into his bucket and tosses a silver disc out into the water, close to where Ben's floater bobs on the surface. The disc lands. It doesn't sink immediately, but instead floats on the water, glinting in the light. Slowly it starts to spin, caught in the pull of the water, sending ripples of iridescence in a circle around itself. A sudden splash and the disc disappears. A second later something tugs on Ben's line. A fish.

"Spinners," Ben exclaims. "My uncles used to always say fish were attracted to anything shiny." She heaves on the rod, reeling in her catch. Slowly at first, and once it breaks the water, faster. Sure enough, a fleshy little smallmouth bass twists on her hook. Once it's in range, Tó scoops it up in a net and dumps it into an empty bucket.

"They're not the only thing attracted to the shine," Tó says. "All kinds of things are attracted to shine. You hear that, Maggie?"

I lean back against the rail, arms across my chest. "I am sure the psychology of fish is all very fascinating, but what does this have to do with me?"

Tó huffs. Throws another spinner into the water. The same process happens—shine, spin, and catch. Which Ben reels in, delighted.

"It's got everything to do with you. It's nature's way, enit?" He takes a handful of spinners and tosses them wide across the surface of the lake. A dozen shiny baubles dancing in the sun. The water starts to roil as scores of fish come for the metal discs. Ben lets out a little gasp of awe, leaning over the railing, the importance of catching anything forgotten for a moment in the storm of fish.

"I'm going down to help Rissa, unless there's something else you want to show me."

Tó spits, clearly irritated that I'm not more impressed. I give him a few more seconds, but when he doesn't say anything else, just settles himself back into his chair, I take that as permission to leave.

# Chapter 33

Later, we eat the fish Ben caught, dipped in blue cornmeal and fried. It's probably the best thing I've eaten in years. Tó also has some sort of water plant he's collected and dried, and Rissa boils it with bits of something sweet that makes it melt in your mouth. But even more than the food, there's the company. Rissa and Aaron sit next to each other, and he fusses over her food, making sure she eats in a way that makes me think that maybe she has a point about him trying to change. Ben tells a literal big fish tale, and Tó tops it with a story about the time he and Nohoilpi tried to convince a bobcat to dance, and before we know it dinner is over.

"Going to check my charts," Tó announces, pushing back from the table. "We should be there any minute now."

Once he's tottered off to the front of the boat, Ben says, "You notice he left before cleanup?"

Rissa laughs. "Of course he did. I don't think he's washed a dish a day in his life." She stands and starts gathering the dirty dishes. "It's fine. I'll do it."

"I'll help," I say, joining her. I station myself at the little sink, and Rissa hands me the pile of dirty plates. I dip the plate in one of Tó's ubiquitous buckets, this one filled with soap and water, then into clean water for a rinse, before handing it to Aaron to dry. He rubs it down with a towel before handing it to Ben, who puts it back on the shelf where it came from. Working together, we make quick work of the cleanup, and by consensus we all end up on the upper deck, watching the sun set across the water.

"This is it," Tó shouts up to us as we pull in close to the shoreline. He's at the helm now, which consists of a steering wheel and a gearshift not so different from the one in my truck. He's turning the boat into the breeze and slowing down as we reach a sort of sandbar jutting out into the lake.

"Where's the dock?" I ask, coming down the stairs.

"No docks out here. You're going have to swim."

"What?"

He chuckles. "A little water's good for you. I didn't want to say nothing, but you all could use a bath. Loved-By-Fish smells like her name."

Ben protests somewhere behind me, but Tó only laughs more.

"I'm not getting my boots soaked," Rissa says, coming up beside me.

Tó gives her a squinty look. She gives him a look back. "For the lady, then," he says deferentially. Rissa gives him a smile that would make grown men piss themselves in fear. Tó only cackles.

We pull up as close to the jutting sandbar as we can get without bumping it. From here, we should be able to make the jump at a run. Rissa wants us closer, but Tó insists that it's as close as he can get.

We throw our packs over first. Aaron shakes Tó's hand and says something about not forgetting to add oil to the engine, which makes Tó nod his head sagely. Rissa's next, with a kiss on the hand. Then Ben, who gives Tó a hug before making the leap.

"Ahéheé, Grandpa," I say as I get ready to make my jump.

"Wait," he says, hand on my arm. I pause. Look back.

"I've got something for your friend. The one you're going up there to rescue."

"Kai?"

"Aoo'. Somewhere here." He pats the pockets of his blue robe, searching unsuccessfully. His hands move to his chest, patting, until his eyes light up in discovery. He reaches into his shirt and pulls out a flask. No, it's more like a hand-size clay pot. Black-and-white, wider at the bottom with a thin narrow neck. It's attached to a rawhide string, which he pulls up over his neck. He hands it to me.

"What is this?"

"A present. For your friend. You give it to him when you see him. Tell him it's from me."

I drop the string over my head, tuck the pot safely under my shirt. "I will."

"Don't forget."

I pat the object. "I won't."

I turn back to the shore. Swing back and forth on the rail to build a little momentum for my jump, and then leap to dry land. I give Tó one final wave.

"Maybe your silver-eyed boy will change my luck," he says under his breath, but I hear him well enough.

I turn, incredulous. "What did you say? About Kai's silver eyes?"

He grins. "Don't forget your fish psychology!" he shouts, waving vigorously.

"What did you say about Kai?" I repeat.

But the boat is already drifting away.

"Tó!"

I hear the engine punch into drive. "Tó!" I shout again over the roar of the engine. I watch it pull away, quickly becoming a diminishing speck on the darkening lake. I linger for a while, wondering who the mysterious old man was. I'm sure I'll find out soon enough.

"Maggie!" Rissa shouts from down the path. "Let's go!"

One last look across the lake and then I'm hurrying to follow my companions, down to whatever awaits us at Amangiri.

# Chapter 34

"That's got to be it," I tell Rissa as I hand her Aaron's binoculars. She takes them from me, shifting for a better look over the rocky cliffs and down into the valley where the Amangiri spreads out below us.

"Looks nice," she says. She gives the binoculars back to Aaron. "Swank. Or at least, apocalyptic swank."

"So, what's our plan?" Ben asks, sounding eager.

I glance over at Ben. In the camouflage pants and Twin Arrows gift-shop T-shirt, she looks like a version of the girl I met with Hastiin, even if the bandanna hanging around her neck is now pink and white, more cowgirl than mercenary. But with her hair back up in a tsiiyéél and that expression on her face, she looks enough like a Thirsty Boy again for me to take her seriously. Which isn't going to make what I have to say next any easier.

"So, Ben," I start, trying to ease into the conversation, "I was thinking that maybe you should wait here."

Her brow wrinkles in confusion. "What? What do you mean?"

"I mean that Hastiin trusted me to keep you safe, and maybe it's safer for you to wait up here on the ridge while we go down and scout . . ."

She's shaking her head, eyes big in disbelief.

"Ben," I say. "I know this isn't easy to hear. But remember what you said to me back at my trailer? When I said I'd let you come along on one condition? Remember that?"

Her eyes lock on me, the same look of betrayal I remember from the mountain when the Thirsty Boy told her to back down. "No! I'm going down there with you. I earned this."

"It's not about earning anything."

"No, Maggie!" She takes a step toward me, that same cold fury rising from her that I felt when I tried to get her to stay with Tah in Crystal. It's intense, desperate, and for a minute I almost waver.

Ben's voice breaks as she yells, "You promised!"

"I didn't promise," I correct her quietly, my voice steady, reasonable. "I didn't promise you anything, Ben. In fact, the only thing I said was that you could come along if *you* promised not to argue with me."

"You don't think I can do it? That I'm not brave enough? I rescued myself from Knifetown, didn't I?"

"You did."

"And I killed that archer woman at Lake Asáàyi. You saw that. You can't deny that." Her hands clench into fists. "But you still don't think I can handle myself in a fight. You saw me with a knife. You were there. You saw me kill her!"

"It's not that." I knew we'd come to this at some point, but I didn't want it to be like this. "I think you're plenty brave, Ben. That's not it."

"Then what?!" She's shaking, her whole body radiating rage. At me. "You want the glory to yourself!" she yells, accusing. "It's not enough that you rescue your boyfriend—you have to kill the bad guy too?!"

"Ben," I say, voice sharp. "Quit it. Now."

"Always have to be the big hero. The monsterslayer. Oh, no. Now it's Godslayer. Godslayer! So stupid!"

"You need to stop, Ben," I warn her, my own temper rising, "before you say something you regret."

"Regret? *Regret?* I already regret. I regret ever trusting you. Ever thinking you were my friend. Ever calling you my auntie. I regret—"

"She didn't die!" I shout.

Ben freezes. Stares at me, mouth hanging open, the color draining from her face.

"You didn't kill anyone, Ben. The archer back at Lake Asááyi? She didn't die! You stabbed her with a steak knife. The wound was surface deep. The handle broke off, remember?"

"B-b-but . . . ," she stutters. "She was bleeding!"

"After we left, the Thirsty Boys took her down the mountain to get medical attention. No doubt she's in jail right now, having to face justice for killing your uncle. And that council spokesperson. But she's not dead, Ben. You didn't kill anyone."

She looks at me one long minute, and I'm sure she's going to burst out into tears. But instead she turns and runs. Fast and Deer People nimble. She scrambles straight up a cliff. Disappears into the darkness in a matter of seconds.

"Dammit!" I shout, teeth clenching. I throw my hands up in frustration, pace away from Rissa and Aaron, ready to smash something.

Rissa waits until I've stopped cursing to ask, "What are you going to do?"

"Let her go," I say. "She's not my problem." And I almost mean it.

"What if she goes after Gideon on her own?" Aaron asks.

I hadn't even thought of that. Surely Ben wouldn't be that reckless. Who am I kidding? That's exactly what she plans to do.

"No, Maggie," Rissa says, guessing what I'm thinking. "You go find Kai. Aaron and I will go after her."

"No. She's my responsibility. I should go."

Rissa shakes her head. "I have a little brother, remember? I know teenagers. Let me handle Ben. She's not going to want to hear anything you have to say right now."

"No. She—"

"Maggie." Rissa clears her throat, and I know whatever she's going to say is going to be bad. "Killing that archer? That meant something to her. It was her redemption. You know she blames herself for Hastiin's death, right? It was her fault, wasn't it, that the archer spotted you on the trail?"

"The clip in her hair," I acknowledge. "Did she talk to you about it?"

"She confessed. When we were at Twin Arrows. And that's the way she put it. A 'confession' that she was responsible for Hastiin's death."

"She told me at Lupton that if she had died in the Energy Wars, maybe Hastiin would still be alive. I took it as survivor's guilt, but now I think she meant it literally." I shake my head, feeling like an idiot. "What else did she tell you?"

Rissa hesitates. Glances over at Aaron, who's looking at his shoes, hands stuffed in his pockets.

"She told me what happened to her as a bride at Knifetown."

Something seizes up in my chest. "Don't tell me . . ."

"No, nothing like that," she says, looking back at Aaron again. "But it was bad enough. Poked and prodded and *graded.* Bishop gave each bride a freaking grade, like a side of beef. That's how he set their reserve price. Grade B would sell for less than an A. . . ."

I wave my hand, disgusted. "I get it."

"It was humiliating. Awful. But no one . . . violated her."

"Brings down the price," Aaron whispers, so low I almost don't catch him. "Bishop don't do that no more. Nobody wants to buy a girl . . . or a boy . . . after that. Soiled like that."

Rissa presses her lips together, gives her good-enough-for-now boyfriend a look that's part compassion and part concern.

"Aaron," Rissa says, voice worried. "Are you okay?"

He glances up, a surprised look on his face. "Yeah, yeah. 'Course. There's no more to Knifetown, is there, 'cept rubble? No more Bishop, maybe? I'm fuckin' great."

She gives him an encouraging smile, and he returns it wider.

"I'll go after Ben," Rissa says after a moment. "Maggie, you go find Kai. And then, please, can we go home?"

Without another word, she turns and heads up the path Ben took, leaving Aaron and me standing there looking awkwardly at each other. He tilts his head, eyes narrowing between white lashes. "We all seen some shit, eh? Done some shit too. I bet you done some dark shit."

I nod slowly, unsure where he's going with this.

"Probably going to see and do a lot more dark shit too."

"Probably."

He reaches into his pocket and hands me something—the brochure of Amangiri.

"It's got a map," he says. "Layout of the facility. Gideon will be in the private residence. He plays rabble, but he ain't common. Not really."

I take it, not sure what to say but, "Thanks."

He tilts his head. "Godslayer, huh." His mouth bleeds into a half smile. "I always knew you were the crazy one in the girl gang."

He gives me a salute and jogs after Rissa. After a moment he, too, disappears into the darkness, leaving me alone on the cliff above Amangiri.

# Chapter 35

The Amangiri Resort and Spa is bigger than it seemed from Aaron's brochure. And colder. Not in temperature, although the desert has dipped to freezing with the sun down, but in architecture. All the buildings are built along sharp angles, the materials not adobe or even wood, but cold concrete. The place has none of the curves of the earth, nothing that speaks of Dinétah, of wooden hogans or warmth. It is entirely foreign. A place made by bilagáanas, for bilagáanas. That is a truth I feel deep in my bones. Bones that plead for me to turn around, that I don't belong here, that this place has no love for a child of Dinétah. But I do my best to ignore the cold dread that warns me to turn back. Because if I don't belong here, Kai doesn't either.

Aaron's brochure turns out to be helpful, giving me a general layout of the grounds. The main hotel building of the Amangiri is a sort of shortened L shape, centered around a pool in a courtyard. The main area at the top of the L shape appears to be the entrance to the building, with a series of rooms for guests trailing down the long body of the L. The spa is a separate building on the other side of the pool, and up the hill opposite us, there's a an individual residence. A mansion, really. If Aaron is right about his brother, that's where I'll find Gideon.

I approach from the southwest, keeping low and moving quickly through the darkness. Large walls of windows face outward to the desert, lit from within. I look for cameras, guards, some kind of security, but there's nothing. Either I am expected and it's a trap, or the White Locust's hubris is as vast as the land around me. I'm able to look into the rooms as I pass. All of them seem to be lived in, if currently empty. There are no bars on the wide windows, no chains forcing doors closed. I stop to test a sliding patio door. It opens easily, a puff of a whisper on an oiled rail. I tense, remembering they could be alarmed, half expecting to hear a warning shrieking into the night sky. Nothing. I could just walk in. Anyone could just walk in. Or out. I slide the door closed and keep moving, looking for . . . something. Some sign that one of these rooms is Kai's and that he's being held against his will. But they are all variations on the modern concrete cube, clean lines and sand-colored furniture, pre–Big Water stylish but entirely nondescript. I don't know how I'm going to tell.

And then I do.

The room is the last one in a long row, closer to the main common area than I'd like. But as soon as I see it, I know it's his. There's no sign of the man himself, but I know this is where Kai's been living. The room itself is the same plain box of concrete and pale wood as all the others, only this room feels warm. Living. A pool of rich golden light falls across an oversize desk, and smaller puddles cascade from tall, thin silver lamps placed around the room, the warmth of light a tonic to the stark concrete. They illuminate books. So many books. Books covering every surface, twice as many as Grace's library. There are books lining floating wooden shelves, books sitting in haphazard piles on the floor, books spread lavishly across the bed, allowing only the edge of a gray blanket to show through at the far corner. And these books look important, totally the opposite of Grace's well-loved paperbacks. These books are thick, hardbound, stacked three or four deep on the desk, higher on the floor. And besides the books, there's maps. Hung on the walls, even a few on the floor, like someone had hunched over them, studying their arcane lines. The maps on the wall have been written on, marred by crisscrossing black lines and scribbled numbers in longitude and latitude, others in letters and numbers that look like math equations. Maps of Dinétah and the Malpais, maps of Page and the surrounding area. I think I recognize the dam, the one Aaron called Glen Canyon, but from out here beyond the glass door, I can't be sure.

My heart beating loud in my ears, hands shaking, I slide the door open.

"Kai?" I call softly, even though he's clearly not here. It feels almost blasphemous to enter his space uninvited, but I've come so far and waited so long. If I can't be close to him, at least I can be close to his things.

I circle the room, trailing my fingertips across everything. The desk, a spiral notebook full of his writing, the gray blanket on this bed. His scent is here, that smell of cedar and clean tobacco, and I close my eyes and inhale it. It calms me, heals me. And makes me miss Dinétah so much it feels like a physical ache in my side. I keep moving, letting my eyes travel carelessly over the maps. And I begin to see a pattern. I was right that one of the maps on the wall was of the dam we crossed to get here. But I see other dams too. The Hoover Dam, which I recognize from school. And smaller ones I'm not familiar with. Grand Valley, Navajo. The routes of the Colorado River and its tributaries are highlighted over in different colors of permanent marker, the places they flow into Dinétah inked the thickest. And next to them, notes on force and time and acre feet. I turn to look at the books. Many of them are accounts of ancient stories—the Hebrew Bible, a story of something called a Tiamat from Ancient Babylon, another book with a Chinese dragon and what looks like a tortoise on the cover. I pick the Tiamat one up at random and flip through the pages. It's a poem, and hard to follow, but it's definitely about a primordial flood.

And a dull worry starts to gnaw at my belly.

I set the book down and pick up a different one. This one has a tan cover and the book itself is flat and twice as wide as a normal book. It's a side-by-side analysis of the story of Noah, a story I recognize from a brief stint in Christian school as a kid. Alarm blossoms at the back of my brain as I realize the stacks of newspapers around me are all accounts of the various events that led up to the Big Water. It seems obvious that Kai is studying the world-ending floods of history, looking for I'm not sure what. But combined with the maps of the Colorado River and its tributaries through Dinétah and the massive dams used to manage the river . . . and I'm starting to see the method to Gideon's madness. And the part that Kai, the one-time King of Storms and student of the Diné Weather Ways, may play in it all.

I leave Kai's room and slide the glass door shut behind me, feeling shaken. Gideon may be some kind of madman, but if he is, why is Kai staying here?

Because Kai is helping him. There's no other way to explain it.

Kai was always smart. Having been raised by scholars meant he knew his way around books and libraries and research in a way that I never did. Never will. And he's helping Gideon with this plan to do what—flood Dinétah?

It's too much. Too different from the Kai I know. And it makes me think that maybe I've misunderstood him. Maybe I don't know him like I thought I did. Maybe I need to admit that even though he was willing to face death for me to be free of Neizghání, perhaps that sacrifice has blinded me to the ways he deceived me when he thought I was the monsterslayer of his nightmares. And maybe there's something true to Rissa's suspicions, to Nohoilpi's interrogations. And instead of feeling a happy nervousness to see Kai again, my body feels heavy, my feet drag, and all I feel is dread.

There's a small fence separating the hotel rooms from the pool area. I vault the gate and move soundlessly, following the line of the building. I turn the corner only to pull up abruptly when I realize that around the corner is a wall of glass. And on the other side of that wall of glass are people. I can hear the buzz of their voices now, rising and falling in conversation. Laughter and the clink of utensils and crystal cups. And under that, music. A familiar song I can't quite place. Something from my childhood, so ubiquitous as to become anonymous, something about the snow or the cold and staying inside near a warm fire.

I hunch down low and peek around the corner, hoping that the bright indoor lights will blind the people inside enough to keep me hidden from a casual outside glance. They are in the main dining room of the hotel. The room is understated. Low-backed modern chairs in shades of honey and sand cluster around sleek modern tables. And on every table, a white candle glows, encased in a glass lamp. Golden boughs made of foil hang tastefully along the walls, interspersed with sprigs of sage. Here and there, big golden ornaments are arranged artfully on piles on the floor, and in the center of the room, behind a massive table that could seat fifty people, is a huge artificial pine tree that touches the ceiling. It, too, is decorated in golds and ivories and long coils of foil. And I realize that the White Locust and his Swarm are having a Keshmish party.

A Keshmish party.

It's so outrageous, so unexpected, that I have to cover my mouth with my hands to keep myself from laughing. I was expecting . . . something else. A militarized force, armed to the teeth with black-market guns and hoarded explosives. Doomsday fanatics in long robes and shaved heads. At the very least, people held prisoner, wings cruelly grafted to their backs, faces caught up in some beatific trance like Caleb.

But these people look normal. Happy. Laughing and drinking at a lavish Keshmish party.

As I look more closely, I see that the decorations are not quite as bright and new as they first appeared. The golden paint is peeling off the ornaments. The white candles are melted-down stubs, reduced to pools of watery wax. The tinsel is frayed and peeling around the edges. They must be the last decorations the Amangiri used before the Big Water, likely stored in boxes for years before Gideon and his people came along to pull them out and string them throughout their dining room.

Gideon's people are dressed in their party clothes. Nothing in comparison to the wealth I saw at the Knifetown auction and certainly nothing as otherworldly as what I remember from the Shalimar. But the people look clean. Well fed. Their clothes well taken care of. A swirl of a red dress here, the shine of a dark suit jacket there. And then there's the wings. Not everyone has them, or at least has them on display, but enough do. They look a bit like fairies, more ethereal than insectoid under the Keshmish lights. They are strange, but beautiful, too. More artwork than grotesquerie.

As I watch, they gather around the huge table, taking their seats as if their places were decided, leaving the head chair empty. The energy in the room seems to climb, a sense of expectancy in the air, like everyone's waiting for whoever belongs to that seat. It has to be Gideon, and I welcome the chance to finally get a look at the monster in the flesh.

And then I hear it. That laugh. The one that saved me so many times. That pulled me from the darkness in my head. That made me feel safe. That saved my life.

Kai is seated at the table, one seat away from the White Locust's chair. His back is to me. He's wearing a royal blue velvet suit jacket that gleams soft and lush in the golden light. His head is bent in conversation with the person next to him. A woman with long blond hair that cascades down her back. Kai's hair is longer, too, grown out in the time we've been apart. It covers his neck, brushes the tops of his ears, and hangs down in a thick wave across his eyes. I watch as he tilts his head back, pushing his hair from his face with long, elegant fingers, familiar turquoise rings catching the light. And God help me, my heart does a little flip-flop. It's not that I'd forgotten the effect he has on me, the sort of otherworldly beauty he possesses. But maybe I had forgotten how susceptible I was to it.

And I'm not the only one.

I watch as the blond woman takes a small bite of something from her plate and holds it up for him to eat. He tries to take it from her hand, but she pulls back teasingly. He gives her a little half smile and opens his mouth. She feeds the morsel to him, her fingers lingering against his lips. And then she leans in and kisses him.

And something inside me free-falls.

She pulls away, giggling. Touches a hand to her chest and rolls her head back, a pantomime of pleasure, and Kai smiles.

I'm on my knees. The rough concrete bites through my leggings, tearing my skin. Nothing, really. Bruised bone and torn flesh. Such a small pain.

Kai slips his arm around the back of the blond woman's seat, leans close to whisper something in her ear. And for a moment his eyes flicker my way.

I press my hand to the glass.

The color on his face drains. His fingers tense, digging into the back of her chair, and his eyes . . .

I wonder what he sees. A girl on her knees just past the glass doors, palm pressed against the barrier that won't let her in. A stubborn fool stuck out in the desert cold, while he laughs and feasts and kisses golden-haired women in the warm light.

He starts to rise from his chair, when something draws his attention back to the room. And then everyone is standing and applauding. A bilagáana man, midthirties, enters. Tanned skin and brown hair. Tall, fit, handsome. He greets people as he moves through the gathering, shaking hands and touching shoulders. He smiles with sparkling white teeth. I hear them shout his name, even from out here. Gideon. He's wearing jeans, a matching denim shirt, a leather bolo with a silver medallion shaped like an insect. A locust.

Kai tries to leave, pressing a hand to the blond girl's arm and mouthing excuses. She looks back over her shoulder, directly at where I am, but I can tell by her expression that she can't see me.

But Kai sees me. I can feel it.

She grabs his hand, not letting him go. He tries again, but now Gideon is there, wrapping an arm around Kai's shoulder and giving him a one-armed hug. And he's saying something, and I can barely follow his lips. But then I do.

Son. He's calling Kai "son."

Kai shoulders fall slightly, but he covers it with a smile. The blond woman gazes at Kai adoringly. And Gideon takes his seat at the head of the table, with Kai on his right.

# Chapter 36

I sit for a while, my feet dangling in the deep end of the empty pool, listening to the party. I should probably be somewhere less visible, but I know Kai saw me. I can only hope he'll come. And if someone else finds me first? Well, I'm not sure it matters.

My breath frosts in front of me, and for a moment I'm surprised I'm still breathing. I'm surprised I'm still alive at all.

I track the path of the stars as they travel across the sky. They're faint out here, so close to all this electric light. Neizghání used to encourage me to learn the names of all the stars, but I was always a terrible student. Náhookos Bika'ii, I recognize. The man lying on his side near what the bilagáanas call the Big Dipper. And Náhookos Bi'áadii, the woman. The man and the woman. Watching over a ruined world.

I hear him before I see him. A burst of conversation, cut off abruptly by the soft *whoosh* of a sliding door. The quiet tap of party shoes. The scratch of a match and the punch of sulfur. And then the scent of mountain tobacco.

He stands there, silent behind me. The only noise is the inhale and exhale of smoke from his cigarette. The night stretches, cold and distant as the stars.

"You're wearing his sword," he finally says.

I flinch at the accusation in his voice.

"It's my sword now," I say, eyes still on the night sky.

He's quiet, and I can only guess what he's thinking. Surely the Goodacres told him that I buried Neizghání alive and took his sword for good measure. Or maybe he thinks it means something else, something about where my loyalties lie.

"It doesn't mean anyth—"

"I can only stay a minute," he continues quickly, cutting me off. "They'll come looking for me if I'm gone too long. Did you get my message?" he asks. "I left you a message at Grace's."

"I got it."

His voice is sad. "Then why did you come?"

*Because you said you loved me, and nobody's ever said that to me before.* "You were missing. There was blood at the guardhouse. I thought maybe you needed—" I stop myself from saying "me." I say "help" instead. I turn to face him. "Plus, last time I saw you, you were dead."

He pales, his hand going to his chest reflexively, the place where I shot him.

"You look good," I say stupidly. Because he does. He's taken off his blue jacket and the sleeves of his black button-up shirt are rolled up to his elbows, the collar loose and open despite the cold. His familiar rings glint in the light, the big turquoise one I like so much. Everything about him is elegant, even the way he holds the softly glowing cigarette between his long fingers.

"You look good too," he whispers, perfectly sincere.

"Not like you." I gesture to his party clothes.

"Your hair got longer," he says.

"So did yours."

He smokes some more, and I wonder when he started smoking outside of ceremony so much. His hands are shaking slightly, and he unconsciously twists a ring around his finger with his thumb.

"When I woke up," he says, voice unsteady. "When I woke up from being . . . gone, I was pretty messed up. I couldn't remember what had happened. Where I was. Just darkness. And pain."

I don't want to hear this, but I know I have to. I know this is my burden too.

"For the longest time I'd wake up every morning thinking that I was back in the Burque. It was like no new memories would stick." He laughs self-consciously. "That was a shit show. But Clive was there, and I remembered him. I did a lot of ranting. And the nightmares," he says quietly, scraping at his throat, as if he were still screaming. Clouds pass overhead, temporarily blocking the stars.

I have to ask. "Did you remember . . . ?"

"That you shot me?" He says it lightly, but I can almost taste the undercurrent of bitterness. "Yes," he says, lowering his eyes, "but I remember that I let you."

I smile, thin and pained. "It was the only way. Neizghání would have never—"

"I know," he says gently. "I remember it all now."

"I'm sorry."

He shakes his head. "There's no reason to be sorry. We agreed. I agreed."

"I need to say it. I need you to know." I need it so badly that it feels like a physical thing, a rip in my belly that won't stop bleeding, a fist crushing my heart into dust.

He looks at me, asking me something. But what? We hold, neither of us saying anything.

"I know, because I also remember the look on your face," he finally says. "When you pulled the trigger. Right before I died."

I close my eyes, and something inside me drops like a ten-ton weight. "Clive didn't tell me any of this."

"No. I told him not to."

The words are out of my mouth before I can stop them. "Is that why you didn't come to me when you woke up? You . . . hate me?"

"No." He shakes his head. "No, Maggie." He takes a step toward me. "The opposite. It's the opposite. I was a wreck. I couldn't come to you like that. I would have been a burden, like I was to Alvaro after the Uriostes. Like I was to my father after my mom died. I wasn't going to do that again, be that person again. I had to get myself together first. And then Gideon showed up, and he had a lot of answers. A lot of smart things to say. I felt like maybe, maybe, if I could learn from him, then I could start to heal. Get better. If I saw you again, I wanted it to be when I was whole."

"If?"

"I needed to heal."

"How did you even meet Gideon?"

"The All-American. He came to the bar one night. We talked over a few beers. He said he could see that I was suffering. That I was . . ." He blows out a breath. "Everyone else had been tiptoeing around it. Clive would listen, but he always had this look on his face."

"He pitied you. The medicine man who couldn't heal himself."

He looks away.

"And Gideon didn't," I say.

"He understood. He'd been there too. A death experience, and he had been reborn. With purpose."

"What is his purpose?"

"He's gathering people to him. People who believe that things could be better in the Sixth World. That the corruption and greed that led to the Big Water was a rot in the human heart, but that it can be cured."

"I've seen his flyers, Kai. That's not about healing. That's about punishment. Fear."

He takes a drag from his cigarette, watches me through the smoke. "He's a good man."

I roll my head on my neck, left, then right, trying to understand what's going on. What Kai sees that I don't. "He's a cult leader."

"He's not."

"He calls you 'son.'"

He pauses, clearly taken off guard. "How did you know that?"

"Who's the woman with the wings?"

He blinks at my change of subject. "The woman? Oh, Jen? The blonde? No one."

"She didn't look like no one."

"It's a party," he says, as if that's explanation enough. "She's been drinking. I didn't encourage her. She wants to get close to Gideon as much as she wants to get close to me."

"She didn't kiss Gideon."

My accusation hangs in the air until he clears his throat. "If you saw Clive, I assume that means Caleb made it back to the All-American?"

"So I guess we're not talking about Jen."

We both hear the door slide open behind him. He curses, hurries back around the corner where I can't see. I hear him whisper furiously to someone, and a female voice answers in concern. Jen. And then his tone shifts, a low, persuasive murmur. I know what he's doing. I can almost see his eyes flash silver. Bit'ąą'nii Dine'e.

After a moment the door closes, and he comes back. This time he walks around to sit near me on a patio chair, one of those long chaise chairs from Hollywood movies. He taps the space next to him, wanting me to join him. So I do. Because even now I want to be close to him, God help me.

He takes my hand, rests it on his thigh, and covers it with his own. "Jen is one of Gideon's favorites. It's important that she like me, that she trusts me. And if that means . . ."

"If that means what?" I ask, tone sharper than I mean it be. But I remember that Kai was willing to sleep with me if it meant I would help him fight Neizghání.

"Not that," he says, looking taken aback. "Maggie, I meant what I said at Grace's."

"But you left."

"Because I had to. Because maybe Gideon has some answers. Because being here, having a purpose, drove the darkness back a little."

"And I don't drive the darkness back," I say, knowing the truth when I hear it. "I just bring the darkness closer."

"You are who you are. I'm not asking you to change. But Maggie, there's so much death on me," he says. voice barely above a whisper. "It's like I can't think sometimes."

I know that feeling, am intimate with that feeling. "You need a ceremony. You don't want to end up like me, Kai."

He nods. "I didn't know. I'm sorry. You were right, and I didn't know."

"You were right too. People can change." I take a deep breath.

"There's something else. Caleb didn't come back to the All-American," I say abruptly. "We found him nailed to the Wall in Lupton."

He blinks, caught by surprise. "Caleb Goodacre? No. Gideon sent him back to the All-American. I helped heal the wounds from the graft, but it wasn't going well. Even with my clan powers, he wasn't healing like he should have. His blood wouldn't clot. We argued about it, but Gideon agreed to send Caleb home. He left him with Ziona in Lupton until he was well enough to travel."

"No, Kai. Caleb was nailed over the gate in the southern Wall at Lupton, pointing us out to the Malpais clear as a ransom note. Did you really not know?"

And from the look on his face, I can tell he really didn't.

"But Gideon promised," he says, sounding defensive. He rubs at the bridge of his nose. "I . . . I made the deal to help Gideon with his work so Caleb could go home, and Gideon promised. I would have never, Maggie. If I'd known, I would have never."

"I know." At least I think I know. I know the old Kai would have never, so I have to believe this Kai wouldn't either.

"Is he . . . ?"

"He was with Clive, headed back to Tah when I last saw him."

Kai stiffens. A shudder rocks his body, and he bends at the waist, head between his knees like he's going to be sick. His cigarette drops forgotten from shaking fingers.

"Are you okay?" I ask, alarmed, reaching for him out of instinct. His back trembles under my hand. "Kai? Kai! What's wrong?"

"What did you say?" he asks, voice thick. "About my cheii?"

He doesn't know. Of course he doesn't know.

"He's alive. Tah is alive." I don't know why I didn't tell him sooner. It should have been the first thing out of my mouth. "He was out shopping when Ma'ii came that morning, and he slipped away in the chaos of the fire. He was at my place after Black Mesa, waiting. He's been living with me in Crystal."

"That's impossible," he says when he finally finds his words. "My cheii is dead."

"No, Kai. He's alive. And he's waiting for you." I rush on, scared that if I stop, I won't say it. "I've been waiting for you too. Both of us. You have family in Dinétah. That's your home."

"But Gideon said . . ." He trails off, shaking his head. I have a feeling Gideon has said a lot of things. Kai looks at me, and there's something different about his posture, something of the man I know. But it's gone almost as quickly as it came.

"What's going on, Kai?" I ask, suspicious. Because that look. I know that look.

"I think I may be a fool, Maggie," he whispers to me. "I think everything I've done may end up being for nothing." His eyes search my face, looking for . . . I'm not sure what. And he looks so alone, so . . . scared, that I impulsively lay my hand against his cheek. He leans into my palm, kisses my bare skin, and desire thrills through me.

"I've started something here," he whispers against my hand, "and I have to see it through."

"I don't understand."

"I know. But can you trust me anyway?" he asks. "I know it's a lot to ask, and things look bad right now, but if you could . . . if you could have faith, just a little longer . . ."

My breath comes short, and something tightens in my chest, because even after what I saw in his room, what I saw at that dinner table, my answer is simple. "I have faith."

He smiles, no doubt recognizing the same words he said to me on Black Mesa." He starts to move away. But it's not enough, this brief touch. This conversation with more secrets than answers. I need more. I need Kai. I lost him once, and I'm not losing him again.

But he's already walking away.

"Kai!"

He pauses and turns back.

I'm on my feet, and I close the space between us, and then I do the only thing I can think to do in the moment. I grab him by the back of the head and pull his mouth to mine, and before he can react, I bite his lip, hard enough to draw blood.

He rears back, surprised. Looks at me like I'm a little crazy, but I do my best to give him innocent eyes. He smiles back hesitantly. Reaches into his trouser pocket and pulls out a tissue. Dabs at the bloody spot.

"Sorry," I murmur. I run a finger over his quickly swelling lip, let his blood paint my fingertip.

"I'm not sure how I'm going to explain that," he says, touching the tender place on his mouth before dropping the tissue back in his pocket. I don't say anything. I may trust him, but an insurance policy never hurts.

A burst of party, a sliding door. Kai gives me a look, clearly trying to say something, and then says loudly, "I'm not going back to Dinétah with you. I have a mission to complete, and I'm going to finish it tomorrow, come hell or high water."

I see a shadow hovering around the corner, and I understand that Kai's words are meant for whoever is listening, not me. Another lie within a lie, but I told him I had faith in him and I meant it.

"I belong here with Gideon," Kai continues. "He's my family now. I'm sorry, but I'm already home."

One last look and then he's backing away, into the shadows. He turns the corner, says something in a voice that sounds surprised, and then he and the owner of that shadow disappear through the sliding door, back to the party.

# Chapter 37

I wait until the sounds of the party have died and the bright golden lights have all gone out to hunt Gideon down. I go back the way I came. Circle around the pool, hop the gate, and make my way past all the little rooms. I don't stop at Kai's. Not because I don't want to. I do. More than anything. But I know that if I want Kai back for good, I have to deal with Gideon first.

Amangiri's private residence is a mansion at the top of a small mesa. The darkness is thicker here, away from the main compound's lights. The once colorful mountains of Canyon Point are rendered into hulking shadows. I scramble up the white rocks, my feet fighting for purchase in the shifting sand. The spill of pebbles under my feet sound like the echoing patter of rain.

Again, there are no guards here, and I wonder if Gideon is trusting, arrogant, or if there's something else about the man that I'm missing entirely. It's not a good feeling, and I pat my weapons again, making sure everything I need is with me.

There's a wall around the mansion. A solid adobe, ten feet at best. I take a few steps and come at it running. Launch myself forward, reaching up hands up to grab the top and haul myself up. And marvel at what lies beyond the wall.

It's not the house. It's beautiful in the stark way I've come to understand Amangiri. A two-story block of concrete in the same style as the rest of the compound, shuttered windows showing no light at the balconies in the back. What stops me in my tracks are the gardens surrounding the house. Sculpture gardens, full of strange metal-wire statues. Some are beautiful, a ten-foot tall angel with delicate feather-like wings that trail to the ground. Some are hideous, hunched monsters with pointed, razor-wire claws. The monsters devour human figures that scream, openmouthed, as they are consumed. And everywhere, metal insects. Locusts mostly. But all kinds of flying insects—bees, dragonflies, wide, flat-backed winged beetles. In another place, under different circumstances, the statues might be beautiful, but here in the shadowy darkness, knowing what I know about their maker, they are grotesque.

I drop off the top of the concrete wall into the sculpture garden. Move silently through to the residence and head for the back of the house that, just like the hotel, is a wall of sliding glass doors. The first one I try is unlocked. I draw my gun and step across the threshold.

I'm in a living room. Modern, clean, but as soulless as the rest of the Amangiri. Low lighting reveals a fireplace big enough to stand in, now cold and banked. White couches and low, armless sitting chairs. A coffee table centered over a white carpet. And more metal statues. Some of these I recognize as images of the Diyin Dine'é, copies of things I've seen on sand paintings or at ceremonial. Although I don't know why Gideon would sculpt statues of the Holy People for his living room.

"Come out, come out, Gideon," I whisper in a singsong. "Time we had a talk."

The room seems to swallow my voice, and it doesn't echo back to me. Just disappears in the stillness.

I leave the living room and round the corner into a dining room.

Metal and wood chairs line a table long enough to sit ten people, but only two places are set. An open bottle of deep mahogany-colored whiskey sits between them, a note perched against the base, written in a flourishing script. I pick up the note and read it: *I was hoping you would come. Join me for a drink. I'll be only a minute.*

"You have got to be kidding me," I mutter.

"I assure you I am not."

The same attractive middle-aged man from the party moves into the light. He's holding a silver serving tray. The elaborate curlicues decorating the handles gleam like treasure in the soft light emanating from the room behind him, which must be the kitchen. And on the tray, what looks like, of all things, a pie. Apple, I think, although I can't remember the last time I had an apple, never mind a whole pie of them. The impossibly rare smell of cinnamon and sugar waft from the dish, and despite the completely surreal moment, my mouth waters.

Gideon smiles, showing even white teeth. A movie star's smile. Or a charlatan's. "You are Maggie Hoskie, correct? I've been waiting for you," he says. "I wasn't sure if the messengers I left behind would be enough to pique your interest, but I am certainly glad they did." He lifts the tray. Breathes in the aroma of the pie. "I made this for you. And the whiskey, of course. Kai told me it was your favorite. He told me a lot of things about you. I hope you don't mind. Because, frankly, it just makes me that much more excited to meet you. It's not every day one gets to meet a godslayer."

Is he trying to flatter me? "Nice speech," I say, bringing the Glock up to eye level, "but I've got a gun."

"Ah, now," he says, his grin shifting to disarming, "you wouldn't shoot a man who baked you a pie, would you?"

"Didn't anyone tell you, Gideon?" I growl, as K'aahanáanii rolls through my veins. "I'm the crazy one in the girl gang."

I pull the trigger.

***

Time slows. The air thickens to molasses, the calling card of Honágháahnii. The silver tray slides from Gideon's hands, the pie tilting toward the floor. Sound rolls from his mouth, thick as raw honey. It fills the room, a physical thing, and that telltale sweetness of a summer memory pours over me, trying to tug me under. I resist. Pull the trigger again. Both bullets seem to slow in the heavy air. Impossible. But it's true, and they catch in the locust song like a drop of dew in a spiderweb, hanging suspended between us. I've never seen anything like it, and for a moment I gape, stunned.

Gideon's still moving. He flicks his wrist in a downward motion. The bullets drop to the floor just as the pie explodes against the tiles. A matter of milliseconds.

He moves his hand again, and my gun flies from my grip so abruptly it takes a layer of skin with it. I stumble, start to fall. Catch myself on one knee that goes out from under me, and I slide sideways on the white tiles, skidding through the pie filling.

I draw my throwing knife. Obsidian, not silver, because I think I understand Gideon's clan power. I release the blade, and a pain tugs at my arm. The wound from the canyon outside Knifetown. I forgot. It throws off my aim, and the blade grazes his neck instead of landing true. A line of red opens across his skin. The locust song cuts off. Everything speeds up to normal in a breath-stealing second, and Gideon roars, "Enough!"

But it's not enough. I gather my feet beneath me and lunge forward, Böker in hand. Aiming for his chest. He gestures with his hand, knocking my knife away with crushing force. I cry out at my fingers bend and crack, my raw palm stinging.

I feel something heavy hit my chest. It knocks me back, leaves me fighting for air. Another strike, across my belly. Something sharp, and cold metal cuts into my skin. Again. Again. And I realize I'm being wrapped in chains. Around and around they circle me, like a living serpent. They pin my arms to my sides until I can't move. Something solid shoves at the back of my legs, and Gideon dumps me unceremoniously into one of the metal dining room chairs. He glares at me, all the calm civility of moments ago torn away. His jaw clenches, and a vein in his forehead beats with the force of his anger.

"What is *wrong* with you?" he spits, his voice vibrating with barely contained rage. "I offered you food and drink. You don't try to kill someone who offers you hospitality!"

I'm panting, some of the blowback of using my clan powers catching up with me. It takes me a moment to answer. "That's not hospitality. That's bait."

The pulse in his forehead grows more pronounced. "I am not—" He stops. He's winded too, no doubt from using his powers. He takes a deep breath and starts again. "I am not your enemy."

"You kidnapped Kai!"

His smile is pained, strain showing around his eyes. "Does Kai look kidnapped to you? He is here by his own volition, I assure you. Whatever lies he told you tonight at the party are exactly that. He was trying to protect you from me, which is admirable but unnecessary."

"I won't leave here without him!"

"My dear," he says, somewhere between bemused and exasperated, "I don't want you to leave at all."

Gideon moves around the remains of the pie on the floor and settles himself in the chair across from me. Touches his fingers briefly to the scratch on his neck and looks at the blood in disgust. He opens the whiskey bottle and pours himself a glass. Holds it to his nose and inhales. And then sets the glass down again, untouched. He folds one hand around the tumbler and rests the other on the table. Steadies himself before he starts talking again.

"I don't want you, or Kai, to leave because I am afraid I need you both." He rattles his glass, sending the whiskey sloshing around inside. He studies me, intelligent eyes moving over my face. "I can certainly see what he likes about you."

"Can't say the same."

He smiles briefly at the easy insult. "Can we agree to set aside the bravado, hmm? Speak to each other openly? You see, I was hoping"—he hesitates, face lighting up again, excited—"I was hoping that you would join me. Join us."

"Is that why you put me in chains?"

"Not my first choice." He glances meaningfully at the pie strewn across the floor.

"I won't help you flood Dinétah. I saw Kai's room. The maps, the books. I know what you're using him for."

His face remains pleasant, but his hand tightens around the whiskey glass. "I could not have done all of this without him. I admit that. I had a vision, but Kai's unique power showed me how to manifest that into reality. I am indebted. But to suggest that I don't care for that young man . . ." He takes a deep breath, visibly calms himself before he continues. "Kai is precious to me, truly. But he still doesn't quite understand the forces at play here. His vision is limited. You, however . . ." Now he grins, big and generous. "You and I are different, Godslayer."

I scrutinize Gideon's face. Aaron said his brother was Diné. From a distance, with the light brown hair and the light eyes, he looks bilagáana. But this close I can see it. A subtle shape of the eye, the bridge of his nose. "Clan powers?" I ask.

He lifts his eyebrows.

"The way you control the metal. The statues, the wings, my guns. It's a clan power, isn't it? You're Diné on your mother's side." And then it occurs to me. "No, you're Diné two ways. That locust song—that's a clan power too."

His surprise turns to something else. Loathing. But I'm not sure if it's directed at me or at himself. "And why would you say that?" he asks, voice low.

"Do you know your clans?"

His nostrils flare in irritation. "I'm afraid my mother didn't do me the honor of sticking around after I was born. As for my father, I can't really say much about him, either."

"I met your foster brother, Aaron."

His whole demeanor shifts. The muscles in his face seem to harden, the line of his mouth thins to nothing, and his eyes—whatever light they had before—snuffs out. "And how is my dear brother?" he asks in a brittle voice. "Not dead yet, unless you did the honors?"

"Not dead."

"Well, if you have met Aaron, then surely you have met Bishop and the whole viper's den at Knifetown. You have seen it with your own eyes, what has become of humanity in this Sixth World."

"I've experienced their hospitality," I admit. "Didn't care for it, either."

He stares at me a minute, eyes narrow, before he barks a harsh laugh. "Hospitality," he sneers.

"I mean, they didn't bake me a pie or anything. But I got out in one piece."

Something ugly crosses his face. "One piece? Are you in once piece?" He lays a heavy hand across my knee. "One need not dismember a woman to break her into pieces. I think you know that."

A deep uneasiness radiates from his touch, and I shake him off. He doesn't force it, instead folding his fingers around his glass. He sighs, and now the look he gives me is all sympathy.

"I don't think you've been in one piece for a very long time, Maggie. But I can help you be whole again. Just like I've helped Kai, as I've helped all my dear friends. I can help you find the one thing that eludes you."

"And that is . . . ?"

"Purpose."

"What?"

"Purpose. Isn't that what you need? If you are no longer Neizghání's apprentice, who are you? Isn't that what you've been asking yourself?"

"How did you know that?"

"Kai told me of your troubles. No, don't be mad at him. He has troubles of his own, and my song is very persuasive. You are the first person that has been able to resist it. Did you know that?"

"Is that how you get your 'Swarm' to follow you? Promise them things that only exist in their imaginations?"

He fingers the metal insect on his bolo. "The locust has much to teach us. They are resilient creatures, dormant most of their lives. But when they rise, they rise in number and they are unstoppable. They change the world, reorder entire landscapes."

"They are devourers."

"Oh yes," he admits. "But where they cleanse the earth, new life grows. They destroy to make room for the new."

"I'm not interested in destroying anything or anyone."

"Says the girl with the gun."

I say nothing to that, and he takes a small sip of his whiskey. "Are you sure you don't want any?" He lifts the glass in my direction. "It's a rare vintage from the cellars here. Better than anything you've ever tasted, I assure you."

I shake my head.

"Suit yourself." He takes another sip before he leans forward, intent. "But answer me this, Maggie, since we're talking. Why do the Diyin Dine'é play favorites? Do you know?"

"No idea what you're talking about."

"No? You've spent most of your life around them. I was hoping you had some insight. For example, why do they build a wall to keep some men out? Why do they favor one woman over another? If all Diné are their children . . . if even I am their child, as you so kindly pointed out, and we all belong to the land, then why am I left to suffer and rot while others prosper?"

"Kai said he met you at the All-American. You've been inside the Wall."

The chains around me tighten, and I gasp. "That is not what I mean." The vein in his forehead swells again. He dips his head and takes a deep breath. "You're certainly no philosopher," he says dryly.

"Sorry."

He laughs a little under his breath. "I have to admit that now that I've met you, I begin to understand."

"Understand what?"

"Not so much the what, but the why. Why your gods have taken an interest in you."

"I don't think it works that way."

"You don't know the way it works," he hisses, his rage bubbling up again. "Or you don't want to admit it. I have been a pawn in their games, just as you have. So please, *please*, don't presume to tell me how it works."

I want to challenge him, tell him that Dinétah is a place just like any other, with bad and good, and that the Diyin Dine'é have nothing to do with whatever offenses he's suffered to bring him to this place. But I'm not sure I believe it. At the very least, he's right that the Diyin Dine'é were instrumental in building the Wall. They instructed the medicine men and the lathers. And rumors have always swirled that Ma'ii or someone else had something to do with the Big Water. And he's right about one other thing. The Diyin Dine'e certainly haven't been shy about interfering in my life. Is it so hard to believe that even now they play favorites?

Gideon's been watching my face, and now whatever he sees there makes him lean back, grinning.

"So, you do see the truth in my words. You feel that frustration, that unfairness inside just as I do." He touches a hand to his chest.

"And now you see my real vision. The flooding of Dinétah is only the beginning. I plan to challenge the gods themselves. And you are the perfect vessel through which to do that." His eyes shift to the lightning sword on my back. "With the perfect weapon."

"The Diyin Dine'e are sacred beings. More powerful than anything you can imagine. You can't defeat them."

"Didn't you?" he asks. "Haven't you, more than once? It's remarkable what you've done, really. I don't even think you appreciate it."

"And I don't think you appreciate how certifiable you sound."

His mouth twists, amusement flickering back to anger just like that. He picks up his glass of whiskey and drinks it down in one swallow. Slams the delicate crystal onto the wood table so hard it fractures. He squeezes, and it shatters, sending shards flying from the table. Something strikes me above my eye, and I wince. Blood trickles through his fingers, but he doesn't seem to notice.

"No more, Godslayer," he grinds out between clenched teeth. "No more will I be a victim. I am going to do what should have been done a long time ago. I'm going to destroy Dinétah, and you are going to help me do it."

He leaves me there, chained in the metal chair. Disappears down a hallway without another word. I try to put the pieces of information together in my head, but a headache is starting to build and I can't focus. Something brushes my eyelashes, and I try to blink it away, my hands still chained to my sides. Drops of blood fleck the table. I must have gotten cut when he broke the whiskey glass. I lean my head back to try to keep the blood from getting in my eyes. Rattle the chains a little, checking to see how loose they are. Not loose enough to get free.

I look around the dimly lit room for something to help me. Some kind of weapon besides wasted bullets and cooling pie filling.

I brace my feet against the floor and rock the chair. It tips up on one thin leg and then swings back to the other. Again, with more force, and I'm falling to the floor. I hit the tile, my shoulder and hip taking the brunt of the impact. I feel shards of glass dig into my thigh through my leggings. I ignore it, using my weight to shift the chair closer to the spot where I can see my Böker against the wall.

My heart is pounding. I can feel the seconds ticking by, knowing Gideon could come back any moment. I wriggle awkwardly, pulling myself across the tiles, feeling the blood flowing faster from the cut on my head, glass grinding as it rolls under my hip and shreds holes in my leggings. The metal wiring cuts into my arms, pinching the skin. But I'm almost there. I almost have my knife.

I'm inches away when I hear Gideon's footsteps. Feel him pause in the doorway, the same one I first saw him in, taking in the scene.

"Remarkable," he says, wonder in his voice, and I think he means it. I make one last awkward attempt for my knife before he reaches with his power and drags the chair, and me, across the room. I slam into the wall of windows with a scream. The glass above me shakes and sways, rippling in its frame.

The chair settles, and I realize that not only is my head throbbing, but my vision is hazy with blood and I'm twice the distance from my weapons as I was before I started.

"This was all so unnecessary," he says, gesturing around the room, at me in the chair. "Do you still not understand that we're on the same side?"

He's wearing white pants and an elaborate metal vest, layers of overlapping steel creating armor. The kitchen light surrounds him, a nimbus of gold. Giant locust wings made of flexible metal flare open, as delicate and beautiful as lace, like some sort of insectoid angel.

I spit a mouthful of blood on the ground, and the small movement makes me dizzy. I struggle to focus. "Let me go," I say, sounding slightly drunk.

His eyes linger on the place where I've defiled his high-end flooring. "Neither of us is stupid, Godslayer. Once today's business is done and Dinétah is no more, I will be back for you. We will try this conversation again. But until then, I think it's best you sleep." He draws a small leather book from the inside pocket of his suit. Unzips it and pulls out a needle. A memory of Knifetown shivers down my spine as he tests the plunger.

"You disapprove of Bishop, but you don't mind his methods."

He fills the needle, unconcerned. "His methods are humane, even if he is not."

"Convenient morality."

A flash of irritation crosses his features but passes quickly. He walks forward and leans in close to me. Not close enough for me to reach him, my arms chained by my sides. But close enough for him to brush my hair from my face. Study the place the glass sliced open my forehead. His breath smells of whiskey and rotted pork. I turn my head, but he grips my jaw and holds it tightly. He pushes against my face with his thumb, as if searching for something under my skin. It's horrific, and too intimate, and I toss my head violently to shake his hand off. He lets me go, some emotion I can't read coloring his face.

"Stay still, please," he says, lifting the needle to my neck. "I will chain your head to the wall if I have to, but I would rather not. This is thiopental. Do you know what that is?" I flinch as the needle pierces my skin. "It will make you sleep until I can return."

He steps back from me. Pulls his black case out and stows away the needle.

"Where are you going?" I ask, voice slurring. The drug, combined with my injuries, is too much, and my world is quickly sliding into darkness. I blink, try to force my eyes to remain open.

As he stands there, he begins to vibrate. His wings open wider. The lace-like lattice ripples, begins to shimmer and flow, and a thousand locusts drop free, plopping thickly to the floor. They mill over one another before lifting into the air. He opens his mouth, and more pour out from his throat, crawling over his cheeks, his eyes. He raises his arms, and they rise from his hands. Locust song fills the room. Thick and warm and bilious, a physical thing. Like drowning in a vat of molasses. The steel beams in the wall of glass behind me rattle in their foundations. The glass shifts under the weight of the mass of insects that have settled on the windows. Cracks in the glass split the air like the shrieks of giants. Gideon hovers feet off the floor, arms extended, and locusts swarm to him, encircling him, lifting him higher.

"I go forth to devour," he says, and his voice is the buzz of a thousand insects speaking as one. "I go forth to remake the known world and bring the very gods to account for their atrocities. I go forth to bring a reckoning."

The last thing I hear besides the deafening drone of locusts is the groan of the steel beams ripping apart as the glass wall behind me shatters.

# Chapter 38

"Is she dead?"

"No. With the right dosage of the counteragent, I should be able to . . . Will you move back, Ben? I need room to work."

Someone grabs my eyelid and pries it open. I see bright lights, faces. I try to pull away, but Rissa's thumb digs into my eyeball. "Let me the fuck go," I mumble, my tongue thick as wool. I work my jaw, trying to draw moisture to my mouth, but all I produce is a groan of pain.

"She lives," Rissa says, grinning and mercifully letting go of my eyelid.

"It's already working," Ben says excitedly.

"Of course it's working," Aaron says. "Gideon was never very good in the Reaping Room. No subtlety. The man would choose a cleaver when a scalpel would do. The dose he gave her must have been twice the recommended—"

"Water," I croak, cutting Aaron off. I hear someone hurry away, probably Ben and hopefully to the kitchen. I manage to get both my eyes open on my own, eyelids scraping like sandpaper. "You came back," I manage to wheeze out.

"We weren't going to leave you to do this alone," Rissa says.

"Good thing, too, because clearly Gideon kicked your—"

Ben's back. She holds a cup of water to my mouth. I gulp it down, grateful. Blink to try to clear the crust from my eyes. Rissa uses a white napkin to wipe blood from my head and then starts to work on loosening the metal wires still coiled around my chest. I wait until they fall to the floor around the chair in a puddle of steel loops. I shake my arms out to get the blood flow to return. Try to ignore the deep gashes in my arms where the metal dug through flesh, the hundreds of tiny stinging cuts all over my skin.

"I'm just glad you're here," I say, feeling something like a sob wanting to break free.

Rissa softens. "Friends, right? Just because you're a solid bitch sometimes doesn't mean I'm going to abandon you."

"I'm sorry too," Ben says, head down. "I know I promised not to argue with you, and a deal's a deal, so . . ."

"I shouldn't have treated you like a child, Ben. I was trying to do what was best for you, but all I did was deny you the right to make your own choices."

Ben looks up, teary-eyed, and before I can tell her no, she rushes forward and throws her arms around me. Pain flares across my chest, and I whimper. Rissa laughs and pulls Ben away. "Leave her alone. She's injured. Plus, I've heard she melts if you hug her too much."

"What time is it?" I ask. "How long was I out?"

"It's a few hours before dawn. Ben made it all the way back to Page before we caught up with her." Rissa shoots her a look. "It took some time to get back. And then when we found the Amangiri empty, we thought you'd probably gone with them."

"Wait, what? It's empty?"

"Like a big concrete crypt," Ben offers. "Furniture's there. Everything looks lived in. But no people."

"Where did they go?"

"Don't know," Rissa says. "But Ben still had a beat on you from Knifetown, and she tracked you here." She sniffs the air. "Does it smell like apples in here to anyone else?"

"Gideon's planning to flood Dinétah," I say. "There were maps on Kai's walls. And he had books, lots of books. Different versions of the end of the world."

"Come again?" Rissa asks.

"Accounts of the Big Water, but also all kinds of apocalyptic stories. From different cultures and different times. He has Kai studying them."

"So you did find Kai?" Rissa puts her hands on her hips, looks around. "But, funny, he's not here with you."

"It's complicated."

Rissa's jaw sets in a hard line, and her hazel eyes darken to a swirl of deep green. "He's helping him," she says, her voice flat. An accusation.

I nod again, slower this time. I want to defend him, tell her that I believe he's lying to Gideon, using his clan powers to trick all of them into thinking he's on their side, but I don't want to explain to Rissa what I saw—the blonde, him seated at Gideon's side, the things he said about Gideon helping him get over the trauma of dying. And all I have for proof is my blind trust. Trust that's been wrong about Kai before. So I just hold her gaze. Ask her to trust me if she can't trust him.

"Why would he be reading those?" Ben asks, oblivious to the tension between Rissa and me. "And helping Gideon with what? I thought Kai was on our side."

"He is," I answer Ben, but I mean it for Rissa.

"Maybe your Kai has his own plans," Aaron cuts in. "Rissa said he was an accomplished liar. Maybe he's a spy on the inside."

I have no idea where that came from, and I'm not sure if it's meant as an insult or a compliment to Kai, but it's close enough to what I was thinking that I'm grateful to Aaron for saying it.

"It's good for a man to have his own agenda," he says.

Rissa glances at Aaron, probably wondering if a man having his own agenda applies to him, too. But Aaron's turned away from us, drifting over to examine Gideon's metal sculptures, which line the walls. He runs a hand over the curving wing of an angel, clearly admiring his brother's work. Rissa's gaze lingers, her lips pursed in thought, before she turns back to me. "You said Kai had maps on his walls. Maps of what?"

"The Glen Canyon Dam, for one."

"Just the Glen Canyon?" Aaron asks, his attention coming back to us. "What about Hoover downstream? Grand Valley upstream? If that's what he's planning, then he'll bring them all down."

"Wait, wait, are we accepting that this is real?" Rissa asks. "He's actually going to try to flood Dinétah? Is there even enough water for that?"

"Before the Big Water, Hoover held thirty-two million acre feet alone," Aaron says, falling into his tour-guide demeanor a bit. "Glen Canyon another twenty-seven million. After the Big Water, that's probably doubled."

"What is an acre foot?" Ben asks.

"Enough water to cover an acre of land with a foot deep of water. So enough to cover twenty-seven million acres under a foot of water. Dinétah is only seventeen thousand acres. Lake Powell at capacity holds more than eight billion gallons, if it helps to think of it that way."

"He's going to create his own natural disaster," I say.

Ben shivers. "Which could destroy Dinétah."

"Even if he did release the water," Rissa says. "Even if he did break those dams, wouldn't it just return the water to where it is supposed to be naturally? Down the Colorado River?"

"It's too late for that," Aaron says. "Landscape's been permanently changed. Add the destructive force of flowing water." He pats at his shirt as if looking for a pen in a pocket. "I could calculate it quickly if—"

"No need," I say. "We get the point."

"That's a lot of water," Aaron says. "My brother can do many things, but he can't just move billions of gallons of water to where he wants to on command."

"Yes," I say, "he can."

"What do you mean?" Aaron asks.

"Oh shit," Rissa says, dropping into the chair next to me. The whiskey bottle is still there. She takes a pull straight from the bottle.

"That could have been poisoned," I observe as she swallows it down.

She lifts one shoulder in dismissal. "Does it matter if we're all about to die?"

"What do you mean, Maggie?" Aaron asks again. "It's physically impossible. Tankers, pipelines. Even if he had them all in place and ready to go, it still wouldn't be sufficient."

"He doesn't need any of those things."

He snorts. "The water's not going to go somewhere just because he wants it to."

"Want to bet?" Rissa quips.

Aaron wrinkles his forehead in confusion.

Rissa tips the bottle up again.

"I'm not following," Aaron says.

"Me neither," Ben adds.

Rissa looks at me. "It's Kai," Rissa says. "His power. I saw it myself. He can control the wind. Why not the water?"

I nod in agreement. "Kai's going to redirect that water wherever Gideon needs it."

"How?" asks Aaron.

"Why?" Ben demands.

"It doesn't matter," I say to both of them. "We have to stop him."

"Uh, this is the guy who can heal himself, right?" Ben says. "How are you going to stop him?"

"You can shoot him again," Rissa suggests. "That put him out of commission for a while last time."

"I'm not shooting him," I say, thinking of the way he looked at me, the haunted eyes, the unspoken accusations. "I don't know why he's doing this, but I'll find a way to talk to him. Besides, the bigger problem is how to stop Gideon. Weapons don't work against him." I look at Aaron. "You could have mentioned that your brother has clan powers."

Aaron's breath hitches. "I . . . I didn't know. He didn't before. When I knew him."

"Well, he does now. He can control metal. He plucked my knife out of my hand like it was nothing. Stopped the bullets from my gun in midair."

Aaron blinks. "He . . ." He sighs, small and sad. "That makes sense."

"What are you saying, Maggie?" Rissa asks. "That guns and knives don't work on him? He's just as invincible as Kai? If that's the case, then we're all going for a nice long swim."

"Not invincible. I've just got to figure out how to get to him."

"If you're right, and you think he's planning to blow those dams today, you better figure it out quick."

I stand on shaky legs. Ben jumps forward, reaching for my elbow to catch me as I stumble, but I waive her off. I'm going to have to be able to stand on my own two feet if I'm going to do this. I give her as close to a smile as I can manage. "I'm fine. Maybe another glass of water?"

She nods and hurries off.

"Are you fine?" Rissa asks, concerned.

"I have to be."

I collect my weapons, moving like a wounded turtle. The sword is still strapped to my back, and I unbuckle it and lay it on the table. Set it down with a kind of reverence that doesn't seem to fade. It's still sheathed in the scabbard Tah had made for it, but its presence seems to fill the room. Gingerly, I place a hand on the hilt. The air crackles around us, suddenly alive. Aaron wipes at his brow, sweating. Rissa whistles in awe, low and impressed.

"When did it start doing that?" Rissa asks.

"Tó showed me how to . . . talk to it."

Her eyes get big, but she doesn't say anything.

One deep breath and I pull the sword free in one smooth motion. Lightning curls around the blade, sending tiny sparks in the darkness. Lightning wraps around my hand where I grip the leather hilt and lightning dances up my wrist all the way to my elbow. It doesn't burn. It just . . . waits. It feels like contained energy, eager for me to direct it. Just like Tó said it would. I straighten and breathe deep as the energy flows through my body. I can feel my wounds knitting closed, my headache clearing, Gideon's drugs melting out of my bloodstream.

"Damn," Rissa whispers, her voice full of awe.

"You're glowing," Aaron murmurs.

"Not just glowing," Ben adds. "You're on fire."

"Your skin," Rissa says. I raise an arm and see that my skin has in fact taken on a deep blue glow. "And all the cuts are gone. Even your head."

I run a hand across the cut on my forehead. Smooth skin. "Holy shit."

I sheathe the sword, and the glow immediately fades from both me and the weapon, leaving us all in the hazy lamplight of Gideon's living room again.

"Now what?" Rissa asks.

"Now we do what we came here to do. Rescue Kai."

"And kill Gideon," Ben says. Aaron's head cocks toward her and I think his eyes narrow, considering, but in the relative darkness, I can't be sure. But I know we can't put this conversation off any longer.

"We need to talk," I say. "About you"—I motion toward Aaron—"and your brother."

"Maggie," Rissa says, a note of warning in her voice.

"No, we need to know the truth."

"Know what truth?" Ben asks.

I hesitate, and Aaron says, "Gideon is my brother. My foster brother. We grew up together in a Mormon foster family in St. George."

"What?" Ben takes a step back from him, hand over her heart. "Did you know, Maggie? Rissa?"

"We suspected," I admit. "And the question, Aaron, is whether your loyalty lies with us or with him."

Aaron shoulders rise on a prolonged shrug. "I got no love for my brother. He and I parted in the worst of ways. Me on my feet and him bearing a dozen cuts from my knife, bleeding him out."

"Something you regret," I say, pushing back.

"Something I regret," he says, nodding. "A man shouldn't knife his brother, no matter his offense. But me regretting ain't going to change a thing. He needed to die then, and seems like he needs to die now." His eyes bore into me, trying hard to convince. Too hard? I don't know.

"And why was that, exactly, that your brother needed killing?" I ask. "What happened between the two of you?"

"Knifetown," he says flatly. "Knifetown happened."

"That's not good enough."

"It's going to have to be."

"You can't expect us to trust you—"

"I don't expect no trust. We have a deal and I'll stick to my deal. I'm good for that."

"I need to know whose side—"

"Maggie," Rissa says. "He's on our side. If he says he's good to his word, I believe him."

I don't. But maybe I don't have to. Maybe Rissa's asking me to trust her, same way I asked her to trust me about Kai. And maybe I owe her the same courtesy, friend to friend.

"Aaron's proven himself," she says. "He helped us at Knife-town, and he found Ben in Page. He's on our side."

All those things could be self-serving. We were a means to an escape from a place he hated, and knowing that Ben was set on killing his brother one way or another, keeping her close would be a smart move. Nevertheless . . .

"Okay. He's your responsibility," I say. "Whatever he does, it's on you."

Rissa touches Aaron's arm possessively. Nods once.

"Aaron," Ben says, her voice no more than a whisper. "You could have told me."

Aaron reaches for the hat he doesn't have anymore, as if to tug it down. Instead he brushes an empty hand across his forehead, smoothing his hair. "Sorry, Ben," he says, and he actually sounds sorry. "Sometimes a man is so used to keeping secrets, he doesn't know how to stop keeping them. We get through this, I'll do better by you. That's a promise."

She nods, but it's clear that his confession is bothering her. Maybe it was easier to want Gideon dead when he was just a bad guy. Harder when he's a real person, the brother of a friend.

"Ben, why don't you come with me?" I say. "I want to go back and get another look at the maps in Kai's room. Make sure I didn't miss anything obvious."

"Aaron and I will head for the Glen Canyon Dam," Rissa offers. "Wait for you at the crossing."

"What if you run into Gideon and the Swarm?"

"I know how to stay hidden," Rissa reassures me. "Besides, we won't engage. Just observe. As long as you two don't linger, we'll be fine."

# Chapter 39

Ben and I head back down to the compound. The solar-powered lights along the footpath are still glowing a pale gold, but the lights in the building itself are off. We reach the wing of rooms where Kai was. I stop and press my face to a glass door randomly. The room inside is deserted. Bed unmade, clothes still visible. I spot a half-eaten apple sitting on a desk. "They left in a hurry. Everything's still here. They didn't even pack."

"So they're coming back?"

"No one's coming back," I say, knowing it's true.

We reach Kai's room, and I push open the unlocked glass door. Step across the threshold. Ben follows. I flick on a lamp and the room lights up. The books are all still here, but the maps on the wall have been hastily torn down, the corners still taped to the walls. And the notebook Kai was writing in is gone.

Ben walks to the wall, puts a hand against the empty space. "How are we going to find him now?"

"Well," I say, stepping over the wealth of books strewn across the floor, "my guess is he went to Glen Canyon Dam, but just in case . . ." I spot a pair of black dress pants draped over the back of a chair. Reach into the pocket and pull out the tissue, exactly where I expected it to be. "We have this."

Ben comes over, curious. "What is that?"

I pull the material apart to show her the bloodstain. "Insurance policy."

She takes if from my hand. Holds it up and sniffs. "How can you be sure it's his blood?"

"I'm sure. I just need you to do your thing."

Her face falls, and she catches her bottom lip between her teeth, clearly bothered.

"No?" I ask.

She walks to the desk chair and sits, weighing the bloody tissue in her hand. "I think I'm ready to tell you how I got my clan power."

Damn. Not the best timing, but she's sitting there with her head down and her feet swinging nervously, and I know I have to hear her out. I walk over to Kai's abandoned bed and clear a spot to sit. "Okay, Ben, I'm listening."

She exhales, clearly bracing herself to tell me her story. "You know my parents were Protectors in the Energy Wars, right? That they died outside Pawhuska, defending Osage land."

"The Little Keystone," I say. "You told me."

She nods sadly. "One night Oilers raided the camp. I don't remember much. Just the chaos. And the noise. The sound of automatic gunfire, my mom and dad arguing, people yelling. And then people screaming as they died. My parents were warriors and they were needed to defend the camp, so my mom told me to hide. Find a place and hide until she came to find me. So I went to hide in the pipeline—"

"Wait, the pipeline?"

"They'd already installed it, when the Osage were tied up in court and couldn't stop them, but the crude hadn't started flowing yet. It was empty and us kids at camp would play in it sometimes. Hide-and-seek, that sort of thing. The adults would yell at us when they found us, and we'd promise never to do it again, but it was still the best hiding place I knew. Plus, it was safe in the pipes. No way Oilers would destroy their own equipment."

It sounds like a terrible idea to me, but I keep my mouth shut.

"I remember crawling in and pulling the port closed. The sound of the lock engaging. My mom had warned me it might be a few days before she could find me, so not to panic. She promised she would come back for me."

"But she didn't," I say, voice quiet.

She shakes her head. "That was the last time I saw her. Or my dad. I waited, you know. I don't know how long. Days? A week? Long enough that the food and water in my backpack had run out and the smell of my own waste was making me sick."

"Jesus, Ben."

"But you know what, Maggie? You can't open those ports from the inside. I didn't know. But that wasn't even the worst part," she says, rubbing her hands against her pants, the scratch of her palms against fabric loud in the room. "Turns out Oilers were raiding the camp to clear it because they got the court order to let the crude flow."

She swallows, her hands making fists. And I can only imagine the horror of being in that small dark pipe for days alone, not knowing if your parents were alive or dead. And then the terror she must have felt, hearing the rush of crude coming for her and not being able to outrun it. Swept away on a dark sea of oil.

"They say I washed up in some refinery machinery for catching dead animals. Turns out animals fall into the pipes more often than you think. They thought I was dead. How could they not? But I wasn't, and when they realized their mistake, they made arrangements to have me sent back to be with my only living relative left."

"Hastiin."

"Hastiin's mom, my shimasani. She was still alive back then.

But she told me that when I first came to her, she didn't have much hope for me. I had crude-oil poisoning. Some brain damage and temporary loss of my eyesight."

"Did you get healing powers?"

"No. I healed at the normal rate. We didn't even know about my clan powers for years. Until my shimasani died from an accident. She'd fallen. Busted her head, blood everywhere in the kitchen. I had to clean it up." She lowers her head, clearly embarrassed. "I saved the towels. With the blood on them. I don't know why. I think I wanted to keep part of her. Anyway, I didn't go to the funeral. You know how old people can be about kids being around death. They didn't want me near it, especially after everything I'd been through. But I wanted so badly to see my shimasani again. So I . . . I found her."

"What does that mean?"

She closes her eyes. "I had those towels, and when I held them, when I . . . tasted them, it was like I could smell her. They had taken her all the way to Tse Bonito, to the funeral home there. Fifty miles from our house in Sheep Springs. But she was there with me, like something on the back of my tongue." She shakes her head. "I show up at the funeral home and everyone is freaked out. I mean, I don't really remember it. I was in some kind of daze. I learned to control it better since then, but I can track people once I've tasted their blood. Do you think there's something wrong with me?" she asks, her voice small and worried. "Like I'm some kind of vampire?"

"I'm not a medicine man. I barely understand my own clan powers. But it sounds like your tracking power awakened because you could have used it to find your mother. Clan powers seem to want to fix things for us. I think yours was trying to do that. So you would never be left alone again. Ever."

She inhales sharply and then sucks on her lip, thinking.

"But right now we've got to go. Rissa and Aaron are probably already at Glen Canyon."

"Oh, right. Do you want me to . . . ?" She holds up the tissue with Kai's blood on it.

"Why don't we just hold on to it for now. If Kai's not where he's supposed to be, then I'll ask you again."

"Do you think Kai can help me figure out my powers better?"

"I think if we get out of this and get back home, we can all figure out what's going on."

She grins, relieved. I fold the tissue and stuff it in my pocket, and we leave Kai's room.

# Chapter 40

We head to the parking lot at a run, Ben doing her best to keep up. Sure enough, the big black SUVs that stood sentinel at the entrance earlier are gone. But there's a dune buggy, a little two-seater meant for doing maintenance work or gardening around the compound grounds. It's not much more than an engine and a chassis on four massive wheels with a roll bar across the top. A quick search of the key box by the front door reveals several sets of keys, and Ben and I grab the handful that are left still hanging on tiny hooks. I pick a key that looks like it might fit, but no luck. I keep going, moving through the likely suspects until I find the right one. One turn and the engine growls to life. Ben dumps our packs in the back and starts to hop in the passenger's side.

"I want you to drive," I tell her, stepping out of from behind the wheel.

"You do?" Her face lights up.

"I may need to move quickly, and I don't want to be stuck. Besides, the sword doesn't fit, and I'm not taking it off. I'll sit in the back and scout for trouble." I position myself along the open back wall of the vehicle as Ben slides into the driver's seat. "Give me the shotgun too," I tell her. "Just in case."

She does as she's told. Puts the vehicle in drive with only the slightest grinding of gears.

"Sorry," she says, but she's smiling, damn close to happy. I find myself smiling too, glad I could distract her from having the relive the horrors of her life. But my smile vanishes when she hits the accelerator. I lunge for the roll bar to keep from falling out the back.

"Slowly, Ben!" I shout. "Won't do us any good if you kill me first."

Her next try has us pulling out of the driveway smoothly and then gaining speed as we head down the narrow road away from the Amangiri and down the road toward Page. At the top of a rise, I think I can see the lights of the dam in the distance, and farther east than that, the sky starting to lighten from black to indigo, a thin band of white signaling that dawn is close. Way I figure it, we've got an hour tops before sunrise. Not a lot of time.

I tap on Ben's shoulder. She looks back at me.

"Go ahead and open her up. Let's see what she can do."

She laughs and gives me a thumbs-up. I grab the roll bar with both hands as the buggy lurches forward. We take a sand dune at speed, and for a moment we're airborne. I grit my teeth as my ass lifts off my already precarious perch and I come down hard enough to rattle my bones. Ben laughs, a wild joy, and I find myself grinning again as we go flying across the desert like a shotgun blast straight out of hell.

# Chapter 41

We hit the north entrance to the dam forty minutes later. Ben slows, and the buggy comes around and the massive dam comes into sight. It looked different when we crossed from the eastern side and from the driver's seat. I had been too nervous to get a good look at it. But now I can see it in all its massive glory.

It's enormous, ten times higher than the Wall, high as a mountain. Seven hundred and fifty feet and an almost sheer wall of concrete. It is an arch, curving upstream at the narrowest gap in the canyon, which is still, as Aaron had informed us, a little more than a quarter mile wide. Behind the arch lies Lake Powell at its capacity, all eight billion gallons of it. And along the concave side of the dam, something Aaron didn't mention. Dozens of small pearlescent dots littering the sheer surface of the dam. I stand up in the buggy to try to get a better view.

"What are those?" Ben asks, seeing the same shimmering spots, no doubt. "They're beautiful."

And they are. In the light of the new sun they look like shining drops of dew strewn along the face of the concrete like jewels on a necklace. One every fifty feet or so, moving steadily down the face of the dam like drops of rain against a windowpane. Every once in a while a drop of pearlescent dew breaks free, shattering the beauty of the scene with a sudden violence as it goes rolling down the wall headlong. A quickening plummet, faster, faster, until the tiny pearl-like figure ruptures against the rocky shallows hundreds of feet below. And as I watch, others are tossed back and forth across the vertical surface of the dam, caught in crosswind. Their strange ballet is mesmerizing until I realize what I'm looking at. And that those shiny dewdrops aren't dewdrops at all.

"Let's go, Ben," I say, tapping her shoulder.

"Is that a person?" she asks, coming to the same realization I did, her voice suffused with the same soft horror that's making my stomach curl.

"I think that's the Swarm."

"But why don't they use their wings?" She looks back at me, her face contorted with the insanity of it. "Why are they falling?"

"I don't know. Maybe the winds are too strong out there, maybe once gravity and speed get a hold of them, those wings don't work so well after all." I don't tell Ben, but I'm thinking that they just don't care. Gideon's brought them here to watch the end of the world. Maybe setting explosives on the dam face is volunteer work, same as letting yourself be nailed to a turquoise wall. Maybe dying like this is an honor. Maybe it's their purpose.

I sit back down in the buggy.

"Let's go, Ben," I say, more insistent.

"But . . ."

"There's nothing we can do for them. We've got to find Kai. My guess is he'll be somewhere close, near the control tower, so head in that direction."

Ben is silent as she drives us over. Once we're at the gate that blocks entry across the top of the dam, I motion for her to stop. The gate's been chained shut, closed to vehicle traffic until the Alt-Rangers arrive for their morning shifts. But nothing's keeping us from walking out over the roadway. I climb out of the buggy. Check my weapons out of habit. Throwing knives. Glock. Big-ass lightning sword. Ben climbs out beside me, and I hand her the shotgun.

She looks at me, eyes wide. "You mean it?"

"Hastiin taught you how to shoot, didn't he? Then you're going to cover me." I point with my lips to the top of a concrete pillar, probably twenty feet high and wide at the top. "Up there."

She nods, her face solemn. I start to walk away but turn back to her, face grim. "Once I'm on the dam, you stay out of sight. If anything happens, like the dam starts to blow, you get in that buggy and you drive like hell back toward Amangiri. Go find Tó. He'll help you."

"Don't die, Maggie," she blurts. Runs forward and hugs me. I let her. She sniffles a little, and I pat her on the back. Give her a second before I gently push her away. I wait for her to climb the ladder to the top of the pillar and get herself in position. I can see the barrel of the shotgun laid out across the top, Ben hunched over, already scanning the landscape ahead of me.

"I love that gun," I mutter, nostalgia hitting me. Because I don't want to admit it, but I've got a bad feeling about this. A bad feeling that I'm missing something important. Some clue or sign that I should have seen. Little to do about it now. I've come this far. So I pull the lightning sword from the scabbard, feel its supernatural energy curl up my arm and around me, and step onto the Glen Canyon Dam.

My feet tell me there's solid ground beneath me, a well-traveled road wide enough to move a semitruck across, but my body doesn't agree. My stomach drops, and a wave of dizziness pulls me up short. I suck in a breath and try to calm the adrenaline that's pumping through my blood. To my right is the lake runoff, a sparkling bed of water a hundred feet deep. To my left is a seven-hundred-and-fifty-foot drop to certain death. The wind picks up a little, and out on this precipice there's no protection from the elements. I lean into the breeze, pushing myself forward. My mind flashes back to the Swarm, falling one by one to their beautiful deaths, and for a moment, I swear I can still hear their screams.

Head down, leaning into the wind, I make my way across the dam. I keep moving, eyes scanning, heading for the tower and hoping Ben has my back. A worrying dread has settled in my gut like black tar, and my breath comes in short pants. The back of my neck itches, like someone is watching me, but so far I can't see anyone.

And then I spot him.

A small figure kneeling on a platform hanging just over the protective railing along the lake edge of the dam. He's in dark jeans and a black Metallica T-shirt. He has his maps spread before him on the ground, the corners held down by rocks. He's fighting the wind, too, as it tries to throw his notebook over the side. I'm close enough to hear him curse as he pushes his too-long hair from his eyes.

I have to school the grin of relief that flashes across my face, calm my heartbeat that speeds up, try not to remember the way his mouth tasted like smoke and wine.

"Kai." I call his name, not wanting to startle him.

He doesn't hear me the first time, so I say it again, louder. This time he turns, her face tight with annoyance at being disturbed. His eyes meet mine, and his face brightens. And then his glance immediately darts to the sword wreathed in lightning in my hand, and his joy fades.

"Friends?" he asks, voice tentative.

"More than friends," I say, grinning. "Partners."

He laughs, tension draining from his body. He sits back on his heels. "I didn't know if you were coming."

"'Come hell or high water,'" I say, quoting his last words to me back to him. "You're not trying to help Gideon; you're trying to stop him."

He nods, relief breaking across his face. "Once I figured out what he wanted to do, I thought I could talk him out of it. Bit'ąą'nii and all. And at first it worked. A day would pass and he would forget. But then it was only an afternoon and then an hour. And I realized if I was going to stop him, I would have to stay with him. See it through to the end."

"Why didn't you tell me last night?"

"I don't trust myself around him. He has a persuasion all his own. We'll be talking and I'll tell him things. Things I don't mean to, even as the words are coming out of my mouth. I had to commit. I had to be convincing so he wouldn't ask." He runs a hand through his hair, fighting the wind to push it from his eyes.

"He's using you. He doesn't have the answers you need, Kai. He can't give you purpose. You're going to have to find that on your own."

He narrows his eyes, squinting into the rising sun. "The Godslayer—that's you, isn't it?"

"So I've heard."

"He wants to use you, too."

"He can't. His powers of persuasion don't work on me. I don't know why not."

His eyes flicker to the sword in my hand.

"Maybe," I admit. "It has other properties. It's possible."

He nods once. The wind whips up, rattling his maps.

"So, what's the plan? You have a plan, right?"

He grins and motions me closer. "I've calculated everything. He wants to blow the dams all up and down the Colorado River. My job is the keep the water on track and running true to her tributaries. Only"—he hunches forward, excited—"I think I can generate enough force to push the water into the atmosphere, to turn it into rain. If I can do that, and spread it wide enough, it should become a natural phenomenon, self-sustaining. Nature will take over and I won't even have to hold it together. There'll still be flooding, some damage, but nothing like what he had planned. I can't save everyone. But I can save a lot."

"How do you know all this?"

"I don't for sure. But it makes sense theoretically."

"But you're using clan powers to do this, not science."

"I definitely need a little luck," he says, the grin I missed so much ticking the side of his mouth up. "Magic, medicine, science, and a little luck. If I had duct tape, I'd throw that in too."

"And if this doesn't work?"

His voice is matter-of-fact. "Then we die."

"Can you die?" I ask before I can think better of it.

"It's one thing to take a bullet. It's a whole other level to be crushed under the pressure of millions of acre feet of water. I'll die."

"Well, when you put it that way . . ."

We sit there for a moment in awkward silence, and then I remember Tó's parting gift.

"I have something for you." I reach into my shirt and pull out the pot Tó gave me. It's the size of my palm and thankfully still intact.

"What is this?"

"Not sure, but a friend gave it to me. Said to give it to the silver-eyed boy. That's got to be you."

He frowns. "I don't understand. A friend?"

"He lives on the lake. Called himself Tó."

Lines crease his forehead as he stares at the pot, turning it over in his hands. "What does—" He cuts off with a gasp, eyes wide. "Did you say Tó? As in Tó Neinilí?"

"Maybe?"

"A curmudgeonly older man, a little bumbling, likes to dance."

"Lives on a houseboat," I say, nodding. "Who is he?"

"He's a god. A rain god, to be specific. One of the Diyin Dine'é. He gave you this?"

"To give to you. Said the Diné could use a good soaking. I didn't get it at the time, but now I do. He thinks your plan is hilarious, by the way."

Kai throws back his head and laughs. Leaps over the railing in one smooth movement and wraps his arms around me. Kisses me, impulsive and wild. "You're a genius, Maggie!"

I grin back. I can't help it. "Well, maybe not a genius, but I can carry a pot real good."

A shotgun blast rattles across the canyon. I instinctively duck, pulling Kai down with me out of the line of fire. I look back over my shoulder, but I'm too far away and can't see Ben anymore. Kai presses something into my hand. Binoculars. I scan back across the dam from the way I came. Find Ben, who's waving frantically and motioning toward the southeast. I pivot and use the binoculars to search the sky, looking for whatever Ben saw. It doesn't take me long to find it.

"We've got trouble," I tell Kai, as a black cloud crosses in front of the rising sun, darkening the horizon. He stands next to me, hand braced above his eyes, trying to get a better view. Trying to comprehend the sudden eclipse. But there is no better view.

"What the hell is that?"

"Locusts."

We watch as the swarm moves closer, an immense unstoppable force.

"It stretches for miles," he murmurs.

I tighten my grip on Neizgháni's sword, letting the swirl of electricity be a comfort. We watch as the first edges of the swarm curve and descend, landing less than a hundred yards in front of us on the roadway.

"Shit," Kai says.

I watch as the locusts form themselves into shapes, thousands of insects melding together into individual human-shaped figures like the one that attacked me at Grace's house. Watch as their arms extend into swords, replicas of the one I hold, but forged from living insects. They move forward as one. Another line forms, and another, until there's a dozen chittering warriors headed our way, and still the swarm keeps coming.

"I think Gideon knows you switched sides, Kai."

"Shit," he says again.

"Well," I say lightly, "looks like you won't be crushed by a giant wall of water after all."

"Should we run?"

"To where?" I look around the dam pointedly. "There's nowhere to go."

"Gideon won't kill us," Kai says, eyes flickering to the locust army. "He still needs us."

"So what are these for?"

"To subdue us. He controls the locusts best when they're in human form. Otherwise they might just eat us."

"Great. That makes me feel great."

He glances down at his maps. "I can . . ." He climbs back over the railing and starts flipping through his notebook. "Can you hold them off, Maggie? Ten minutes. I need ten minutes to build up enough of a storm to take them out."

The locust men have come closer, their high chittering song almost deafening. Ten minutes might as well be twenty. What can I do against a swarm of locusts?

Unless.

"Fish psychology," I mutter. Because Gideon was right. The Diyin Dine'e do take sides. And Tó is on ours.

I sheathe Neizghání's sword so I can draw my Glock. Hit the release to eject the magazine and dump the bullets into my hand. And then into my pocket. Do it again with the extra magazine before I trade the gun for the sword again.

I have two handfuls of tiny gunpowder bombs encased in lead shells. For this to work, I'll need speed.

Speed I've got.

I roll my shoulders, breathe deep. Try not to remember the feel of millions of insects clawing through my hair, biting my skin, trying to crawl down my throat.

I take one last look back at Kai. He's kneeling, eyes closed, singing softly in Navajo. Already in his own world. One hand is stretched out to the lake, the other over the water god's pot.

"Ten minutes," I repeat to myself. "Always with the ten minutes."

I walk forward, letting the tip of the sword trail behind me, sparking fire against the concrete. Once I'm closer, I break into a jog. Honágháahnii wakes and catches, pure potential in my veins. I raise Neizghání's sword. Lightning cracks and flashes in my hand.

And I run straight into the horde.

# Chapter 42

I hit the locust men at full speed.

Duck under reaching arms. Slide on my knees, chopping legs apart as I pass.

The smell of burning locust flesh fills my nose. Blood sizzles. Guts coat the ground.

But it's not enough. They simply re-form.

I rise in the center, hand digging into my pocket. I pull my hand out, fling it open. Bullets scatter, bouncing and flipping across the concrete.

I raise Neizghání's sword. Think about calling lightning to me. Focus on feeling it. Ask it to come.

And lighting answers.

I feel it, hotter than Honágháahnii has ever been. Searing, blinding.

I scream, and my breath is flames. I swing the blade wildly, incinerating every bug within twenty feet.

No. Control it. I've got to control it. I remember what Tó said, to force the fire out. Away. So I do.

Lightning arcs from the obsidian tips, the same way it did for Neizghání before.

Each bullet is a tiny receptor, and as the lightning strikes, they explode. Fire flares in the sky, fifty feet above me. All around me. Rumbling into the earth itself. I stand in a circle of fire that transforms the locusts to less than ash.

The power shudders through me. Hot, electric, with the desire to do nothing but burn.

I think of Gideon. How he hates the world so much all he wants to do is see it destroyed. But his nihilism doesn't tempt me. I'm trying desperately to stay alive.

But I don't know if I can.

The lightning strikes from the sky again, recharging what was lost. Fire pours into my body, and I howl flames. Energy snakes through me, crackling across my skin, wreathing me in a deadly electric blue. I am not Neizghání, a child of the sun god. I am only a five-fingered, playing with too much power.

I drop to my knees, overcome. Somewhere far away I hear my name. Faint. Low.

But all I know is fire.

"Let go of the sword!"

Kai? No. Another voice. Ben.

"It's burning you up, Maggie! Drop it!"

The sword. My fingers flex, and the pommel drops from my hand. The fires extinguish simultaneously, and I gasp air into my lungs. I collapse onto my back, heaving in air like a drowning man, feeling seared from the inside out.

"Are you okay?" Ben asks. I can see her now, kneeling beside me, her brow knit in concern.

"Don't. Touch. Me."

She freezes, hand hovering over me. "I don't think you're burning anymore."

"Bugs?"

"You burned them all, but"—worried eyes dart skyward—"there could be more coming. Can you move?"

"I told you. To run."

"You said if the dam broke to run. It's not broken." As in on cue, the ground rumbles beneath us. Low popping sounds echo across the canyon. The first of the explosives detonating. "But I really think we better move."

I can't move. I lick my lips, looking for moisture, but there's none. The inside of my mouth is raw. My eyes ache as if I've been staring at the sun. I have a sudden absurd thought. "My hair?"

"What?"

"Do I still have hair?"

Ben gives me a look like I've lost my mind. Okay. Still have hair. No matter how charred I feel, it was a supernatural fire. I'm not actually burned to a crisp. And now that I think of it, my body doesn't hurt at all. In fact, my body feels great. Healed. And brimming with power.

The ground shudders and sways. More popping noises and the cracks in the concrete from the lightning strikes start to widen. Shit.

Ben gingerly tugs at the collar of my coat. "Maggie. I think we'd better go."

Something hits my face. Wet. My first thought is bug splatter, but Ben's still talking and tugging at me, and I can't hear the locust song.

"Stop spitting," I mutter to Ben as another drop hits my cheek.

She frowns. "What?" Her hand flies to her own face, touching. She pulls it back and stares in wonder. "It's water."

We both turn our eyes to the sky, where the black cloud of locusts has been replaced with thick roiling storm clouds.

"Kai." I get to my feet. "Where's Kai?" We both look around frantically, but he's not where I left him. "The locusts didn't . . . ?"

"No," Ben says. "He was at the edge of the dam. Facing the lake. I saw . . . There!"

She thrusts her hand out, finger pointing, but she doesn't have to. I see him too. A figure floating in the clouds, held aloft in the storm. A bright nimbus of white light surrounds him, and his eyes flash with the silver of thunder. The rain starts to fall in earnest, fat drops splattering the ground like the heavy tread of angels.

Another *boom*, and Ben and I watch a chunk of the dam break off, tumbling off the edge. Another, and another, and concrete rips apart to cascade over the edge. We stumble backward, toward the eastern side of the dam, as the world starts to crumble beneath our feet.

Ben screams. The ground tilts and she slides. I grab her hand, pulling her off the cracking concrete. But the dam is breaking around us, and soon there will be no safety anywhere in sight. To my right the lake is rising, waves rocking high over the railing, grasping greedily for their own freedom.

Thunder booms. I look up to see Kai throw out his hand, palm forward. He curls his fingers in, making a fist, and slowly lifts his arm upward. I stare, dumbstruck, as the shoreline changes course, rising into the air at his command. A wall of water rises, as if dragged skyward by an invisible force. It's both beautiful and terrifying. But it doesn't stay there long. I expect him to fling it back upon itself, but instead he spreads his fingers sharply. Water shatters to mist, evaporating into the desert air and rising up to fatten the bulging storm clouds, catching rainbows in their impossible spray.

"Fucking hell."

Rainbows.

And I know how to get us off this crumbling dam.

"One more blessing, old man," I mutter as I pull Ben tight against me and, with only a moment of hesitation, wrap my free hand around Neizghání's sword. Fire travels up my arm, fills my veins, the power of the storm saturating an already oversaturated vessel.

The world tilts, the edge of the dam coming up fast, a fall into oblivion. I backpedal, trying to keep my balance and my hold on Ben and the sword, but I can't. My feet lose their purchase. And we fall.

I scream to the lightning, desperate as a deathbed prayer.

Ozone fills my nose, something inside me ignites, and I shatter into flame.

# Chapter 43

Lightning strikes the command tower on the west side of the canyon, and Ben and I stumble onto solid ground. Ben collapses, vomiting. I'm not much better. My whole body feels like it's going to shake apart. With unsteady hands, I sheathe the sword in the scabbard on my back. Stomp my feet to try to dissipate some of the raw energy around me.

"Did we just . . . ? Did you . . . ?" Ben stutters out once she's left the contents of last night's dinner at her feet.

"I think so," I admit, my voice as shaky as my hands.

"And you've never done that before?"

"Once, with Ma'ii, but he was driving, and it was a lot smoother. Sorry for the bumpy ride."

She shakes her head. "Don't be sorry. Look." And I look where she's pointing, back to the center of the dam, where we were just moments ago. Most of the dam is still there, still holding the water back, but there's a V-shaped chunk of concrete probably fifty feet wide missing in exactly the spot where we were standing. Lake water pours through the break in a powerful rush that cascades down seven hundred and fifty feet to the rocks below. It looks peaceful from here, beautiful even.

I scan the sky, searching the clouds, but I can't see Kai anywhere. I know he must be there, embraced by the storm, controlling the flow of water with whatever supernatural powers he's harnessed from Tó's pot and his own power.

The rain is steady now, a cold curtain of a downpour that's already starting to chill. It's been so long since I've felt rain, I can't help but turn my face upward, let it wash over me. Ben's not as charmed. She's running to the nearest shelter, the guard tower. I take one last mouthful of rain and then hustle after her.

Ben's rattling the doorknob, trying to open the guard tower door. "It's not locked," she explains, "but there's something heavy blocking it." She leans in with her shoulder. "If I could just . . ."

I add my shoulder to the push, and together we open the door a foot. Ben peeks in the narrow opening. "Maggie, wait!"

"What is it?"

"There's somebody there. Blocking the door. A body."

I look in, and sure enough, there's someone lying on the floor, blocking the doorway. I see long legs sheathed in familiar brown leathers, big biker boots, and the edges of two thick red braids.

"It's Rissa," I say, voice grim.

I move Ben back and reach through the opening. Try to push against Rissa's shoulder to get her off the door, but I can't muster enough power to move her, and she only flops forward at the waist before she falls back again.

"Is she dead?" Ben asks, her voice scared.

"I . . . don't . . ." I sit down, stick my foot through the door and kick Rissa in the side. This time she stirs, and I think I hear her groan. "She's alive," I tell Ben. "But hurt."

We need another way in. There's a window on what looks like the second floor. Narrow. Too narrow for me, but not for a sixteen-year-old Deer clan girl. I explain what I'm thinking to Ben. "Can you make it?"

She nods, eager. I position myself under the window, and Ben steps back about ten feet to get a running start. The rain is quickly oversaturating the parched earth, turning the ground to mud. I plant my feet wide, brace my back against the tower wall, bend my knees, and cup my hands in front me. Give Ben the go-ahead nod.

She doesn't hesitate. I grunt as I take her weight in the makeshift steps my hands make, then I lift and push. Her foot on my shoulder is surprisingly light, as if she's suddenly weightless, and she scampers up the wall. Grasps the windowsill with ease, flipping herself over, and kicks through the glass in one smooth movement. After a moment she leans out the open window to give me a thumbs-up, and then I can hear her quick footsteps on the stairs as she makes her way to the front door.

"Careful," I warn her as she grabs Rissa by the armpits and drags her out of the way. Once she's moved, I join them both inside.

"Her pulse is good," Ben says, relief evident in her voice. "And I don't see any wounds."

"Check her neck." I have a suspicion.

Ben gently turns Rissa's head, lifting her hair out of the way. And sure enough, there's a small needle prick at the base of her neck. Ben frowns. "Gideon got her?"

"Or Aaron."

She sucks in a breath. "Do you think he betrayed us?"

I motion for her to be quiet and I sit back, listening. I can't hear much over the steady pounding of the rain. I walk over to the winding staircase. Take a few steps up, straining. And there is it. Dim but definite. Voices.

"Stay here, Ben," I say as I start to shed myself of metal weapons: Böker, gun. I even unbuckle the scabbard and lay my sword near Rissa's feet. The only thing I keep is my obsidian knife. "Watch Rissa. My guess is Aaron wanted to have a little one-on-one talk with his brother."

"What are you going to do?"

I start up the stairs. "Interrupt them."

"Maggie," she says, her voice soft but urgent. I look back. "You don't have to kill him. I know before I said . . . but it's okay. I'm okay."

The truth is that Gideon is going to be hard to kill. Conventional weapons won't work, and the lightning sword is too dangerous and my control too erratic to wield it in such a small space. I'm just as likely to burn everything to ash—guard tower, Gideon, and everyone else inside.

"What about your purpose, Ben?"

She places Rissa's head in her lap, cradling her gently. Her eyes are downcast. "I don't know. I know before I said I thought it was my purpose, but I think I'd rather just get out of here and go home. With you and Rissa both alive. So if it means you could get hurt . . ."

Ben runs a hand over Rissa's head, smoothing her hair down, and says, "Your life means more to me than his death. Does that make sense?"

A warmth spreads through my chest, that same feeling I got back at Twin Arrows when Rissa offered me her friendship. "It makes a lot of sense."

"Okay, then." She presses both hands over her heart, something I remember Hastiin doing with the Thirsty Boys before a bounty hunt. A blessing he learned on the frontlines of the wars.

"What does that mean?" I ask.

"It means come home safe. It means we're family."

# Chapter 44

The staircase winds up through an opening in the center of the tower. I've never been in a lighthouse, but I've seen pictures, and I imagine the inside is a lot like this. I move silently upward, any sound I might make drowned out by the thunder outside. Each step seems to take me deeper into the storm. The rain that was a steady downpour now slashes violently against the windows, demanding to be let in. Lightning streaks across the sky, followed quickly by the boom of thunder.

Kai's out there somewhere, the living heart of this tempest.

I have to trust that he will be all right, that he knows what he's doing, or at least that he can take care of himself. And I have to trust that when this is over, I will see him again. Touch him again. I have to believe that.

The voices reach me now, barely loud enough to be heard over the growing gale. Gideon and Aaron, but mostly Gideon. Aaron's voice is weaker, only a whisper compared to the roar of his older brother.

"Do you know what the locusts did to me?" Gideon shouts. "Out there in the desert? I was lying there. Within feet of the Wall. Covered in my own blood. Blood drawn by the hand of my own brother.

And all I can think about is what that social worker said. That my mother was Diné. And if I was Diné, then why wouldn't they let me in? Why couldn't I get past that monstrous Wall?

"And then I feel this . . . pinch. Amid all the other pain, all the razor cuts you gave me. It was nothing. But then there were more, Aaron. And more. And then I realize they're coming out of the ground. Insects. Hundreds of them. And they're biting me. Attracted to my blood and eating me alive. And I'm so weak and so tired that there's nothing I can do about it but lie there and let them."

"I'm sorry," I hear Aaron sob, barely a whisper.

Gideon moves, footsteps across the room. "I experienced a miracle that day," he says, voice filled with wonder. "I suppose I should be thanking you. If you hadn't betrayed me to Bishop, if you hadn't given in to your baser impulses . . ." His voice rises, his emotions barely contained. "If you hadn't murdered me!"

Silence, and when he speaks again, his voice is back to controlled, civil.

"A locust crawled into my mouth," he says, "and I couldn't stop it. I could feel its feet on my tongue, the flutter of its wings against my teeth. Their incessant chatter in my ears. Inside me. And I knew it would devour me . . . if I didn't devour it first."

A sound like a chair being dragged across the floor.

"Did you know that the Diné traditionally considered the locust a messenger? He led the way into the next world. And as I was lying there dying, Aaron, the guts of a half-chewed locust dripping from my lips, I realized I, too, could be a messenger. That I didn't have to die. The locust could eat away that which was rotted and old and make way for the new. The new that was me. I could live. And if I lived, I could take you and Bishop and the whole of Dinétah down with me. I just had to have the will, the desire, the goddamn *fortitude* to persevere."

"But why destroy it now, Gideon? We can go home."

Silence, like the room is holding its breath.

"What did you say?"

"I made a deal, and you can come with me. We can start again, in Dinétah. Prodigal sons, like you used to say."

I risk a peek around the corner. Gasp silently in horror. Aaron is nailed to the wall. Metal spikes through his shoulders, same as Caleb. Another through his abdomen, and he's bleeding freely. Two more through his upper thighs, blood pooling under his feet. Gideon sits in front of him like a man studying a particularly fine painting hung on a wall. There are locusts in his hair, crawling on the collar of his metal vest. More on his hands, circling his wrist, climbing his arms. Boiling out over his bare feet.

Thunder booms outside, the rain still pelting the windows in a constant steady beat, the storm rattling the walls. So loud I almost miss Gideon's words.

"You *child*." He leans in close to Aaron, caressing his cheek. "You think I want their pity? That I would return a puppet when I can be a king?"

Gideon stands abruptly, and I drop back, out of sight. He strides over to the windows, throwing them open one by one. The storm roars in, sending papers flying. A bookshelf tumbles over loudly. Thunder cracks through the room.

"Dinétah's days are at an end!" Gideon shouts. "Once I have cleansed the land, I will challenge the gods themselves. I will take what I was denied, what should have always been mine."

He comes back to Aaron. Leans in and kisses him. Aaron struggles weakly, but Gideon holds him still. Gideon's jaw unhinges and locusts pour from his lips, rushing down his brother's throat, surging over his face like a shimmering black cloth. Aaron chokes on the insects, tries to scream, but he's buried by the swarm.

I yell his name, but my voice is lost in the roar of the wind through the open windows.

“Good-bye, brother,” Gideon shouts as he backs away. I watch as he steps up on the open window ledge. His wings flare open, and I realize he’s going to jump. I take off running, and just as he launches into the air, I fling myself out the window after him.

# Chapter 45

I catch him in midair. He grunts in surprise, and we tumble through the sky.

I tear at his clothes, his metal wings, grappling for purchase. He screams incoherently and tries to pry me loose. We fall, spinning, unable to tell up from down, blinded by the torrential rain. It seems like an eternity until we slam into the earth below.

The rain has turned the red dirt around the guard tower into a mudslide, and the once firm earth slips out from underneath us, sending us down the side of the hill, straight toward the dam and the drop beyond. We both fight to stop. Nothing is solid, everything is chaos, and we rush unhindered toward the edge.

I can't stop. I'm going too fast. I lose sight of Gideon as he tumbles past me. I try to scream, but my mouth is filled with mud. A river roars in my ears.

Something strikes me across the stomach, and I grab for it. Cold metal under my hands. A pipe of some kind, planted vertically in the ground. I hold on tight, drag myself up, struggling to get my head above the mudslide.

I've caught hold of the cross section of a guardrail, anchored down in the concrete observation deck. Another twenty feet and I would have slid right off the edge. I cling to the railing, wiping mud from my eyes and spitting wet earth. I look for Gideon.

He's at the edge, slowing pulling himself along the same metal railing farther down. His face and hair are slicked red, the delicate lace of his wings clotted with mud, and his white clothes are stained ochre. He hasn't seen me yet. I check my moccasin wrap, and my fingers close around the obsidian knife still tucked between the layers of suede. But before I can draw it, Gideon spots me.

His eyes narrow. He yanks at the air behind me, and the railing I'm clinging to rips free of its moorings. Metal piping slams into my back.

I'm sliding again, more controlled this time, head above the fray. I'm barreling toward the edge . . . until Gideon plucks me from the river of mud. Tosses me against the netting behind him—the last hope for those unlucky enough to fall from the deck. The flow holds me pinned, dangling out over the edge. The structure moans under the pressure, threatening to break at any moment.

"Where is the sword?!" Gideon shouts.

"Somewhere you won't find it!"

He's panting, leaning against what's left of the rail. "Why are you fighting me, Godslayer?" He sounds truly bewildered. "Don't you want to be out from under their thumb once and for all? Don't you want to be free?"

"No! Free is lonely. Free is having no one who cares for you, no one who will sacrifice their own lives to protect you. Free is no one having your back even when you're a solid bitch. I don't want that kind of free!"

A vein throbs in his neck and his hand clenches. "Weakness. Dependency. Human frailty. Why wallow in your humanity when you can become a god?"

There's movement behind him, out over the open sky. Something coming in quickly, a dark smudge in the sheeting rain, blurred and indistinct.

Gideon's still staring at me, his breath coming is gasps, waiting for my answer.

"Because I'm just a five-fingered girl," I say finally. "And I need other people."

"They cannot make you whole."

"They don't have to."

"Kai told me about you. How they treat you because of your power. You are a pariah. A monstrosity. They'll never accept you!"

"You're wrong, Gideon," I say, thinking of Rissa on a curb outside of the Twin Arrows, the two of us laughing over a shared cup of coffee. Of Ben, her hands over her heart, calling me family. Of Kai, who loves me broken, dark, exactly as I am. "They already have."

Gideon sneers at me. Raises his hand to rip the netting open and send me tumbling to my death. Behind him the figure in the rain solidifies. Jeans, Metallica shirt, eyes made of quicksilver.

A bolt of lightning streaks from the sky, striking near Gideon's feet. He stumbles back.

Kai lands, putting himself between us. He lifts his hands, fingers pressed together, and then jerks them apart. The water crushing me recedes abruptly. I tumble to my hands and knees, exhausted. I want to rest, but I make myself move, crawling across the netting toward land.

Gideon's eyes light on Kai, and he smiles. "You've come back, my son. I knew you wouldn't desert me."

"You've got to stop this, Gideon," Kai says, his voice both storm-dark with power and full of pain.

"No, Kai. No. Do you see what you've done? What you can do?" He lifts his face to the rain. "More power than I thought possible. My God, boy. You are magnificent."

"I don't want the power," Kai says. He drops his head, and when he looks up again, I know that his eyes have lost their uncanny glow.

Gideon's mouth turns down in disgust. "Then what do you want? Not more sentiment, like the girl." He sneers in my direction. Kai looks at me too, and I'm close enough now that he holds a hand out to pull me up. I get to my feet and we stand together, side-by-side.

"I want you to come back with us," he says.

"Kai . . ." I start, but he touches my wrist, a plea, so I hold my tongue.

"This is your last chance, Gideon," he says. "Terrible things have happened here. The Swarm, they're all dead. And that can't be changed. But it's not too late for you. Come home with me. Meet my cheii. He can help you."

"Help me do what?" he sneers. "Become the father you so desperately miss? So that you can disappoint me, too?"

Kai flinches, and a soft rage bubbles up inside me. "He's giving you a chance to live. Take it."

"He can't give me anything," Gideon spits, "except failure." He flexes his shoulders, and his wings spread open behind him.

"He can fly!" I shout to Kai, but Kai's already moving. He covers the distance to Gideon in three long strides and wraps his arms around him to hold him tight. Gideon freezes in surprise. Kai whispers furiously in his ear, his cheek pressed tight against Gideon's, skin-to-skin. His right hand grips the back of his head. The older man's eyes widen, a look of pure wonder on his face. Tears gather in his eyes. Kai rocks him gently in his arms, turning Gideon until his back is to me.

Kai's voice has been too low to hear, but as he looks up at me over Gideon's shoulder, I hear one thing, loud and clear. "Good-bye."

And I know that's my cue. I throw my obsidian blade. It lodges into the back of Gideon's head, at the base of his skull. He doesn't even scream.

Gideon slumps in Kai's embrace, and for a moment, they stand together. And then the White Locust is melting, dissolving into thousands of locusts, all just as dead as their namesake.

Insect carapaces strike the ground, the sound of them hitting the earth lost in the steady fall of rain. They are caught up in the river of mud, and they wash down the incline to plummet off the edge to the depths below. I step out of the way and watch them go.

Kai drops his hands to his knees, head bent, dark hair dripping rainwater. I join him, bending to dig through the mess of bugs and mud to find my knife. I clean it and put it back where it belongs.

"You okay?" I ask.

It takes him some time before he straightens. He pushes his hair from his face. "It was too late for him. I should have seen it earlier. All this is my fault."

"No, Kai. He made his choice. We all have choices."

He nods, but he doesn't look convinced.

"What did you say to him?"

"I told him his clans. Who his parents were. I told him he was loved."

"How did you know?"

"Gideon had his own birth records. He just refused to read them, always too angry or afraid of what he might find. I took the liberty of reading them." He squints through the rain, looking out of Glen Canyon. "I wanted to give him some peace."

"Medicine People Clan."

He looks over at me. "I'm sorry I asked you to do that."

I shrug. "It's what I do. Like you said, I am what I am. No use fighting it."

He looks thoughtful before he says, "A monsterslayer."

"Pretty good at it, too," I say with a grin. "But it never hurts to have a sidekick."

"I had it handled."

"Sure you did."

He chuckles and pulls me close. Kisses my forehead. We lean into each other as we turn to trudge back up the hill.

"So you can fly," I murmur.

"Well," Kai says, "it's more like hovering, being held up by the winds—"

"And shoot lightning from the sky."

"I can direct what's already there if—"

"Kai," I cut him off as we reach the top of the hill. "It's badass. That's all I'm saying. Very"—I glance down at his T-shirt, clinging to his wet skin—"very metal."

He smiles, a little sadly but at least I know I haven't lost him. "I saw you destroy an army of locust men with a lightning sword. That was pretty metal too."

I raise a hand in a horned salute. He laughs.

"The others are in the guardhouse," I tell him. "They need medical attention."

"Others?"

"Rissa and Ben. Ben's Hastiin's niece. You'll like her. She never listens to anything I say, and she's got a catalog of old pop songs to torture you with. She's fun."

"Sounds like you've been busy."

"Yeah. But it's time to go home."

"Yeah, Mags," he whispers against my hair. "Let's go home."

# Chapter 46

The morning dawns bright and crisp on Keshmish, but I wouldn't know because I slept in. Kai tells me later that he and Tah had been up for hours, putting the finishing touches on his new hogan. They wanted to get it done before Grace and the family come over for dinner. Ben's been in the kitchen for hours, whipping up a feast, allowing me in only for a cup of coffee. The coffee is Grace's Keshmish present to Tah for nursing Caleb back to health. Tah informed us that Caleb's keeping his metal wings for now. The youngest Goodacre is still not convinced that Gideon was all wrong. I know Kai's planning to talk to him about what happened, about Gideon's Armageddon, and I'll leave him to it. It's not a conversation I'm interested in being part of.

I did promise Rissa we'd have a remembering ceremony for Aaron. She brought back his aviator's cap and she thought it would be nice to make a memorial to him, back here in Dinetah, where he always wanted to be. Ben immediately volunteered to cook something special to feed his spirit, too, so after dinner, we'll get together and do that.

There's a blanket of snow on the ground. Not like we used to get back before the drought, but it's a least a few inches. My dogs run crazy through the white stuff, barking and spinning and throwing themselves down hills. I watch them for a while from the window, sipping my coffee and wondering how I got this lucky.

"You okay?" Kai asks, coming up behind me. He presses a hand against my shoulder and his lips briefly brush the top of my head. I lean into him, just a little, and he takes my weight. Pours me more coffee and hands me a cookie that Ben made, dusted with cinnamon and anise. No idea where the spices came from, but there have been lesser Keshmish miracles.

I take a bite. It's divine.

"Yes," I say. "For once I think I'm okay."

# Chapter 47

The thin layer of ice covering Black Mesa cracks under his moccasins. The winter wind blows feral, tossing his long raven hair around his shoulders. Snow whirls in the air, chilling him beneath his flint armor, but he is not deterred. He has been searching for weeks, chasing every rumor, every whisper.

He finds the spot. A stretch of earth like any other. Unmarked, unremarkable. He slings the pack off his back. Pulls the shovel free and begins to dig.

The day stretches long, the sun wheels across the winter sky.

He is about to give up, concede another story proven false, when he sees it. A feathered hoop. Mica glittering in the harsh light like flakes of shattered rainbow. He grasps it in his muscled hands. Pulls. At first it won't come. But then it loosens, and he sees it is tied around a man's neck. He gently clears the dirt away. Gets down on his knees in the hole he's dug and wrenches the hoop wide. Slips it from the buried man's head.

The earth begins to bubble and roil. He scrambles back as the sand collapses around him, rushing in to fill the space as the man rises from the earth. There are other hoops holding him, and he hurries to clear those, too. Until the man stands before him, finally free.

"Brother?" he whispers, hopeful.

Neizghání's eyes open. "Brother," he echoes. And then, "Where is she?"

"She has used the sword."

"How?"

"She had help. The Water-sprinkler, Tó Neinilí."

Neizghání's face darkens. "Meddling old man. Then it is as we feared."

His brother Tóbájíshchíní's face is grim.

"The world is out of balance. We must prepare for war."